To Rachel, Jaina and Poppy – the best family anyone could ever wish for. Thank you so much for your love and support, without which this book would never have been possible. The three of you make me feel like the luckiest man alive.

And to the real Alan Garrett - thank you for letting me use your name, and for your friendship throughout the years.

A long time ago, through a stroke of luck, I was introduced to the sport of hockey. It changed and shaped my life beyond measure. Those of you who play any sort of team sport will undoubtedly know what I'm talking about. Those of you who don't, should try taking one up - you might like it! To players of all team sports everywhere...this book is dedicated to you. Enjoy!

Paul Cude
www.bentwhistlethedragon.co.uk

Bentwhistle the Dragon
in
A Threat from the Past

PAUL CUDE

An Authors OnLine Book

Text Copyright © Paul Cude 2011

Cover design by Steve A Roberts © 2014

British Library Cataloguing Publication Data.
A catalogue record for this book is available from the British Library

ISBN 978-07552-0678-0

Authors OnLine Ltd
19 The Cinques
Gamlingay, Sandy
Bedfordshire SG19 3NU
England

This book is also available in e-book format, details of which are available at www.authorsonline.co.uk

Contents

1

Dragon Sleighing

Plumes of dark smoke billowed into the air across the city. The sickly smell of smoke and death wafted on a gentle breeze across the market square, tugging at the canvas of the overturned market stalls scattered haphazardly amongst the raging fires.

Off to one side stood the giant archway, which for hundreds of years had been regarded as the main entrance to the city. Normally a giant monster of an oak gate and portcullis hung, attached to the weathered archway, providing a reassuring air of safety to all the residents of the city. That had all changed about fifteen minutes ago. Now all that remained was the splintered outline of the huge beast, where it had casually walked through both oak gate and metal portcullis, as easily as a knife would slice through butter.

Steam rose from the dark cobbles of the market square; some glowed yellow and orange with the heat. A trickle of water could be heard coming from the debris which not more than ten minutes ago had been the ornate fountain, the grand centrepiece of this magnificent square. The remaining buildings were on fire; the smell of burning flesh and bones was everywhere, but despite this the people still alive were mesmerised by the sight before them.

At the entrance to the square, with wreckage on either side of it, hovering a few metres in the air, was a giant dragon. The dragon was matt black all over with a wingspan in excess of fifty metres, and flame was dribbling down both sides of its colossal jaws.

In spite of its size the dragon was clearly agitated, roaring occasionally, scraping the large claws on its feet along the top of the rubble on either side of it, and banging its tail into the ground intermittently. The object of its agitation stood directly opposite, on the other side of the square: out of breath, clad from head to toe in chainmail armour, and clutching a rusty shield in one hand and a shining sword in the other. The knight was sweating profusely and parts of his armour were blackened from fleeting encounters with the dragon's flame over the past few minutes.

The knight seemed to have spent the last few seconds deciding on a course of action and, in one swift motion, dropped his rusty shield and threw his helm to the ground. He then proceeded to remove his gauntlets and the armour around his feet. You could almost hear a collective gasp from the city folk left alive, as the armour came off and the knight appeared to mouth a silent challenge to the giant beast on the other side of the square. Impossible as it may seem, the dragon appeared to understand the knight's whispered challenge from over three hundred metres away, and with one huge flap of its wings propelled itself forward, creating such down force that stone, wood and dead bodies were hurled across the square. At exactly the same time, the knight started sprinting towards the dragon, with most of his armour now removed and just his shining sword for company.

Time seemed to stand still as the speeding dragon travelled towards the knight, just above the ground, emitting a thunderous cone of fire in front of it. As the city folk watched in awe, it seemed there could only be one possible outcome: that the knight would be obliterated by the mighty beast.

As the apparently inevitable drew closer, the sprinting knight managed to find a little more speed and at the split second before hitting the tip of the flame, dived headlong towards the cobbles. The extra speed had caused the dragon to miscalculate and as the knight rolled underneath the dragon, he managed to turn over and thrust the heavy two handed sword into its dark underbelly with just one hand.

The flames died away instantly as the dragon thudded awkwardly to the ground, its massive body narrowly missing the exhausted knight. The dragon let out a low pitched holler that could be heard citywide, as its jaw cracked against the stone of the square. The knight hauled himself up from the ground, visibly panting as he did so. He slowly walked along the side of the downed dragon, as if inspecting it, only stopping when he reached its head. Kneeling down he started to recite some words only he and the beast could hear. Seconds turned to minutes as the knight continued to whisper to the fallen dragon.

Meanwhile, the city folk appeared to be recovering from the shock of previous events by helping the wounded, putting out fires, and comforting those people mourning the loss of a loved one.

From one side of the square a group of people, headed by the mayor, made their way cautiously towards the knight through the burning rubble, thick black smoke, and numerous bodies. As they approached, the knight finished his whispered conversation and a soft purple glow slowly spread from the dragon's head to the tip of its tail, finally encompassing its whole body.

The knight walked back along the dragon until he got to its belly. Crouching over, he put two hands on the hilt of his sword and swiftly pulled it free from the dragon's body. As he did so, about a dozen tiny scales clattered onto the stone cobbles. These scales had dropped from the immediate area around the sword's entry wound and were each about the size of a man's fingernail. Quick as a flash, the knight scooped them up and poured them into a silk bag which he had produced from beneath his armour. He then sheathed his sword and turned to face the newcomers.

"Is it dead?" asked the mayor, nervously.

"For all intents and purposes, yes," said the knight.

"How can we ever repay you for what you have done here today, brave knight? That vile beast would surely have destroyed everything had you not stepped up, valiant Sir," whispered the mayor.

"I require no reward. I'm sorry for the loss of life and damage to your city," the knight replied in a heartfelt manner. "I have companions who as we speak are making their way here with great haste to assist with what has happened this day, among them healers and engineers. I ask that they are allowed to help out as best they can, and also that you not address me as Sir, as I have not yet earned that title, but by my name: George."

The group of dignitaries nodded their agreement in unison and told George that lookouts would be posted to greet his companions, before hastily rushing off, clearly still frightened by the body of the giant dragon.

Over the next two days things progressed quickly. All the major fires were put out using water from the city's surrounding rivers, as the people formed giant human chains to pass the buckets along. Those not involved in controlling the fires helped the wounded, either in the hospital, by escorting them there, or by collecting herbs and roots outside the city to manufacture new medicines. The bodies of the dead were collected and taken to giant pyres that had been erected outside the walls of the city. The spire of the city's magnificent cathedral, fortunately undamaged, cast its long shadow over the city square, as if joining in the people's collective sorrow.

During this time George's companions started to arrive on their own and in pairs. They were easily identifiable because they all wore the same tunics as George. These tunics were white with a bright blue trident running diagonally across them. Upon arrival they were taken through the bloodstained boulevards to the overcrowded hospital, where George was helping to tend to the seriously wounded in a dark, dank, death-smelling ward.

George, seemingly in charge, dished out assignments to the new arrivals straight away. The healers stayed in the ward to assist the injured, most doing so immediately even though they had travelled for many days and were hungry, tired and weary.

Other arrivals included planners, politicians, and engineers. The planners and politicians worked closely with the mayor and his advisors to try and co-ordinate the rebuilding effort and temporarily re-house those folk who had lost their homes.

The engineers, meanwhile, seemed to be working miracles. Working around the clock, they designed and built two massive conveyor belts, spanning the entire circumference of the square, powered by an array of shire horses. They had also taken the one decaying crane that belonged to the city, reinforced it so that it could lift ten times the weight it had been able to bear previously, and made it mobile.

People watching the efforts of these men whispered in hushed tones that they were doing the impossible and that they must be using some sort of... magic.

During all of this, the giant body of the broken dragon lay in one corner of the square, eagerly avoided by everyone. Its magnificent black wings were lying at an excruciating angle with its delicate, flimsy arms tucked in under its bulging belly. If anyone had bothered to look closely at the corpse, which of course they didn't, they would have noticed that its scales had taken on a shimmering purple hue.

As the days passed, the progress in repairing the devastation was phenomenal.

The crane moved around the square lifting debris onto the conveyor belt. Usable building material was taken off at different points of the belt, while anything with no value was left on until the end and then taken away by horse and cart. In the meantime the planners had drawn up a blueprint of where the new buildings would go, agreed it with the mayor and his advisors and passed it on to the engineers who would implement it.

In the hospital all the minor injuries (broken bones, burns, concussions etc) had been taken care of and the patients discharged. Seven patients remained in the ward; all had been critically ill when they came in. The doctors and nurses performing triage had given them absolutely no chance of survival at the time, and moved their blood soaked bodies into a mouldy, shadow-ridden corner of the ward. The patients all remained alive now because of George. He had found them, waiting to die in that corner, and tended to them personally. The good doctors and nurses had gone about their work, dismissing George's actions as a waste of time because the patients seemed too far gone. But remarkably, one by one the patients' conditions seemed to stabilise, much to the delight and surprise of everybody on the ward.

With less work to do in the hospital, George spent more time checking on the rebuilding work and conversing with his companions. As he moved through the streets of the city, people would approach him, men shaking his hand, women kissing him on the cheek, all offering thanks for the seemingly amazing feats he and his companions had achieved. They were all grateful that George had managed to halt the mighty dragon before it destroyed their beautiful cathedral. Everybody in the city remarked what a true and inspiring leader of men he was. If only they knew the truth...

It was in the early hours of the morning on the seventh day after the battle with the dragon, that in the shadows of one of the partly rebuilt houses on the edge of the square, George held a meeting with his companions.

"How long until everything here is complete?" he asked.

Hannah the chief politician replied,

"Two full days from now the whole thing will be finished; the city will be as good as new, if not better."

"What about the chamber? Will it be ready on time?" enquired George.

"As far as we know preparations are in an advanced stage and it will be ready when we get there," answered Hannah.

"Have we procured any transport for Troydenn?" was the next question George asked, directing it towards the engineers. From the back of the building out stepped a short, fat, balding man with a great big, thick, grey beard. Although nothing special to look at, this man clearly commanded great respect, as well he should, for he was renowned as one of the best engineers that had ever lived. His name was Axus.

He moved through the crowd to the front so that he could address George.

"We've asked the mayor if we can have two of the massive freight sleighs that they use in winter to transport goods up the main road and through the pass. I don't think there will be a problem as they will still have six left and as it's only spring, they will have plenty of time to build replacements. We know how to convert the runners on the bottom of the sleighs to work effectively on road, grass and mud. The biggest problem we have now is that because of Troydenn's massive frame the sleighs will have to be attached so they run side by side and must be reinforced dramatically. At the moment we have no way of doing this. I've sent word back home and they are going to send someone out to us with a couple of new mantras to try. All seven miles of the route to the cave have been checked for any obstacles that may impede the sleighs, and the two miles inside the cave have been reinforced and lit up. Guards have been posted discreetly along the entire length of the journey."

On hearing all of this George gave a huge sigh of relief.

"You've all done a fantastic job over the past days, but as you know the hardest part is almost certainly still to come. I ask that you all continue the effort you've been making for two more days so that we can finish our tasks for these good people. Also, I'm sure we all know to be extremely vigilant. Anything out of the ordinary, no matter how small, should not be overlooked, because if they get him back, this will all have been for nothing. Let me know if there's anything else I can do."

As everybody started to sneak back to their accommodation, George pulled Axus to one side for a quiet word.

"Is there any word on how or why he's changed colour?"

"Not so far," replied Axus. "The council are working hard to find out though. Nothing like this has ever happened before as far as anyone knows, so they are sifting through the royal library, the dragonkin database and asking the relevant people if they know anything, but nothing as yet."

"Okay, let me know if you hear anything," whispered George, as they slid out of the building and into the night-time shadows.

The next day, the building work continued at a frantic pace. All of the buildings were nearly finished and the last intricate pieces were being added to the almost totally rebuilt fountain, the square's centrepiece. The mayor told the engineers that they were welcome to take the sleighs that they needed. He added that because that night was due to be their last in the city, a massive feast would be laid on to thank them all, and in remembrance of all those who had lost their lives.

Late in the afternoon a visitor arrived on a horse, asking to see Axus. Once guided to him, through the hectic preparations for the feast, the visitor dismounted, pulled three large cylindrical objects from his saddle bags, and handed them over. All the engineers gathered round as Axus opened the first cylinder and pulled a large sheet of parchment from it. From this point onwards the group of engineers looked more like a party of naughty school girls, all huddled together, whispering, sighing, even giggling at one point. They stayed like this for the rest of the afternoon and well into the evening, pausing only to obtain food and drink from the feast.

The feast itself was a great success. The food and drink were wonderful; the fires crackled and the scent of roasted meat swept across the city. The sound of music and dancing filled the air on this warm spring night. Towards the end of the evening, the mayor gave an emotionally charged speech, naming all those who had lost their lives in the attack, praising George's courage in confronting the dragon, and thanking him and his companions for their help in restoring the city to its former state. He also announced to everyone that George's entourage would be taking the dragon's corpse with them when they left the next day.

As the sun rose early the next morning the city seemed to be a hive of activity. The smell of freshly baked bread wafted down the streets as people cleaned up from the night before, dismantling stalls and marquees, collecting all the litter, washing shop fronts and streets. George made his way towards the nearly finished square, eager to talk to the engineers about their progress. On arrival he was confronted by a group beaming with pride but looking much the worse for wear after the previous night's merrymaking. Axus appeared to one side of the group.

"Blimey, that wine was potent last night. My mouth feels like a badger's bottom," he said, looking completely bedraggled, with chunks of meat and bread littering his unkempt beard. "Still, could have been worse I suppose. Poor old Hopkins spent most of last night whispering sweet nothings to those two sacks of flour over there. He even came over at one point to tell us that he thought one of them might be marriage material. Haaaa haaaaa, I don't think he's going to live that down for quite some time!" muttered Axus hoarsely.

"Anyway, onto important matters. It's done! One of the mantras sent out did the trick nicely. The two sleighs are as one and look as though they have always been that way. We've been up all night testing it to make sure it's okay. Only a matter of getting him on there now!" exclaimed Axus.

As George listened to what Axus was saying he noticed out of the corner of one eye a small boy appear from between two buildings and cautiously make his way towards the dragon's body. George stood riveted to the spot. None of the city folk would go anywhere near the dragon; most refused to even look at it.

As the boy got closer he seemed to be pulling something from his belt. Quick as a flash George had moved to put himself between the boy and the dragon.

"What exactly would you be up to, young sir?" asked George politely. The boy stood looking rather sheepish, suddenly realising that not only had he attracted the attention of George, but everyone else in the square as well.

"Well…. um, I, er... my name is Sam, Sam Smithers. My dad is Elron Smithers, the city's best known butcher. I um…. thought it would be such a waste, you know, what with some of the not so well off people in the city not having enough food and all. I thought it would save you the trouble of having to take it away as well."

"Let me get this straight," exclaimed George dubiously, "you were going to skin it!"

"To make sausages," added Sam.

The group of engineers burst into laughter as one. Everyone else looked on in astonishment as Sam's face turned a deep shade of scarlet. George ushered the crowd to quieten down.

"Young Sam, you seem full of noble sentiment which I admire greatly. But unfortunately there is a bigger picture which, because of your age, you fail to grasp. Perhaps you would take your knife and try and skin the dragon for me? If you succeed you can keep all the meat you like," declared George.

With the eyes of all those around on him, Sam pulled his knife from his belt and headed determinedly for the beast. With the knife in his right hand, Sam put his left hand on the dragon's right thigh to brace himself and, drawing his arm back, he thrust the knife at the flesh.

At the first point of contact the knife buckled in on itself, and the shock from the impact forced Sam to drop the now useless blade onto the cobbles. Sam stood with a look of absolute amazement on his face.

George wandered over to where the bewildered Sam stood and put his arm round his shoulders.

"Sorry Sam, that was a bit mean, but I thought a demonstration would be more effective than anything I could say to you. The reason we need to take the carcass away is that it requires very special measures to dispose of a dead dragon. And since you've ruined your best knife you can have this as a replacement," George said, slipping a gleaming dagger made from white gold, encrusted with tiny jewels, from his tunic and into Sam's shaking hands.

Sam managed to squeak a "Thank you" before heading gingerly back through the crowd towards his father's shop.

With the excitement over, everybody went about their work with a quiet dignity, knowing that they had all contributed to a job well done.

By early afternoon all of the building work was complete and the city's giant crane perched over the body of the outstretched dragon, like a huge heron waiting to rip into the water to catch a fish. Leather harnesses crisscrossed the dragon and met in the centre above him to form a gigantic net. The horses that George's companions had arrived on had been tethered together and attached to the front of the double freight sleighs that now occupied one corner of the square. Axus was busy co-ordinating the efforts of all the engineers. Time ticked by slowly as the crane took up the slack in the gigantic net. The creaking and groaning of the crane's timbers could be heard all across the square as the dragon was raised a few metres into the air.

It seemed the whole city had come out to see this happen. People were crowded onto the city walls overlooking the square, hanging out of windows, and packed onto balconies. With the dragon suspended in mid-air, the sleighs were guided very slowly into position underneath. The dragon was gently lowered onto the transport after about forty minutes, and the watching crowd let out a resounding round of applause.

Axus and the engineers checked the sleighs to make sure everything was secure and then formed up behind them. The politicians and planners had lined up in front of the sleighs to form a convoy headed towards the rebuilt east gate of the city. George shook hands with the mayor and took his place at the head of the convoy, leading them towards the exit, to the sound of a fanfare from the trumpeters, high up on the city's walls.

It took an agonisingly long time to reach the gate, at the slow pace they were going. But as George crossed beneath it, he reflected on all that had happened in such a short space of time. The good folk of the city waved him off believing that he had conjured up some sort of miracle to defeat the dragon. If only they had known the truth: that he too was a dragon, along with all his companions, just in their *mutatio* form at the moment.

Being a dragon in human form (*mutatio*) gave George enormous advantages over normal humans, such as superior strength, stamina, intelligence and agility. Also his metabolism could heal him faster, he had a higher tolerance for pain and he was tougher, making it harder to wound or injure him.

That's not to say it was a fair fight by any means. The dragon in its natural (*solitus*) form is virtually impossible to kill. A normal human would have no chance of killing a dragon as there is only one spot to strike on its entire body where it would be vulnerable, and it would take a perfect strike to actually slay it. Even a blow to injure it is remote, as generally the area of vulnerability is very small.

George was able to discern the exact point where Troydenn, the dragon, could be hurt or killed when they fought, because he was a dragon himself and whether a dragon is *solitus* or *mutatio*, another dragon can always see that special weak point. When George thrust his sword into Troydenn, he knew it wasn't a killing blow because of the angle the sword went in, purposefully inflicting a massive amount of pain and incapacitating the dragon for a short period of time.

As George pondered all of this, the giant sleighs with the matt black dragon attached made their way out of the city and into the countryside at a slow pace, escorted by George and his companions.

The troop travelled for the next five hours before finding a suitable place to stop for the night, just before sunset. The place they had found was a clearing near a small brook, off the main road, if you could call it a main road that is. As the horses were released from the burden of pulling the sleigh and led to the brook for water, George told everyone what they needed to do.

"We need lots of torches lit. Plant them into the ground to form concentric circles all the way to the edge of the road, with Troydenn right at the centre. I don't want anyone sneaking up on us tonight. If they are going to come for him I want to see what's going on. We will fight them here and we WILL win. Also we all need to get used to this, because at our present rate of speed we are going to spend at least two more nights in the countryside with only ourselves to depend upon before we reach the cave."

With guards posted all around the clearing and the horses tied up by the brook, a small fire was set up in the middle for cooking and warmth. As the food was cooked and eaten, people not on sentry duty tried to get some rest as best they could in the centre of the camp.

As George sat to one side quietly eating, Axus trudged across from the fire to sit beside him, bread in one hand, a mug of water in the other.

"No bloody wine again, huh! I know, I know. Need to be sharp and all that. Still what's an old... man supposed to do?"

As they sat eating, Axus gave a nod towards the dragon at the centre of the camp.

"Slightly ironic that you were sent to bring him back I suppose. I mean what with you growing up in the same nursery ring and then being in the council's royal guard together and all that."

There followed a great silence between the men. All that could be heard was the crackling of the fire, the meat sizzling on the spit and a few whispered conversations from around the camp. Axus, not normally one to worry about what he had said, started to have serious misgivings about the situation because the silence had lapsed into minutes and George still sat there with a faraway look on his face. A few more moments passed by and George let out a deep breath, a look of relief on his face.

"It was no coincidence that I was sent to confront him and bring him back. The council knew after what happened at Panama that it had to be me. Not only that, but apparently there are prophecy mantras that predicted that all of this would one day happen, depending on who you believe."

Axus, visibly stunned, sat on the ground shaking his head as George continued. "What I don't understand Axus, is how anyone is capable of doing what he has done. As you said, we practically grew up together; I've fought alongside him on a battlefield, letting him watch my back. I would have laid down my life for him at that point. Believing that he was capable of that level of deception and those atrocities was never really an option for me, until I saw what happened firsthand at Panama. It had to be me that confronted him and returned him to the others. I never really believed it before but I know it now."

The noise in the camp had died down. Only the sound of the burning torches and the cooking fire could be heard as the two men contemplated what had been said.

After finishing their food and drink George piped up with a question, keen to move away from thoughts of the past.

"Can I ask about the area in Antarctica?"

Axus, clearly happier at talking about an engineering subject, replied,

"What do you want to know?"

"Well I know that it's a containment area, only to be used as a last resort, but that's about all I do know. Perhaps you could tell me a bit more, as it seems increasingly likely that it will come down to that."

Axus stroked his beard thoughtfully as he answered.

"About fifty years ago, some of our best geologists were in southern Chile looking for new laminium deposits. They were looking at two volcanoes in particular, Monte Burney and the more southerly Fueguino. Now although no new deposits were found, the cutting edge technology that they had with them kept giving off very strange readings. Instead of putting the readings down to a fault with the equipment as most would have, the geologists decided to investigate and made a startling discovery. Running from Southern Chile, out towards the Falkland Islands, was a large underground channel. The channel was about half a mile wide, running approximately two miles under the ocean's surface. Just before it reached the Falkland Islands the channel branched, with one branch leading to a surface entrance on the Falkland Islands and one twisting sharply and heading directly south towards Antarctica. The geologists were amazed and had never seen anything like it. Most bewildering of all was that these highly skilled individuals could not tell if the phenomenon was naturally occurring or not. The group kept following the channel south but eventually came up against a problem they were not equipped or prepared for."

"Of course," said George quick-wittedly, "the temperature."

Axus grinned wildly.

"That's right. And with low temperatures having such an adverse effect on us dragons, sapping our strength, energy and stamina as well as clouding our minds, wisely the group stopped before the temperature plummeted too low. At that point they decided to set up a camp there, while two of them returned to fetch specialist protective mantras. After discussions with all the leading experts (and more than one visit to Gee Tee's Mantra Emporium), appropriate mantras were found, although because of the difference in volume between *mutatio* and *solitus,* the mantras were deemed most effective in human form. Once everything they needed was procured, and the council informed of what was happening, the geologists set off into the channel heading towards Antarctica. They continued for many days and nights, only able to survive because they were in human form, protected from the cold that would almost certainly have cost them their lives, solely by the protective aura of the specialist mantras they had returned to get.

As the group trudged on, the temperatures plummeted even further and the channel became more treacherous. Two of the team succumbed to frostbite in their feet and had to turn back, accompanied by one of the healthy geologists to make sure they returned to the camp safely. By now things were looking really bleak for the team but they were desperate to find out more about this phenomenon. As they sat round the make-shift camp fire eating nearly the last of their provisions, they concluded that they could travel for another twenty four hours before they had to turn back. The group set off early in what their body clocks told them was morning. As they set off into the darkness, the floor of the channel started to descend quite steeply. Weaving their way through giant stalagmites growing up out of the floor and ducking down at times to avoid even bigger stalactites hanging from the ceiling, to the group it looked just like giant jaws about to swallow them whole. At the point when it looked as if they would have to turn back defeated, the path ahead of them opened out into a gigantic cavern, like nothing any of them had ever seen before. This was as far as that group got, due to the cold and the fact that they had run out of food."

George let out a long breath that crystallised in the cold night air as he contemplated what he had heard.

"Any tales that have something to do with cold always send shivers down my tail no matter what form I'm in."

"Aye," chuckled Axus, "but that's not the end of it. After that startling discovery, more expeditions were sent to see what else they could find out about the place. Six expeditions over a fifteen year period finally revealed all. The cavern that the geologists came to the entrance of, below Antarctica, is believed to be the biggest on the planet. It's in excess of five hundred square miles and has a depth in places of over two miles. Unusually it has underground fresh water streams running through it, the source of which has yet to be determined. Another odd fact is that there is no geothermal activity whatsoever, with not a single trace of any known mineral deposit anywhere in or around the entire cavern system. The channel seems to be the only entrance into the cavern and the temperature never gets above -10° C, which is ideal for the purpose the council has in mind, I think you'll agree George."

George ran both hands through his long black hair as he considered everything Axus had told him.

"It just feels so permanent, Axus. I really hope it doesn't come to that, and that the council can find another solution."

"Aye, I know what you mean son, but these are undoubtedly the darkest times we've ever faced as a race. Even all the trouble that went on in South America pre-Balfor, pales into comparison with all of this. None of this sits that comfortably with me George, but I trust in the wisdom of the council and so should you. Once they've made their decision, whatever that should be, we can be confident that the hard work of so many has left us all well prepared. The cavern is well stocked with everything needed to survive well into the future. Individual shaped charges have been laid, starting at the exit of the cavern, going ten miles back into the channel at five hundred metre intervals. They have been carefully tested so that they only bring the roof of the channel down and do not disturb the ocean above. If it's decided that Troydenn and his followers should be incarcerated then they will be, well and truly, in that cavern."

"Well, I appreciate you telling me some of the details Axus. Let's trust in the council's judgement and wait to see what they decide," George said firmly. With that the two parted company for the night, George to go on guard duty and Axus to get some sleep.

As the sun rose over the camp, those sleeping were woken, bread and cheese passed out, and the horses watered, before the day's journey started. The convoy continued as it had started the previous day.

The journey over the next two days proved uneventful. The convoy passed many people, including travellers, salesmen, and farmers, during that time, most of whom didn't seem surprised to see a giant matt black dragon being pulled through the countryside on a massive sleigh. When these people were passed, sometimes sly hand signals were exchanged, sometimes a look was enough, or maybe even a whistle. All the cloak and dagger business with the passers-by, showed that the way ahead had been checked for any danger and that none had been found.

In the middle of the afternoon on the third day, the convoy left the muddy main road at the point where a blue trident had been inconspicuously painted on a large boulder, and headed across an open field in the exact direction the trident pointed. After crossing the field, the group came to a coppice and noted the same trident carved into a tree, pointing in another direction, and duly followed it. This went on for about two more hours, until they came over a rise and into a meadow. In the distance, beyond the long swaying grass dotted with flowers, was a large rocky outcrop.

Just as the convoy entered the meadow, hundreds of warriors and archers appeared silently from within the grass and on top of the outcrop. Bows and swords appeared from nowhere in the hands of all members of the convoy as they formed a defensive position around Troydenn, even though they were massively outnumbered. A tense silence enveloped the meadow and the outcrop; the only movement was that of the long grass rippling in the wind. George stood up from his kneeling position in front of the massive dragon with his shining sword in his hand. As he did so, a loud horn could be heard all across the meadow. One of the foremost warriors stepped forward from the long grass, sheathed his sword, walked towards George and clasped his free hand. George and the warrior exchanged whispered greetings while all around them bows and swords were stowed. The soldiers in the field parted swiftly, forming a huge path straight to the rocky outcrop. The convoy followed the path to the outcrop where the entrance to a massive cave was revealed; as they did so the soldiers in the meadow behind them closed in to form a great ring around them.

As everybody gathered at the cave entrance, the exhausted horses were untethered and led off into the meadow to graze. Meanwhile ropes appeared from the well-illuminated cave and were threaded through the sleigh on either side via a series of pulleys. More ropes were attached to the back of the sleigh and then led out into the meadow.

Once everything seemed satisfactory to Axus, most of the warriors in the meadow picked up the slack on the ropes in two lines and a large horn was sounded deep inside the cave. The rope in and around the pulleys on the sleigh began to go taut, and the sleigh with its giant burden moved slowly forward through the cave's entrance. Moving at a funereal pace, the convoy began its descent into the cave's massive interior. Daylight from the entrance gradually faded the further the group moved, being replaced by small circles of yellow light on either side of them, coming up from the stony surface they all walked on. Every twenty or so paces, jewels the size of a man's fist throbbed with bright yellow light from their place on the floor by the cave wall. These jewels lined the path all the way to the party's destination, just over two miles away. The rate of movement was incredibly slow and very occasionally a tight hairpin bend would have to be negotiated, which meant that distance was measured more in inches, rather than miles, per hour.

After what seemed like an eternity, but was actually just over eighteen hours, the weary travellers reached their destination. The winding path opened out into a gigantic underground cavern, which seemed to be filled with a lot of people. The same jewels that lit up the path were placed all over the floor of the chamber and up the walls at intervals as far as the eye could see; nevertheless, it was still impossible to discern the ceiling. Far from being damp and cold, the chamber was warm and a subtle breeze flowed through the whole area. The reason for this may have been the sporadic sections of molten lava around the edges of the chamber and oozing down parts of the shiny stone walls.

Shuffling feet could be heard in the dimly lit arena, as men and women moved to the edges to let the sleigh through to the middle. Once there, those who had travelled with the convoy from the city gradually moved away from the massive sleigh towards the edges of the cavern, merging with those already there, with the exception of George. Little men came scurrying out of the shadows, surrounded the sleigh and started to inspect it purposefully.

After much whispering, one of the men asked George to step back from the dragon, which he duly did, while the other men circled the sleigh and began chanting. It started as a quiet whisper but soon reached a crescendo of raised voices, all in unison. All of a sudden there was a huge BANG!!!!!

In the subsequent near silence, it would appear that instead of a scene of utter devastation, the only thing that had happened was that the double sleigh on which the captive dragon had been resting had completely disappeared, leaving the dragon lying on the cold stone floor.

Unexpectedly, huge stone doors swung in on themselves right in front of George and the dragon. Through them walked a tall man leading twenty four other men. As the crowd in the chamber saw this, they as one all started to kneel down and bow their heads, realising it was the dragon king and his councillors.

The king in his *mutatio* form looked nothing short of amazing. He was nearly seven feet tall with long golden hair flowing down past his shoulders, colossal muscles protruding from under his tunic, which was bright purple in colour and had a bright blue shimmering trident on the front of it. Most stunning of all though, was the real trident the king was carrying in his right hand. It was as tall as he was and appeared to be made of a bright blue metal that quite literally seemed to have a mind of its own, visibly flowing in different directions all the time, while also somehow remaining solid. An eye catching ring pulsed with different colours on the king's left hand.

The king thumped the trident onto the stone floor and spoke.

"Be upstanding everyone," he said. "You should all know why we are here. Let the proceedings begin," he bellowed.

One of the councillors approached Troydenn, pulled some parchment out from under his robes, and started reading the mantra on it. Everyone in the cavern could see the purple glow throughout the giant dragon's body recede more and more as the mantra continued. After finishing the mantra and slipping the parchment back into his robes, the councillor addressed Troydenn for everyone to hear.

"Will you voluntarily turn back into human form?" The dragon's mighty skull moved slightly, dragging its massive chin along the black stone floor, while two dribbles of flame came out of its nostrils.

"I'll take that as a 'no' then shall I?" replied the councillor, stepping aside to let the king through. A little quiver seemed to run through the defiant dragon as the king raised the trident and pointed it at his head.

"Since you won't change of your own free will, I will force you to change which will be most unpleasant... something I had hoped not to do."

With that, shimmering beams of blue energy lanced out from the tips of the trident towards Troydenn. When the beams hit his body they formed straight lines all along it, from head to tail. All the while Troydenn remained motionless, except for his eyes; they flicked from side to side, betraying the fear he felt.

Once all the horizontal lines were in place, the energy seemed to 'flip over' and form vertical ones that crisscrossed the horizontal ones, giving the impression that a giant net encased the dragon. Troydenn mustered all his strength in a panicked attempt to get to his feet as though sensing what was yet to come. The shimmering net of blue energy crackled ferociously as it began to shrink, causing Troydenn to let out a blood-curdling wail.

With Troydenn's pain echoing around the cavern and the contracting lines of energy crackling, sparking and smoking, it became very hard to see what was happening inside the energy net. Certainly a change was taking place because the area the net covered had diminished to about a third of the size it had been originally, and the wails and screams coming from within it were now much less those of an animal and much closer to those of a human.

The transformation only took a few more seconds to complete. Lying slumped on the cold stone floor, gasping for breath, was a stocky bald-headed man with a goatee beard and strange black tattoos on his cheeks and neck.

A low murmur of disbelief rippled through the crowd after what they had just seen. Most people realised that it was history in the making, as the last time a dragon had been put through this was nearly three hundred years ago.

Unsteadily the man got to his feet, all the time taking in his surroundings as if he had just woken from a long sleep. As he gazed over the king's left shoulder, Troydenn looked into the pale blue eyes of George, standing only a few feet away.

"Traitor!" he shouted, as he lunged towards George with a crazed look on his face, only to be stopped inches away by hulking guards that appeared from the shadows. Troydenn spat in George's face and wriggled and kicked in an attempt to break free from the guards' vice-like grip.

George wiped his face, desperately trying to maintain a façade of calmness and serenity, even though every muscle in his body screamed to fight. With his feet dragging along the ground, the guards hauled Troydenn back to the spot in front of king that he had previously occupied. A red beam of energy shot out from the trident, hitting Troydenn in the foot, and curled upwards towards his head, forcing him to stand bolt upright.

"Enough!" roared the king. "You will stand and listen to the charges brought against you and your supporters."

Out of the darkness, above the giant stone doors, a balcony suddenly appeared, illuminated by an eerie green light. Dressed in scarlet robes lined with purple, and a matching hood over her head, the magistrate appeared, gavel in hand. She smacked the gavel onto the stone balustrade in front of her, causing a THUD to echo around the giant cavern.

"Troydenn, formerly of the high council's royal guard, you are charged with the gravest of crimes. Your followers have already admitted that they murdered, maimed, kidnapped, stole, threatened and embezzled, all on your orders, for your own sordid purposes. The one thing that is sacred to us as a race, taught to us throughout our formative years in the nursery rings, is that we as a society are here to protect and guide humans at all times because of their potential. Throughout dragonkin history, nearly all dragons have strived to obey this founding principle laid down in our law.

I declare that you, Troydenn, are not only guilty of the crimes previously mentioned, but of the worst crime possible in our civilization............ manipulation of humans for your own selfish purposes. Since nothing on this scale has happened in over fifteen hundred years, the punishment will be decided by the king and his council," said the magistrate, clutching her gavel tightly.

As the magistrate stood on the balcony overlooking everyone, the eerie green light that had illuminated her started to fade away, after a few seconds making her indistinguishable from the stone walls behind her. Simultaneously the same light appeared around the king and Troydenn.

With his long golden locks, backlit by the soft green light, the noble features of the king's face turned from quiet contemplation to steely determination as he prepared to speak.

"The council and I have spent the last two days discussing the sentence that should be imposed on you, Troydenn. I can honestly say that this has been the hardest thing that the council members and I have been required to do during our tenure. I believe the outcome was reached in a fair and unbiased manner, considering all the relevant options and circumstances, although it should be pointed out that the decision was not unanimous, but reached by a majority of twenty four to one. The council hereby decrees that, YOU, Troydenn, and all of your conspirators currently in custody, will be transferred forthwith to our secure, remote detention facility, where you will remain for the rest of your natural lives."

A huge 'GASP' echoed around the cavern from all the shocked dragons in their human forms. In the shadows, a few feet behind the king, George stood rooted to the spot, absolutely shell-shocked. Not for a moment did he believe the sentence would be so harsh or absolute, despite his earlier conversation with Axus.

Throughout all this, Troydenn had remained totally impassive, with his jaw jutting out and piercing eyes not moving from the figure of the king.

The king continued speaking.

"Because of the natural constrictions of the facility, you will all be extremely limited in using your powers or any '*ediscere*'[1]. Provisions and equipment will be on hand to prevent any unwanted fatalities; however you will have to work hard and manage the limited resources available to you constantly, to ensure your continued existence. If you have anything meaningful to say, Troydenn, any words of regret or apologies, you will now have your chance to do so." The red beam of energy holding the evil dragon in place faded away.

Troydenn held up his arms and turned around as if addressing everyone in the chamber. The green light cast an ominous shadow over his malevolent face as he snarled,

"We will break free from whatever prison you confine us in and when we do, we will destroy your precious dragon society and visit terror on all your little human pets. Whether it takes ten years or five hundred, we WILL find a way."

"Enough!" commanded the king. "The sentence has been passed. Secure him for his flight with the rest of them."

"Yes, Your Majesty," said the leader of the guards, as Troydenn was surrounded and then bundled away by the rest of the soldiers.

---

1   Mantras that are memorised, as opposed to those that are written down.

A booming THUD resounded around the cavern as the magistrate smashed her gavel against the stone balustrade in the darkness of the balcony high above and declared,

"This tribunal has ended."

As the people left the cavern via variously concealed exits, George stood with a heavy heart, on his own in the darkness. Tears started to stream down his face and he didn't really understand why. He realised that the crimes committed by his former comrade in arms were amongst the most serious his kind had ever seen, and on an intellectual level he understood that the sentence was probably the best thing for dragons, humans and the whole planet in general. But somehow he couldn't help thinking that this was a sad day in dragon history and that this might have serious repercussions in the future.

Suddenly a well muscled arm appeared around George's shoulder. Immediately alert and ready to fight George pulled away, turned, and squared up to..................... the king.

"I'm, I'm, I'm sorry Your Majesty," George muttered, dropping his fighting stance.

"George my boy, less of the majesty, please," said the king.

"Sorry," replied George, wiping his tear-stained face on his sweat covered tunic.

"Listen, son. I know you have reservations about what's happened here today and that's understandable. I also know you did a wonderful job bringing him in and repairing the damage to that city. It's no surprise that it's affecting you badly considering how close the two of you were. That's nothing to be ashamed of. But try and think about the bigger picture. The pain will ease over time and gradually fade altogether, but it might take a while.

You're a good dragon, George, one of the best in fact. One day you will make it onto the council and I think you'll go on to become a great king, mark my words. But tell anyone I said that and I'll have to have your tongue cut out, as I'm supposed to be entirely neutral in these matters," said the king, winking and smirking at the same time.

George finally broke into a smile, for the first time in days.

"Thank you, *Majesty*," he emphasised with a grin.

The king smiled and said,

"That's much better," and broke into a great big belly laugh.

The light-hearted moment was over as quickly as it had begun, the bond between the two concealed, as one of the councillors approached.

"The flight has gathered with the prisoners, Majesty, and is ready to take off on your command. A tracking station has been set up in the magistrate's main office so that we can all monitor their progress to the detention facility," said the councillor sombrely.

"George and I will be there shortly Osvaldo. Thank you for letting us know," replied the king.

The councillor nodded and walked back the way he came, giving George a disapproving look as he did so.

"Hmmmm…," whispered the king. "There's something about that dragon which bothers me, always has done, but I just can't seem to put my finger on it. He's always done his work well, acted responsibly, helped others, and been a model councillor in fact. But just recently the way he's acted and some of the things he's said have been really out of character." Osvaldo Rosebloom had been the one councillor who opposed Troydenn's sentence.

"Anyway, no time to think of that now. Let's get to the magistrate's office and get this over and done with."

George followed the king through the concealed exit that Osvaldo had left by, and along a maze of corridors, in almost total darkness. After a few minutes, the king stopped suddenly and started to run his hands along the wall high above his head. Just as George was wondering what was going on, there was a sharp 'CLICK' from overhead and amazingly part of the wall silently slid away to reveal a brightly lit room bustling with activity.

Against each wall of the square office was a big desk, with a dragon in human form sitting wearing a shiny metal helmet connected by coloured wires to a machine at that desk. On the desk in front was a great big map of the world with different locations lit up and marked on it. A couple of dozen or so leather-clad stools had been arranged in the middle of the room. The main door to the room was exactly opposite where George and the king had entered. A tall wooden bookcase stood next to the door, piled high with old books, looking strangely out of place.

The king entered the room and, avoiding the stools in the middle, immediately headed for the far corner where the other councillors were gathered. As George stepped into the room and tried to make out what was going on, a little part of him recognised that the door through which he and the king had arrived had closed completely, without making any sound, or showing any sign now that it even existed at all. George was baffled and had never seen anything quite like it. He made a mental note to himself about this and promised himself he would try to find out more when he got the chance.

George regained his focus, and through all the noise of people talking and moving about the busy room, he heard the familiar gruff tones of Axus. His no-nonsense approach was always totally refreshing.

"We have four dragons flying separately from the rest of the flight, Majesty. Their job is to transmit the images that they are seeing directly to their opposite number in this room. Once the images are received, they will be passed on through the wires in the receiver's helmet to the tiny screen in the projection device. Light-emitting crystals will then shine through the tiny screen, thus projecting the nearly real-time images onto one of the four walls of this room."

George looked around the room and seemed to get the gist of what Axus had been telling the king. The flying dragons would travel with the guards carrying the prisoners to the detention facility, but their job would be to transmit telepathically the images that they were seeing so that everyone here could make sure the prisoners were successfully incarcerated. George knew that all dragons had telepathic abilities, but he figured that these four were probably stronger than most in that department due to the importance of this assignment. Perhaps they even worked for The Daily Telepath itself, or were in some other way enhanced.

The Daily Telepath was known to every dragon outside of the nursery rings, (as those still in the rings are deemed too young to receive it) as a daily news bulletin that is transmitted telepathically throughout most of the world, although dragons would find it increasingly hard to receive in either remote or very cold places. Reporters gathered and collated the news from all over the world, and it was then edited into a kind of telepathic newspaper to be distributed to those that wanted it. Those who worked at the Telepath were generally exceptional in their field of study, particularly if that field of study was telepathy. The ironic thing about the Daily Telepath was that its offices were situated directly beneath the Daily Telegraph offices in Fleet Street, London, England. Dragons in their various guises worked for the Daily Telegraph, making sure that all the news collected about the human world there was available to the editor of the telepathic news bulletin, as well as everything dragon-related.

Once edited, the bulletin was broadcast, at precisely five fifty eight am GMT daily, via giant thought-amplifying transmitters located in the basement of its offices. Having left the basement, the information travelled throughout the underground world of the dragons, using massive crystal boosters, powered by geothermal power, located strategically throughout the world. The day's issue was stored in small crystals throughout the land, then over written the next day. The crystal storage system allowed dragons to access their local paper and pick up a copy. A typical Daily Telepath bulletin consisted of the main news story, (sometimes dragon, sometimes human, sometimes one and the same) usually with a bold headline. Weather warnings played an important part: not local warnings, but global warnings, about weather systems such as typhoons, blizzards, and tidal waves. Sport was also on the agenda, as just about all dragons were keen on sport, particularly laminium ball. There was also a letters section where dragons commented on just about everything, and an obituaries column where dragon death notices were placed. These, in particular, were very important as dragons very rarely die; when they do, dragons can travel from far and wide to attend the normally extravagant funeral proceedings. Any news to do with the king or the council would also feature heavily in an edition of the Daily Telepath, and a selection of human news from around the globe was also included.

The system seemed to work quite well for the most part, and dragons can often be heard in human and dragon form discussing subjects from that day's Daily Telepath. Just recently the Telepath had been experimenting with images and had tried incorporating them in the news bulletin. Even though dragons can successfully pass telepathic images in colour to one another, the images tried by the Telepath in their experiments were in black and white and had turned out to be quite poor in comparison. Most dragons complained that the images were blurred and barely visible when the bulletin was looked at. This had apparently been put down to the fact that the boosters that transmit the bulletin around the globe could not handle the extra information entailed in the images. It now looked like most dragons were not going to get to see pictures of their favourite laminium ball stars in the bulletin on a regular basis.

George's mind, having wandered off, was brought back to the room by hearing Axus finish off telling the king about the projection system.

"So you see Majesty, this was the only way to use the boosters in that area and keep the transmission secure. We certainly don't want every dragon in the world viewing the captives on their way to being incarcerated, do we?" asked Axus seriously.

"Not with some of Troydenn's followers still unaccounted for, no we don't," replied the king, gravely.

Axus clapped his hands to get everyone's attention.

"Could everybody please move to the centre of the room, as that's where you will get the best view of all four projections. Dim the lights and start the projectors please!" ordered Axus, loudly.

All the people gathered in the room moved to the stools in the centre, except the projectionists, Axus, the king, and strangely Osvaldo, who remained where he was, casually leaning on the bookcase next to the room's main entrance. As the room plunged into darkness, the walls became alive with moving images. It took George a little while to process exactly what he was seeing on the walls of the room.

On the 'main wall' in front of those gathered, was an image from a dragon that was right in the middle of the convoy. The image showed dragons flying to the left, to the right, above and below, all flapping their gigantic wings to propel them along. The flying dragons all had tightly fitting harnesses strapped to them, with anything from one to three sedated dragons in human form unwillingly attached to them.

On the 'left wall' the view was from a dragon clearly flying at the back of the pack, high on the right hand side. It showed all of the dragons and their cargo from above, flying at break-neck speeds through a large open cavern.

On the 'right wall' the view was from a dragon skimming along the surface of the cavern, underneath the left side of the dragon flight. As the dragon looked up, he could see the giant underbellies with the prisoners strapped to them and the bones and muscles in the dragons' wings working furiously to keep them aloft and propel them along at about five hundred miles an hour.

On the wall behind the gathering of people, the scene showed the dragon convoy from quite a distance away. The dragon projecting this image seemed to be trailing the large group by about one and a half miles, with the dragons only really showing up as small dots, but dots which appeared in corresponding shades to those dragons in the convoy. The captives attached to the dragons could not be seen from this view because of the distance involved.

Those gathered in the centre of the room all seemed to have a different idea about what was the best projection to view the proceedings from. George found himself gazing at the 'behind' view most of the time, while the others kept swivelling on their leather clad stools. The limited light in the caverns that the convoy was flying through made the spectacle of the dragons look like stars in a dusky night sky.

Progress was seemingly slow, but dragons were renowned for their patience and understanding. Everyone in the room knew that this was only the start of a long journey. The underground route for the convoy involved flying south west from Europe, towards Africa's eastern coast. Once there, the dragons would head south under the coast until they reached the capital of Sierra Leone, Freetown. Turning south west again they would then fly under the south Atlantic for about three thousand miles, before arriving under the outskirts of Rio de Janeiro. Following the coast of Uruguay they would head towards Buenos Aires in Argentina before heading directly south towards the Falkland Islands and joining the massive trench there that would take them all the way to the detention facility in Antarctica. The entire journey was over eleven thousand miles long and would take about twenty two hours in total.

Most of the dragons in the room had let their concentration slip and their minds wander more than a little. It had after all been an extremely intense and historic day, and the most important part of the journey and the incarceration would be at the very end, from the Falkland Islands onwards, so trying to relax now was by no means a bad thing. After all, dragons had the ability to become instantly alert at a split second's notice anyway.

George was no different from the others, and found his concentration waning in a room where the only noise was that of Axus, who was constantly circling the room, whispering instructions to each projectionist, adjusting the tiny light crystals or fiddling with the wires that joined onto the dragons' helmets. Occasionally Axus would inform everyone where the dragon convoy was in the world and how far they still had to go.

"So far the convoy has flown under the Mediterranean and along the coast of Morocco. They have just passed beneath Casablanca and shortly you will see from the projections increased magma activity as the group skirt around our Canary Island geothermal power plant," said Axus with authority.

George could see from his preferred view, the long distance one, that the bottom of the cavern systems now being traversed by the party was growing increasingly bright. Giant slithers of molten lava weaved along the floor and lower walls, making it look like an enormous spider had spun a mammoth fluorescent web.

George, like all other dragons, knew all about geothermal power; he had after all spent months studying it in the nursery rings like every other dragon. The subterranean dragon cities were all powered and heated using geothermal power and had been for many centuries. Huge underground areas had also been specifically heated to exacting temperatures, so that they could grow a diverse range of crops all over the world, just like giant underground greenhouses. Although these achievements were amazingly clever and interesting, most dragons' favourite part of the geothermal process was the HOT SPRINGS……..

Ahhhhhhhhh.

Just thinking about hot springs made George's tail wave around in delight, even though he was in human form. Whatever form he was in, George remained convinced that a dragon's tail was like its soul, and that you just could not be parted from its essence. So much so that sometimes he even had to look behind him to check that he wasn't dragging it along the ground when he was disguised as a human. This thought, it must be said, was totally private and not something he would ever want other dragons knowing, for fear of ridicule.

"Hot springs," he thought, "are just pleasure personified to a dragon — that, and chewing your way through a mound of charcoal....totally the best draggony things to do on the whole planet."

If there's one other thing that most dragons like, it's gossip. Dragons are always sharing the latest rumours about anything and everything. There was undoubtedly always talk about the next big project to use geothermal power. George had overheard some of Axus' engineers gossiping back at the city after the fight with Troydenn. They were speculating on rumours of a planet-wide transport system being built underground, which harnessed the geothermal power. Pure fantasy of course, thought George. Just like the idea of different flavoured charcoal and that absurd rumour about each city getting its own automated dragon wash. Madness indeed!!!!!!!!!

With regard to geothermal power, it is widely hoped and believed within the dragon community, that with the right guidance and a gentle nudge or two, humans in the coming decades and centuries, as they develop and become more advanced technologically, will take up the mantle of geothermal power because of its abundance and pollution-free properties. Most dragons hark back to Roman times and point out that the Romans themselves were subtly nudged in the direction of geothermal power and achieved it quite successfully, especially at Pompeii, that is until the catastrophic eruption of Mount Vesuvius in 79 A.D.

George's wandering mind was once again interrupted by one of Axus' updates on the dragon convoy's progress.

"The convoy has nearly reached Freetown and will soon be changing to a south westerly heading," muttered Axus, with distinctly less enthusiasm than an hour ago.

Over the course of the rest of the day, the dragon convoy followed the planned route and made good time, with no extraordinary occurrences. Axus continued with the regular updates, while some dragons in the room paid more attention than others; some closed their eyes and meditated, while others, chiefly Osvaldo, left for short periods and then returned.

Once the convoy entered the trench at the Falkland Islands, the tension in the room became apparent. Dragons shifted on stools, paced the room and held whispered conversations with one another, betraying the nervousness everybody felt. Even Axus was more agitated than George had ever seen him before, not being able to stand in one place for more than two seconds and constantly berating the technicians flitting in and out of the room. Only one person seemed unaffected by the tension and the pressure: the king. He sat on one of the stools in the centre of the room looking like he didn't have a care in the world: the calm centre of a hurricane raging all around him.

"Majesty, the convoy are about five hundred miles out from the entrance to the cavern and should be there in approximately one hour," announced Axus.

"The detention facility is fully stocked with provisions and equipment for the criminals. It should just be a matter of the guards releasing them from the harnesses and using the mantras to bring them round. Once the mantras have been activated, it will take about five minutes for the fugitives to recover completely. The first thing the captives in their human form will have to do is to set up all the cold weather gear we left there, as they will not have the benefit of the protection mantras, unlike the guards dropping them off. By that time the guards will be long gone and the shaped charges will have been set off, trapping those remaining behind a permanent wall of rock and ice."

George knew the whole sorry episode was nearly at an end now, but as he looked around the room at the different projections of the convoy on the different walls he couldn't help but pity those dragons being carried to their internment, to live the remainder of their lives in that horrifying environment, so totally alien to all and any dragons. Even worse, to know that you would end up dying there as well, with absolutely no chance of ever mating or reproducing at all. A wave of sorrow washed over him and once again he thought of Troydenn and wondered how it had all gone so horribly wrong.

Everybody in the room continued to watch the convoy moving towards their final destination. As the minutes progressed, the images on the walls seemed to deteriorate, sometimes becoming blurred, sometimes cutting out altogether for a few seconds at a time. Axus was working even more frantically than he had been before, something that had to be seen to be believed.

"What seems to be the problem, Axus?" asked the king, calmly.

"It's the telepathic boosters, majesty. We've increased the power output on them all to as much as they can handle, but the range is just too great. The cold may be having an effect as well. The pictures will continue to break down I'm afraid, and there's nothing more we can do from here."

"How long before the convoy reaches the cavern, Axus?" asked the king.

Axus strode over to the great map on the desk at the front of the room and began to study it carefully. As he did so the projections on the walls around them began to cut out and flicker more frequently. After a short period of time, Axus turned from the map to face the king, grinning wildly.

"They're only a few minutes from the entrance, Majesty," he said, sounding relieved.

The king nodded his head and everybody went back to focusing their attention on the projections.

Although George could see the left and the right side projections out of the corner of his eyes, he remained concentrated on the back wall and the view from the dragon flying far behind the main convoy. It seemed that there was less interference with this projection, maybe because it was further behind than the other images, making it easier to take in what was happening.

All of a sudden Axus pointed at the front projection and roared,

"There it is, the entrance to the cavern!"

Everyone in the room, even George, turned to look at the projection on the front wall. Through the distortion and interference they could just make out the gaping entrance to the detention facility, back-lit by the artificial light put in there for the captives' benefit by Axus and his team of engineers.

At that exact moment............ALL HELL BROKE LOOSE!!!!!!!!

It was difficult to tell quite how it started because of the poor quality of the images that were being projected onto the walls, but the captives were all turning from their human form (*mutatio*) to their dragon form (*solitus*). Everybody in the room looked slack-jawed and stunned at this shocking turn of events: that is, everybody but the king and Osvaldo Rosebloom.

Some of the prisoners had broken free of their harnesses and had turned back into their dragon form while dropping towards the ground at great speeds. They could be seen heading towards the ground as a human, dropping like a stone, only to transform on the way down and swoop back up as a dragon, ready to join the fight. Others, however, were turning back into their dragon form while still attached to the guards in their harnesses, bursting free and taking their guards completely by surprise.

In every projection it was the same, dragon fighting dragon. Streams of flame spewed from the mouths of the different dragons, looking like tiny candles high up in the cavern entrance from the dragon projecting the images from furthest away. Dragons were head-butting, biting, and crashing each other into walls and stalactites, or using their talons to rip through each other's wings, sending their opponent spiralling to the icy cavern floor way below. Some were also using their tails to deadly effect. In the middle of it all was the terror-inducing sight of the huge matt black dragon that was Troydenn going on an absolute rampage.

"Where are the closest reinforcements, Axus?" asked the king calmly, never taking his eyes from the scene of carnage and mayhem before him.

"Not close enough I'm afraid, Majesty. The prisoners would easily be able to get back to the Falkland Islands and escape in plenty of time before we could get any kind of force even vaguely close," Axus replied, shaking his head gloomily.

George noticed Osvaldo out of the corner of his left eye. Unlike everyone else in the room who looked shocked or horrified at the turn of events, Osvaldo just looked................SMUG.

All of a sudden the projection on the left wall cut out totally. The operator at the desk on that wall fell off his chair to the floor and in a panic-stricken way scrambled to remove his headset, before letting out a blood-curdling scream and losing consciousness. Some of the technicians watching the carnage rushed over to aid their colleague. A medic arrived within a minute or so.

Everybody in the room could see what had happened from the images on the back wall. There, through a crowd of dragons, flying, fighting and roaring fire at one another, in the middle of the cavern entrance was a pale dragon with bright flecks up its back and tail. Its long slender neck was being gradually crushed by the giant vice like jaws of Troydenn. The two dragons hovered in mid air with the chaos ensuing all around them, long after the life had left the pale dragon, which had been projecting images back for all to see. Drawing a gasp of horror from all in the room, Troydenn's gigantic jaws finally clasped together, totally severing the poor dragon's neck, and letting the two pieces of the body swirl to the darkness at the bottom of the cavern. The dragon sending the images back that was furthest away from the action, focused in on Troydenn. Flapping his massive matt black wings in mid air, he had a crazed look in his eyes and a huge grin on his face.

In the monitoring room you could cut the atmosphere with a knife. In the stony silence that followed, everybody looked towards the king. He stood and with his left forearm smashed a vacant stool halfway across the room.

"ENOUGH!" bellowed the king. "Blow the explosive charges now!" he shouted across the room.

Axus turned timidly towards the king. "But Majesty, what about the guards? They'll be trapped along with the prisoners," he stuttered.

With a look of absolute fury on his face, the king roared, "**DO YOU THINK I DON'T KNOW THAT THEY'LL BE TRAPPED AND LOST FOREVER? THINK HOW MANY HUMANS AND DRAGONS ALIKE WILL BE KILLED IF TROYDENN AND HIS FOLLOWERS ARE**

ALLOWED TO LEAVE THAT PLACE. I COMMAND YOU TO BLOW ALL THE CHARGES AT ONCE. NOWWW!!!!!!!!!!"

Despite the fact that all the blood had drained from his face, Axus turned and walked over to the table with the giant map on it. From a drawer underneath he pulled out a small box and flipped open the lid. Closing his eyes and shaking his head, he depressed the small red button that lay inside.

Bright explosions blossomed across all three of the remaining projections. Dragons were pulverised by flying rock, ice and super heated air. The explosions encompassed everything in sight, causing two of the remaining projections to cease almost immediately, signalling the deaths of two more of the dragons that were projecting the images back to the gathered few. The room became a whole lot darker with only the projection on the back wall remaining.

George knew that everyone else in the room, just like him, could do nothing but stare wide-eyed at the image on the back wall. What he saw made his green blood run cold.

The lone projectionist had turned away from the cavern entrance and was now flying as fast as he could along the trench in the direction of the Falklands. Swerving erratically to avoid the giant stalactites and stalagmites, the dragon appeared to be flying at break neck speeds in the comparative darkness, clearly aware of the fate of those behind him. While still flying ahead in the trench, the dragon took a brief glance over his shoulder. The image showed huge amounts of rock and ice crashing down on one or two other fleeing dragons. The cascading barrage of rock and ice caused by even more explosions was steadily catching the dragon up, even though he seemed to have found a little more speed from somewhere.

Without realising it, everyone in the room, watching the heroic efforts of this dragon had been holding their breath.

Moving incredibly fast now, it seemed that the only possible outcome was for the dragon to outrun the wave of death behind him. Until, that is, an explosion went off about ten metres in front of him. The last thing those in the room saw before the wall went blank was of a torrent of rock, ice and fire heading towards the brave dragon.

Now plunged into darkness, the room was as silent as a crypt in the dead of night.

"Lights!" commanded Axus, and immediately they came on.

George had never seen dragons so sombre. The shock and horror at what they had witnessed here today would stay with each of them forever.

"Report," commanded the king.

Axus studied the information on the map table before turning around and addressing the king.

"All the charges detonated, Majesty. Anyone still alive will remain encased in that hell hole for the rest of their lives."

George was in emotional turmoil. The trial of Troydenn itself was bad enough, but this – this was beyond belief. Guilt, sadness, remorse, relief - was it even possible to feel all of these things at once, he asked himself. On reflection, he knew his emotions would always overwhelm him when he thought of the events that surrounded the last week or so. But today the greatest threat his race had ever faced had been thwarted for good, finally. And that in itself must be the most important thing. At least that's what he continued to tell himself.

*   *   *

"And that, students, for those of you who didn't already know, is the real story of George and the Dragon. Nothing like the dismal tales you will hear on the surface from the humans, if and when you finally get up there. That will be all for today. Lessons will resume in the morning," said the 'tor. The students all got up from sitting on the cold marble floor and slowly made their way back to their living quarters.

2

A Tail of Humility

Peter leapt down from the thick, rock wall of the nursery ring onto one of the wide paved walkways that littered the underground domain of the dragons. It had been some three years since he had left his nursery ring (this particular one in fact), but something always seemed to draw him back from time to time. He always tried to turn up late in the afternoon if he was going to visit, knowing full well that the young dragonlings always had the chance to choose the subject matter at that particular time of day. Dragonkin lore always seemed a popular choice with the younglings, along with myths and magic. Peter wasn't sure how many times he had heard the legendary tale of George and the Dragon, probably several hundred by now, but even so he always ended up being spell-bound, with goose pimples running up the length of his tail, just like the pupils in the class. As he made his way in human form along the walkway towards the monorail station, enjoying the heat from the molten lava running through the gaps in the paving stones beneath his feet, Peter thought back to his time in the nursery rings.

Dragon families and relationships, unlike those of the humans on the surface, would appear to have no rhyme or reason. Some parents visit their children in the nursery rings every day, while others just deposit the newly laid egg there and never return. Peter had never met his parents. After hatching from his egg, the nursery ring became his home and the *praeceptors,* or 'tors as they were known, became his family. The *praeceptors* act as tutors to the young dragons, only in a much more holistic way than in human schools on the surface. Their guidance not only covers the academic studies that the dragons will learn in the fifty year compulsory attendance period, but other much more personal skills, that include learning to fly, changing shape, grooming, diet, family history, economics, relationships and social skills (dragon and human). Most dragons tend to form a really strong bond with their 'tor due to the time spent with them and the intensity of their relationships, and dragons who have no recollection of their parents quite often come to think of their 'tor as a parent or guardian figure.

A dragon's rate of growth far exceeds that of a normal human being. Physically a dragon can reach full grown maturity by the time he is ten years old, and most two year old dragons have a far greater intellect than the average full grown human being. Peter reached his tenth year maturity celebration in the nursery ring without any great fuss. He hadn't really excelled at any one particular thing; he didn't really know what he was going to do when he left the nursery rings (not that many dragons do at that age as they have at least another forty years of learning ahead), and although he admired and respected his 'tor, he hadn't built up the kind of relationship that the other dragons around him had. There were two things that tended to stand out in his mind from that time in his life though. The first was the friendship he had formed with two of his classmates, a friendship that was as strong today as it had been at that time, some fifty two years ago.

Richie Rump was a beautiful female dragon. She had hatched only a few months after Peter and just a few months after that they seemed to have formed an incredible bond of friendship. As dragons go, Richie was a real eye catcher. While Peter was short and round with a longer than average neck, a small jaw and great big floppy undragon-like ears, Richie was petite, sleek and perfectly formed, with a gorgeous sparkling emerald green hue, except on her tummy, where the green gently blended into a lovely soft shade of yellow. What she lacked in stature, she more than made up for in grace, speed and determination. From an early age, Richie had always out-performed anyone else at anything physical. She was the first in the ring to master flying and even now can out-fly dragons twice her size, matching them easily for speed and skill. No slouch on the academic front either, most of the young dragons knew better than to challenge Richie to anything, physical or mental, because it was almost certainly going to end in humiliation, for the challenger anyway.

Peter's other friend was called Tank. Although relatively naïve, (as were most dragons still in the nursery ring), Peter thought Tank was the most caring, thoughtful and considerate dragon in the whole world. A huge mountain of a dragon, Tank could easily fit Peter's squat little frame under one of his gigantic wings. Had he more speed and dexterity, Tank could possibly have been groomed to be a professional laminium ball player, as he was most certainly the right size and shape for it. Tank seemed to have a great affinity for anything to do with nature. He always knew more than even the 'tors seemed to about plants or animals, much to their utter amazement. He was also always the first to jump in and stand up for his friends in any sort of argument or confrontation, not that Richie ever needed any help in that department, but Peter often found himself on the end of a lot of taunting and teasing from the other dragons in the nursery ring, some of which would end up going a little too far. Although the 'tors were nearby almost all the time, they very rarely interfered with anything like that, preferring to let the young dragons sort it out of their own accord, classing it as part of their learning experience. Hence the reason Peter supposed the bond between him and Tank had grown as strong as the one between Richie and himself. The three of them seemed almost inseparable.

The second thing that Peter remembered vividly was the dragon that often came along in human form to watch the lessons and see how the young dragons were getting on, much in the same way that Peter tended to turn up and watch whenever he got a chance. Even though Peter had no family to speak of, he always thought kindly of that particular dragon, and although they had only ever exchanged a few polite words, he always got the impression that the dragon was keeping an eye out for him in some way, shape or form. He always appeared in the human form of an old man with long, straggly, grey hair flowing down past his shoulders, and a walking stick made of a light coloured oak. The walking stick always stood out in Peter's mind when he thought back. It was the kind of walking stick that if you had a million walking sticks of all different shapes, sizes and types, this was the stick you would choose. It seemed somehow...special.

The old man would turn up and watch lessons at the nursery ring, sitting on the wall much as Peter had done only moments ago, and would also turn up at Lava Falls and watch the young dragons practise their aerial technique and impromptu laminium ball matches.

The last time Peter had set eyes on him was on the day the whole class graduated from the nursery ring. Graduation traditions vary from nursery ring to nursery ring across the whole world, but they all have them. Peter's nursery ring was no different, and so on this special day all of the young dragons found themselves atop the highest cliff at Lava Falls, watched by all the staff and 'tors. The dragons were all in their human form, standing over a mile above the bubbling lake of super-heated lava. Peter could distinctly remember feeling the heat and the steam on his face, even at that distance. He also remembered very clearly turning and looking behind him at all the staff from the nursery ring and just out of the corner of his eye, catching sight of the old man, who, when their eyes met, gave Peter a wink and a smile. Peter had little chance to dwell on it at the time, as he was caught up in the mad rush of graduating dragons running at full speed off the cliff in their human forms. Peter, caught up in the rush, ended up diving head first off the cliff, a very scary feeling in his human form, even though it was quite tame compared with the kind of flying that most of the dragons had practised.

The idea behind this particular tradition was that the dragons would leap off the cliff in their human forms and on the drop down would change into their dragon forms and fly up into the air to celebrate. Changing shape halfway through a drop like this would have been taxing for an experienced adult dragon. Thus there was a definite element of danger to the whole thing. Peter remembered the effort he had to put in to effect the change to his dragon form. He also remembered the sheer exhilaration once he had completed the change and had zoomed up into the air, after being only metres away from the bubbling lava, with all his classmates.

After a few minutes of flying around celebrating, Peter's classmates all flew down to meet the staff and 'tors for a final meal that had been prepared and laid out on the cliff side. As they did so, Peter sought out the old dragon hoping to have a friendly chat, but much to his surprise he was nowhere to be seen. That was the last time Peter had seen the old man, and he often found himself wondering what the old dragon was doing now, and if like Peter he still visited the nursery ring to watch the other dragons. Looking back, Peter assumed that the old man/dragon must have been taught at that nursery ring and liked to visit, just as Peter did.

From his tenth year onwards, lessons at the nursery ring, as far as Peter was concerned, became a lot more interesting. Up until then, their education had consisted of the kind of things the humans on the surface would learn: maths, languages, history, science, economics, and a broad range of religious and human studies (everything about the human world that had not already been covered). They had also covered the dragon basics such as flying, grooming, mating, diet, dragon beliefs and the founding principles. From now onwards the young dragons got to cover subjects such as dragon lore, self defence, moral standing, spatial awareness and mantras in all their shapes and forms.

Mantras were the one subject guaranteed to put a glint in a young dragon's eye. All had heard about what they could achieve; only a few had ever seen examples in real life. Mantras could do anything from healing humans, dragons, animals and plants, to repairing any sort of machinery, complex or simple. The most common and nearly every day use for mantras that most dragons had was to change their form from *solitus* to *mutatio*. The ability to change from a dragon form into a human form was one that required the utmost concentration and took years to perfect. This was basically what the next forty years in the dragon ring would be all about, learning to swap forms, and more importantly maintain that unfamiliar human form indefinitely without any flaws or imperfections. Once the young dragons had mastered that they then had to learn how to make the subtle changes in their human bodies that would allow them to blend in with the normal humans on the surface and not stand out at all.

Peter remembered his very first mantra lesson with great clarity. He was sitting on the cold marble floor in the giant courtyard attached to the nursery building with all of his nursery ring classmates. Their 'tor had explained and demonstrated how to use the mantra properly, and the students were all standing around expecting to repeat the actions of the 'tor. The nursery ring was never a particularly quiet place even when it was supposed to be, but you could hear the sizzle of flames dribbling from some of the more nervous dragons' noses, as the dragonlings all watched each other to see who would be brave enough to go first.

A small dragon by the name of Tempest was the first to try. Sitting nearly in the middle of the courtyard, Tempest took a deep breath, unrolled the parchment and, closing her eyes in concentration, recited the mantra. Even though they were all supposed to be getting on with their own mantras, all of the other students watched Tempest eagerly.

The single most important aspect of nearly all mantras is not just reciting the words, but channelling the concentration and belief behind the words. This is what causes the mantra to succeed or fail. This also determines how successfully the mantra will work. For example, a healing mantra being used on a deep open wound, if used by an experienced healer, will heal the wound, destroy any infection and remove any scar tissue. The exact same mantra used by someone less experienced, and not directing the same sort of concentration or belief into it may not have the same effect. It may fail to close the wound properly, leave an infection, or it may heal it all up but leave a massive scar. The difference between total and faltering concentration and belief is staggering; the results can lead to the mantra working in the way it should, only less effectively or sometimes producing unpredictable side effects.

Now the dragonlings had all been taught this, but most had not really paid attention; they were too excited about the prospect of performing their first mantra. That was why the 'tor had started with this particular mantra and why, if the students had looked closely at their tutor, they would have noticed a slight smile developing at the bottom of his huge jaw, something that rarely happened as he was a most serious dragon and took great pride in his work.

Tempest, although she tried, clearly hadn't put enough belief and concentration into her mantra and was just starting to discover how unpredictable the side effects could be.

When the 'tor had demonstrated the mantra about five minutes before, his five metre long tail had, starting at its tip, shrunk until it was no longer there. That was the particular effect this mantra should have had if used well. Known only to the 'tor was the fact that this mantra was unbelievably specific and amazingly sensitive to incorrect pronunciation or not enough channelled belief. A look of utter horror and humiliation was etched on Tempest's face at the moment, as not only had her tail began to grow bigger but it had also split into three parts, all of which were now growing and snaking across the courtyard of their own accord. Students occupying the area directly behind Tempest were dumbstruck momentarily. This soon changed as they were forced to dive and roll out of the way of the ever expanding tails and flee back into the indoor teaching area or try and make a dash to get round the front of the horror stricken Tempest.

Looking back on the whole thing, Peter thought it was absolutely hilarious, but at the time the incident had seemed anything but funny to the young dragons. Eventually the tails stopped growing larger, but not before each had split into three again leaving poor Tempest rooted to the spot in the middle of the courtyard, with nine giant tails embedded firmly in the broken marble floor.

The lesson had ended there that day and the class had been dismissed and sent off to Lava Falls to practise their aerial combat techniques. Everyone was aghast at what had befallen Tempest, with very little flying being done and most choosing to sit on the cliff side and dwell on the aforementioned events. That night Tempest was missing from her dormitory, with nobody in authority seeming to know anything about her whereabouts or wellbeing. The next morning all the students except Tempest sat waiting nervously for the 'tor to arrive for the morning's lessons. The 'tor walked in with a big beaming smile on his face, followed closely by a very healthy looking Tempest, much to the surprise of all the students.

The missing pieces of the puzzle soon began to fall into place. The 'tor had undone all of the trouble with the tails in a matter of minutes after the students had left the previous day. He then proceeded to repair all the damage to the marble in the courtyard and the surrounding walls and buildings. With everything back to normal the 'tor had treated Tempest to a slap up meal and persuaded her to stay in alternative accommodation that night to make the other students 'sweat a bit'. The whole scenario had been designed to show the students what could potentially happen if mantras were not used with enough conviction, stressing the importance of belief and concentration over merely reading the words from the parchment. Peter was sure none of the students who witnessed the events of that afternoon would ever forget it.

Peter's thoughts of his friends and past events faded, and reality came flooding back as the walkway he was on started to widen and fill up with dragons in their natural form and in various human guises.

The nursery ring Peter had been to visit was part of a dragon community called Purbeck Peninsula. This community is one of the oldest dragon enclaves in Britain, second only to London itself. It is based beneath the south coast of England in a region that covers the area from the east of Bournemouth through to the west of Swanage, as far south as the most southerly point of the Isle of Wight and as far north as the northern reaches of Wimborne Minster. Purbeck Peninsula dates back over three thousand years and draws its name from the fact that its centre is located directly beneath the Isle of Purbeck and because the underground area on which the community is built is surrounded by layers of molten lava, making it almost inaccessible from other underground dragon communities.

Originally it was built with only one point of access underground, from the north side, which in itself is remarkable as most dragon enclaves across the world have at least five or six main entry points. This is because the dragons, despite all their knowledge and power, still acknowledge that they are susceptible to natural disasters and unforeseen circumstances. Although there is only one underground point of access to Purbeck Peninsula, like all dragon-inhabited areas there are hundreds, if not thousands, of entrances to the surface above. Most of these surface entry points are tiny ones from houses or shops, but other slightly larger ones exist in more out of the way spots on the surface, so that unsuspecting humans don't stumble across them accidentally. Some of these around Purbeck include caves, mines, secretly activated entrances in various ruins, two or three rather creative underwater entrances, and some very interesting ones, based around puzzles.

With only one main underground route into Purbeck Peninsula it was no surprise that the monorail station was a terminus. But it wasn't just any terminus: the place was huge even by dragon standards and that is no mean feat. The path that Peter was on peaked on the brow of a hill and dipped sharply, allowing him to take in the sight of the busy terminus and the bustling city from above.

Directly opposite from where Peter stood, embedded into the rock face of the hill on the other side of the terminus and overlooking the whole complex, was the main office that controlled all the monorail cars as they came into the station. From that point, dragons made sure that the cars arrived and departed on schedule, and that they all reached the correct platform after coming down the single monorail line into Purbeck Peninsula. The station itself took the form of a giant plaza, with eight different overhead support rails branching off the main one, which itself appeared from a huge circular tunnel carved from the rock face. As each individual car arrived from a different destination it was guided into a particular berth on one of the eight branches and gently brought to a standstill just above the ground, to allow passengers to disembark. In between, monorail cars filled up with dragons wishing to embark and when a scheduled space became free the car would hurtle off from its resting spot at the end of one of the eight branch lines. The giant overhead points would change accordingly, allowing the monorail cars to smoothly make their way onto the main line and out of the community via the huge tunnel.

The overall sight was made more impressive by the speed with which this was all accomplished. The cars themselves could travel at up to six hundred and fifty miles an hour over longer journeys, and although by necessity the cars travelled much more slowly in the terminus, it did all happen in nearly the blink of an eye. A mere human would not have been able to comprehend what was going on, let alone keep up with all the information constantly changing on the big LCD screens embedded into the rock at regular intervals to keep passengers appraised of the monorail's timetable. The monorail system had been up and running for over sixty years now, and connected every dragon community in the whole world, via a network of subterranean tunnels.

Peter couldn't remember a time when the monorail hadn't been available for transportation purposes. Often while the young dragons were studying in the nursery ring, the 'tors and other accompanying adults would use the monorail to take the whole class on field trips to faraway places. In some of their dragon history lessons the youngsters would learn facts about the monorail system, such as how it took over two hundred years to construct, and about the techniques used to develop it and keep it operational. On top of all of that you generally tended to find at least one of the 'tors during these particular lessons would drone on about how in his or her day they had to fly everywhere and not be pandered to with fancy transport systems.

As Peter walked briskly down the hill, he spotted a silver monorail car come speeding out of the tunnel and noticed that it was heading for platform six. He speeded up, as this was where his car would depart from. He arrived at the car just as it docked and the electric doors opened with a WHOOOSH! All the passengers leaving exited from one side of the car, leaving the other side clear for dragons to get on.

"Nice and orderly, or dragon-like," Peter thought. "Absolutely nothing like the chaos up top," he laughed to himself.

Once inside the car, Peter sat down on one of the long sofa-like seats that ran the length of the carriage on either side, and waited for the monorail to leave the station. The seats themselves were designed to accommodate either human or dragon form, with some seats even having special holes for dragons' tails. However, most dragons boarding the monorail tended to do so in their human form. Peter didn't have long to wait. Some fifty seconds after he boarded the car, the doors whooshed shut and smoothly the car picked up speed, negotiating the points until the windows went dark as the car entered the tunnel on its way out of Purbeck Peninsula.

Through the windows of the carriage, Peter could see the dark rock face whizzing by on one side, only inches away, while on the other side dragons in both human and dragon form walked along the old path that had been the main entrance to Purbeck Peninsula for hundreds of years. The old path ran parallel to the monorail track for some fifteen miles before splitting up and winding off in several different directions and a lot of dragons came from miles around just to walk along the path and learn about its history. The path itself had just been the bottom of the tunnel that the dragons used to fly in, long before the monorail had been built.

The monorail was going so fast now that the dragons walking along the path were only a blur, and even with his heightened dragon senses, all Peter could really see were the bright crystals illuminating the path, with odd patches of molten lava showing up from underneath the paving stones from time to time.

Peter's destination was a city in southern Wiltshire, some fifty miles away, called Salisbridge. This was where Peter worked and lived and had done so ever since he had left his nursery ring. Had Peter been travelling on the surface, the journey time from Purbeck Peninsula to Salisbridge in a car or bus would have been over an hour, but here on the monorail it would take a little over eight minutes.

As the monorail track peeled away from any of the pedestrian walkways the carriage got significantly darker, only occasionally lit up by the odd patch of molten lava. When the monorail was built the dragon designers had wasted no time at all in deciding that only bigger caverns or areas where the monorail travelled close to pedestrian walkways would be illuminated, leaving the vast majority of travel through tunnels in solid rock to take place in near total darkness, punctuated occasionally by a monorail car heading in the other direction, although even a dragon might miss it if he blinked. Sometimes on these journeys Peter closed his eyes and tried to imagine what it would be like for an ordinary human to experience a monorail trip. He knew of course that it could never happen, but he guessed that it would feel akin to a really scary powerful rollercoaster ride, only soooo much more.

There were many reasons why a human would never experience dragon monorail travel, but the main one was the fact that no human could survive the intense G forces that the monorail generated. This was not a problem for dragons, because in either human or dragon form they can withstand intense pressures, hence their ability to perform amazing aerial feats, such as flying at speeds of up to six hundred and fifty miles an hour, performing tight turns at speed, or pulling out of death-defying drops at the last second.

Dragons' physical capabilities were taken into account by the monorail designers, so they tended to build the tunnels in the direction of where they wanted them to go, only changing direction for any insurmountable obstacles, such as a big lava flow or a large vein of a problem metal or gas. This meant that the monorail would travel in a straight line for much of the time and then suddenly all sorts of twists and turns, drops and ascents would kick in, just to avoid a problematic geological area. Most dragons barely noticed it, but no human would ever be able to survive it intact.

Peter could feel the monorail car slowly starting to decelerate and knew that they were approaching the Salisbridge monorail station. The darkness of the tunnels was suddenly replaced by the soft orange glow of the multi-platformed station. As smooth as always, the carriage pulled up just above the platform and the doors whispered their usual whoosh, opening to allow all the departing passengers off the monorail. Peter made his way across the platform and up a set of very worn marble stairs. By the time he had reached the top, the doors on the carriage had whooshed closed and, with hardly a sound, the monorail was accelerating out of the station.

At the top of the stairs, the station opened out into a vast courtyard with nine walkways going off in all directions from it. Although the Salisbridge station was relatively small compared with the likes of Purbeck, London and Glasgow, the painstaking detail with which it had been decorated put all the others to shame. On opposite sides of the courtyard, twelve tall marble pillars supported the cavernous ceiling above. Carved into each pillar was a legendary figure from history, with their dragon form on one side of the pillar and their human form on the other side. The pillars were all made of black and white marble, to match the expanding floor of the courtyard, but where the pillars turned into the dragon legends, the marble had a very distinctive gold fleck as if gold leaf had been mixed with the marble to make it twinkle like golden stars in a black and white night.

As Peter reached the top of the stairs from that particular platform, he always found himself directly opposite the huge marble pillar that depicted the famed George from the George and the dragon tales. He sometimes wondered to himself if he were not somehow linked to the story in some way, as at times like now it seemed to be everywhere around him. He shook his head slightly to himself, knowing that the very thought was absurd. Dragons did not believe in fate or destiny. They were a practical race, more concerned with the present than the past or the future.

Peter's fanciful thoughts seemed to be blown away as his highly attuned senses started to come under assault in a variety of different ways. The sickly scent of some of the Mediterranean plants that were dotted all around the courtyard made his nose tingle and little squirts of flame threatened to dribble out from his nostrils. Plants from much warmer climates always seemed to be used in the underground areas, as the conditions better suited them, Peter supposed. A loud whirring noise from one of the five or six vendors that inhabited the courtyard made Peter turn to his right to investigate. Sure enough, just as Peter had thought, the vendor had just primed his machine to start making fresh charcoal doughnuts as the passengers from the monorail had come up the stairs. Peter watched as the noisy mixer whizzed the dough around and around, pausing now and then for different coloured bits of charcoal to be added to the mixture. Peter watched, mesmerised, as the mixture was poured into a funnel and then a doughnut shape was forced out at the other end into the hot fat. The doughnut bubbled its way along the machine until about halfway along it was suddenly flipped over so that the other side of it could be cooked. As Peter's mouth watered in anticipation, the vendor looked at him with a knowing gleam in his eye that almost said 'gotcha'.

Concentrating so hard on the doughnut, Peter had only just begun to realise that the sickly pollen scent had started to be replaced by something much nicer. His very sensitive nose had picked up the delightful aromas of lemon, cinnamon and slightly burnt charcoal. Turning away from the doughnut maker, Peter looked at the next vendor along, just as the spindly-framed dragon tossed a giant pancake into the air, flipping it over expertly so that it landed on the hot plate to a loud sizzling noise. Peter, now fully enthralled by the pancake, slowly moved towards the next stall, much to the indignation of the doughnut vendor.

Peter's nostrils seemed to have come alive in the last few seconds as more gorgeous aromas started to waft over from the other side of the courtyard. Glancing over, he could see two more vendors cooking. One was baking magnificent multicoloured bread that smelt like fresh candy floss and toffee apples all rolled into one. The other was frying mouth-watering chunks of dark brown meat, in a skillet with all sorts of wonderful fruit and vegetables, creating a silky sweet, barbecue smell that made his stomach rumble.

Peter's inquisitive nature kicked in again and he wondered if the vendors had some way of knowing that he not eaten all day. After another minute or so of being assaulted by all the food sensations, he chose the pancake over the doughnut, the bread and the meaty fajita. With his pancake wrapped in a cardboard cone, he made his way across the courtyard to the narrowest of the walkways and started to follow it along its incline. After two or three minutes Peter found himself in relative darkness. The path's twists and turns had now cancelled out any remaining light from the bright courtyard of the station, the only remaining illumination being provided by tiny fluorescent crystals embedded into the three foot high wall, at thirty foot intervals. With the incline becoming more pronounced, one or two gaps in the wall started to appear at random intervals.

Peter walked on for another three or four minutes before stopping at one particular gap in the wall. This was the underground entrance to his house. He slid through the gap in the wall while wolfing down the last of his pancake and started to make his way, in what was now total darkness, up a very narrow and steep set of stone steps. The darkness didn't bother him at all as he had done this part of the journey many of thousands of times already in his relatively short life, and besides if need be he could enhance his vision using his dragon senses. The further up the stairs he went, the narrower the passageway became.

"Good job I don't have to do this in dragon form," he thought to himself. Not even his tiny dragon frame could negotiate this tight space, let alone a reasonably sized dragon.

Peter found himself in total darkness on the top step, facing an apparently solid wall of rock. Peter brought his left hand up along the wall beside him until it was just above his head. The thumb and the ring finger on his left hand found two small indentations on the wall at exactly the same time, and in the confined space and the pitch black, he forced his fingers into the indentations and squeezed down with both digits instinctively. There was a soft 'click' and the sound of tiny gears turning far away. A huge chunk of the solid rock in front of Peter moved silently upwards and out of sight. Ducking his head ever so slightly, Peter moved through the gap and found himself in a dusty cellar. Cobwebs hung down from the wooden beams that ran across the ceiling, while fluff adorned the light coloured dust sheets that covered all sorts of different shaped objects that littered the room. In the far corner, a black ornate spiral staircase rose from amid the covered belongings and wound tightly up to the ceiling, where it just.............stopped. The ceiling was totally intact and there was nowhere for anyone to go if they bothered to climb the Victorian staircase.

This didn't perturb Peter. He dodged all the dusty objects and squeezed himself onto the first rung of the staircase. As he did so, the gears moved the chunk of solid rock back into place, plunging the room into total darkness. Circling round three times on the staircase, Peter stopped just before his head touched the ceiling. His right hand moved down below the banister and took hold of a rust-covered black flower that was part of the Victorian design. He twisted the petals anti-clockwise, and as he did so a small hole in the ceiling gradually started to get bigger. Peter poked his head through and started to climb the remaining rungs.

Once through the hole, Peter emerged into what looked like a very ordinary, very small, modern day sitting room. He stepped out from the corner of the room and made his way around a light brown coloured piano. Reaching over the keys he yanked hard on a glass Galileo thermometer, which sat on top of the piano, causing all the coloured balls inside to crash violently against the glass, but surprisingly, not to break. Nothing happened for a few seconds, but then the hole through which he had just climbed started to close back up, and once it did so, the whole piano slid around ninety degrees on the wooden floor, to sit snugly in the corner of the room on top of the concealed entrance/exit. The thermometer also went back to an upright position. All of this took only a few seconds and anyone now entering the room the conventional way would be none the wiser.

Peter lived in a small terraced house that had two bedrooms (some would describe it as three bedrooms as there was a small study in the roof, but he always thought of it as two), a sitting room, a small kitchen, a bathroom on the ground floor and a sixty foot long narrow garden.

At the turn of the century the terraced houses where he lived had all been railway cottages as Salisbridge had always been part of a big human railway community. The city's railway station sat on the main line from London to the West Country and the railways had always provided a lot of work for the local community. The house that Peter lived in had always been owned by one dragon or another, hence the concealed passage to the world below. As far back as the Romans, and maybe even further, dragons have sought to live side by side with humans, to blend in and find out everything they could to fulfil their pledges to look out for and guide the human race because of the so-called potential that it possesses. Throughout history, homes bought by a dragon often have some sort of access to the underground world. That access is nearly always hidden, more often than not in some completely obscure and bizarre way that nobody would ever stumble across in a million years: from revolving wardrobes to hollow bottomed washing machines and fridges that you could climb into, entrances in gardens hidden by all manner of plants and animals, to showers where the base folds back to reveal a long slide leading to the dragon world.

With their natural affinity for all things mechanical, and armed with all sorts of different mantras, virtually nothing is beyond a dragon when they set their mind to it. The main challenge throughout the years has been to put a modern spin on all of these things and constantly update them so that they blend in with their contemporary surroundings. The piano, for example, had been in Peter's house for many decades, but that was not really so unusual for a piano. Whereas the lever that had originally started the whole process from inside the house had been an old fashioned candelabrum, that most definitely would look out of place now, so replacing it with something so much more modern (the Galileo thermometer) causes the whole thing to look totally innocuous to an innocent bystander or visitor. The thermometer was specially crafted by an expert in modern mantras, based in Purbeck Peninsula, and fitted by one of the many dragon designers that routinely update dragon abodes and are always in demand.

Peter glanced at the rocket shaped clock on the wall above the twenty six inch flat screen television. Nearly twenty to seven it told him.

"Hmmmm," he thought to himself. "Better get a move on or I'm gonna be late for training." With that he raced up the stairs to the first floor, dashed into the main bedroom and quickly changed into his hockey kit.

Peter was a keen hockey player and was a member of the local club. He played for them on a Saturday (mainly for the second XI) and always attended club training on a Tuesday evening from seven o'clock. Having thrown on his shirt, shorts, socks, and tied his astro trainers up, he grabbed his shin pads from the top of the chest of drawers and picked up his stick bag from behind the bedroom door as he headed for the car. It was then that he caught sight of himself in the full length mirror next to the bedroom door. Pausing briefly, he gazed into the mirror, thinking about the complex mantras that held the delicate human form in front of him in place. Long wavy black hair adorned the top of his head. It was something straight out of the eighties he knew, but then it was in that period of time that he had been perfecting his human mantras and this was how he liked his hair. Of course over time he knew he'd have to tweak the mantras just a little to add some grey, let the hair thin out a little, or both. The light line of stubble around his chin he was particularly proud of. "That damn mantra was so hard to perfect," he thought to himself, shaking his head. Apart from that, everything else was rather 'run of the mill'. He'd gone for an average face with an averaged sized nose and no distinctive features. He was of medium height, not at all skinny, but certainly not overweight. And, he decided, he looked good in his hockey kit. Nodding his head in the mirror, he turned and sprinted down the stairs to the car. The drive to the sports ground took less than five minutes. Situated on one of the main roads out of the city, it was just outside the city limits, away from immediate residential areas. It consisted of a large two storey pavilion that overlooked an Astroturf hockey pitch, a grass rugby pitch and a grass lacrosse pitch. A large tarmac car park serviced the pavilion on the opposite side from the sports pitches and changing rooms for all the sports teams were separate to the main clubhouse. Inside the pavilion there was a huge bar and dining area on the ground floor that looked out onto all three sports pitches. On the first floor was a members' only lounge, a committee room, the chairman's office, a storage area and a bar with a balcony that looked out over the sports fields.

As Peter turned off the main road and into the car park, he couldn't help but be dazzled by the giant floodlights, shining onto each of the pitches. Not only was it training night for the hockey club, but for the rugby and lacrosse sections too, meaning that Peter would hopefully see both Richie and Tank tonight, as Richie played lacrosse here and Tank played for the rugby team, so both would be training tonight.

The training session went reasonably well, with Peter larking about with those members of the second XI that had turned up. Afterwards he spent well over an hour in the bar, catching up with Richie and Tank. It was nearly quarter to eleven by the time Peter got home, just enough time to have a quick shower and head off to bed. He drifted off to sleep, wondering what the next day at work had in store for him.

3

A Major Disappointment

Peter was woken abruptly by Radio One blaring out of his radio/alarm clock, as always at seven o'clock. Rubbing the sleep from his eyes he wandered from the bedroom, downstairs to the bathroom, and began cleaning his teeth. Gazing into the mirror, he decided that he most definitely was not a morning person, as he did about the same time every morning. After finishing brushing and flossing his teeth he smeared some gel into his hair and headed back to the bedroom to get dressed. He grabbed a tie from the rack in the wardrobe and slapped the off button on his clock radio, on his way out of the room. Leaping down the stairs three at a time, he turned into the kitchen, feeling much better than he had ten minutes ago.

Pouring himself a bowl of cornflakes, he took the milk and a strawberry yoghurt from the fridge and sat down at the small pine dining table in the middle of the kitchen. Peter drizzled milk over his cornflakes and munched his way through the whole bowl, before quickly wolfing down his yoghurt.

With a little time before he was due at work, Peter decided he would catch up with events in the dragon world. Sitting back in his chair with that contented feeling of food in his stomach, he closed his eyes and began to concentrate. The sensation that followed felt very much like flying in his dragon form. Reaching out with his mind, he searched for the nearest crystal booster, which not only had the power to amplify the information being sent out, but also was able to store information so that dragons could access it and retrieve it at will. Sitting at the table with his eyes closed and small beads of sweat forming on his brow, Peter's consciousness rose above the roof tops of the houses in the street and momentarily hovered until finally zooming off in a south westerly direction looking for the nearest crystal booster, the one that he normally used. Even though it was only his mind that was racing through the air above the streets, Peter could swear he could feel the cold breeze brushing his arms, causing goose bumps to appear, and the hairs to stand on end.

After thirty seconds of searching he finally caught sight of what he was looking for. On the outskirts of the city, a wonderful set of gardens wandered along one of the main rivers, revealing amazing views of the fantastic cathedral and water meadows. The gardens included paths and seating, wonderful open areas and playgrounds for children of different ages, all next to the beautiful winding river.

Just opposite the children's play area, in the middle of the river, was a small island with a giant oak tree growing on it. That oak was the destination for his mind. Swooping down and across the park, Peter's consciousness headed towards the end of a large branch on the cathedral side of the tree. Heading straight towards the tree at high speed, Peter always seemed to notice that this particular branch, instead of tapering off to a point, just had a hole in the end of it. A hole through which Peter's consciousness was now entering. After the vivid colours of the park the world now became pitch black. All that remained was a sense of moving along at a great speed. Having done this so many times Peter knew what to expect next, and he wasn't disappointed. Brilliant bright white light assaulted his senses. The sensation of speed passed and his mind was now meandering down a long, tunnel-like corridor. On either side of him were hundreds, if not thousands, of huge wooden filing cabinets. Most were shut, but one or two he passed were open and had hundreds of pages fluttering out, seemingly going nowhere. Each cabinet had massive italic writing on the front to signify what it contained. As he traversed the corridor Peter passed *Sol (April-May)*, *Speculum (March-April-May)*, *Liber (April-May)* and *Stella (March-May)*.

Finally he found the one he was looking for............... *The Daily Telepath (April-May)*. Peter concentrated on the drawer of the filing cabinet and it slid open towards his consciousness. He swooped up and dived into the drawer, rifling through the pages. Suddenly he felt as though he was swimming through a book where someone was flicking the pages really fast. Whizzing past him were pages from last month's copies of the paper that he recognised, so he immersed himself even more until he eventually got to the copy of yesterday's paper.

Slowing himself right down he found the front page of today's copy, got a tight hold on it with his mind, and leapt right out of the cabinet. As he did so he could feel the explosion of information grab hold of his consciousness and follow it back, the way it had come, across the park, over the roof tops, down into the house and back into his head where it belonged. Once the information was downloaded, Peter found it easy to access in his head. It was just like turning the pages of a real newspaper, but mentally rather than physically. The front page of today's Daily Telepath looked like this:

The Daily Telepath

Britain's Oldest Telepathic Newspaper   Issue No 252171

New Theme Park Opens in Hawaii

By Rainbow Swan

Yesterday saw the opening of the fabulous new lava theme park Mauna Loa Falls underneath the Island of Hawaii. It features raging lava rapids, forty super size lava plunge pools, three cleansing steam caverns, the lava geyser challenge flying course and the amazing star attraction 'Molten Meltdown'.

The spa has its own eight crescent spa pool. Treatments include full body scale polishing, stomach descaling, tail sharpening and nostril enhancement therapy. Visitors are advised to book early to avoid disappointment. The main park entrance is only a short flight from the Honolulu monorail station.

Monorail Preliminary Test

By Tawny Clockface

Three new test bore holes have been drilled, two in Europe, one in Australia. The idea of having a monorail link that goes straight from Europe,

through the Earth's crust, narrowly missing the core and heading directly to Australasia took another step forward yesterday. Four sites in Europe have been determined as having the potential for the proposed cross planet link, with the engineers involved having already solved the problems caused by stress tolerances, seismic pressure and power requirements. It only remains for the team to find a route for the proposed monorail that satisfies safety and stability requirements. A spokesdragon for the engineers involved said that "the project was progressing at a satisfactory rate and that the real possibility of a direct transplanet monorail could only actually be a decade or so away." Apple Pink, speaking on behalf of the dragons against technology movement, was quoted as saying "of all the disastrous ideas, this seems to be the most ridiculous. The current monorail infrastructure is already damaging the planet's core. This potentially threatens the safety of the whole planet and every dragon should wake up and realise this. We will not sit by while the King and his Council jeapardise every living organism on the planet, just so that dragons can travel from A to B just that bit quicker." More test bores are planned for central Australia next month.

New Rule Change?

By Rushton Boat

The world Laminium Ball Association (WLBA) is understood to be considering changing one of the main rules to our beloved sport. At the moment the goals each end of the giant cavern are formed by six huge stalactites and stalagmites, meeting up to form six columns of rock, with each team aiming to use the laminium ball to destroy as many columns as possible. The WLBA is thinking of extending the six columns to eight. Outrage surrounds the plan as six columns have been the standard since Roman times. Watch this space for regular updates on this most important matter.

Council to Discuss South Pole Warning

By Chief Political Correspondant Briony Ingham

The next monthly meeting of the King's Council will raise the issue of global warming at the South Pole. Ever increasing angst amongst human scientists over the issue has seen

Councillor D'Zone table the issue for the next meeting. Top level dragon specialists will be consulted on how best to proceed, with some already calling for a fact finding mission. At this moment in time the council seems split on whether already overstretched dragon resources can cope with what would be a long and potentially waste of time and invaluable equipment. For the first time in a while, it may be that the King has the final say in the matter with his casting vote.

Envoy to the Nagas

By Pliers Appleworth

The King's special diplomatic envoy has been dispatched to the Southern Hemisphere to try and re-establish diplomatic relations with the notoriously nomadic Naga community. The Nagas were last seen over two hundred years ago in the vicinity of Isla de los Estodos, off the Eastern coast of Argentina. The council are keen to offer out an 'olive branch' in the hope of forming a friendly, diplomatic relationship.

After having a quick flick through, Peter decided to store the rest of the paper to read later. Concentrating hard on the edition in his mind, he mentally screwed the paper into a ball and threw it into a large green bucket with LATER marked on the front. Next to that bucket was a red one twice the size, full to bursting with screwed up paper balls; it was marked RUBBISH.

Getting up from the table, Peter grabbed his sandwiches from the fridge, walked into the hall and took his waterproof sports jacket from the coat stand before leaving the house. Jumping into his five year old Ford Fiesta, he turned the ignition which much to his surprise, started first time. Switching on the radio, he headed off to work.

Peter worked at the biggest employer in Salisbridge, Cropptech: a highly specialised and world renowned supplier of precious metals and valuable stones. The main Cropptech facility was located on the western outskirts of Salisbridge, comprising a large office complex, a small industrial area and a warehouse and logistics setup. The office complex housed the company's marketing department, accounts and payroll, sales and administration, technical support, training and web management teams. The industrial aspect of the site dealt with polishing and cutting gems and experimenting with rare and unstable metals. Distribution of the gems and metals to the customers after having been refined was the responsibility of the warehouse and logistics department, as was the collection and safe delivery of the raw materials to the main Salisbridge site.

As well as this all-encompassing site, Cropptech owned numerous mines, small specialist production facilities, experimental bore holes and tiny offices all over the world, making it one of the leading companies in its field. The company had been set up some one hundred and twenty years ago and had been a family run business ever since. The man currently in charge at Cropptech was the last living descendant of that family, a man named Al Garrett. A confirmed bachelor in his late forties, Garrett was a plain man that wouldn't stand out in a crowd. His lean frame and shiny bald head with just a few etchings of grey hair around his temples was neatly complemented by a ferocious looking grey moustache. He was known affectionately by his staff as the 'bald eagle', because he never seemed to miss anything that was going on at the Cropptech site.

When Garrett inherited the site around twenty five years ago, the company had been on the verge of bankruptcy with very few future prospects. Al Garrett had single-handedly turned that around and made Cropptech a market leader in nearly everything it did. As well as having a brilliant business mind and acquiring a large personal fortune, (much of which he donated to charity), Garrett had become renowned for his generosity and the favourable way in which he treated all his staff. Everyone that worked for him always thought of him as approachable and caring with a sense of humour that was legendary.

Both Peter and Richie worked at Cropptech and had started there straight from the nursery ring, some three years ago. Richie worked in the training department in the office complex, teaching anything from the latest payroll software to new health and safety procedures. She seemed to positively thrive in such an environment and had already been promoted twice. Peter worked in the security department. Starting off as a guard on the nightshift, Peter's dedication and enthusiasm for the job had seen him also promoted twice since being there, just like Richie. So now he only occasionally had to pull a nightshift, mainly for holiday cover or if someone was off sick. His official title was Assistant Security Co-ordinator. He had his own small office on the ground floor of the office complex, just across the road from the main security gate outpost. Peter's office consisted of a desk with a workstation, a bank of security monitors and an array of filing cabinets, beyond which he was afforded a great view of the main gate into the facility and the security outpost attached to it.

Peter's relatively new role within the company thrust an enormous amount of responsibility onto his very young shoulders, (lucky for him he was a dragon,) with only the chief security co-ordinator and Al Garrett above him in the chain of authority.

For the last four weeks or so Peter had been reporting directly to Garrett as the chief security co-ordinator had been off sick with a mysterious virus. Prior to his direct contact with Garrett, Peter had heard all the rumours about him and suspected they were grossly exaggerated. He was sure nobody could be that caring and considerate to their staff all the time. However since he had been reporting to Garrett, these past four weeks, he was forced to admit to himself that he had been very wrong in that estimation. Dealing with Garrett on a daily basis, Peter had witnessed firsthand his consideration and generosity towards his staff, himself included. Peter felt he had developed a rapport with

Garrett and was constantly being told by the 'bald eagle' to call him Al and not Mr Garrett.

Everything, Peter had to admit, was going swimmingly at work. His working relationship with Garrett was excellent, and the staff under him seemed to be happy and motivated, while respecting him as their superior, despite his young age. Peter couldn't wait to get into work every day.

After parking his car, Peter walked briskly across the car park in the biting wind towards the security lodge at the main gate. Although there was no real need for him to go to the lodge, it was something he'd gotten into the habit of doing, to check that everything had gone smoothly on the nightshift and to see how his staff were doing. Smiling to himself, he also knew he went there because of the witty banter the staff offered in his direction first thing in the morning. He was sure there wasn't a more cheeky department in the whole company.

"Just as well they're all excellent at their jobs," he thought to himself. Twisting the handle on the white double glazed entrance door to the security lodge, he squeezed through and was glad to be out of the harsh wind. Walking up the short corridor, past the water cooler, toilets and photocopier, and round the corner he stopped at an open plan area.

"Good morning slaves!" he shouted with a tone of mock authority in his voice, fully expecting numerous funny and/or x-rated replies. All he got was a mumbled, "Morning."

Turning to Jessica Freeman who was in charge here at the moment, but also happened to be sitting closest, Peter leaned towards her and whispered,

"What's going on?"

Jessica replied in low voice,

"Not sure really, but Mr Garrett wants to see you ASAP."

"Mr Garrett?" replied Peter.

"Hmmmmm that's right," said Jessica, looking straight at Peter and rolling her eyes.

"Okay, well thanks Jessica. I'll catch up with you later," Peter said as he stood up from the desk, turned and headed for the door. As he walked across the road that separated the security lodge from the main office complex, he was most puzzled.

"Something very unusual is going on," he thought to himself.

Stopping briefly in his office to hang up his jacket and put his lunch into his desk drawer, Peter then headed for the lift and Al Garrett's office which was located on the fourth floor. On the way up in the lift, Peter caught his reflection in its interior mirrored walls and began straightening his tie nervously. On exiting the lift, Peter headed down the long oak panelled corridor past Garrett's personal secretary, whom Peter smiled at, his feet sinking luxuriously into the thick, expensive carpet. Stopping at the oak door and facing the brass plaque that said 'Al Garrett Chief Executive', Peter took a deep breath and knocked twice. A growl of 'ENTER' reverberated from the other side of the door. Peter turned the brass handle and went in.

The first thing Peter noticed as he entered the room was how gloomy and dark it was. Apart from the fact that there was a large stocky man looking out of the window, blocking out most of the light, the normally bright, clean and airy office seemed dark and dreary. A strange aroma hung in the air throughout the room. As he walked towards Garrett's desk Peter tried to figure out what it was, without much success. Al Garrett slowly looked up from his desk, over his reading glasses.

"I've implemented some changes, effective immediately, that you need to know about Mr Bentwhistle," Garrett said forcefully.

"From now until further notice, every department head, yourself included, will report directly to Major Manson. Major Manson is from Darktech Technologies, a leading security consultancy. He will be carrying out a full review of our security and operational procedures. I expect nothing less than full co-operation from you and all your staff. Do I make myself clear?"

"Absolutely Al," replied Peter instantly, smiling.

"That's 'Mister Garrett' to you," a haughty voice from behind Garrett said, dripping with condescension.

"He's right," said Garrett.

Peter looked straight into the dark, unforgiving eyes of Major Manson as he turned round from the window, using all his self control to hold his temper in check. In the lightless environment it was difficult to see in great detail, but Peter quickly used his enhanced dragon sense to get a clear impression of Major Manson. Manson appeared stocky, but about the same height as Peter. He had brown straight hair, or "used to", Peter thought with a smirk, as most of it now was receding rather rapidly. He was clean shaven with an almost square jaw. His eyes though, there was something about his eyes that was just.......................wrong.

Garrett cleared his throat and jolted Peter from his train of thought.

"Sorry Mister Garrett," Peter said, with just a tinge of sarcasm.

"That will be all. You're dismissed," Garrett said, without looking up from the paperwork on his desk.

Peter wheeled round and headed for the exit without giving the other two a second glance. Walking out of the office, he barely managed to resist the urge to slam the door on his way. As he returned along the corridor towards the lift his head seemed to be swimming with thoughts.

"What the hell is going on?" was the first one. Garrett was acting very strangely indeed. The lighting in the room, the strange smell, and the whole 'call me Al' one day, and then 'Mister Garrett' the next, were all very peculiar.

"Very strange," thought Peter, as he travelled down in the lift. As for Major Manson, well….. when Peter had looked straight into Manson's eyes, he was half expecting to sense some sort of evil dragon there. Something about him seemed so…..unusual. At that particular moment, Peter had stretched out with all his dragon senses but had detected nothing out of the ordinary. Dragons know when somebody else is a dragon in human form and there is no way to disguise it. It simply isn't possible. Nevertheless there was something very wrong with this whole situation, in particular Major Manson, Peter mused as he stepped out of the elevator.

Peter spent the next few hours skulking in his office, doing paperwork, signing off time sheets, and generally making sure everything was in order. During that time he spotted Manson on three occasions. Once going into the security lodge, where he stayed for six and a half minutes; once walking past his window on the way to the distribution depot, and again walking into the staff car park and getting a big black box out of a shiny new black Mercedes. Each time Peter noticed that Manson walked with a limp and carried a walking stick made of dark wood with a silver ornament of some sort on the top. Peter was not sure what the ornament was, as it was very difficult to see from so far off, even using his dragon abilities.

After lunch, Peter paid a visit to the security lodge just across from his office. Back in the familiar office, Peter once again noticed that everyone was keeping their heads down and nobody was larking about at all: most unusual.

The atmosphere was most out of place as normally it was a well run, efficient, happy place to work in or visit.

Having delivered his paperwork and spoken to the members of staff that he needed to, Peter walked down the corridor towards the exit. Weaving his way past the big photocopier, he felt like banging his head against the wall in frustration. He was sure, from the atmosphere and the way everyone looked, that they all felt the same way about these new developments, but nobody wanted to even speak about it. He was determined to get some answers as to what was going on. He resolved to speak to Richie tonight.

When it came to the end of the day, Peter did his normal trick of staying a bit later to avoid all the queues out of the car park. Because most staff were on flexi-time, people started to leave any time from four o'clock onwards. This certainly helped with the leaving congestion; nevertheless there were still queues for the first part of the journey home from ten to five until at least half past. Peter liked to wait until about quarter to six before leaving, and tonight was no exception.

For the best part of the last hour he had only been gazing out of his office window, trying to gauge the mood of everyone leaving Cropptech. With a good view out on people heading to their cars, he had unsurprisingly seen lots of glum faces on the way to the car park. However, he had to admit to himself that those glum faces were in the minority and that most people from the different departments of the company looked their normal cheerful selves. He wasn't sure if that bothered him more or not after the kind of day he had been through.

At precisely a quarter to six he grabbed his jacket and lunch box, and with his phone in his hand he headed towards his car. On his way across the car park he began to text Richie on his phone, to see if she wanted to meet for a drink later that evening. He stopped at the door of his car as he finished typing in the rest of his message. (For a dragon, who was supposed to be unbelievably proficient with any kind of technology, he was amazingly bad at texting and using mobile phones in general.) Slipping his phone into his pocket, he turned the keys in the lock and as he did so noticed out of the corner of his eye that Major Manson's black Mercedes was still in the car park, albeit in a different parking bay from earlier. Shaking his head, Peter got into his car and drove home.

Once home, Peter cooked himself some tea, and while doing so received a reply from Richie saying she would meet him in the bar of the sports club at eight-thirty. After eating his tea, he slouched on the sofa watching the news for an hour and before he knew it, it was time to leave to meet up with his friend.

Walking through the giant double glass doors into the sports club, Peter passed numerous notice boards, a deserted reception area/shop, and continued until he turned the corner into the bar area. The scene that greeted him was a riot of colour and noise. A raucous pool game was taking place, in between some drinking. An even noisier battle was taking place between two stocky chaps on the arcade "shoot-em-up" game off to one side. As well as this there were the sounds of drunken men enthusiastically playing two fruit machines and a dozen or more track-suited men all taking part in a drinking game involving flipping a matchbox over and drinking beer as fast as was humanly possible.

Peter closed his eyes and shook his head.

"Oh PANTS!!! It's Wednesday," he thought to himself. A rugby coaching course had been going on all day. That explained the chaos. He weaved in and out of the chairs and tables, narrowly missing the pool game that looked like it might turn into a contact sport at any second. Upon reaching the bar, he asked for his usual (large diet Pepsi, lots of ice) and turned to face the rest of the room to search for Richie. It didn't take long to spot her tucked away in the far corner nursing her drink. "Even from this distance," Peter thought, "she looks striking." Her long dark brown curly hair flowed down the back of her neck, framing her ever so cute face. This was all completed by a freckly complexion and a petite body that brilliantly mirrored her dragon form. Peter stood captivated for a few seconds, wishing at the back of his mind that perhaps one day they could be something more than best friends. Sitting close to Richie, two young rugby players were arm wrestling each other, clearly trying to impress her with their strength and macho deeds. With all thoughts about their relationship dismissed from his mind, carrying his drink, Peter made his way over to Richie and sat in the chair opposite her. As he did so, the two arm wrestlers scowled at him and one said to the other,

"Look it's one of the juniors from the hockey club." The other replied,

"You would think it would be well past his bedtime."

They both seemed to think this was really funny and sat there waiting for some remark back from Peter. Richie leant over the table towards Peter and nodded her head at the two rugby players.

"Aren't you going to say something?" she whispered to Peter.

"It's not worth it," he replied, hoping the whole thing would just go away. With the two rugby players laughing louder than ever now at Peter, and with most of the people in the bar looking to see what all the fuss was about, he suddenly noticed a mischievous glint in Richie's eye. Before he could stop her, Richie stood up and said to the two laughing rugby players,

"You two so-called real men think you're tough eh? I'll arm wrestle you both at the same time and win, how about that?"

By now everyone in the room was focusing their attention on what was happening, including all the staff. If nothing else, the challenge had wiped the smile off the two rugby players' faces, because they, like most of the people there, were well aware of Richie's reputation, not only as an athlete but as somebody who always seemed to be able to 'pull a rabbit out of a hat' so to speak. The two rugby players looked up at Richie's diminutive frame standing over them, and in particular at her skinny little biceps.

"No problem," one said, as they both slammed their fists down onto the table.

As everyone slowly gathered round to watch, the two rugby players took a seat next to each other, opposite a smirking Richie.

"You sure you wanna do us both at the same time luv?" the more drunken of the two queried. Peter could see a dozen people in the crowd clearly shake their heads at this, knowing full well the amount of humiliation that was about to come raining down on the two macho fools.

"We'll try not to hurt you luv," said the slightly less drunken one, winking at her as he did so.

Richie sat in her chair, smiling at the two fools. She put both her elbows on the table and offered out her petite hands. Once each of the rugby players had taken a hand, someone in the crowd started counting down....

"5, 4, 3..."

The rugby players' biceps positively bulged as their arms tensed.

"2...." The smile still on her face, Richie closed her eyes and................

"1!"

SMASH!!!!!!!!!!!!!!! The two rugby players yelped with pain as their bruised hands bounced up from the undamaged table.

"Thanks guys," Richie said, as she got up and performed a mock bow. The entire clubhouse erupted with applause and laughter.

The two large rugby players headed off through the crowd, all the time taking huge amounts of abuse from those in the busy bar.

Taking her seat opposite Peter, Richie took a big swig of her drink.

"That's how to handle them," she said, after finishing her drink.

"That's not really the way we're supposed to do things," Peter whispered, rolling his eyes for effect.

"If the council ever got to hear about stuff like this you would be in so much trouble."

"Yeah, yeah, blaady blaady bla," Richie replied cockily. Leaning over so she could whisper into Peter's ear, she muttered,

"Some of these humans desperately need some lessons in manners."

Shaking his head, Peter sat up straight, realising that someone was approaching their table. Richie grinned wildly as the two shamed rugby players approached their table. The whole clubhouse looked on silently.

"Drinks for both of you," one said as the other produced fresh drinks for them both.

"We're both very sorry and...um... have learned a valuable lesson today," the other stuttered as they both turned away. With the natural balance of things restored (that is, Richie looking cooler than a polar bear in the Arctic, sponsored by Ferrari), everybody went back to what they were doing in the bar.

With the ambient noise in the clubhouse having dropped considerably since he came in, Peter decided now was the best time to talk to Richie about work.

"So how's your day been Rich?" he asked casually.

Sitting back in her chair still smirking from her easily won victory over the rugby boys, she pondered the question for a few seconds and then replied,

"Pretty quiet really. Had some health and safety training to do this morning but that was all over by lunch time so it was quite an easy afternoon."

"So you haven't heard about the new consultant guy that Mr Garrett's brought into the company?" Peter enquired.

"Oh you mean Major Manson."

Peter frowned and said,

"That's right."

"What a lovely man. We all met him this afternoon when Al showed him around our offices."

"WHAT!!!!" exclaimed Peter, nearly knocking his drink over. "You've got to be kidding me!"

With a worried look on her face, Richie leaned across the table and took hold of his hand and said,

"What is it Peter? What's the matter?"

Peter pulled his hand away from Richie's and sat there shaking his head slightly. Richie decided she would wait for Peter to tell her what the problem was. After a short while Peter took a breath and a sip of his drink, looked Richie in the face and said,

"Did you not see how he was manipulating Garrett?"

"What do you mean?" replied Richie, puzzled.

Sighing ever so slightly and trying to calm himself, Peter said,

"Major Manson, the guy from Darktech, has got some sort of hold on Garrett. I'm sure of it."

"What makes you say that, Peter?" Richie responded, more confused than ever.

Peter then spent the next fifteen minutes explaining what had happened earlier that day, particularly the encounter with Manson and Garrett in Garrett's office. During that time, Richie listened intently, but by the time Peter had finished she seemed more puzzled than ever. Now it was Peter's turn to listen. Just as Richie had listened to his account, he afforded his friend the same courtesy.

Richie explained how Al Garrett and Manson had toured the office complex this afternoon and that Garrett had introduced Manson to nearly every member of staff and he had seemed kind, considerate, witty and charming. Almost the perfect gentlemen you could say. Peter was struggling to come to terms with how much Richie's account differed from his own experience. This seemed about as far away from the person he had met earlier as you could possibly get.

Richie rounded off her tale by saying that Al Garrett had come back to the office complex much later on and asked the staff what they had all thought of Manson and if they were happy to be reporting to him for the time being. The staff, she went on, had only positive things to say about Manson and they all seemed happy to answer to him. Garrett even went on to explain that the reason for Manson being there was to get a fresh perspective on the way the company operates and to take a little bit of responsibility and pressure away from himself. All the staff agreed after Garrett was gone, that Manson taking some of the workload off Garrett could only be a good thing.

When Richie had finished recounting her story, both she and Peter sat there in silence for a good few minutes looking into the bottom of their nearly drained glasses. By this time the clubhouse had emptied considerably; most of the noisy rabble had gone, leaving only a couple of people sitting on stools chatting at the bar.

Peter looked around the bar to make sure nobody could hear what they were talking about. Once he was confident that nobody could listen in, he spoke up.

"Listen, Richie. I know from everything you've told me tonight that you can't see anything wrong with what's going on. But I swear to you on our friendship that something very wrong is going on with that Manson guy." There was a long pause as Peter considered his next words very carefully.

"It's almost like he's .... one of us."

"Are you INSANE?" asked Richie, lowering her voice immediately.

"We'd know if he was a dragon; we would sense him, and he most certainly isn't."

"I know he doesn't feel like a dragon, but ..... there's something else that just makes him feel really wrong to my dragon senses."

"Have you considered the possibility that your dislike for him stems from the fact he's just waltzed into Cropptech and you've got off on the wrong foot with him?"

"I know it sounds a bit like that Rich. But there's more to it than that I'm sure. You have to believe me ....please. I've never been so sure about anything in my entire life," Peter pleaded.

"Enough with the begging, alright," Richie said, sounding fed up. "I suggest we both try and keep an extra special eye on him and if either of us finds anything suspicious or anything that might lead us to think we were.... mistaken, we tell the other straight away. Agreed?"

"Agreed," Peter said cheerfully.

"Now, I think it's time for me to go home for some well earned rest," Richie said, stifling a yawn.

With that, the two friends deposited their empty glasses on the bar and headed out to the car park. After a quick goodnight embrace they both went their separate ways.

Driving back home, Peter wasn't sure what to make of the evening's conversations. He was glad that Richie had agreed to keep an eye on Manson, but was concerned that she and the rest of the office staff thought that Manson was a decent chap. Perhaps things would look better after a good night's sleep, he told himself as he turned off the car's engine upon arriving home.

Waking up the next morning, Peter went through his normal routine. It wasn't until he walked into the hall to get his jacket that he realised the big difference today. For the first time ever he was not looking forward to going to work, quite the opposite in fact.

Thursday and Friday at Cropptech passed without much fuss. Peter noticed that the atmosphere in the security department was still the same, with the majority of people keeping their heads down and doing their work, without the little jokes or quirky humour that Peter really enjoyed. He made a point of touring the whole Cropptech facility on Friday, something that wasn't so unusual, as he was in charge of security. He made out that it was about being extra vigilant with security measures, whereas really it was more to do with gauging the mood of the employees everywhere else in the facility.

Finding the workers everywhere else happy and productive, Peter didn't really know what to make of the situation he found himself in. He kept asking himself, could he have made a mistake and reacted badly to what had happened? Could it all have been completely innocent and maybe he was the one who had blown things all out of proportion with his vivid imagination?

On the other side of the coin, Al Garrett had stayed in his office during working hours, both on Thursday and Friday, all day long - something unheard of since Peter had been with the company.

"Very unusual," Peter thought to himself as he wandered the facility. Peter had also been trying to keep an eye on Manson from the security monitors in his office whenever he was there, without much success. He would catch the odd fleeting glimpse of him walking down a corridor, but it was almost like he could tell that he was being watched and would quickly move out of the way of the camera. The only times Peter seemed to manage more than just a glimpse came when he either walked down the main corridor to Al Garrett's office or came back out and walked back down the same corridor.

Every three to four hours Manson would go and sit in his car. He would stay in it for approximately five minutes but it was hopeless trying to tell what he was doing, even with the well placed security camera in the car park, as the black Mercedes had darkened windows throughout and it was impossible to see in at all.

Peter pondered all of this on his drive home from work on Friday night. His head felt like it was buzzing with everything going on. The one thing he did know was that he was glad it was the weekend.

4

A Ticket to the Ball? Laminium Ball

The walk from the car to the front door cleared Peter's head of all the doubts and confusion he faced at work. Turning the keys in the lock was like a breath of fresh air. Like cogs in a machine suddenly clicking into place, he realised that it being Friday night, he and Tank had tickets to tonight's big match.

With renewed energy filling his body, he sprinted upstairs and changed his suit for jeans and a T-shirt. Cheered up by the realisation that his hunger, which was causing his stomach to rumble rather loudly, would be quelled, not by something frozen he cooked himself, but rather by something tantalising from the food stalls at the ground, he galloped down the stairs two at a time.

He pulled all the curtains in the house and then checked that he had his wallet, keys and phone, (often he found himself forgetting one or the other). He then raced into the sitting room and pulled hard on the glass Galileo thermometer atop the piano. Silently the light-coloured piano swung out from the corner of the room. Seconds later the bare floor parted in a concentric pattern to reveal a gaping hole in the corner. The first step of a Victorian spiral staircase could just be glimpsed through the darkness. Peter tugged again on the thermometer and quickly made his way down the stairs into the darkness.

Before reaching the bottom of the staircase, the light from the sitting room faded as the hole above closed behind him. Peter made his way through the dusty cellar without needing any light at all. Moving along the left hand wall in the darkness, Peter reached up with his left hand upon nearing the end.

Running his hand along the uneven wall, he finally found a small finger sized hole next to a beam. Putting his finger in as far as it would go, he heard the welcoming sound of gears and cogs turning, which he always associated with a pleasurable return to the underground world of the dragons.

Making his way down the narrow stone stairs, he vaulted the wall at the end and landed on the walkway that led back to the monorail station. A quick walk later up the barely lit path and he was making his way across the plaza of the monorail station, trying desperately hard to ignore the assault on his senses from the food being cooked there. He was more concerned with finding Tank, as the station was starting to get busy now with more than a few people going to the game by the look of things. Looking at his watch, he was starting to feel a bit nervous now, as his friend had the tickets for the game and it was fast approaching time to leave. Startled, as a large hand fell onto his shoulder, Peter whirled around, only to end up staring right into his friend's chubby, smiling face.

"Crikey, you're a bit jumpy aren't you?" enquired Tank.

"Sorry," Peter replied. "Bad week at work. Must be getting to me." Peter patted Tank on the back.

"It's great to see you. We need to hurry if we're going to get there in time for me to grab some food before it starts."

Tank let out a raucous laugh, so much so that nearly everybody in the plaza looked in their direction.

"That's what I love about you Peter. For someone so tiny, you're always thinking about your belly."

"It's true," Peter thought, smiling. "I am always thinking about my next meal."

Tank, a bit like Richie, mirrored his dragon form when disguised as a human. He was huge. Well over six feet tall, with a body that was packed with muscle, rugby was definitely the right sport for him to choose. He had sparkling light blue eyes and what would have been a wild array of floppy blonde hair, had it not been cut so short. Always clean shaven, his face looked like a cross between desperate Dan and action man, apart from his nose, which looked like it had taken one too many punches on the rugby pitch, either that or he'd been chasing parked cars in his spare time.

The two friends hastily made their way across the plaza and into the final carriage of the monorail headed to Burton-upon-Trent. Burton was nearly two hundred miles away but of course that was only about twenty-five minutes away when travelling by monorail.

Tonight's match was taking place in a huge underground cavern below the Peak District and the tickets that the friends had were for seats on the Burton side of the cavern. All the way there, the friends argued about the outcome of the match they were going to see.

"Well I think Steel will be man of the match and that we will get through to the Global Cup 4-2," said Peter excitedly, clutching the ticket Tank had just given him.

"Steel is good, but I think Silverbonce's experience will play a vital role and he will be man of the match. We're gonna win 6-2 to go through," replied Tank, grinning wildly.

"Six? You think we will get six? You must be mad. How many times have you seen a laminium ball match where any team scores six? Eh?"

"At least we can agree that the Warriors will win and get through to the Global Cup for the first time in their history," said Tank.

And that was how it progressed all the way to Burton monorail station, lots of friendly banter about the game, all thoughts of anything else forgotten.

Now for those of you that don't know what laminium ball is, perhaps I should explain. Since before records began, dragons have been playing this as a sport and soooo much more.

Laminium ball is the equivalent of a human football match. The game itself is played in specially designed caverns that are located all across the world. The playing zone in each cavern is two miles long and three miles high, with a sea of molten lava underneath. At each end of the two mile long zone, halfway up, embedded into the cavern's walls are the 'mouths'. Each mouth is made up of six stalagmites and six stalactites joined in the middle. These are known as the 'teeth'. The game can last up to two hours and whoever has knocked down the most teeth is the winner. However, if one team knocks down all six teeth before the two hours is up then the game is over and they are declared the winners. It is incredibly rare for any team to knock all six over and perhaps happens once every decade or so.

The dragon teams competing against each other consist of four flying outfielders and one 'mouth guard'. The outfielders are allowed to control the laminium ball with any part of their body, but most prefer to use their tails. Their tails can be used to dribble, slap, roll, slam, tackle, intercept and do tricks with the laminium ball.

Once any of the outfielders think they are in range, they can attempt to shoot at the mouth. The mouth guard can stop the ball hitting the teeth with any part of his body, from the tip of his tail to the end of his nose.

The ball itself, as the name suggests, is made of laminium, covered in a coat of ionised platinum, making it all but unbreakable. It can even sustain a substantial amount of time submerged in the lava that extends beneath the playing area. Some teams make good use of this and perform dangerous 'flying dives' that start high up in the arena and end with the player diving into the lava and popping up somewhere near the opposition's mouth. This makes it very tricky for the mouth guard to stop, as he has no idea where the opponent will surface, therefore making it very hard for him to position himself correctly.

The laminium at the centre of the ball is a very precious and rare metal, valued highly by dragonkind because of its magical properties. It is only found in exceedingly small quantities, very deep underground and usually in remote and inaccessible areas. This prized metal is one of the things that Cropptech specialises in mining. Often it can only be found in extremely cold conditions, meaning that the dragons have to rely on human help to extract it. The properties that cause dragons to describe it as magical include enhancing the mental capabilities of dragons like their telepathic talents, making mantras much more powerful, giving a boost to natural dragon abilities (such as making them stronger, enhancing stamina, etc) and a host of wicked side effects on top of all of the above.

During a laminium ball match, the precious metal inside the ball can enhance any or all of these attributes belonging to the dragon flying with the ball, thus making it amazingly hard to take the ball away from a particular individual.

For each team to be recognised by the spectators during a match, the players in that particular team all have an aura added to their bodies before the game starts, to give off a particular colour, normally blue and red for the respective teams. The dragon in charge of upholding the rules, or the referee to you and me, has a green aura for the duration of the game.

Laminium ball games are much more than just a sport to most ordinary dragons; laminium ball has become a way of life. The games are reported in all of the telepathic papers and receive an amazing amount of coverage. The players involved are treated like gods and are selected from the nursery rings to be groomed from a young age in the art of laminium ball. The youngsters are selected for their size, strength, agility, flying ability, and if you haven't guessed by now, the fact that they are male. Most never actually make it far enough through the rigorous training to become professional laminium ball players. Only a small percentage succeed and go on to become the best of the best.

Once a dragon is selected to be a laminium ball player he spends the rest of his life being treated like a rock star or a sporting god. He wants for nothing and is adored by most. Probably his biggest sacrifice would be the fact that professional laminium ball players are not allowed to go to the surface, ever. They are valued so highly that no risk whatsoever can be taken with them, so they must always stay within the safety of the dragon world. That, coupled with the fact that while most dragons were learning how to attain human form in the nursery rings, these guys were learning how to play laminium ball.

The match that Peter and Tank were going to watch was being played between the Indigo Warriors (Southern England) and the Crimson Crusaders (Northern England). The two friends were mad keen on laminium ball and had always been huge supporters of the Indigo Warriors because they live and were brought up in Southern England.

Each laminium ball player is as famous as any sporting icon from the human world above. They all receive amazing amounts of fan mail, offers of bonding or mating, and endorsement opportunities every week. Not a day goes by when one or other player isn't featured heavily in all the telepathic papers: their black and white pictures blazed all over the papers; talk of a new mate, new scale colouring, a new home, or some exotic new training regime that will make their team win the Global Cup.

The Indigo Warriors were no different and regularly featured in the telepathic papers. The team were all legends to their fans even though they had won nothing for the past fifty years and had similarly under achieved with their current squad in recent years. The Warriors team was as follows: Steel (Captain), Flamer, Cheese, Barf, Silverbonce (Mouth Guard) and Zip (Substitute).

Laminium ball players are given new names once they reach the rank of professional. These names can be given for any number of reasons and are chosen by a panel of experienced dragon judges, who decide their new names when a dragon has reached the required standard and has the necessary drive and ability to make it as a professional laminium ball player.

After turning professional, a dragon then has to wait for his chance to be selected to play in a team. This may take many years and for some very unfortunate dragons may never come at all, if the right positions or opportunities never become available. Once selected for a team, even as a squad substitute, that's when fame and fortune take hold and their lives change forever. Even the most reluctant fans know how all of their team's players have earned their names.

Peter and Tank could recite every detail of the Indigo Warriors team. The captain was named Steel because he had nerves of steel and had proved so many times, never ducking a challenge or tackle, and sometimes winding up with the most horrendous injuries. Flamer was so named because of his highly powered breath which produced the most extraordinary amount of heat and flame extension - something many of his opponents could attest to. Cheese only ever seems to eat cheese and claims this diet is what gives him his incredible surge of speed when he needs it, although some fans of other teams often claim that it's because he smells of cheese. Also he never seemed to appear in a photograph without a piece of cheese; ever so slightly eccentric, but incredibly popular with the fans.

Barf got his name because of his sheer resilience. In the final match to choose which dragons were going to make it as professionals, Barf was quite seriously ill (incredibly rare for a dragon). He shouldn't even have been at the game, let alone been playing. His desire to become a professional convinced the judges to let him play against their better judgement. Having played quite poorly by his own high standards for most of the game, he was beginning to feel that his chances of selection were decreasing by the second. Determined to give it his all for the remaining few minutes of the game, he produced the tackle of the game, which unfortunately for him took place during a steep power dive towards the lava. Just as he was approaching his opponent, the speed and angle of descent caused his poorly stomach to react with violent consequences. Even though he was throwing up with power not seen even in most human babies, he went on to make the incredible tackle and be selected to become a professional. Hence the name Barf.

Silverbonce, the mouth guard, gained his name from the colouring of silver that adorned the top of his skull and flowed halfway down his back, standing out rather vividly from the rest of his pale green body. He was not only the oldest player of the team, but also the oldest professional laminium ball player in the world. Having constantly seen off competition for his place in the side from players less than half his age, more often than not he could save the day for the Warriors by pulling something from his bag of tricks gained from his years of experience.

Zip was the last member of the Warriors and the squad substitute. His name stemmed from the mottled cream and gold colouring that travelled the length of his belly, so that from underneath when he was flying it looked like a giant zip ran across his stomach.

With a poor league season, by their standards, nearly finished, the Global Cup represented the only chance for the Indigo Warriors to win something. Just qualifying would be an achievement of sorts as that had not happened in their history, but the Crimson Crusaders would be no pushover. The Crusaders finished second in the league and had been playing recently like they were on fire, so to speak. For their heroes to get this close to qualifying and fail would be devastating for Peter and Tank, not to mention the tens of thousands of other Indigo Warriors fans.

The two friends had left the monorail at Burton and had made their way along the walkways towards the underground stadium, along with all the other spectators. Carried along in the midst of a throng of other dragons, most of whom proudly displayed some sort of object to show their allegiance to one team or other, Peter and Tank marvelled at how crowded the walkways were, as they edged towards the game.

After rounding a sharp bend, the walkways began a shallow descent and eventually opened up into a giant mall. The throng of dragons in both forms started to spread out, given a bit more space, but even so it was still incredibly tightly packed, with many tens of thousands of *mutatio* dragons entering the stadium from this side to see the game.

On either side of the mall, wide burrows had been carved out of the rock faces and these had all been set up as shops, with an amazing assortment of vendors plying their trades. Market stalls had also been set up in the middle of the mall, forcing all the dragons heading for the stadium to meander through like a river, making the stalls in the middle look like tiny islands of merchandise. Peter and Tank stayed close together and started browsing some of the shops and stalls, ignoring all those selling Crimson Crusader memorabilia.

The first shop the friends came to appeared to be selling some sort of mantras. Pushing their way through the crowd, the friends tried to get as close to the front as they could to see the owner demonstrate his wares to the laminium ball fans. Looking over the shoulder of a rather tall gentleman in front of him, Peter could see the owner reading one of his mantras aloud and wondered what all the fuss was about. Suddenly there was a loud WHOOSH as a blue firework shaped like a dragon flew straight up in the air from nowhere and then exploded with a loud BANG. Bits of exploding dragon floated down from the sky and then amazingly formed the words STEEL IS THE BEST in blue writing, which then began to glow brightly after which it caught fire and burned itself out from one end to the other.

"We have these for every member of the Indigo Warriors team, including Zip," shouted the owner of the shop, out across the crowd. A mad scramble ensued with everyone trying to get to the front to get the mantras that they wanted. Three minutes later the crowd had thinned out and both Peter and Tank emerged relatively happy having got a mantra each; Peter had the last one for Steel and Tank had got one for Silverbonce.

The pair continued through the mall, browsing the stalls and shops at a leisurely pace. By the time they reached the end of the mall, as well as the mantras they each ended up with a big blue floppy hat that said 'INDIGOS RULE' on it, and a huge bucket of flavoured charcoal.

There the two friends were confronted by a massive courtyard that had four main entrances leading off it into the stadium. At each entrance there was a ticket booth and the queues to get in were starting to build up. The main purpose of the courtyard was to act as a food court, in much the same way as in the main monorail stations, with lots of vendors and seating set up in the middle so that people could enjoy food before and after the match. Once again Peter's sensitive dragon nostrils were assaulted by the sensual aromas of the food being cooked around him in the food court. With his stomach growling with hunger, Peter cast his eye about like a predatory eagle looking for that solitary fish.

"Don't tell me you're hungry…" Tank said, catching sight of Peter's eye-popping gaze at all the food on offer.

"Sorry, I didn't eat earlier," Peter said.

Tank shook his head.

"Gosh I'm shocked. Well I'm going to the seats. I don't want to miss the start."

"I'll be really quick," said Peter. "Can I get you anything?" he asked.

"No I'm fine thanks," said Tank, turning away and heading towards the number three entrance and ticket booth.

Peter had a quick scout around and decided to join the queue for the delicious-smelling charcoal and bacon omelettes. Being about tenth in line, he waited patiently and listened as a voice came over the PA system announcing that the match would start in ten minutes. Suddenly, out of nowhere a foot kicked him on his left leg, just behind his knee. It was all Peter could do to stop himself from falling onto the shiny floor. Turning swiftly round he came face to face with three chuckling youths all wearing the colours of the Crimson Crusaders.

"Ah, look who it is guys. It's Bentwhistle!" one sneered, as the other two burst into laughter.

"Where's your two girlfriends then? Richie and Twonk, I mean Tank." The three were doubled over at this, all clutching at their stomachs with mirth.

Peter closed his eyes and shook his head, wishing the ground would open and swallow him whole. The three dragons in front of him were from his nursery ring and used to pick on him a lot when Tank and Richie weren't around. He hadn't seen Theobald, Fisher and Casey since those far-off days, and by the look of things not one of them had matured at all since leaving. The same sense of dread and foreboding rushed into his body, just as it had when he was being bullied by them all those years ago.

"So Benty, what have you been up to in all these years?" snarled Casey.

"Sewer cleaner I bet," chipped in Fisher.

"Probably had to work his way up to that," blurted Theobald, punching Peter in the shoulder.

Peter fought back a grimace. Although the punch didn't look very much,

Theobald had clearly added more than a little dragon power to it, intending to inflict as much pain as possible, but doing it in a sneaky, playful kind of way to make sure that nobody paid too much attention in this very public place.

Forcing a smile to his lips, Peter said,

"I'm head of security at Cropptech, actually."

"They must be employing monkeys then, if you're head of security," Casey said smirking.

"Perhaps we should see how tough the head of security really is?" growled Theobald with a menacing look in his eyes.

Abruptly Theobald was hoisted three feet into the air by the scruff of his neck. Swiftly turning round, Theobald raised his fists ready to strike, until he gazed into the large steely eyes of ....Tank.

"Is there a problem, Tiny?" asked Tank softly.

Theobald looked to his friends for support, but they had backed off some way and were looking distinctly uninterested in getting involved now Tank had shown up.

"Umm.......errr..........I......... No problem. Just catching up on old times. Isn't that right Bent........I mean Peter?"

Theobald hung in the air, looking submissively across at Peter. By now lots of people, not only in Peter's queue but all across the food court, were gazing at the commotion the five of them were causing.

Peter imagined Tank using his big fist to punch Theobald all the way across the food court, sending him smashing into one of the ticket booths. He knew it was wrong to think such violent thoughts, but they did give him a momentary feeling of satisfaction.

"It's okay Tank. We were just........................catching up," said Peter, almost reluctantly, secretly wanting Theobald to hang there indefinitely.

"Ah........well if that's the case..." Tank said, lowering Theobald gently to the ground.

Once his feet were firmly on the ground and he was out of Tank's giant grip, Theobald's expression turned to one of rage, making his face turn a lovely shade of scarlet.

"Nice seeing you both again," he blustered, and then mouthed the words, "I'll get you for this!" to Peter, making sure he was turned away so that Tank couldn't see. He quickly staggered into the crowd, looking for his friends, who mysteriously had developed an acute case of spine-turning-to-jelly and had legged it.

Tank turned to Peter and asked,

"You okay?"

"I'm fine. Thanks," replied Peter.

"You know you should just stand up to them," Tank whispered, as they both shuffled forward towards the front of the queue.

"I know, I know," said Peter. "It's just not that easy. As soon as I saw them my legs went all floppy and my stomach just started doing somersaults…the same feelings I used to get when they bullied me in the nursery ring."

Tank put his hand on his friend's shoulder and said,

"I know it's not that easy, but I also know you have it in you to stand up and be counted."

"Thanks, that means a lot coming from you," Peter said sheepishly. "Just out of curiosity, how did you know I was in trouble?"

Tank gave a great big belly laugh and looked down at Peter with a big grin on his face.

"I didn't know. I just changed my mind about wanting something to eat." The two friends chuckled all the way to the front of the queue.

Having bought an omelette each, the two dragons made their way to the ticket booth and then into their seats with just seconds to spare before the match started. The lighting in the roof of the stadium, generated by thousands of tiny crystals, slowly dimmed, leaving only the lava at the bottom for illumination. A trumpet fanfare started to echo around the giant cavern in the build-up to the player's arrival.

Suddenly, five red blurs came shooting out of five round holes in the edge of the stadium below where Peter and Tank were sitting. At exactly the same moment across the other side of the stadium the same thing happened with five blue blurs emerging at speed from rounded holes. The blurs flew across the surface of the lava, performing a giant circuit of the arena. The hundred thousand strong crowd went wild, cheering, shouting, banging anything they could get their hands on, some even letting off mantras at this early stage, just like the ones Peter and Tank had.

Both blue and red teams were performing circuits of the stadium now, skimming only a couple of feet above the lava and separated by precisely half a lap. Just as suddenly as they had begun the teams stopped their circuits and flew up to about a mile high, right in the middle of the cavern. As they did so the commentator announced over the public address system that the Crimson Crusaders would be playing in the red auras and the Indigo Warriors would be playing in the blue auras. The two teams hovered flawlessly in the middle of the stadium, their brightly glowing auras making them stand out like stars in the night sky.

A countdown of ten red coloured crystals above each mouth started to gleam and then individually wink out. As it did so the crowd began to chant. "9…..8…..7…..6…..5…..4…..3…"

The noise became almost unbearable.

"2…..1…"

The crystals in the roof came back on, illuminating the whole cavern. Out of a hole in the roof shot a glowing silver ball about the size of a football. As quick as a flash the dragons were onto it, batting it with their tails and moving faster than the human eye could possibly see, but presenting no problem for the dragon audience. As the outfielders fought for possession of the laminium ball, tackling, blocking and dodging as if their lives depended on it, the mouth guards made a hasty retreat towards their given areas so that they would be ready to save any shots at the mouth.

The game itself was a scrappy affair; to say it was by no means a classic was the understatement of the year, if not the decade. But the fans loved every minute of it and were at the edge of their seats constantly, no doubt due to the amount at stake. At one point Barf made an awesome interception from one of the opposition's outfielders and sped toward their mouth, beating the guard and earning a shot at an open mouth. As he did so, Tank and Peter stood up and willed him to score, but unbelievably he missed by quite a margin. Tank raised his hands to his head in dismay, but as he did so he realised he had just let go of the remainder of his omelette. He spent the next few minutes apologising profusely to the nice family sitting in the row in front of him, much to Peter's amusement.

Silverbonce made some absolutely stunning saves throughout the match and nearly everybody agreed, whether at the match or in the newspaper reports the next day, that the Warriors would have been heavily defeated if not for him.

In the end the game, scrappy as it was, was decided in one moment of brilliance. Silverbonce slapped the ball to Steel who was high up, right at the top of the cavern. Steel brought the ball beautifully under control with his tail and ducked into a steep dive, ball tucked under his tail, towards the lava. This caught everyone off guard, even his own players as he was still in his own half of the pitch and much too far away to perform a 'flying dive'... or so everyone thought. With nobody being in range to tackle him, Steel had a free run at the lava and by the time he hit the surface he was travelling at an almighty speed. Everyone looked on in disbelief. The Crimson Crusaders thought it was some sort of bluff as nobody had ever got close enough from that far out with a flying dive to score. As the seconds drained away and still Steel did not appear, the Crimson Crusaders' mouth guard looked at first perplexed and then worried. Fearing that something dreadful had happened to Steel under the lava, the mouth guard lost his concentration momentarily. As he did so, up popped Steel behind him and knocked down one of the teeth with the ball.

Everyone in the whole cavern went absolutely mad, even most of the Crusader supporters. Peter let off his STEEL IS THE BEST mantra and was joined by everyone else who had bought one. The glowing blue words lit up every corner of the cavern. Nobody had ever seen a goal like it. The Crimson Crusaders all stood absolutely dumbstruck. With the confidence drained from them, the Crusaders did their best to get back into the game, but to no avail.

As the final horn trumpeted, fans of the Indigo Warriors began to celebrate like never before. Their team had made it through to the Global Cup for the first time in their history and had a shot at becoming the best team on the planet.

The party continued well into the night, with most Warriors fans choosing to stay and celebrate at the stadium's food court and mall. Peter was glad it was Saturday tomorrow and not a work day. As he was playing hockey at home in the afternoon, he would have a big lie-in the next morning.

Much later, well into the early hours of Saturday morning, Peter and Tank sat on the monorail heading back to Salisbridge. Surrounded by a mixture of fans coming back from the match and people travelling normally (the monorail runs twenty-four hours a day, every day of the year) the friends were ecstatic about the great evening they had enjoyed.

"We'll have to try and get tickets for the first round of the Global Cup," Tank shouted over all the noise in the carriage.

"That would be great but it could be anywhere," replied Peter, as the words 'SILVERBONCE FOR KING' came whizzing down the carriage, narrowly missing Peter's floppy hat, and casting an eerie blue reflection in the windows of the monorail car. Clearly not all the mantras had been used at the match.

The monorail pulled into Salisbridge station at 4.10am. Peter came to the conclusion that even with a lie-in he still wouldn't get very much sleep. The two friends went their separate ways at the station, each knowing they would see the other at the sports club later that day, with Tank playing rugby and Peter playing hockey. Within ten minutes Peter was tucked up in bed, dreaming of the fabulous goal that Steel had scored and wishing that he could perform something amazing like that on the hockey pitch the next day.

5

Smokin'

The alarm went off at twelve-thirty. Peter slammed his hand on the off button and tried to go back to sleep but the bright sunlight streaming in from around the ill-fitting curtains seemed determined to prevent that. After hiding his head under the pillow a couple of times, he knew sleep had now left him for the time being, even though he felt exhausted. Grudgingly he got up. Slipping straight into his hockey kit, he stopped only to grab a quick bite to eat before getting into his car and driving to the sports club.

On arrival he found the car park nearly full, not uncommon for a Saturday afternoon. Walking to the changing rooms he bumped into some of his human team mates who gave him a ribbing for looking rougher than a sandblasted tramp.

"If only they knew what I'd really been up to," Peter thought to himself. Ten minutes in the changing room came and went, as he put on his shin pads and hand guard, while listening to the captain talk about tactics.

The team stripped off and in matching orange kit all walked outside to the Astroturf hockey pitch to begin their warm up exercises. Usually the Astroturf pitch was fully booked up on a Saturday, from around nine-thirty in the morning to nearly six at night with the use of the giant floodlights. Today was no different and Peter found that the men's first team were already playing on the pitch. A small area of Astroturf was attached to one side of the pitch, used for teams to warm up and warm down. Peter's opponents were already out on it warming up and hitting hockey balls to each other. Peter did some warm up stretches for about five minutes and then got out his hockey stick and started to hit a ball back and forth with one of his team mates. The rest of the team did likewise until it was nearly time for the two teams currently playing on the Astroturf to finish.

Gathered around with the rest of his team, there seemed to be some discussion as to the identity of a new player that nobody recognised, playing at the moment for the first team. Peter listened in as he continued to warm up the muscles in his legs.

"Well I've never seen him at training," said one of Peter's team.

"There's a surprise," said another.

"You should know by now that not all first teamers have to come to training," said another sarcastically.

Finally the cheekiest of the lot quipped,

"Perhaps he's the captain's new boyfriend." With this the rest of the group just shook their heads and wandered away a little.

"Whaaaaat?" said the cheeky one, but he was practically standing on his own by now.

Peter hadn't been paying much attention really but now that he had finished warming up decided to take a look at the newcomer. Glancing over to the very far 'D', he couldn't believe his own eyes. There, rushing about in a full first team kit, was Major Manson. Peter's heart sank. What the hell was he doing here? A sudden tap on Peter's shoulder made him turn round with a start.

"Are you alright Peter?" asked Andy, the captain of the second team. "You look like you've seen a ghost."

"Ahh......I'm fine. Must have been a dodgy kebab last night," replied Peter, still reeling from seeing Manson on the pitch.

"Okay," replied Andy, giving Peter a sneaky wink.

Peter took a large swig of water from his bottle and tried to compose himself. As he did so, the whistle was blown on the pitch to signal the end of the first team game. Peter's team raced out onto the Astroturf to warm up in front of the goals and do their last minute preparations. Meanwhile the teams that had just finished playing were warming down and collecting their kit from the sidelines. Peter hung about by the entrance to the pitch, pretending to adjust his shin pads. Eventually the players started to trudge off the pitch, most carrying grazes or burns on their knees, legs and arms. As Manson picked up his kit and walked around the edge of the pitch, Peter prepared to head through the narrow gated entrance just as Manson was reaching the other side. Talking to one of his team mates, Manson had just about reached the other side of the entrance, when Peter stood up and walked through, making himself as wide as possible. With no option but to wait, Manson gazed directly at Peter as he strolled through the gate. Peter looked straight ahead as he did so, noticing that Manson made no effort to even acknowledge him. Peter continued round the pitch and put his kit bag down with the rest of his team's kit. Sneaking a quick glance over his shoulder, Peter noticed that Manson didn't even look back at him, and had gone straight into the changing rooms. And it was only dimly in the back of his mind that he realised there was no sign of Manson's limp or walking stick now. Peter became even more convinced that there was something very unusual about that man.

"Come on Peter. Let's go. It's nearly time to start," Andy, the captain, called from the pitch. Peter checked his hand guard and headed out on to the pitch, thoroughly fed up and distracted.

The game of hockey did not go at all well. The opposition were rather good and Peter had his mind on other matters. Seeing Manson playing had been the worst preparation possible and had led to Peter playing like a drain. Within ten minutes his side had been 3-0 down and by half time it was 4-1. Andy the captain made the decision at half time to substitute Peter and although he stayed in his kit, ready to go back on (rolling substitutes are used in hockey, meaning that a player can come off and go back on as many times as he or she likes), he knew because of the way he had played that no matter how desperate his team were, he would not get called back on.

The team fought back in the second half as Peter watched on from the dugout, but only went on to lose 5-4. Those early goals had cost the team the game and everyone, especially Peter, knew it. The atmosphere in the dressing room was subdued, whereas normally it would be full of mucking about and laughter.

Once showered and changed, Peter took his kit out to the car and thought about driving straight home. He knew if he did it would be perceived as sulking and unsportsmanlike. If nothing else, he considered himself very sporting and knew he needed to go and chat to their opponents for ten minutes and have a drink, even though he feared that he would run into Major Manson in the bar. His fears were unfounded, as Manson had already left, so Peter got himself a drink and went and chatted to some of his opponents. After some fifty minutes or so the opposing team left to return home and Peter only then realised that he was having a good time and had forgotten all about his worries. With the bar getting busier and busier he thought about heading home and getting something to eat. Abruptly he received a well timed pat on the back.

"Nice job Peter," said Andy the captain.

Peter just stood and looked puzzled.

"Socialising with the opposition," said Andy, noticing the expression on Peter's face.

"Ahhh," said Peter.

"Now, about the game today," Andy said, putting his arm around Peter's shoulders and slurring his words just a little. "Everyone has a bad game from time to time. The secret's forgetting all about it and just playing your best next time. Some of the team thought you were going to drive off after the game in a huff."

Peter smirked a little knowing that he nearly had.

"But you didn't," continued Andy. "You came in and behaved really well which was the best thing you could have done. It's good to have you in the team Peter. I'll see you at training on Tuesday. Now you'll have to excuse me as there's a rather nice lacrosse player that needs me to entertain her," he said, winking, as he disappeared into the crowded bar.

Peter just smiled. He was very glad he had stayed. The bar was now absolutely heaving with people, with practically all the chairs in the place being filled. Sky sports news was on the massive flat screen television at one end of the bar and most of the people were watching, as it was just about time for the full time football results. The arcade machines in the corner boomed every now and then, while the 'ching, ching, ching' of money coming out of one of the fruit machines provided an occasional interruption. Pool balls crashing together and the sound of friendly rivalry also filled the lengthy room.

Peter just stood and soaked up the atmosphere. There was something very special about all of this and he loved being a tiny part of it. As he took in all the sound and the rowdy atmosphere he found himself thinking of the one thing he most certainly didn't miss. This time last year the atmosphere would probably have been about the same, only a huge blanket of cigarette smoke would have hung in the air throughout the room, infecting everyone's clothes, hair and skin with its disgusting aroma. Thankfully the current human government had chosen to implement a ban in public places recently; the sports club in Salisbridge had only sought to comply at the very last minute, and then reluctantly, unlike a lot of other establishments in the area who had gone smoke-free long before the deadline came into force.

The humans' constant propensity to harm themselves never ceased to amaze the dragon community. Generally not a week went by without some story or other appearing in one of the telepathic papers showing how the humans had discovered some other way to do themselves considerable harm. If not smoking then drinking, drugs, chemical additives in food or unhealthy diets. Over the years dragons have tried to guide the humans in the right direction with all of these so-called vices, but it seems the will of the people and the money behind it all are very hard to stamp out once and for all. In recent years the dragons have had more luck in reducing the impact of tobacco through encouraging awareness campaigns, restrictions on sales, government taxes and the kind of blanket ban that currently exists across England and other countries in the world. Even Peter could see the slight irony in the fact that the dragons have tried so hard for such a long time to stop humans from smoking, when they themselves can produce mighty flames from a single breath and enjoy nothing more than chomping on a whole load of charcoal. The difference, most dragons would tell you, was that the dragons' flaming breath was essentially pure, although it could cause smoke if it set fire to anything (i.e. wood, plants, plastic, etc). The flame itself gives off no chemicals at all, thus causing no damage to the environment or any other animals or plants. However the modern day cigarette contains a cocktail of chemicals including nicotine, carbon monoxide, tar, acetone, ammonia, arsenic, benzene, cadmium and formaldehyde, all of which are pretty harmful on their own, let alone when combined.

What fewer dragons and virtually no people at all realise is that the introduction of tobacco to the civilised world in the middle ages was no accident. Columbus thought that he and his crew had stumbled across it in 1492 when they first set foot onto the New World. Sir Francis Drake brought tobacco back from the Americas in 1573 and then introduced Sir Walter Raleigh to it in 1585. The group of people who thrust tobacco at Columbus and Sir Francis Drake were actually a band of dragons known as the *obscures* (which means 'darkling'). Their plan was to try and take over large parts of the civilised human world by tobacco addiction and by controlling the supply of it. Fortunately the dragon council learned of the plan and managed to head it off eventually, but not before tobacco had been introduced across the whole globe, and compromised a large percentage of the population.

The *obscures* actually invented tobacco with the sole purpose of corrupting human society, and by and large did quite a good job, only being stopped right at the last. Ever since, the dragon council and its kind have been trying to rid the world of tobacco, without much success. These facts have only come to light quite recently in dragon society, (over the last twenty years or so) due to important relevant documents being discovered in a deserted part of the Council's Grand Library. The story of the introduction of tobacco is now told in the nursery rings so that young dragons can hopefully learn from it and prevent the same mistakes that were made generations ago. It was there that Peter learned about it, only in his last few years in the nursery rings when the information was first discovered.

Jolted back to reality, Peter felt a sharp pain in his posterior. He was so surprised that he dropped his half empty pint glass. He watched in slow motion as the glass and its contents headed comically towards the beer stained carpet, waiting for the roar from all the patrons that normally accompanied such a travesty. To his utter amazement it never came. Out shot a slim graceful hand and caught the glass without spilling a single drop of the remaining contents. Richie handed him back the glass with a big grin on her face and proceeded to smack him on the same place that she had just pinched.

"Ohhhhh nice bum Peter," she said raising her eyebrows at him.

Shaking his head and suppressing a smile Peter replied,

"I might have known it was you. Crikey Rich, you gave me such a start."

"Lighten up Peter. It's only a bit of fun."

"Yeah, I'm sorry, I know," said Peter with a tiny smirk. "How did you get on today Rich? Did you win?"

"Of course we did, dopey. 9-4! Guess who scored the winning goal and a hat trick?" Richie said, raising her glass in his direction.

"Um............ let me see. Was it that beautiful redhead Charlotte by any chance?" Peter said, wincing and knowing what was coming next.

STAMP!!!!

"Ouch!" yelped Peter, hopping madly as Richie stamped on his foot.

"You know full well it was me. And I won man of the match," Richie said proudly.

"Nice," said Peter, nursing his sore foot.

"How did you get on?" asked Richie taking a gulp from her pint of lager.

Peter's expression turned from happy to sad in the blink of an eye.

"Don't ask," he mumbled.

"No go on. Tell me," Richie persisted.

"We lost 5-4," Peter whispered, looking at the floor.

"That's not too bad," replied Richie inquisitively.

"I was subbed at half time. Not brought back on either."

"Oh," said Richie, just beginning to understand. "Ah well. Everyone has bad games Peter," she said. "Well...............except me that is."

Peter smiled at this. "Do you want to know why?"

"Sure," replied Richie.

"When I got to the pitch, who should be playing in the game before for the first team but.........Manson." Peter whispered the last word, looking around the room as he did so.

"Hmmmm.......... so?" said Richie.

"Well, what the hell is he doing here? Don't you find it just a bit odd?" pleaded Peter.

Richie just shrugged.

"Not really. I did mention it to him on one of his tours of the office," she said nonchalantly.

"WHAT!!!!!!!!!" exploded Peter, turning a furious shade of red.

"He just kinda got talking about sport and mentioned he was a keen hockey player and I told him all about the sports club and the setup here. Supposedly he talked to the first team captain on the phone and mentioned the standard he had played at previously and the captain put him straight into the team on those grounds," Richie said, nonplussed.

Peter remained a very violent puce colour and, shaking his head, let out a long breath.

"You've got to be kidding me Rich. Do you have any idea of the misery he's made my life at work since he's come along? And now, the one place on the surface I go to enjoy myself and relax and he's here, playing for the flippin' first team."

"Calm down Peter. It's no big deal. So he's here. It's not the end of the world."

Peter stood in the middle of the crowded bar, staring at his feet, looking like a petulant child. He seemed in utter turmoil, and if anybody in the clubhouse had bothered to look closely they may have thought he was going to cry. Reining in his emotions, he lifted his head and looked Richie straight in the eye.

"I thought you understood Rich? Something's happening here, something big. I can't put my finger on it but this is something that affects us all, I'm sure of it."

"Peter, you can't fathom that just from the fact that you don't get on with the guy!" Richie leaned in closer and added,

"He's not a dragon Peter. Just an ordinary bloke, doing his job. This is the first time since leaving the nursery ring that anyone has challenged you over anything. And you don't like it! You have to remember what we were taught, to blend in and to act like normal humans," she said in such a hushed voice nobody could possibly overhear.

With the fury returning to his face, Peter looked like he might explode.

"Me! Remember what we were taught? That's a laugh. You constantly abuse your powers, in front of the whole world. Arm wrestling rugby players and God only knows what else! If the dragon council found out about half the stuff you get up to you'd be for it. Anyway, it's not just being challenged by Manson that's got me riled. We were taught to always be vigilant and look for the unusual. This is what's happening with Manson and you're too caught up in playing the 'beautiful, kick ass heroine' that you're blinded to the reality of the situation," Peter said angrily. This was the first time ever that he and Richie had ever had cross words, with Peter never normally saying 'boo to a goose.'

As Peter turned to go, Richie reached out to grab his arm. Peter shrugged her off, and hastily made his way through the patrons towards the exit.

"Hey, Peter," said Tank merrily stepping into his path. Tank, having played rugby that afternoon, looked like a bomb had hit him. Sporting a black eye, bruised lip and a bandage across his hand, he still had the happy go lucky smile that always seemed to adorn his face.

With Tank in his path, you might have thought Peter would have stopped and spoken with his friend but he didn't. Instead he swerved at the last minute and quickly threaded his way through the throng of people and into the car park, where he jumped into his car and raced home, tears streaming down his cheeks. Tired, hungry and emotional, he decided to skip having a meal and went straight to bed, wishing that he worked and lived a long way from Salisbridge.

Unusually, Peter woke up really early and couldn't go back to sleep. He decided on a big breakfast and then a walk around the city. It being a Sunday, not many people were about at this early hour. Peter passed a few joggers and people walking their dogs as he wandered slowly across the old path that crossed the beautiful water meadows of Salisbridge, taking in the view of the Cathedral as he did so. He mentally chastised himself as he continued his walk for not doing this more often. The scenery was absolutely stunning. With it being the start of April, the air was a little crisp, freezing just slightly as he exhaled. Despite this he was still dressed in his favourite grey shorts, a T-shirt and his hockey tracksuit top.

He continued to follow the winding path until it reached the point where the river turned into a little waterfall and deposited itself into a much wider section of the river right below the historic old restaurant that sat on the main path through the water meadows. Taking a seat in the park opposite the restaurant, Peter sat down and watched the ducks and their newly hatched chicks swim in the shallow waters.

Sitting in this idyllic scene, he felt like something from a Constable painting. Losing all track of time, Peter just sat and let the world go by about him. He watched more people passing, parents taking their children for a Sunday morning walk and listened as teenagers behind him began a game of football in the park, using their jumpers as goal posts. He thought of all the wondrous scenes he had witnessed in the dragon world below ground that were so skilfully concealed from these fragile human beings, and on this glorious April morning had to confess to himself that very little came close to the natural beauty that he was witnessing here today.

The ringing bells of an ice cream van to the theme of a children's nursery rhyme pulled him out of his daydream, only then realising that it was early afternoon and he had sat there for well over four hours. Shaking off the pins and needles in his thighs, he stood up and started his walk back home, grabbing an ice cream from the van as he did so. Ambling at a leisurely pace he was amazed at how different the walk back was from his journey over there earlier this morning. The narrow path was full to bursting with walkers and cyclists of every conceivable age. He noticed that a lot of the people were tourists, using their cameras and camcorders to capture these magnificent sights, and then it dawned on him that he was exactly like them, a tourist, only not from America, Europe or Japan, but from the humid depths of the dragon world.

Arriving home, he hung his tracksuit top up in the hall, having carried it all the way home; it was such an absolutely gorgeous day now, it could almost be mistaken for summer. He noticed that the light on his answering machine was blinking, indicating that there was a message. It must be Richie he thought, wanting to apologise. This brought him well and truly back to reality after the rather surreal start to the day, reminding him of work, Richie, Tank and particularly Manson!!!

He pressed the green button and waited patiently as the electronic voice said, "You have one new message." He was surprised to hear Tank's voice rather than that of Richie.

"Hi Peter. Just phoning to see if you're okay - you seemed a bit fed up when you left last night. Rich told me what happened and I just wanted you to know if you want someone to talk to, then I'm here for you. I'll be in all morning but I'm doing some rugby coaching this afternoon that might go on until quite late. Give me a call when you get up, you lazy git," Tank said mischievously.

Peter deleted the message after listening to it, smiling as he did so.

"Lazy git indeed!" he thought to himself. Pleased that Tank had phoned, he was aware that he couldn't care less that Richie hadn't left a message apologising. Knowing that Tank would be off coaching somewhere, Peter thought he might finish work early tomorrow so that he could seek out Tank for a well needed chat.

6

A Sign of the Times

After an uneventful day at work, Peter left at half past two, using up some of the flexitime that he had accrued over the past couple of months. He drove home and, without bothering to change, hastily made his way to the monorail station via the concealed entrance underneath his house. At the station he boarded a monorail car that was destined for London. Twelve minutes after boarding, the carriage pulled into the Fleet Street station where Peter alighted and headed for Tank's workplace.

Leaving the station and joining one of the little alleyways that littered the place, Peter always marvelled at how space was at such a premium here. Small shops lined either side of his route, with more shops and homes above, feeding off higher walkways on either side. It was also more noticeable that almost everyone he passed and saw through the windows and doorways of shops, had reverted back to their natural dragon forms, making it very interesting walking along these narrow alleyways. Even though it meant lots of ducking and weaving out of the way (not to mention lots of scraping against the walls and doors of shops when two larger than average dragons encountered one another going in opposite directions in these confined spaces) the dragons just carried on and took everything in their stride.

Every time he came here Peter always struggled to get his head around the little nuances that made London very different from anywhere else that he had been to in dragon Britain. In most places, such as Salisbridge and Purbeck Peninsula, it was accepted that assuming human form was the norm, just mainly to save on space, and you would think that with space being so restricted here in London the same policy might be adopted… but no.

In fact, by appearing *mutatio*, Peter seemed to be the one out of place and was definitely the subject of many stares and occasional wing pointing. Knowing full well that the dragons around him could sense that he himself was a dragon, he came to the conclusion that it must be the fact that he was in a suit that made him stand out so much and that's what all the pointing and the staring was about. Most dragons despised any kind of clothing that restricted their movement very much and although a lot had to wear a suit to blend in with the human population at work and at formal events, very few would ever wear a suit willingly underground when they did not have to.

Feeling ever so slightly claustrophobic as the buildings loomed larger and the walkways got narrower, Peter began to wish he was wearing something more comfortable, as the temperature and humidity were rising steadily.

"Most dragons like it hot," he thought to himself, "but this is getting ridiculous," he concluded, with his shirt and tie now dripping with sweat. Rounding a corner and crouching to go under a small arched stone bridge, supporting a walkway above it, he took a sharp left into Camelot Arcade and followed it down until a sign in the distance read 'Gee Tee's Mantra Emporium'.

Walking up to the building, Peter turned the squeaky metal handle on the old wooden door and was greeted with a rush of cool air as he entered. In contrast to the shadow filled narrow walkways outside, Peter found himself in a very well lit, open, shop floor, surrounded by ancient wooden bookcases, twenty feet high, covered with dust and cobwebs and filled from floor to ceiling with old books and parchments. The counter at the front of the shop seemed abandoned, with just a solitary pile of dusty books resting there. Peter wandered between the bookcases and noticed that most of the cobwebs he had spotted when he entered the shop, were actually hosting at least one spider each, none of which were particularly small. Indeed there was a web just behind the shop counter that appeared almost five feet wide. Sitting just off-centre, in the sparkling silver strands of a glorious web, was what looked to Peter's untrained eye very much like a rather large tarantula. Peter knew the fear he suddenly felt was completely irrational, but even accepting that was no help at this present moment.

He decided to stay away from the seemingly deserted shop counter at the moment and resume his search of the bookshelf aisles. Tentatively he made his way down another aisle in search of Tank or anyone else that worked here. Walking around the store, he started to doubt whether coming here was a very good idea at all. Perhaps he should have waited until Tank got home to have a chat with him, but he had to admit to having been more than a little curious to see where Tank worked during the day, particularly as this place was legendary.

"Just like its owner," he thought to himself. Only rarely had Tank talked to Peter about his work and even then he had always been quite vague about it. Peter already knew that the store was once the most renowned and respected in the mantra business with its owner and proprietor, Gee Tee, being not only extremely wise and knowledgeable about mantras, but also being unbelievably old as well. Rumour had it that Gee Tee had seen out over six centuries, which Peter thought was pretty much impossible, even by dragon standards. When he had tried to quiz Tank on the subject all he would say was that his boss was a great employer, but rather misunderstood due to eccentricities and all his idiosyncrasies. He had once gone so far as to say that if you didn't know the dragon then he could be quite scary. Not something Peter wanted to dwell on at this moment in time, as he wandered all alone around his seemingly empty store.

Coming to the end of another aisle and once more being able to see the counter and the entrance to the shop, Peter thought that it might be best if he just left and caught up with his friend later, especially as that huge spider behind the counter was glancing in his direction. Taking a step towards the exit, Peter was startled by somebody clearing their throat.

"Hhhuuurrgh ….hhhuuurrmm."

Peter searched, wide-eyed, for the source.

A large dragon head with long wavy grey hair, wearing a pair of large square spectacles, peered around the dusty piles of books on the counter at the front of the shop. Relieved at finally finding someone, Peter changed direction and headed towards the counter.

"Before you take another step, child, you can take that thing off," the dragon boomed, pointing at Peter's body.

"We do not tolerate those in this shop, EVER!"

Peter stood fixed to the spot, lost for words. The dragon just continued what he was doing below the counter. It might have been reading or writing; he was too far away to tell. Peter quickly considered his options. After a few seconds he realised that the only real choice he had was to take off his clothes. If it offended that much then that's what he would do. Off came his tie and jacket which he neatly put on the bookcase he was standing next to. Next he began to unbutton his shirt. As he did so he glanced around uncomfortably. He did a quick double take. The huge spider above the counter had winked at him, he was sure. Pausing for a moment to check the spider again, he looked up and the spider was facing the other way, busy spinning a line of web. He didn't consider himself to be easily spooked but he was tempted just to leave the rest of his clothes and run away. Deciding against it he continued undoing the buttons and removed his shirt. Off came his shoes and socks followed swiftly by his belt and trousers. Standing only in his white Y-fronts, Peter was unsure how to proceed. Seconds seemed like days as he waited for the shop keeper to look up. He thought about whistling or clearing his throat but in the end managed to squeak a meek, "Is that better?" in the direction of the counter. Simultaneously the shopkeeper and the spider above him looked up from what they were doing. Peter swore the spider winked and smiled at him this time. The shopkeeper looked aghast.

"What an earth do you think you're doing, CHILD?" he cried.

"Ummm.........just what you told me to," Peter quivered.

Standing up straight, taking his large square spectacles off, the dragon spoke to Peter with thunder in his voice.

"I told you to take off THAT terrible outfit," said the dragon, still pointing at Peter's naked chest.

"I don't understand," Peter whispered apprehensively.

The dragon's arm swung around until it pointed towards the entrance.

"Look at the sign above the door, child," he said, exasperated.

The sign (which Peter had not seen when he entered) read 'ONLY THOSE IN SOLITUS FORM ARE WELCOME HERE'.

Immediately Peter understood. It wasn't his clothes that he was expected to get rid of, it was his human form. Only dragons in their natural state were accepted in the shop. Both dragon and spider glared in his direction. Peter knew immediately what to do. Closing his eyes he concentrated on unlocking the dozen or so bonds within his DNA that regulated his appearance as a human. It wasn't very often that he did this, preferring instead to remain in human form most of the time.

The complete transformation took less than three seconds and started with a warm tingling feeling all over that progressed to a kind of citrusy flavour inside his body and ended up with the swirling noise of what felt like a hurricane being heard from within his ears. Looking down, the first thing he noticed were his ripped Y-fronts hanging off one of his talons.

"Oops!" he thought to himself. "Looks like I'm going home commando tonight."

"That's better, child," said the shopkeeper. "Come closer so that I can get a better look at you."

Kicking off the ripped Y-fronts, Peter plodded over to the counter at the front of the store. He understood now why there was so much space in here. If only dragons in their *solitus* form were allowed in, then the room would have to be increased accordingly. Peter himself was a comparatively small dragon, as dragons go, as some can have a wingspan of over one hundred feet and be forty feet tall.

The shopkeeper made his way around to the front of the counter and gave Peter the once-over.

"Hmmmm............ nothing special," he said as he lifted up Peter's left wing. Peter tried to pull away, but the old dragon had a grip of steel and would not let him go.

"Ahhh..........what's this then?" he said, looking below Peter's left wing at the markings on his belly. Peter's belly was predominantly white, although on the left hand side there was a strange pattern made up of matt green scales. It was unusual for any one dragon to be the same colour all over, pretty much unheard of in fact. When the coloured scales on a dragon's body formed a pattern that was recognisable, sometimes the dragon took that pattern or shape as his or her name. This was just so in Peter's case. The matt green scales stood out to look like a whistle. A whistle where the part that you blow into was crooked or bent. Hence Peter's dragon name was Bentwhistle. And his full human name was Peter Bentwhistle.

The old dragon continued to poke at Peter's scales that formed his marking.

"I know this from somewhere," he said, frowning. "I know. You're Tank's friend. He's told me all about you, you know."

Peter smiled at this.

"Has he really? Is he about at all?" asked Peter. "It's just that I wanted a little chat with him if that's at all possible."

"Of course, of course, my young fellow," replied the dragon, stepping out from under Peter's wing. "He's been here all the time," he added with a wicked grin.

Turning around, the dragon went back behind the counter and reached up into the silver web and retrieved the big spider. Peter took a step back, not sure what to expect. Putting the spider on the counter, the dragon picked a red book from the dusty pile and began sifting through it. Having found the right page by the look of things, the dragon put the spider on to the tip of his wing. Peter looked at the spider perched on the dragon and noticed for the first time the same inane grin that Tank wore most of the time.

"It can't be, can it?" Peter thought to himself.

The old dragon started muttering in a language that Peter had never heard before and then right in the middle tossed the spider into the air with one flap of his giant wing, while still muttering the strange words. The spider tumbled in the air and then started to spin around and around, as if trapped in a vortex. Spinning round faster and faster in front of the shop counter, the spider seemed to Peter to be getting taller, although it was becoming mighty hard to tell because the speed at which the spider was now travelling was dizzying even by dragon standards.

Yes, definitely taller, but changing in colour now. The mini tornado, because that's what it now looked like, roared around and around, faster and faster. The old shopkeeper had been chanting all the time but now paused and looked up from the book. Moving his glasses further down his nose he watched the swirling mass and then finished his chant with one word.

CRASH!!!!!!! Tank was thrown out of the mini tornado and into the nearest bookcase. A hail of books toppled down onto his head as he tried to sit up against its base. None of this prevented him from having his usual stupid inane grin.

"Excellent, excellent!" cried the shopkeeper, appearing at the front of the counter.

"A morphic mantra from Roman Times," he said to Tank as he picked himself up from the pile of books.

"Quite a find, even if I do say so myself," the dragon said to no one in particular as he turned away. "You can tidy the books up later. Take your friend into the workshop and have your chat now. Don't be too long though, we have that Aztec flying mantra to test later," the shopkeeper said, wandering off among the bookcases into the depths of the shop.

"That was unbelievable!" Peter said as Tank came over.

"Just run of the mill here I'm afraid Peter," Tank said grinning wildly.

"Really?" asked Peter in disbelief.

Tank put his wing around Peter and led him behind the counter and to the back of the shop, into a big room that was packed full of stuff. Four oversized desks were cluttered up with high piles of books, torn or damaged parchments in all shapes and sizes and a huge variety of specialist writing equipment including oversized dragon pens, ink, brushes and paper. Oversized dragon-shaped chairs accompanied the desks.

"What happens here?" Peter asked his friend curiously.

"This is where we repair broken mantras and try to create new ones sometimes. It's the workshop."

Peter gazed on in wonder.

"I didn't even know it was possible to repair a broken mantra."

"Most people don't," said Tank, matter-of-factly. "It's not something that's needed very much. A lot of mantras nowadays can be memorised or can be carried on mobile phones, laptops or PDAs. This is all quite recent, but before all of that came about, mantras would need repairing, especially important ones that only had a one-off use. This was where most people would come to have it done."

"You mean they don't come here anymore?" said Peter.

"Oh the odd person comes in to have a really rare or old mantra fixed, valued or researched. But sometimes we don't see a customer for weeks on end."

"That's really sad," said Peter, concerned.

"It's just a change in the times, or so Gee Tee says," said Tank quietly. "These new dial-a-mantra services haven't helped very much either."

"Must have missed that," replied Peter, bemused.

"Trust you," said Tank to his friend. "You must have seen all the billboards and the adverts in most of the telepathic papers."

"Nope," said Peter, shaking his head.

"Well, anyway, it's very much like the dial-a-ringtone the humans have for their mobile phones, but instead of getting a new ringtone to download, you get the mantra that you require and then you can store it in your phone as a text message to be used whenever you need it," Tank said in a disappointed manner.

"So it's affecting business then?" queried Peter.

"Yeah, I've never known it so quiet. Gee Tee's already laid off two of his staff and it's only me and him left now."

Peter paused for a moment and then said,

"I'm sorry Tank. I had no idea. You should have said."

"It's not something I like to talk about. Besides, it's not like Gee can get rid of me. He needs my help, as you've already seen," Tank said, grinning.

"That must have been some special mantra to change you into something that small," Peter said, changing the subject.

"Apparently the Roman dragons had a knack of doing it. They were famed for it, but like so much information it's been lost over a period of time. Dragons have never been renowned for their information storage skills, at any point in history and it's not much better today," Tank said, pointing his wing over his shoulder back towards the front of the shop.

"Anyway if I feel miserable about the lack of customers, I can just visualise you standing in the front of the shop in just your Y-fronts," Tank said with tears of laughter beginning to stream down the front of his face.

Peter held his head in his hands, blushing with embarrassment.

"Yeah, thanks for that. I'm sure it will always help me to think of you as that spider."

"Anyway, what brings you to these famous premises Peter?" Tank asked, throwing his wings open wide and turning around.

"Well I wanted to talk to you about Richie and my work," Peter said, frustrated.

"Ahh…….I thought it might be something like that. Richie told me on Saturday night that you had argued, and why," Tank said, sitting back in one of the oversized dragon chairs in the workshop.

Peter slouched in a chair on the opposite side of the room and let his wings droop over the side, until they nearly touched the floor. The two friends started chatting, with Peter explaining to Tank all about Manson and how he seemed to be controlling Al Garrett and manipulating him and some of the other staff at Cropptech. He also tried to convey his belief that Manson was evil and dangerous. Tank listened to Peter for more than forty minutes as he poured his heart out over his troubles and worries at work, and also expressed the regret that he felt for arguing and falling out with Richie. When Peter had finished and sat dejected in his comfortable chair, Tank considered carefully what he had heard from his friend before he spoke.

"I think the first thing I should say, Peter, is that Richie feels as bad as you do about your argument on Saturday. She told me exactly that at the weekend and wants nothing more than to go back to being best friends again. So I think you should stop worrying about that for starters."

This brought a smile to Peter's face, followed by a tiny dribble of flame from his nostrils. The realisation that he had been worrying about nothing dawned on him, making him see quite how stupid he had been.

"As for Manson," Tank continued, "You must understand Peter, that it's very hard to gauge what sort of person he is without having met him. I know what you think, but just maybe Richie's right and it is just all a case of getting off on the wrong foot."

Peter sat silently and just nodded. Having learnt his lesson about falling out with one friend, he had no intention of doing it with another.

"Or maybe you're right Peter. Maybe Manson is a conman or a criminal and is planning some kind of crime at Cropptech. Either way things aren't as bad as you seem to think. If Manson is simply a human crook, then you should have no problem in apprehending him at the appropriate time," Tank said, smiling. "After all, your superior intellect as a dragon gives you a huge advantage over any human. Remember, no dragon has ever been bested by a human in our entire history. The guy stands absolutely no chance. It's not like he's anything other than a human. Both you and Richie would have sensed it and you haven't, right?"

Peter let out a long sigh.

"He's not a dragon. It's just that..........that.........well, he just feels different, almost.....................evil. I can't really explain it, but that's the only way to describe it."

"As long as he's not a dragon, you've got nothing to worry about," Tank said reassuringly.

A coughing noise came from just inside the door. The friends turned round and saw that Gee Tee was standing there with a stern look on his face and his large square spectacles dangling from the end of his nose.

"Are you really worthy of being my apprentice?" the old dragon turned to ask Tank. His velvety smooth voice did little to hide the real edge that his words carried.

Tank was used to the eccentricities and sometimes mischievousness of his employer, but here and now he knew that the old dragon had something more on his mind than games or mucking about.

"If it's what I said about knowing my job's safe, I......apologise," said Tank nervously.

A small frown, practically unnoticeable, developed behind his spectacles.

"No it's not. But I'll bear that in mind," the old dragon said.

"Why don't you tell your friend about the mantra you found last month. You know, the one that produced the purple emperor butterfly, or as you like to call it *apatura iris.*"

Peter recognised the tone in Gee Tee's voice that implied Tank had been showing off with the butterfly's Latin name. Having spent decades with Tank in the nursery ring, nobody knew better than Peter how annoying it could be to spend ages learning about some plant or animal, and then up would pop Tank, knowing its correct Latin name, out of nowhere. Clearly, Peter thought, whatever had happened with the mantra, Gee Tee had taken offence at Tank's special talent.

"Would you perhaps prefer it if I told him?" Gee Tee asked Tank in a tone that was more an order than a request. Tank sat dead still and nodded his head.

"Well young Bentwhistle, one day my apprentice here was sorting out some of the Egyptian mantras out on the shop floor. Sorting through them he spotted one that he recognised, or so he thought. I was away at the time, buying some more ink and paper for the shop. So anyway my clever apprentice thought that he would use the mantra he had found to produce the emperor butterfly that I mentioned earlier. Reciting the mantra correctly, for it was nearly all in ancient Egyptian, he managed to produce a lovely butterfly that lovingly followed him all around the shop."

Peter looked over at Tank and saw his friend squirming with discomfort.

"Now I'm sure I don't have to tell you about my apprentice's love of everything living," Gee Tee said, looking over at Peter. Peter just nodded.

"When I came back to the store later that morning, I could scarcely believe my eyes. Flying around my shop was an Egyptian morphbeetle. One of the most dangerous beings the world has ever seen. And to make matters worse there was my clever little apprentice, petting it at every opportunity. Needless to say we had to call in the King's Guards to get rid of it, what with it being a Class 9 mantra and all. Eventually they managed to facilitate its capture and subsequent termination but managed to wreck half my shop in the process, something they all seemed to take great pleasure in. I thought at the very least my apprentice might have learnt a valuable lesson from said incident, but upon overhearing part of your conversation it would appear that no such lesson was learned."

Tank sat up straight and tried to put the pieces of the puzzle together, the lesson and the relevance to the conversation. Try as he might, with his employer bearing over him, his mind just went blank.

"For Bentwhistle's sake I shall put you out of your misery. The valuable lesson you should have learned, was that evil comes in many shapes and forms, and that not all those shapes and forms are always visible to everybody. You thought the butterfly was real because that's what you wanted to, but as soon as I came in the door I recognised it for what it was," Gee Tee sighed as he finished.

Peter thought he knew what the old dragon meant.

"So what you're saying is that I could be right about Manson and that he could be immensely evil, even though nobody else can see it!" Peter cried enthusiastically.

"That's one way to put it, I suppose," said Gee Tee. "But perhaps you need to expand your narrow way of thinking somewhat. Tank thought the butterfly was real but it wasn't. What if this 'Manson' is not all that he appears to be? What if, like the butterfly, something much more sinister lies beneath?"

"Are you saying he could be a dragon?" asked Peter, wide-eyed.

Tank quickly butted in and said,

"But that's just not possible. They would sense him if he were a dragon."

"Would they indeed...?" said Gee Tee. "If history teaches us nothing else, it's that you can always expect the unexpected, my naïve apprentice. Dragons throughout the ages have hidden themselves before, and I don't doubt that at some point they will do it again."

"Really?" said Peter, fascinated.

"Of course," said Gee Tee. "It can be done. It's very difficult, but it can be done. Anyway, I'm sorry to cut short this meeting but I need Tank, I'm afraid. We have many more books to sort out. You can start on the 'Mechanical Repairs' section, after you have shown your friend out," Gee Tee told Tank. Gee Tee turned to Peter.

"It's been a pleasure meeting you, child. Consider yourself welcome any time. It's not like it's a busy time for us at the moment or anything," the old dragon said sadly. "I hope you sort out your little problem at work," he added, bowing as he turned and went back to his dusty shelves.

Peter rose from his chair and followed Tank back through to the shop. The friends bade each other farewell and Peter, remembering to collect his clothes from the dusty bookcase, made his way back to the monorail station to head home.

That night Peter sat at home in front of the television, trying to unwind. His visit to Tank's place of work had been absolutely fascinating in many different ways. Learning from Gee Tee that it was possible, however hard, for a dragon to conceal their dragon-ness was just breathtaking. Peter eventually headed upstairs to bed at just past 10pm, his head spinning with thoughts from an astounding afternoon. Before he nodded off he vowed to himself that he would keep an open mind about... everything.

7

Security Sweep (Sooty or Sue?)

Peter woke the next morning at the same time as usual. He went through his normal routine and, while eating breakfast, he decided to send out his consciousness to get a copy of the Daily Telepath. He didn't get the paper every day purely because he was too lazy, but today was an important one because the details of the Indigo Warriors' first game in the Global Cup should be announced. Sending his mind off in a kind of autopilot way, it wasn't long before it had retrieved said paper and was able to access it. The front page looked like this:

The Daily Telepath

Britain's Oldest Telepathic Newspaper   Issue No 252231

Are Teaching Standards in our Nursery Rings Declining?

By Mike Frame

More young dragons leaving the nursery rings are being turned down for top jobs because they just don't make the grade. A report commissioned by the SDC (Scientific Development Centre) states that the quality of applicants for entry level jobs has dropped by nearly ten percent in the last five years. The number of applicants failing to get posts attached to the King's Council has also risen by fifteen percent. Nursery ring development coordinator Leyla Buttercup said, "the nursery rings strive to move with the times and constantly aim to provide young dragons with the best education possible."

Charcoal Targets Announced

By Pedro Rodrigez

Councillor for 'above ground resources' Professor Enzo Thorndagger has announced new targets for the effective management of dragon charcoal consumption. The guidelines refer to coppicing. This had been regarded for several hundred years as the best way to sustain and manage the woodland required to supply charcoal to dragons throughout the world. While coppicing has been used by most suppliers, one or two have recently been found to be taking wood for charcoal production from non-sustainable resources, something which the dragon council finds wholly disturbing. With charcoal consumption reaching an all time high last year, the council feels that it is high time to increase the previous ninety percent coppicing target to ninety eight percent. Despite opponents insisting the target should be raised to one hundred percent, the council feels this would be unrealistic and that the targets should be reviewed on a yearly basis. For great new and innovative charcoal recipes, see our twenty eight page Sunday supplement.

Latest Success- The Giant Lau Lau

By Holly Origin

European Ped Labs claim to have followed the success of growing the star fruit underground by announcing successful trials of sustained growth of one of the dragon community's most desirable delicacies - the giant lau lau. The subtle sweet taste of the large, crunchy, well flavoured fruit has long been one of the most sought after foods of the dragon domain. Demand has long since outstripped supply for this brightly coloured fruit, which up until now has only been found to grow in Papua New Guinea and some of the other pacific islands. Although still in its early stages, Ped Labs claim to have used one of their underground greenhouses to grow the equivalent of one year's worth all in one go, despite a few problems still surrounding the seeds, some of which can lose their viability quite rapidly. A spokesdragon claimed, "the research is progressing on schedule, with giant lau lau supplies set to treble in the next four years." Ped Labs, made famous by their amazing fruit embued charcoal, the recipes of which are still a secret to this very day, are always way ahead of any competitors in their field. When ruthlessly questioned on what their next project might be the comunications dragon declined to comment but gave a very knowing smile when the phrase 'melt in the mouth chocolate flavoured charcoal' was mentioned. Don't forget folks........you heard it here first.

South Pole Timetable

By Chief Political Correspondant Briany Ingham

The King's Council met over the weekend, with one of the subjects on the agenda being global warming and in particular the South Pole. The Council all agreed that the issue needed further study and Councillor D'Zone was appointed the task of putting together a group of dragons to form the expedition by the time of the next meeting. The Council's overwhelming agreement on this issue has come as a surprise to most but has been welcomed in practically every quarter. Further news on the make up of the experdition when we get it.

New Plant Opens

By April Brown

Yesterday a new geothermal power plant opened beneath Mount Fuji, just west of Tokyo. The turbine used is the biggest on Earth, making this new plant the second most productive in the world. The plant will provide energy for the entire Southern Hemisphere's monorail.

105

"Wow," Peter thought, after studying the Global Cup section. The Warriors are playing the Coral Rock'ards. It would be a tough game he knew, but as it was a one-off contest he was sure they could win and progress to the semi final.

"I wonder if Tank can get us some tickets?" he thought on the way out of the house, a big smile blossoming across his face.

Arriving at work, he got on with some staff timesheets and found himself missing the old atmosphere that used to prevail before Manson had arrived. Only a relatively short time ago he would have known exactly where and when to go for a laugh and a joke but at the moment you could hardly buy a smile from any of his staff, let alone a comic moment.

Later that morning the phone rang and Peter promptly picked it up. It was Dr Island, head of the scientists on the Cropptech Industrial site. Peter prided himself on the fact that he got on pretty well with all the heads of department, or he had done, until the arrival of Manson.

"Hi Peter, it's Sheridan Island here from industrial," came the troubled voice down the phone.

"Good morning Dr Island. What can I do for you today?" replied Peter politely.

"Could you come on over please? We seem to be having a bit of a problem with some of the guards."

"What sort of a problem?" Peter asked, immediately concerned.

"They seem to be conducting some sort of security sweep, and it's interfering with our work rather a lot," said the good doctor.

"That's rather bizarre," said Peter. "I've authorised no such thing, I'm sure."

"Uhhhh......... I don't think it's you," said Dr Island. "The delightful Mr Manson is behind it according to the guards," she added, dripping with sarcasm.

Peter let out a long sigh that clearly wasn't missed by Dr Island on the other end of the phone.

"I'll be over as quickly as possible doctor," Peter said.

"Thank you very much," said Dr Island, and with that the phone went dead.

Peter stood up from his desk and on his way out noticed it was raining, so grabbed his coat from the wooden stand as he made his way out of his office. Leaving the building he headed for the industrial unit which was right at the opposite end of the complex to Peter's office, and involved a five minute walk around the office complex to get there. On his way Peter wondered what the hell Manson was up to. Did he not realise that these scientists were a special breed of people? They carried out some of the most critical work on the site and Peter had learned from experience, and from those around him, that it was best to try and let them get on with their painstaking and exacting work with as little fuss as possible.

Getting thoroughly drenched, despite his coat, Peter arrived at the industrial unit and made his way past the reception desk into the interior. Peter's senses always seemed to get confused whenever he came into this building. On one hand the environment was very clinical and sterile. On the other hand there were massive machines moving around, spraying hot metal and giant sparks all over the place. Was it a laboratory? Was it a factory? Somewhere in between, his brain reluctantly told him.

Amongst all the machines and equipment, scientists in lab coats stood around in disbelief, looking on as a dozen guards wandered in and out of all the heavy equipment. Peter walked up to Dr Island and put a hand on her shoulder.

"I'll try and sort this out straight away," he said in a calm manner, noticing that the doctor looked like she was about to pull out all of her long dark hair.

Peter strode over to the guard who looked like he was reluctantly in charge of all the rest.

"What's going on, Phillips?" he whispered, knowing how far the sound travelled in this environment.

"Just following orders, boss," Phillips replied anxiously.

"We can't just come in here and interrupt their work whenever we like," Peter said, still maintaining a whisper.

"But that's exactly what we *can* do," boomed a snarling voice from the opposite corner of the unit. Everyone looked round as the voice reverberated about the equipment. Out from behind some of the larger machinery walked Manson menacingly, tapping his walking stick on the polished white floor as he did so.

"Did you not understand when Mr Garrett put me in charge, Bentwhistle?" Manson asked demeaningly. "I am in charge of security here now, and I can perform a security sweep of any part of the complex, any time I like. Do you understand, Bentwhistle?" Manson used Peter's surname like it was some kind of embarrassing fungal disease you might have in your unmentionables.

"Yes sir, I understand," Peter said, humiliated, with the ten scientists and the dozen or so guards looking on.

"You had better," said Manson with steel in his voice, "or you'll be looking for another job. Now, what I've seen today is nothing short of disgraceful. The security here is woefully inadequate, laughable in fact. Any of these workers could smuggle equipment or valuables out of here at practically any time."

"Now you listen here…" started Dr Island, looking as though she was about to erupt like a volcano. "How dare you accuse any of my staff of impropriety? Every last item is always accounted for, and my staff are all as honest as the day is long."

"Have you quite finished, woman?" Manson said with contempt.

Peter and everyone else couldn't believe what they were hearing. In all the time that Peter had worked here, he had never heard anyone speak with such rudeness as this, and by the look on the faces of all the others present, neither had they.

"I'm not standing for this a second longer!" said Dr Island, absolutely furious. "Nobody speaks to my staff that way, especially not some jumped up, snotty nosed ex-officer. I'll have you know that I have worked here for nearly thirty years and I've never been treated like this. Al Garrett is going to hear about this straight away." With that, Dr Island turned around and stormed out of the building.

Manson just stood there twisting his finger in the air.

"One down, several hundred to go," he said grinning. "You can all get back to work," he said to the remaining scientists. "I will be introducing my own set of specialised guards for duty here, so you had all better watch yourselves," he added.

The scientists, clearly distressed, made it look as though they were going about their jobs, but were more likely waiting for Dr Island to come back from seeing Al Garrett.

"You can all resume your normal duties," Manson told the guards, who dispersed as quickly as Peter had ever seen. He couldn't blame them. Manson turned and looked Peter straight in the eye.

"I wouldn't bank on the good doctor having too much success if I were you," he remarked before turning to leave. Peter hoped with all his heart that Dr Island was explaining things to Al Garrett right at this very moment and that Manson would be on his way shortly.

How very wrong he was.

Peter went back to his office and stayed there working and eating his lunch, all the time wondering how Dr Island had got on. He didn't have to wonder for too long. As he ate, he noticed a new email come into his inbox. "Great," he thought, "notice of Manson's departure."

Opening the email with a click of his mouse, Peter was aghast at what he read. The email was from Al Garrett to all department heads and said that Dr Island had been fired this morning for a severe breach of discipline and that the department, being without a head at the moment, would be run in the interim by Major Manson.

Peter thought his day had got just as bad as it could. But later that afternoon, he received more bad news. Chief security co-ordinator Mark Hiscock, another dragon who had been off sick for some time now, had died last night. Peter was shocked to his core. It was very rare that a dragon died and he had never known anyone, human or dragon, who had passed away. He sat in his office all afternoon, overcome with grief.

8

The Faint Whiff of... Octopus

Unable to concentrate on anything at all, Peter felt like he was in a constant daze. The first thing he had done on Wednesday morning was to check the telepathic papers for details pertaining to Mark's passing away. Sure enough, in two of the more reputable editions he found obituaries for his dead colleague. The funeral, holding with dragon custom, would take place exactly ten days after his death. Dragons that knew him would need time to prepare and journey from all over the globe. Peter himself planned to attend, likewise the funeral that would be held for Mark on the surface for the humans that knew him in that form.

Staff at Cropptech were also finding it difficult to come to terms with his death. Every time Peter ventured out of his office to some part of his department he caught someone weeping or just recovering from doing so, trying to conceal their puffy, upset eyes. He also kept chastising himself for not going to see Mark and for not realising how serious the problem was. Dragons rarely get ill, but even when they do, it is never usually very serious. Peter had expected his colleague to resume work and had no reason to suspect anything like this would happen. What made it even more surprising was the fact that Mark was relatively young in dragon terms, only 120 years old.

It didn't help that the hockey season had just finished, something else that made Peter a little sad, particularly in light of the way work was going at the moment, so he had nowhere to let off steam. Peter had phoned Andy, the second team captain and let him know that he would not be able to play in the last game of the season or make the last training session. Andy was fine about it and Peter confirmed to him that he still wished to play next season, so Andy told him that he would see him at pre-season training, towards the end of the summer.

The human funeral for Mark Hiscock was scheduled for Friday. Cropptech staff had contributed towards a wreath and Peter knew many of the people in the security department were planning to attend. On his travels during his days at work, Peter had taken to opening up his dragon senses and, using the superb hearing he and all other dragons possessed, he would eavesdrop on other people's conversations as he travelled around the Cropptech facility. Although this practise would probably be frowned upon by dragons in general, Peter got around this by telling himself that he was doing it as part of his security role and that it was for the greater good of the company, which is essentially why he was here in the first place: to safeguard the limited supply of laminium.

The day before the funeral, Peter made more of an effort than ever to wander throughout the facility and see what people were gossiping about. The only downside to doing this was the fact that he could bump into Manson at any point - not something he was keen to do, but he already had a mental list of excuses as to why he was touring the buildings, that he hoped would be enough to keep Manson off his back.

As he wandered, selectively picking up on conversations between people, he noticed a definite theme. Most of the staff talked about Al Garrett and the fact that he had not appeared in this time of need. They seemed to think it odd, as normally when something like this happened, Al would take the initiative and offer assistance in any way possible to the family, while also touring the facility reassuring the staff and listening to what they had to say, as well as praising the deceased and recognising the contribution that they had made to the company, however big or small.

Although Peter had not been with the company long enough to remember anything like this happening, plenty of staff had and they were all amazed that nobody had seen hide nor hair of Garrett all of this week. Most of the whispers doing the rounds though were centred on whether or not Al Garrett would attend the funeral. In the past this question would have been unthinkable, but with his current odd behaviour nobody was sure what would happen.

The day of the funeral arrived and Peter found himself walking across the crisp grass of the crematorium in his new black suit. One of the first to arrive, Peter sat in a pew at the back of the room on his own, nodding to a few of the staff that he recognised and getting a nod or a subdued wave back in acknowledgement. As the minutes passed by, more people filed in and sat in the wooden pews. Peter tried to look unaware of what was going on and who was there but that couldn't be further from the truth. He noted everyone that came through the door and was particularly interested to see whether Garrett would attend.

With the crematorium half full and Al Garrett nowhere to be seen, the vicar in charge checked his watch and reluctantly started. Peter sat at the back and listened to the kind words being said. Looking around he saw members of staff in various states of emotional distress. It brought home to him just how much deception was involved in a dragon's life. People here were genuinely upset at the death of a man they probably in reality hardly knew, because at the end of the day he was a dragon. And being a dragon would have meant that he would be keeping numerous secrets as well as not revealing most of his true personality. And yet he had still made friends, friends that were now sitting here grieving for him. Peter felt so confused, especially when it occurred to him that Mark's body wasn't actually here. His true body was being prepared for the dragon service. The dragon council were clearly at work here, deceiving the humans into thinking Mark's body was in the building.

Once the service had finished, Peter found himself in the courtyard outside, making small talk with some of the staff that he knew. Milling around and chatting to different people, Peter realised the mood had changed from utter sadness to one of quiet contemplation. Staring out at the well maintained grounds, Peter felt a tap on his shoulder. Turning round, Peter stood face to face with a well dressed, middle aged gentleman, whom he didn't recognise.

"Excuse me, but are you Peter Bentwhistle?" the gentleman asked.

Suspicious of everything at the moment, Peter suddenly became alert to everything around him.

"I am," he replied, cautiously.

The man offered his hand to Peter.

"Good morning. I'm Oliver Burns. Of Burns and Haybell solicitors."

Peter looked bemused. Shaking his hand, he said,

"Nice to meet you."

"You don't know why I'm here?" asked Mr Burns.

"Sorry, no," said Peter.

"We're handling Mr Hiscock's will," whispered Mr Burns.

"What has that got to do with me?" replied Peter, suspiciously.

Mr Burns frowned.

"Mr Hiscock made you the executor of his will. You didn't know?"

"I had no idea," said Peter shocked.

"Well it's a little unusual," said Mr Burns, "but never mind. Basically Mr Hiscock has left his whole estate to charity. There's some paperwork to do and then you need to arrange for his possessions to go to the charity in question."

"Can I ask what the charity is?" Peter enquired.

"The children's hospital over the other side of town," replied Mr Burns.

Peter nodded thoughtfully.

"I wonder why he chose me."

Mr Burns flipped open his paperwork and began to scan through it.

"It says here that as well as working for Cropptech, you are both of the same descent."

Panic raced through every fibre of Peter's body. He wanted to grab the papers and destroy them, but instead stood very still in this most public of places.

Mr Burns looked closer at the documents. Peter's heart was in his mouth.

"Ah yes. Here it is. It says that you are both originally of Irish descent," said Mr Burns looking up.

Relief, as well as steam, poured off Peter.

"That's right," said Peter, relieved. "I'd forgotten I'd even told him about that."

"Well, that's cleared up why he selected you," said Mr Burns happily.

Peter signed the paperwork that he needed to there and then, and told Mr Burns that he would go round to Mark's house and sort his belongings out. Mr Burns told Peter to make an appointment to see him, once he was ready, and handed him the keys to Mark's house.

Having left the crematorium, Peter was sure that he couldn't face going back into work this afternoon, as he had planned to do. So instead he phoned up and told them he would be back on Tuesday, having already booked the day off for the dragon funeral on Monday. Peter went home and thought that he might go round to Mark's house later that afternoon to sort out the things for charity, but the more the afternoon wore on, the more he decided he really couldn't face it at the moment.

The weekend passed really slowly. With no hockey to play, Peter didn't really know what to do with himself. He thought about going up to the sports club, but knew it would be quiet, as the rugby and lacrosse had finished for the summer as well. Instead he moped about the house, doing some cleaning and washing, things that he normally put off until they could be put off no longer. On Sunday he went for another long walk, this time shunning the beautiful water meadows for the solitude of the countryside. Driving his car up to an ancient hill fort, about eight miles outside of Salisbridge, he parked it there and proceeded to do a circular walk, nicknamed the Pilgrim's Oval, that took in a great deal of the stunning countryside and was about six miles long. He ambled along at not far off a snail's pace and noted how different this was to his walk last week. Whereas the water meadow path was crowded with hundreds of tourists all wanting to take pictures of the Cathedral, today out in the countryside he must have passed only about two dozen people, in the four hours that he had been out here, with not a camera in sight.

With his head cleared a little from the fresh country air, Peter again thought about going round to sort out the things in Mark's house. He really didn't want to go, making up all sorts of excuses for himself, like 'it's not the sort of thing to do on a Sunday, better to wait until after the dragon funeral' and even pretending that he had more housework to do and that it was imperative that it be done today.

Realising on the drive home that this was all a load of rubbish and that he could continue to put it off for a long time to come, he decided to stop by at Mark's house and make a start. He told himself that was the least that he could do, as the guy was no more and Peter hadn't thought of visiting him even once during his illness.

Checking in the glove box of his car to make sure he still had the key to the house that Mr Burns had given him, he proceeded to drive through the deserted suburban streets towards Mark's residence. He got to the junction of Winchester Road and Romany Road and turned left into Romany Road, looking for number seventy-two. As he drove down the road he concentrated on looking out for house numbers, which was more difficult than it seemed because most of the houses he was looking at either had their number obscured by a large hedge or tree, or had a house name instead.

Between focusing on that and his driving, he found that he had gone some way past Mark's house, but only when he had reached number ninety-six. He opted to park the car and walk back as there was a convenient space where he was, and he knew that he was only going to pack a few things up, rather than take anything away.

As he walked back down the street, looking for number seventy-two, the feeling of butterflies returned to his stomach, a feeling he strongly associated with being bullied at the nursery ring. A quick glance over his shoulder showed him that there was nobody around, least of all those thugs from the nursery ring.

Abruptly, he stopped dead in his tracks. The feeling in his stomach increased tenfold. There, parked right outside number seventy-two Romany Road was the black Mercedes that Manson drove. Peter didn't even have to double check that it was Manson's as he recognised the number plate and prided himself on being good at recognising cars, along with the fact that nearly all dragons have a photographic memory. With his stomach now doing somersaults, Peter realised that he couldn't stand in the quiet street for too long without sticking out like a sore thumb. Tank's words came bubbling back to the top of his mind. 'I know you have it in you to stand up and be counted,' Tank had said to Peter just before the start of the last laminium ball match, when the three stooges had tried once again to bully him.

"Well," he thought, "I'm not at work at the moment and I have every right to be here. So I *will* stand up for myself," he told himself, opening the squeaky garden gate and stepping onto the crazy paving path that led to the front door.

Clutching tightly onto the key as he climbed the two steps at the end of the path to the green front door, Peter took a deep breath, unsure of what he was about to find. Turning the key sharply, he pushed open the door and decided it was best to make as much noise as possible. Peter stepped over the threshold and looked down the long hallway that clearly led to the kitchen. Sure enough, a door quickly opened from the left side of the hall, about halfway down. Manson stepped out into the hall, slapping his walking stick on the bare wooden floor boards as he moved. Framed by the open front door behind him, Peter stood still and waited for Manson's next move.

"What are you doing here?" Manson sneered, his top lip wriggling like a caterpillar that had eaten one too many poisonous leaves.

Using all his courage to compose himself, Peter replied,

"I might ask you the same question."

Manson appeared to consider the response carefully, something that concerned Peter rather a lot.

"Mr Hiscock and I were friends," Manson said, changing his tone from disdain to blasé.

"He even gave me a key," said Manson, smiling and holding up a shiny new key that looked identical to the well-worn one Peter still clutched in his hand.

"Still doesn't explain what you are doing here," said Peter, trying not to show that his confidence was starting to wane.

Manson's tone turned back to one of contempt and he screwed up his face as he replied.

"I lent Hiscock a book and wanted to retrieve it before it was thrown away. It's very important and has been in my family for generations."

"Where is it then?" said Peter with a faint smile on his face.

"It doesn't appear to be here," Manson said with murder in his eyes. "You still haven't told me what you are doing here," he added suspiciously.

Peter held the key up in front of him and said,

"I'm the executor of the will. I'm supposed to be here, to sort out all of Mark's things."

A tense silence enveloped the hallway. Manson appeared to be weighing up his options. Seconds passed as both men stood in silence, glaring at one another. Finally a look of resignation crossed Manson's face.

"Well, I'll be going now," Manson said smugly. "If you find my book, give it away with the rest of the stuff if you like," he said, barging past Peter on his way out.

Peter watched him go. As he walked through the garden gate, Manson turned round and shouted back to Peter, with an evil expression on his face,

"I expect I'll see you at work."

Peter stood in the doorway and watched the black Mercedes roar off down the street, narrowly missing a cyclist on its way past. Shutting the front door, Peter proceeded down the hall to the room that Manson had come out of. Unmistakably this was the living room. But it looked as though a hurricane had cut a path through it. Books were strewn across the floor, DVDs were thrown across the sofa, some open with the discs all mixed up. Cupboard doors on the dresser were open and the entire contents emptied out in front of it. The television had been pulled away from its socket and turned around the wrong way. There was also a very strange smell that seemed to be ingrained in just about everything.

"What the hell has Manson been doing?" Peter thought. There was definitely something very …how would the humans say it? Something very…crabby? No…eely? No…octopussy? No….Ah yes!…Something fishy going on.

Peter toured the rest of the house and found that every room was in the same state as the living room. Peter started the thankless task of tidying up and sorting out, but the more he did, the more concerned he became about Manson's actions. After about an hour, he became so concerned that he phoned a twenty four hour locksmith and got them to change the locks on the house.

Peter eventually left at 9.30pm, having tidied up about half the house and got the locks on both the front and back door renewed. It was only as he was driving home that he realised that the smell that permeated the house was the same as the one coming from Al Garrett's office. Confused and tired, he drifted off to sleep that night, focusing his thoughts on the spectacle of the dragon funeral the following day.

Peter awoke the next morning after the worst night's sleep of his entire life. Well it wasn't so much sleep as a series of twenty minute naps with an hour of being awake in between each. Tired and emotional, he found the brightest cloak he had in his wardrobe (tucked away at the back, beneath several dozen shoe boxes) and in nothing but his birthday suit made his way through the concealed entrance and out into the steamy dragon world. Once he had made his way down the narrow steps that led to the walkway by his house, he stopped and changed from his human form into his dragon form. Having changed, he then attached the gaudy looking bright green cloak around his neck. With his cloak billowing behind him as he walked, Peter made his way to the monorail station. His destination was the Dragon Bereavement Grotto at Honister Pass Boulders in Cumbria, over three hundred miles away.

In the dragon community, every country in the world has its own bereavement grotto. Some even have more than one, such as the United States, Russia and China. These grottos are the final resting places of dragons who have passed away. The word grotto implies something small and cosy, which in some cases is true. Take for example Liechtenstein. The grotto there is only fifty metres long and thirty metres wide, and is full of water with a small lava pool at the southern end. It has a stunning waterfall at one end, that trickles down a rock face imbued with marble and gold, meeting the small lava pool at the bottom, producing huge plumes of steam that carry all the way to the surface nearly two miles overhead. This grotto is also only accessible from under the water, so when a dragon's life is celebrated there, the colourful parade of dragons that come to pay their respects have to swim along an underground river to access the grotto, all in human form, which is most unusual. It is said that there are few more enchanting sights than seeing a bereavement ceremony in the country of Liechtenstein, although no dragon has died there for over one hundred years, so you can see that it is not used very often. Taking the other extreme, grottos in some of the larger countries can be the size of laminium ball stadiums.

No matter what their size, all of these grottos have several things in common. First is the fact that somewhere inside them is an area of lava that must be large enough to submerge a fully grown dragon. Secondly, the roof of the grotto must be able to accommodate one dragon scale from each dragon that is submerged there. And last but not least, the grotto must be looked after and guarded so that it is only used for these ceremonies, being such a sacred place.

Peter waited on the correct platform for the monorail to arrive. The journey would take about fifty five minutes he knew, but only because he would have to change monorails three times, first at Birmingham, then Manchester and finally at Windermere; from there the monorail would travel straight into the reception area of the grotto.

Once on the monorail, Peter closed his eyes and tried to relax, and not think of everything going on around him. After the first change, Peter noticed more people going to the funeral (easy to spot because of their colourful cloaks, which were traditional). By the time he alighted at the grotto reception area, there were literally hundreds of dragons, all wearing brightly coloured cloaks. Having never been to anything like this before, Peter just followed the crowd. Thankfully, that proved the right decision, as they all moved from the reception area through a single tunnel and into the grotto itself. As the throng of people came out of the other side, a very tall, serious looking dragon handed each one a silver horn, from a large wooden table that was stacked high with them.

Peter accepted his when it was handed to him and nodded a thank you to the serious dragon. Moving further into the grotto now, Peter became aware of just how beautiful this place was, as an usher led him towards his seat on a rock ledge at the side of the grotto. All of the seats looked out over a swirling mass of bright orange lava that continually twisted and writhed, forming eddies and whirlpools every now and then. The bright light from the lava's intense orange glow reflected off the high grotto ceiling, making it look like the surface of a strange planet in a distant galaxy, littered with tiny stars. To Peter, the effect was mesmerising. He knew that what appeared to be stars high above him, were actually scales from dragons, long dead. Each dragon has a scale removed from his or her body when they go through the funeral rite and that scale becomes part of the ever changing starscape that visitors to the grotto will always remember.

The steady trickle of dragons entering the grotto died away. The silence was only interrupted by the occasional bubble or hiss of molten lava moving about below them. Peter sat back on the rock ledge and looked up at the glistening scales, high above. It was such a peaceful moment. Taking a sneaky look at the dragons around him, Peter noticed that they were all doing the same thing. Some were even whispering a silent prayer by the look of things. He could now see why the grottos were so sacred and why working in them was such a highly valued occupation.

Brought out of his musing by the sound of rock grating on rock, Peter looked to his right and made out a huge circle of rock rolling along the wall, revealing a dark passage behind it. Peter could detect movement in the darkness with his highly developed dragon sight but not much more than that. Rapidly, a line of dragons flew out of the darkness, eight in all, with the last two carrying the perfectly preserved dead body of Mark Hiscock in *solitus* form by the wings. The dragons flew in formation around the grotto for more than five minutes, swooping in low at times so that everyone could get a good view of the deceased. As one the flight of dragons stopped in the exact centre of the grotto. Peter looked left and right and saw all the other dragons bowing their heads in respect. Peter immediately did the same and said a silent farewell to Mark. As they did so, the master of the bereavement grotto flew silently up to Mark's dragon body, and took a scale from his tail, using a ceremonial instrument reserved only for this purpose. He flew up to the grotto's ceiling and attached it there, to shine along with the scales of the other deceased dragons.

The overwhelming silence was broken by the ting of a triangle echoing gently round the grotto. As one, all of the dragons watching instantly stood up and put their silver horns to their lips. Peter did the same, but was a split second behind everybody else. As the last note of the triangle faded to nothing, all of the dragons blow into their horns simultaneously.

At this exact moment the two dragons holding Mark's corpse, released it and let it tumble down into the lava below. The giant dragon body hit the lava with a mighty splash and floated on the surface for a few seconds, before sinking slowly, and with one final gurgle was gobbled up by the lava forever.

The horns stopped playing. The formation of flying dragons did one more lap before disappearing back into the dark tunnel, which was in turn covered back up by the moving circle of rock.

As the rock crunched back into place, the grotto became a whole lot brighter and the dragons began to file back out towards the reception area, handing their horns back in as they went. Peter followed and handed his horn in to the serious looking dragon, and with that, walked through the tunnel and emerged at the reception area. Peter looked around and realised that was it. The dragons were already boarding the silver monorail carriages, and heading off to different destinations. Standing on the shiny stone floor, Peter felt… empty. Although the service had been absolutely stunning and filled with emotion, Peter felt that the closure he had expected to experience just wasn't there. With nearly all the dragons having departed, Peter reluctantly hopped onto the last monorail carriage bound for Manchester.

He sat in a comfortable seat, hurtling along at nearly five hundred miles an hour. Dragons all around him were chatting, laughing, joking and just getting on with things. He, on the other hand, just felt miserable. The monorail pulled onto the Manchester concourse and Peter stepped off looking for the carriage to Birmingham. As he did so he noticed the carriage opposite was just about to depart for London. "Tank," he thought. Wishing for nothing else than to speak to his friend, he jumped through the whooshing doors of the London bound monorail, just as they were closing.

Forty minutes later, he found himself walking through the narrow, shadow filled streets, on his way to Gee Tee's Mantra Emporium. Buoyed by the thought of seeing his friend, Peter quickened his step, smiling as he realised that he was even in the right form to enter the shop without getting an ear bashing from the owner, unlike last time. Turning into Camelot Arcade, Peter made his way along until he reached the old wooden door with the squeaky handle. Opening the door, he stepped in once again to the much brighter surroundings. The shop looked exactly like it had last time, right down to the last cobweb Peter thought, wishing that somebody occasionally did some dusting. Ignoring all the aisles of bookcases this time, Peter made his way straight to the front of the shop, all the time keeping a lookout for any strange or exotic animals. Once at the shop counter, he leaned as far over as he could to see if anyone was about. "Why don't they get a bell on the front door?" he thought to himself. At least they'd know then when a customer came in. Tapping his wing on the counter he decided to blow some flames from his nose, in the hope that the noise would attract some attention.

"Hello child," came a voice out of the blue.

Peter nearly choked on his own flames. Emerging from a bookcase just behind him was Gee Tee, the owner of the shop.

"Uhh.....hi there Mr…Tee," said Peter nervously.

"Hello again child," whispered Gee Tee in his velvety voice. "What can we do for you today?"

"I was hoping to speak to Tank," said Peter.

"I'm afraid he's not here at the moment……..child."

"Oh….ok. Can you just tell him I'll catch up with him later?" said Peter disappointed.

"Certainly child," said Gee Tee, sensing Peter's disappointment. "Is there anything I can help you with…child?"

"No I don't think…well actually, maybe yes," said Peter.

"Is it regarding the man you work with that we discussed last time?" said Gee Tee, peering over the top of his precariously placed square plastic glasses.

"Yes it is," said Peter, keen as mustard.

"Right, I'll tell you what. You help me put some books back on the shelves and I'll listen to what you have to tell me. Deal?"

"Sure," replied Peter, wondering just what he had let himself in for.

121

Gee Tee led Peter back into the maze of bookcases until eventually they stopped in front of one that said 'Mantra Additions For The Human Form' on top of it, and had a pile of dusty books as high as Peter's shoulder next to it. Gee Tee explained that the books needed to be cleaned and then returned in alphabetical order, from the top of the pile. With his feather duster clutched in one hand Peter picked up the top book entitled 'Abdominal Flab And How To Coax The Beer Belly Out Of You', and gave it a quick clean.

"So child, why don't you tell me what troubles you?" said Gee Tee, blowing a whole load of dust from the front cover of a book entitled 'Nose Hair – How To Grow It Like A Jungle'.

"Well, it's like this......" began Peter, updating Gee Tee on his encounter with Manson at the industrial unit, telling him about Dr Island's shock dismissal and about discovering Manson at Mark's house. All the time the two dragons continued to put books back on the shelf after having cleaned them, with the latest clutched by Peter, called 'Double Chins – The Best A Man Can Get'.

After having listened intently to everything Peter had to say, Gee Tee put down the next book that he was holding, took off his glasses and scratched his nose vigorously.

"Well child, it does all sound very suspicious indeed. Tell me, can you describe exactly what the aroma in Garrett's office and Hiscock's house smelt like? Were they identical?"

"It's difficult to describe the aroma. It was really bitter and overpowering with just a touch of ....something...citrusy......I think," said Peter concentrating hard.

"Have you ever had problems smelling anything else?" said Gee Tee.

"Nope," replied Peter certainly. "Passed all the senses tests in the nursery ring with flying colours."

"How odd then that you should struggle to identify this mysterious scent now," Gee Tee said with a faraway look on his face. "How very strange indeed, but then again perhaps not. Most poisons are designed to be hard to trace or identify, particularly slow acting ones, so maybe we shouldn't be quite so surprised."

"You think Mark was poisoned?" Peter said, startled.

"It does seem to be at least a possibility," said Gee Tee.

Peter let his big dragon bum slide down the wall beside the bookcase, until he landed on the floor with a 'thump' and just sat there dejected. With his tail curled up and his wings folded over his head, he looked a forlorn sight.

"I can't believe all of this is happening to me," he said from beneath his wings. "What am I supposed to do? I'm pretty sure there were no lessons in this, in the nursery ring. Who do I trust? Who will believe me?" he said, now holding back the tears.

Gee Tee let out a little chuckle. From beneath one wing, Peter looked up at the old dragon, rage building on his face.

"It's all right child. I'm not laughing at you. It's just that this whole situation reminds me of something I've been involved with before. The other person I helped was a lot like you."

"Does this mean you're going to help me?" said Peter, his face brightening.

"Ummmmm...I suppose so......yes," said Gee Tee, smiling, "but I'm not sure exactly how much help I'll be, as I've never even taken human form, let alone met a real human in person, or even been to the surface. I've only ever read about their customs and beliefs so I have no real firsthand experience of what you're talking about."

"Who cares?" said Peter grinning from ear to ear. "Someone that believes in me, how fantastic is that?"

"Well you can blame Tank partly for that," said Gee Tee, getting back to business. "You see, although I may think you're okay, the fact that Tank thinks of you as his best friend counts for rather a lot. In all the time I've known the young fellow, the only time that I've known his judgement to be suspect was the incident with the Egyptian morphbeetle that I told you about. Normally his judgement of people, plants and animals is spot on. So if I can't help his best friend, who can I help?"

Gee Tee offered out a wing and pulled Peter up.

"Perhaps we had better devote our time to something more productive than stacking bookcases," the shop owner said to Peter. As the two of them made their way back through the maze of bookcases towards the shop counter, Gee Tee said,

"It's such a shame dragons don't do autopsies. If they did, and had one been done on Mark, just maybe we would have found some poison residue. Never mind, never mind. We'll just have to find another way," said Gee Tee, leading

Peter behind the counter and into the workshop again. "Now tell me child, do you have to go back to Mark's house again?"

"Yes," replied Peter. "I have to finish sorting out all of his stuff and then take it to the children's hospital as per his wishes."

"Well," said Gee Tee, rummaging through the bottom of a stack of books, "I'm not sure being exposed to whatever is in that house for a prolonged period, is a very good idea."

"But.....but..." Peter started to protest.

"Yes I know. You have to go back and sort it all out. Ahhhhh....here it is. Just what we need," Gee Tee said enthusiastically. "Now let's have a look and see if this will do," he said, sweeping books, pens, paper and bottles of ink from the nearest desk onto the floor with one flick of his giant wing. Opening up an old rolled up sheet of parchment, he began to carefully study it.

Peter waited in silence, trying to catch the occasional glimpse of what it was he was reading over Gee Tee's shoulder. After a few minutes of muttering and mumbling under his breath, the old shop keeper turned around to face Peter.

"It's not quite what I had in mind, but I think it will do," Gee Tee said, grinning wildly.

This was the first time in his two visits that Peter had seen the old shopkeeper smile, and looking at the parchment on the desk had clearly put a spring into the old dragon's step.

Gee Tee guided Peter to the centre of the room with one large wing and asked him to stand still. Going back to the table he stretched out the parchment once again and put a book at either end to hold it flat. Turning to the very puzzled looking Peter he said,

"This mantra is not designed to specifically protect against poisons but I think it will be strong enough to grant you temporary immunity to whatever evil lurks in that house. I strongly suggest you try your best to keep anyone and everyone away from the house in general until we can come up with a way to neutralise whatever it is that was being used."

Poking his glasses high up his nose, he turned to look at the parchment on the table and said to Peter,

"Stand perfectly still, this will only take a few seconds." Turning round with his eyes closed, Gee Tee muttered words in a language Peter had never heard before, made all the more remarkable because dragons learn to master some twenty different tongues when in the nursery ring, and they have a basic understanding of a lot more than that.

Concentrating on standing perfectly still in the middle of the room, Peter chose to focus on Gee Tee's square plastic spectacles. As he did so, he noticed beads of sweat, from the effort, running down the old dragon's nose.

"These words seem to be taking a lot out of him," Peter thought. Finishing the last few words, Gee Tee staggered over to the table and fell into one of the large oversized chairs. Peter, who by now was tingling all over, came over and knelt beside the old dragon.

"Are you okay?" asked Peter worriedly.

Struggling to catch his breath, Gee Tee replied,

"I will be in a few minutes, child. Reciting ancient Polynesian mantras takes a lot of energy, and I'm not as young as I once was," added the old dragon, smiling and wheezing at the same time.

Unexpectedly a voice from the doorway behind them, interrupted.

"Oh my god, what's happened here?" said Tank, rushing in and barging Peter out of the way, so that he could get to his employer's side.

"It's all right my apprentice," Gee Tee said, still wheezing. "I was just showing your friend here a mantra or two."

"You know you're not supposed to cast mantras, particularly highly draining ones, when there is nobody else about," said Tank in his best school master voice, while glaring daggers at Peter.

Gee Tee smiled.

"There was somebody about," he said pointing his wing at Peter, who was now really confused as to what was going on.

"You know what I mean," Tank said with a really serious expression on his face.

"I know, I know," said Gee Tee remorsefully. "Why don't you take your young friend here and make us all some steaming hot charcoal?" Tank knew better than to argue when he heard that tone of voice.

"Come on Peter," Tank said, motioning to the door with one of his wings. Peter followed Tank out onto the shop floor and once again through the maze of bookcases, heading towards the deepest, darkest part of the shop. In between two of the dustiest bookcases Peter had seen so far, was a dark red wooden door. Tank turned the handle and walked inside. Peter followed and found himself in a very small ramshackle room used as a makeshift kitchen. Tank lit the gas stove with a tiny streak of flame from his mouth and put a copper coloured kettle filled with water on to boil.

"What went on while I was away, Peter?" asked Tank.

"Well I came to see you and you weren't here so Gee Tee and I talked and I told him all about what was happening with Manson and then he agreed to help me, and then he cast a mantra on me to protect me from the poison and…."

"Whoa, whoa. Poison? What poison?" Tank asked worriedly.

Peter explained what had been happening regarding the funerals and him being the executor of Mark's will, as Tank carefully sorted the ingredients of the hot charcoal into three oversized, ultra thick mugs, with huge handles so that a dragon could grip it. Peter smiled as he noticed that Gee Tee's mug had a script he didn't recognise going all the way round it, while Tank's mug had a tiger morphing into a butterfly on it and the remaining mug, that Peter assumed was for him, was just plain purple and had obviously seen better days.

As Tank poured the steaming water onto the contents of each mug, he turned to Peter and said,

"There's something you need to understand, Peter," said Tank, sombrely.

Peter nodded to his friend and urged him to continue.

"Gee Tee won't reveal his true age to anyone, but it's thought that he's over six hundred years old."

Peter nearly dropped his mug in surprise at what his friend had just told him.

"Over six hundred years old! I think someone's been pulling your tail Tank," chuckled Peter. "No dragon can live that long."

Tank just stood with a sombre expression.

"It's true Peter. He is over six hundred years old. He's also very frail and gets tired incredibly quickly. When I told you the other day that I wouldn't lose my job, it wasn't only because of the work I do here. It's because I help look after him as well. The doctor visits once a week and he's on all sorts of medication. He may act all tough and arrogant, but he's really not like that at all. He shouldn't be wearing himself out performing crazy protective mantras when they are not required."

"I didn't make him do it, honest Tank," pleaded Peter.

"I'm sure you didn't Peter. But it makes no difference. By spinning him your tale, he thinks he can help and turn things around. He's not willing to admit to himself how ill and frail he really is," Tank said softly.

Peter took a big slurp of his drink and looked up at his friend.

"I'm sorry Tank, I had no idea."

"I know you didn't Peter," replied Tank. "Hardly anyone does. All I'm asking is that you try not to get him too excited and involved in stuff. By all means talk to him and pick his brain, but try not to wear him out, and quit if he starts to look too tired."

"Sure thing, Tank," Peter agreed, as the two friends headed back across the shop floor with their hot drinks.

Tank smiled at his friend.

"So, a protection mantra, eh? Just one more thing you should be aware of Peter. Gee Tee is probably the world's expert on everything and anything to do with mantras. The mantras in this shop are unlike any others found on this planet. Some of them date back thousands of years and Gee Tee is the only one that can make head or tail of them. That being said, even the great man can make mistakes casting his mantras, especially when he's feeling tired and hasn't taken his medication when he should."

"What are you saying?" said Peter looking anxious.

Tank smiled in a way that made Peter feel very nervous.

"Be thankful that you didn't end up in the body of a spider," Tank said, giving his friend a wink.

Most of the time Peter could tell when his friend was being serious or whether he was joking, but at this exact moment he really didn't have a clue. The two dragons returned to the workshop to find that Gee Tee had fully recovered from his exertions and was gathering up all the things he had so wantonly strewn on the floor earlier. The three of them each took a chair and sat sipping their drinks in comparative silence.

With the minutes passing, the silence turned from pleasantly relaxing to frustratingly awkward. Peter really wasn't sure what to say, and so decided to keep quiet. The silence continued and Peter thought to himself that the best thing for everyone was probably for him to leave. Having nearly finished his drink (only the big whole blobs of charcoal remained at the bottom of his mug), he started to think of the best way to extricate himself from this uncomfortable situation, when his thoughts were suddenly interrupted.

"I knew there was a reason I continue to employ you," said Gee Tee, smiling at Tank and licking his great big jaws. "In all my years I've never come across anyone who can make steaming hot charcoal like you do."

Tank's moody expression seemed to soften slightly, particularly when the old shop keeper let out a resounding 'BURRRRRP'.

Looking directly at Tank, Gee Tee pushed his glasses as far up his nose as he could with the tip of his wing and said,

"I know you only have my best interests at heart apprentice, but I'm not quite as frail or infirm as you seem to think I am."

Tank's softened expression turned back to one of moodiness, and Peter could see that his friend was just about to lecture Gee Tee again, when the old shop keeper held up his wing to stop his young apprentice.

"I appreciate the way you look after me, child, even if I very rarely show it," said Gee Tee looking straight at Tank, "but I've lived for a very long time and have a great many experiences to call upon. My experience now tells me two things. One is that your friend, Peter, has got himself tangled up in something very unusual indeed and needs OUR help. And two, despite my vast years, I'm still a very long way off joining the great river of lava."

At this last comment, Tank broke into a real smile, the first time Peter had seen him do so today.

"So," continued Gee Tee, "we will continue our research here, and try and find a mantra that will totally neutralise what we think is poison in Mark's house on the surface. While you, young Peter, must practise caution. If indeed Manson is not as he appears, then he could be potentially very dangerous. If I were you, I would continue to gather more information and avoid any unnecessary confrontations with him."

Peter nodded in agreement and left the Mantra Emporium feeling genuinely happy for the first time in as long as he could remember. He would continue to watch Manson and with the help of his friends, old and new, he was sure he would thwart whatever evil Manson had in mind.

9

Here Today, Gun Tomorrow

The first thing Peter did when he arrived at work the next morning was to email Richie and see if she would meet him for lunch in the staff restaurant. She must have been checking her emails at the precise moment that Peter's arrived as her response was near instantaneous and she agreed to meet at lunch time. Peter spent the morning doing staff appraisals in his office and worrying about what he was going to say to Richie when they met. Occasionally he would check the security monitors in his office to see if he could pick up any sign of Manson's whereabouts, but the smug ex-officer remained elusive all morning, despite the fact that his car was in the car park.

At five to twelve, Peter logged off his computer and walked through the building towards the staff restaurant. Most of the time Peter preferred to bring sandwiches into work, not because of the price (as the restaurant was heavily subsidised and a three course meal could be bought for as little as ninety-five pence) but mainly because he could then eat his lunch and work at the same time or sometimes not eat until mid-afternoon.

Rounding the corner, Peter caught sight of Richie standing outside the entrance, people pouring into the restaurant either side of her. Noticing his approach, she flashed him a classic Richie smile and he knew everything was going to be fine. They greeted each other with a hug and unusually Peter gave Richie a kiss on the check, which managed to pleasantly surprise Richie, something she commented on as the pair of them each took a tray from the pile and joined the end of the queue. Shuffling forward as one, the two friends eyed up the menu for today.

Richie went for lasagne, while Peter thought he would make the most of not having to cook a hot meal today and went for the roast of the day which turned out to be his favourite, beef. They both added a soft drink to their trays and, upon reaching the checkout, Peter offered to pay for both his and Richie's meals, thinking that it might go some way to making amends for falling out. Richie didn't put up a fight, which Peter thought strange, right up until the very pleasant lady on the till announced that the grand total for the two meals and drinks was a hefty £3.45. Blushing upon realising his mistake, Peter paid quickly and made his way to one of the few remaining free tables, with Richie following. As the two friends sat down, Peter said,

"I didn't really think that through did I?"

Spooning a large chunk of lasagne into her mouth, Richie smiled and waited until she had finished her mouthful until she replied,

"What a friend. Treating me to a slap up meal at one of the best restaurants in town," she said sarcastically.

"How about I promise to take you out somewhere really nice? You can choose. Whenever you're next free in the evening," Peter said, taking a bite out of a Yorkshire pudding that was nearly the size of a football.

"You don't have to do that Peter," Richie said, looking across the table.

"I know I don't have to. But I really want to, to...... make up for the way I acted," Peter said awkwardly.

"A meal with my best friend would always be most welcome," Richie said, enjoying her lunch. "We were both at fault for what happened. Let's just leave it behind and move on. Our behaviour is always put to shame by Tank - good job we've got him to look after us and show us how to behave."

Peter nodded and said,

"Yeah he always seems to know what to say. I bet his pet plants don't give him nearly as much trouble as we do, though."

Richie laughed and replied,

"They know not to give him any trouble, because if they do he'll just spend more time talking to them and they can't run away. He puts Prince Charles to shame on that front."

"That sounds about right," Peter said, mopping up the last of his gravy with his remaining piece of roast beef.

A figure loomed over the friends' table.

"Sorry to disturb you Mr Bentwhistle, could I have a quick word?"

Peter looked up into the face of one of the scientists from the industrial area, and try as he might, he just couldn't remember the man's name.

"Of course you can um…."

"It's Jake Brown," said the scientist, concerned.

"Sorry Jake. What can I do for you?" Peter said showing his best smile.

"Well it's the uhhh…….the new guards. We're all finding it quite hard to concentrate with… you know."

Looking as puzzled as ever, Peter replied,

"You're going to have to be a bit more specific, Jake."

"The new guards and their new… equipment. It's making everybody over in industrial very… nervous you might say," Jake said, looking up at the ceiling.

"I really don't know what you're talking about Jake. What exactly is making everyone so nervous?" said Peter.

The scientist leaned in close and looked around to make sure nobody was listening in.

"The guards, they've all got… well, see for yourself," Jake said, standing up and pointing towards the entrance of the restaurant.

All around the restaurant heads turned and conversations suddenly dried up, as everybody started to notice the pair of guards that stood at the back of the queue. Dressed from head to toe in a light blue uniform, the guards certainly stood out from the mixture of smart casual that most of the other employees wore. That however, was not the main talking point. Strapped around both of the guards' waists was a shiny black belt that held a holster on one side. Poking out from the holster, the handle of a gun was just visible. As if to make matters worse, dangling from the back of each belt was a serious looking baton, a handheld radio and a silver pair of handcuffs. Peter was visibly taken aback.

"What the hell…?" he muttered to nobody in particular. Shaking his head and giving Richie a kind of 'I told you so' look, he got up, mumbling,

"This just can't be happening…"

With the restaurant reaching perhaps its busiest time, nearly two hundred people watched, fascinated, by what Peter's next action would be. Taking a deep breath, Peter started to make his way through the mass of tables and chairs, winding like a snake as he headed for the two guards at the end of the queue, all eyes watching him like a reality TV show freak. Eventually reaching the guards, by now his mood had darkened no end, which was highlighted by the scowl on his normally friendly face. Peter leaned in close and whispered,

"Can you please tell me what the hell is going on?"

"Step back please, sir," said one of the guards, in a rather patronising tone.

Feeling unbelievably lonely and realising that not a single sound could now be heard in the whole of the restaurant, Peter began to get just a little hot under the collar. The situation rested on a knife edge and was rapidly becoming as tense as walking into the bathroom for a shower, and catching your granny in nothing but her beard.

Poking his finger into the guard's chest, Peter said,

"Listen sonny, do you know who I am?" for all to hear.

The other guard began to finger the cover of his holster nervously, not sure quite what to do with this steamed up man close to abusing his colleague. Peter spotted the second guard's hand straying towards his gun and something inside him just snapped. Feeling like a volcano was erupting inside him, Peter sought to convert all of his built up rage into dragon power and knock these two idiots fully across the room. The two guards faces looked panic stricken and confused as Peter finally looked like he was about to lose the plot.

Out of the blue, a slender freckled arm weaved its way around Peter's shoulders and pulled him gently away from the guards.

"You'll have to excuse my friend," said Richie, leaning away from Peter but towards the guards. "I think some of his roast beef went down the wrong way," she said, smiling like butter wouldn't melt in her mouth, and with that she whisked Peter out through the double doors before he had a chance to say a word. Richie's vice-like grip on Peter didn't diminish even though they were now out of the restaurant and standing on the polished floors of the adjacent corridor. Maintaining her grip, she guided Peter subtly along, until they reached a glass door leading out to a very small secluded courtyard, set right in the middle of the building. The courtyard was about half the size of a tennis court and was awash with many varieties of ferns and other large plants, which provided a lot of shade and a certain degree of privacy. A small rectangular shaped pond, packed to the brim with koi carp of every different colour was hidden away in the far corner, camouflaged by the giant oversized green plants that towered above it.

Richie led Peter out into the courtyard and steered him through some fern leaves and round a huge raised flowerbed, to a small wooden bench that looked as though it could do with a new coat of varnish. Peter looked up and could just about see a couple of clouds through the tangled mess of leaves and branches. It took a few seconds for it to dawn on him, but then he realised that he was right, smack bang in the middle of the office complex. Looking more than a little perplexed, he also realised that he had no idea that this place even existed. Richie had taken a seat on the bench and with her elbow resting on the arm of the worn old seat, she looked at him in a very peculiar manner.

"This is a turn up for the books," she said, a big smile blossoming onto her face. "Me having to take you away before you do something you'll regret for a very long time."

The surprise of finding this place and the relaxing sound of the tiny movements of water in the pond had drained Peter of all of his pent up aggression and anger. As quickly as his rage had appeared it was now nowhere to be seen, and the normally quiet and reserved, awkward youth was back to his shy self.

Rolling his eyes and pointing discreetly with his finger in an upwards direction Peter said,

"Uh Rich, we're surrounded by three storeys of windows on all sides. I'm sure everyone at their desks won't want to listen in to our conversation."

Richie just sat there and smiled at him.

"The windows are all double glazed and all of the ones facing out onto the courtyard don't open up at all. I can't believe you don't know about this place," said Richie, in a pretending-to-be-shocked voice.

Peter looked up at all the windows looming over the courtyard, trying to confirm what Richie had just said.

"Of course I knew about this place," he said nonchalantly.

"Oh please, don't try and hide it from me. I could feel your shock the moment we came out here," said Richie. "You had absolutely no idea it even existed, did you? Call yourself head of security," she said mockingly.

Peter just nodded his head. He knew it was impossible to hide anything from his friend.

"I can't believe it. It's like a little oasis of calm, tucked away where no one would find it."

"So anyway, back to what happened in the restaurant," said Richie, knocking Peter out of his day dream.

"Yeah, sorry about that," said Peter, not able to look his friend in the eye.

"And thanks for pulling me out of there before I lost my temper and did something stupid."

Richie shook her head and laughed.

"I just kept looking at your aura with my dragon abilities," she whispered.

"It looked like you were going to explode at one point. I thought it best to get you out of there… although I have to admit a big part of me was desperate to see the dashing Peter Bentwhistle, head of Cropptech security, in handcuffs," she said with a big toothy grin on her face.

"Wasn't gonna happen, trust me," said Peter determinedly.

Winking, Richie said,

"You should give it a go. You don't know what you're missing."

Shaking his head and starting to blush, Peter replied,

"You know my feelings about that. One day, you're going to get into so much trouble with your… your… human dalliances."

"Not gonna happen, trust me," Richie said, imitating her friend and smiling. "Seriously though, Peter, what happened? I've never seen you lose your temper at all. You were ready to finish those guards off if I'm not mistaken."

Peter sat on the old bench and held his head in his hands. Letting out a long breath, he put his head back and looked up at the big fern leaf above his head, noticing a brightly coloured ladybird crawl across its arched centre. Keeping his eyes firmly fixed on the ladybird's progress, Peter said softly,

"This is the last straw. Head of security my arse! Oh I might sign off the timesheets, do the appraisals, but obviously I'm no longer in charge of security here."

Richie sat and listened to her friend intently, knowing that her lunch hour was long since over, but not really caring much.

The ladybird unfolded its wings, looking like it was about to take flight. As it did so, Peter marvelled at how delicate and precise its flimsy-looking wings actually were.

"Guns, armed guards… What the hell is this place coming to? The security provisions that were already in place were more than adequate for the site we have here," Peter said, as if to no one. "In its entire history, Cropptech has never been the victim of a major theft or incident of any kind."

The ladybird in the meantime had decided not to fly away and was just fluttering its wings for no apparent reason.

"I know you might have disagreed with me before about Manson's motives Rich, but can you not see now what's going on? Something here is very, very wrong. I just can't seem to work out exactly what it is. It's as if, as if... the answer is right in front of my face, but for the life of me I can't seem to see it. It's just so... frustrating."

Richie studied her friend, while he in turn continued to study the ladybird on the leaf above him. She had been friends with Peter for such a long time and had never seen him so... out of sorts. Not wanting to upset him, and particularly not wanting to fall out again, Richie considered her words carefully.

"I know it seems strange Peter, but perhaps Manson is just doing his job. Perhaps armed guards are a little over the top, but the Cropptech industrial unit does house a variety of valuable metals and gems. Not to mention the laminium, and we both know how valuable that is in the right hands," she added, raising her eyebrows.

"It's so much more than that, it really is," Peter whispered in frustration. "Don't ask me how I know, I just do."

Not wishing to press the point any further and also recognising that Peter seemed to have reached the end of his tether, Richie leaned over and kissed her friend smack in the middle of his forehead.

"Well if there's anything I can do to help don't hesitate to let me know. I've got to get back to work now. Think you can find your way out?" Richie asked sarcastically, to lighten the mood.

Waving his mobile phone in the air, Peter replied,

"I'll call you if I get lost." The two friends waved goodbye to each other and Peter remained in the courtyard a little longer, trying to decide on a course of action. What could he do about the situation? Ranting and raving at Manson would clearly get him nowhere; it might even get him fired, like Dr Island. Al Garrett was about as visible as a needle in a haystack at the moment so it wasn't as if he could just bump into him somewhere and raise the issue. What he needed was an excuse, an excuse to go and see Garrett and then tackle him about these armed guards and Manson in general.

Peter racked his brains trying desperately to come up with something work-related that would require him to actually go and see Garrett, but after ten minutes he gave up. Nothing he could think of would be important enough to get him a one to one with the boss and still be credible enough to fool Manson, or at least not give Manson a reason to have him fired.

Sitting in the shade watching the fish glide about one another, Peter started to think of the other things he had to do, besides work. Top of his list was to go back to Mark's house and finish packing stuff up to take to the hospital and then confirm with the solicitors that it had all been done. Before he did that though, he was waiting to hear from Tank to see if Gee Tee had made any progress with a mantra to rid the house of whatever evil was in there and had potentially harmed the unsuspecting Mark.

"That's it!" he thought. "Mark." Why hadn't it occurred to him before? The perfect excuse that he needed was right in front of his face. He could go and see Al Garrett about having some sort of memorial at Cropptech in Mark's memory. It had after all been done plenty of times before in the company. The surrounding grounds were littered with benches and statues in memory of people who had worked for the company and had passed away. Better still was the thought that Manson wouldn't even be able to object to the idea, as he claimed to be Mark's friend when Peter had caught him at the house.

"Perfect," he thought, "absolutely perfect." So perfect in fact, that he was going to march up to Al Garrett's office right now. Ducking in between the giant green leaves of the ferns, Peter made his way back to the glass door. Instead of turning left and heading back towards the restaurant and his office, he turned right and headed for the nearest staircase. Once there he climbed to the top floor and made his way through the open plan offices of the accounts department, towards the executive part of the building.

Peter smiled to himself as he exchanged the world of notice boards and narrow corridors filled with photocopiers and printers, for a world of lush carpets, hi tech coffee machines, oak panels and polished brass. Turning the corner, he spotted the shiny doors to the lift that he normally used to travel to Al Garrett's domain. He headed straight down the corridor towards the boss man's office, with a confident swagger in his stride. He knocked on the door with confidence, knowing that whoever was in that office would already be expecting him, having already noticed one or two of the CCTV cameras tracking his movement as he made his way here. A husky voice shouted,

"Come."

Taking a deep breath and forcing a smile onto his face, Peter turned the handle and entered. The office was as dark as it had been before, with the blinds on the giant double glazed windows only open enough to let tiny slivers of light through. Peter was struck dumb by the overpowering stench that pervaded the office. If he hadn't been totally convinced that it was the same smell as in Mark's house before, he was nothing short of one hundred per cent sure now.

Walking through the gloom, he stopped in front of Garrett's desk and looked intently at the old man staring back at him. Although it hadn't been long since Peter had last seen Al Garrett, the physical change in the man seemed quite remarkable. Before, Peter would have regarded Garrett as being in pretty good shape for his age, but now he looked positively ancient. His skin was pale, clammy and gaunt, and his moustache and the small amount of hair on his head looked slick with grease, as if they hadn't been washed in weeks. A closer inspection revealed to Peter that Garrett's eyes were very bloodshot and a smell of severe body odour was wafting, well nearly walking of its own accord, across the desk.

Peter stood patiently and waited for either the seated Garrett, or Manson who was standing up by the window behind Garrett, to address him.

"It's… it's… Bentthistle isn't it?" Garrett said, leaning across the desk to get a better view.

"Bentwhistle sir," replied Peter loudly, standing up nice and tall.

"Ahhhh… Bentwhistle," said Garrett, as if trying to remember something important.

"What is it you want Bentwhistle?" Manson asked sharply, still looking out of the window.

Addressing Garrett, Peter said,

"It's about Mark, sir. Some of us in the security department wondered if you had made any plans for a memorial of some kind."

Garrett sat at his desk and looked bewildered.

"Mark, who's Mark?" he asked, puzzled.

"Mark Hiscock sir," said Peter. "You know, ex head of security. Died about two weeks ago."

"Died… why wasn't I informed?" snapped Garrett angrily.

Peter took a step back, shocked.

"How could Garrett not know?" he thought.

Manson moved away from the window, like a giant dark scorpion, searching for its next unsuspecting victim. Putting a hand on Garrett's shoulders he said,

"It's alright Al. You've had a lot on your plate. We did tell you but you've been so busy it must have slipped your mind."

With Manson so close by, Garrett's mind seemed to be struggling to take in the situation.

"Yessss… slipped my… mind," said Garrett groggily.

"I'll personally make sure he gets the memorial he deserves," said Manson, still with his hand on Garrett's shoulder.

"Was there anything else, Bentwhistle?"

Peter knew there was no point in bringing up the armed guards, here and now. From the look of it, Garrett looked like he was struggling to stay awake, let alone manage to hold a meaningful conversation. Peter looked Manson directly in the eye and said,

"No I think that was everything."

"You'll have to excuse us then, Bentwhistle. We have a lot more work to be getting on with," said Manson, waving his hand as if to dismiss Peter from the room.

Peter turned around and headed for the door, determined that Manson wouldn't see the worry on his face that he actually felt in his heart. As he put his hand on the door handle to open it, Manson called out from behind him,

"I do hope you like my new guards, Bentwhistle." He always managed to make the word "Bentwhistle" sound like something you scrape off your shoe after a walk in the park. Peter turned the handle without looking back and made the long walk back to his own office, all the time thinking about the sorry state of Al Garrett, and what he could possibly do to make a difference.

Once Peter got home that night, he decided he was going to start keeping a diary of all the things that happened at work, relating to Manson and Garrett. Before cooking himself some dinner, Peter found a suede fronted notebook that he had won in a Christmas raffle at the sports club and had never used. Opening up the front page, he began jotting down all of the day's events, in particular how poorly Al Garrett had looked when Peter had left his office.

Just as Peter had finished writing up the day's occurrences, his phone chirped to indicate that it had received a message. Looking at the phone's display, Peter saw the message was from Tank. He hurriedly opened the phone up, hoping for news from Gee Tee regarding a mantra to neutralise the toxin in Mark's house. Peter felt a mixture of relief and disappointment when he looked at the message. Tank said that he would be coming round later that night to drop something off and also that he was unable to procure tickets to the much anticipated game that they both wanted to see.

Peter deleted the message after reading it and proceeded to cook himself some tea. After tea and doing the washing up, he booted up his computer so that he could spend the time waiting for Tank to come round, playing games on his computer, something he found very relaxing. Just recently he had found himself becoming 'hooked' on MMO's (Massively Multiplayer Online) games. The chance to explore worlds and team up with other people in a computer game was just fantastic and had kept him up into the wee small hours ever more increasingly just lately. He'd tried out a few different games before settling on one that he really, really liked, but what they all seemed to have in common, which amused him no end, was the fact that at some point in each and every one of these games you would wander across a dragon and no doubt have to slay it. "If only these humans knew the truth," he thought to himself.

At about twenty to nine there was a knock on the door, and Peter answered it to find a very out of breath Tank, in a gopping red tracksuit, all sweaty and dishevelled. Tank briefly explained that he had run over from his house, in preparation for rugby training which started in two weeks' time. Peter rolled his eyes and gave his friend a 'you really don't need to be doing that' look, but it just went straight over Tank's head.

With his breathing slowly recovering, Tank handed Peter a wooden prism, or as Peter liked to think of it, a Toblerone-shaped box. Tank explained that his boss had gone to great lengths to obtain the box and its contents. He added that the items were very old and possibly unstable, and that the fine powder needed to be used in conjunction with the first item, but both should be fit for purpose. Peter thanked his friend and asked him to pass on his regards to his boss. Tank then headed off into the night on the return leg of his run home. After watching Tank's giant frame disappear into the distance, Peter returned to his gaming, not the least bit tired, and stayed hard at it until the early hours of the morning.

10

An Unusual Request

The next morning Peter sat at the table eating his breakfast, tired from his hours of gaming the night before. Although weary, he was happy that Tank had come round and dropped off a mantra for him to try at Mark's house.

Gee Tee had said that the mantra, if used properly, should get rid of anything toxic that lurked in the house. He had also passed on a second mantra that would confirm the area, or house in this case, was totally safe and free of any contaminants. Peter was eager to try it and had decided to go round to Mark's house on Friday afternoon to finish clearing the stuff for the hospital. It meant using some more of his built-up flexi-time at work, but on the plus side he would have an afternoon off, and at the moment any time away from that place at all was a bonus as far as he was concerned.

Taking another mouthful of his cereal, Peter decided he would download the Daily Telepath and read it later when he got home. Closing his eyes, he concentrated and sent his mind off on its usual route to find the newspaper. Doing it on autopilot as he was, meant that he was able to finish munching on his cereal. Halfway through a huge mouthful, Peter realised something was wrong with the downloading. Squeezing his eyes together tightly, he managed to catch up with his outstretched mind to see what the problem was. He had encountered problems like this before, and they generally tended to be quirks or difficulties at the other end, like the time the newspapers started sending out black and white pictures for the first time, or when a huge lightning storm had destroyed two of the crystal storage nodes. When those problems had occurred, he had caught up with his mind and found giant worded messages flying from the filing cabinets telling everyone about the problems and announcing when a fix would be in place. Although this produced the same feeling in him, it did feel slightly more…urgent.

Linked with his mind once more, he expected to see the giant messages flying around in the air, but this was not the case. Instead, there was a blinking red arrow pointing him in the direction of an old wooden filing cabinet that looked like it had seen better days. With an air of caution, Peter guided his mind over to the wooden cabinet and very carefully opened it up.

He pulled back a little, fully expecting an array of information to come flooding over the top as it normally does with the newspapers, but not so here. Out of the top, flew a little paper plane, dancing and swirling in the air, and then doing loop the loops, before finally flying straight into Peter's consciousness. Peter used his mind to unfold the plane and read the message contained within.

YOU ARE SUMMONED TO A MEETING WITH COUNCILLOR HITCH ROSEBLOOM OF THE DRAGON COUNCIL ON SATURDAY AT 5.30PM, ROOM 54367 OF THE COUNCIL CHAMBERS. PUNCTUALITY IS EXPECTED.

After he had recovered from the initial shock of receiving such a message, Peter filed it away in his subconscious and whizzed off to retrieve the newspaper he had been looking for in the first place. Once he had successfully downloaded that, he let his mind return to him at home and finished off his breakfast wondering what the meeting with the councillor would hold. Once at work, he booked Friday afternoon off and continued to try and track Manson's movements.

The rest of the week passed without event and although Peter had tried very hard to keep tabs on Manson, he had only managed to catch passing glimpses of him going in and out of Garrett's office for extended periods of time. Friday afternoon came along and Peter changed into the casual clothing that he had brought with him, before getting into his car and driving round to Mark's house.

He had already decided to pack up all the smaller, more valuable things to be donated to the hospital before using the mantras that Gee Tee had provided him with. That way, if there were any unforeseen side effects, all of Mark's valuable things would be safely packed away in the car. Not that there should be any side effects, it was just that Tank had warned him that Gee Tee was a little forgetful in his old age and these things had a tendency to go wrong even when performed by experts and let's face it, Peter was still in his infancy in dragon terms.

After a couple of hours, Peter had logged and neatly packed all of Mark's belongings and put them safely in his car. He had searched the house as thoroughly as it was possible to do and had not come across anything that Manson would have been interested in. The only thing he had discovered was that the foul smelling toxin was absolutely everywhere, even in the dank, dark old loft and the tiny cupboard under the stairs that contained only the gas meter and the Hoover.

Content that everything of value was in the car, Peter went to the living room and opened the wooden Toblerone-shaped box that Tank had given him the other night. He pulled out a small packet of powder that was wrapped in a sheet of parchment. Unfolding it, Peter noticed that Gee Tee had written at the top: before use, make sure you open all the windows and doors. Peter went through the house and opened them all as instructed and then made his way back to the living room. Having memorised the mantra during his brief glimpse of it, Peter opened the packet of powder and poured it into the palm of his hand. By the look of things, Gee Tee had not only translated the mantra into English, but had also made it rhyme to add more power to it. No wonder it had taken the old dragon a little while. Translating was one thing, translating and rhyming was something altogether more complicated. "No surprise he's the best in the business then," Peter thought. Changing his focus from the old shopkeeper to the matter quite literally in hand, Peter closed his eyes and started to recite the words of the mantra.

"Powder of bat, essence of lynx,
Do your job and be rid of this jinx.
Seek it all out and blow it away,
Once gone for good, away it will stay."

Feeling the cold rush of air on his skin, Peter opened his eyes to see several mini tornados whirling around the room, making the cushions on the sofa bounce around the room and the wooden legs of the dining table creak in despair. After whizzing around the room three times, the tornados made their way out of the door and split up, all going in different directions. He retrieved the cushions and sat down on the sofa, waiting until he could no longer hear the flapping of curtains or the rustling of blinds. He did a quick tour of the house to check that all the mini tornados had disappeared and then went back to the living room, noting on the way how fresh and clean the house now smelt. Opening up the prism and taking out the second mantra, the one that would check that the house was now safe, Peter took a quick glimpse and then closed his eyes and began to recite the words, chuckling to himself that Gee Tee had done the same with this mantra as he had with the last.

"Oh wonder of wonders, check all of this dirt,
And see that there's nothing to give cause for hurt.
Check everything here is protected and clean;
A message from you we wait to be seen."

As the last word trailed off, a small ball of intensely bright light appeared in the centre of the room. From it, two dozen fluorescent blue dragonflies zoomed and swarmed throughout the house. Peter waited in the living room with the pulsating ball of light, and after a few minutes the dragonflies started to return one by one.

As the last dragonfly entered the ball of light, it began to spin violently. Beams of light started to burst from it until Peter had to shield his eyes. Then there was a loud 'POP' and Peter opened his eyes to reveal a giant worded message flying around the room. In bright fluorescent blue, practically the same colour as the dragonflies, the words 'ALL CLEAR, ALL CLEAR' flew around the room, weaving in and out of the lampshades, lifting the curtains away from the windows and again sending the cushions across the room. After a minute or so the letters in the message started to fade, and continued to fizzle out for another twenty seconds or so. Peter stood in the middle of the room and breathed a heavy sigh of relief. The house had been made safe, and could now be sold on without endangering any innocent bystanders, the clearance men could safely collect all the furniture to be sold, and the monies could be transferred to the hospital as Mark would have wanted.

Peter pulled out his phone and flipped it open. Looking in the directory, he pulled up the number for Burns and Haybell solicitors, and pressed the call button. Eventually he got through to Mr Burns and informed him that Mark's house had been cleared of everything but the large furniture which was being picked up tomorrow morning by the house clearance company. Mr Burns in turn informed Peter that he would have to go to the solicitor's offices to sign some forms to arrange for the funds from the sale of Mark's effects to go to the hospital, which would complete the whole process. Peter and Mr Burns arranged to meet just before five o'clock that night.

Peter entered the offices of Burns and Haybell at exactly ten to five and although he was shown to the waiting room by the receptionist, he only had about thirty seconds to wait before Mr Burns escorted him to his office. Peter handed over the new key to the house and all the relevant paperwork, confirming that the hospital had received all the goods, bar the furniture, and would receive the money from its sale. Mr Burns checked that everything was in order and asked for a couple of signatures from Peter. Once it was all completed, Peter got up to leave, but Mr Burns ushered him back into his chair.

"There's one last thing that I have to do," said Mr Burns. With that he walked over to a large cabinet and opened it up to reveal a safe inside. Making sure that he obscured Peter's view, Mr Burns entered the digital code to the safe. The door swung silently open and Mr Burns pulled something out, before closing the door and returning to his seat.

On the table he carefully placed a small wooden jewellery box. Peter wondered what was going on. Mr Burns looked across the dark mahogany desk at Peter and said,

"The last request in Mr Hiscock's will was that you should take possession of this item after completing all of the deeds as executor." With that he pushed the small wooden box across the shiny table towards Peter. As Peter picked up the box, Mr Burns stood up and offered out his hand.

"Our business here is complete, Mr Bentwhistle. Do have a lovely weekend." After shaking Mr Burns' hand, Peter left the offices and walked back to where he had parked the car, more than a little intrigued as to what was in the box. Once he got into the car, he put the keys into the ignition to start it up, but then hesitated. With an unbridled curiosity burning inside him, Peter found he was unable to resist any longer. He made sure nobody was about and then opened up the wooden box. His eyes grew wide with surprise. Inside was a silver chain with a tiny, sparkling trident hanging from it.

Peter stared in wonder as he held the trident up in the palm of his hand. Although it was made of some sort of metal, the colour it gave off was purple. Not only that, but it kind of... pulsated. Peter had never seen anything quite like it.

After spending a few minutes just looking at it in the car, and making sure no passers-by could see what it was he was holding, Peter eventually put it back in its box and started the car, so he could go home. Once there Peter spent the rest of the evening thinking about the necklace. He searched the internet in vain, trying to find anything even remotely like it but came up empty handed. By the end of the evening he had decided to wear it around his neck, even though he had never felt the need for any jewellery of any sort before. In fact he had always thought of it as a bit of a burden to be honest, because if he had necklaces or rings on when he changed from human to dragon form, they would all drop off, or worse, be destroyed during the transformation. This necklace that Mark had left him was different though. It was as if he was meant to wear it and he could almost feel the power radiating from it. With the time fast approaching midnight, Peter gave up looking on the internet for anything relating to his new found possession and decided to get as much sleep as he could in preparation for his meeting with Hitch Rosebloom the next day. After brushing his teeth he fell into bed with the necklace firmly attached around his neck, glad that he had completed Mark's last wishes.

Peter got up late the next day and dossed about the house, watching television, tidying up and doing all the other household chores that he had ignored all week. During all of this Peter felt a sense of nervousness building up inside him. It was unusual to be summoned to see any of the councillors and he had to wonder why his presence had been requested. Peter made sure that he had eaten something before setting off for his meeting, leaving in plenty of time to reach the council chambers which were, of course, located in London.

He took the monorail and instead of alighting at the normal stop to go and see Tank, he continued on to Buckingham station. As the name implies, the station itself is located almost directly beneath Buckingham Palace. Peter had never been to this part of London before and was surprised at the difference between here and the area where Tank worked. Here the buildings all seemed to be relatively new, as well as being rather spacious and........decadent, Peter thought. In contrast, in the area where Gee Tee's Mantra Emporium was located, the buildings were practically all single or double storey, run down and surrounded by tiny cramped passageways, unlike the wide, clean, polished streets that Peter now found himself walking down towards the council chambers.

Turning a corner between two rather tall buildings, Peter let out a short gasp. The other buildings had stood out from the run of the mill dragon buildings that he had ever come across, but what stood before him now was something else altogether. The building before him must have been thirty storeys high, and for the first time since arriving at Buckingham, Peter noticed that he couldn't see the roof of the cavern here.

"Remarkable," he thought. The height, however, was not the most amazing aspect of the building. Most dragon buildings (whether they are houses, shops or workplaces) are made out of stone, carved into rock or very occasionally made from the remains of spectacular lava formations. Peter knew from the odd telepathic newspaper report that this building was regarded as special, but this was not what he had expected at all. The building itself, as well as being tall, was a creation of curves. There was not a right angle in sight, and the whole construction was seamless. No join, no gaps, nothing. As for the material that it was made of, Peter could only imagine. It couldn't possibly be made of metal, Peter knew, but that was how it looked, with incredible reflective properties that made it seem metallic or maybe even glass-like, gleaming with an oil slick rainbow of colours.

Peter stomped his tail on the path in awe, as he continued to walk up the main walkway towards the entrance. Just when he thought it couldn't get any more surreal, he stumbled across two gurgling pools of lava on either side of the steps, made from the same material as the building in front of him. Dragons entering and leaving the building approached the pools from all directions with most stopping and staring in quiet contemplation as they passed. Some paused to sit on the edge, content to gaze into the steaming mass.

Peter continued on and passed through the giant arch of an entrance to the building, noting the two enormous dragon guards stationed on either side. They were the most ferocious and frightening looking dragons that Peter had ever seen, and from the colours adorning the shining pikes that they carried, he knew they were part of the King's Guard. Peter continued into the building, feeling more than a little bit guilty, even though he hadn't done anything wrong, much the same way totally innocent humans feel guilty around a policeman in uniform.

Weirdly, the lobby of the council chambers was much the same inside as it was outside. Every part of the building had this metallic sheen to it, and the highly polished floors of the lobby only emphasised this even more. The whole thing felt very space age to Peter, who had always been happy with things the traditional dragon way.

Or so he thought. It then struck him that he thought Gee Tee was stuck in his ways for only letting dragons in their *solitus* form enter his shop, when here he was wishing that the very modern building he was in, was something much more low tech. Smiling to himself, he realised that he was much more like Gee Tee than he ever imagined, although he certainly wasn't going to admit as much to the old dragon himself.

Tearing himself away from his thoughts, he turned his attention to the row after row of touch screen LCD televisions that occupied the lobby. Wandering up to the nearest one that was vacant, Peter scrolled through the display. He brought up a map of the council chambers and found that the office he was looking for was about as far away from the lobby as you could get, the furthest corner of the twenty ninth floor to be precise.

Instantly he memorised the route he would need to take to get there. Peter then noticed a button at the bottom of the screen that was marked 'route planner'. He pressed the button and the screen asked him to input the office number that he needed to find. He typed in the number of Hitch Rosebloom's office and suddenly a huge green illuminated arrow appeared on the floor in front of him. Bemused, he took a step forward onto the arrow. Another arrow appeared in front of him again. Shaking his head he took another step forward. Again, another arrow, and again, and again. Peter ended up following the arrows all the way to his destination. They guided him on a totally different route than the one he would have taken, but it did seem to get him there very quickly, he thought as he took a seat in one of the dragon sized silver chairs in the corridor outside Hitch Rosebloom's office.

"Not as comfy as the ones in Gee Tee's workshop, but not too bad as oversized chairs go," he thought to himself.

Unlike a human waiting area, there were no books or magazines to read: there didn't need to be because nearly all dragons had access to papers and other reading materials via their telepathic abilities. Peter thought about accessing the latest edition of the Daily Telepath, but looking at the clock on the wall which read 5.22pm, he decided against it. He was feeling nervous enough, without starting to read a paper and forgetting about the time, so he decided just to sit and watch the clock and wait for it to reach 5.30.

As the minutes ticked by, all sorts of thoughts ran through Peter's head as to why he had been summoned here, most of them bad. Perhaps it was because he was spending too much time in his human form. Much like any young dragon, he'd heard the rumours doing the rounds in the nursery ring, that it was possible for dragons to become almost addicted to being human shaped. Sometimes it got so bad, or so it was rumoured, that subconsciously they could not use their powers to turn themselves back into their dragon forms. On these very rare occasions, a specialist unit kept on standby here at the dragon chambers would be called in to forcibly change the dragon back using unique and varied mantras. These incidents had happened quite some time ago, according to the rumours, and nowadays the council kept a close eye on dragons who remained *mutatio* for long periods of time, especially younger ones.

Peter shuddered at the thought, hoping that it wasn't that. More likely, he thought, it was probably some of Richie's antics that had been stumbled upon and he would be grilled about her arm wrestling rugby players, or the incident with the gang of youths who tried to relieve Richie of her mobile phone late one night in the car park of the sports club, who all ended up in hospital with several broken bones each, or heaven forbid the day she took on three of the biggest, most obnoxious rugby players in the whole world at a tug of war, and singlehandedly and in front of a huge crowd, beat them hands down.

"Please don't let me have to talk about Richie's actions," Peter thought.

The clock now showed the time to be 5.27 and Peter wished it would just get to 5.30 as he was now letting off a lot of steam, a distinct sign of nervousness in a dragon. It was everywhere, coming out of his nose, his ears and from the top of his head. The occasional dragon would plod down the hallway and go into another office, and all who had passed him so far had given him a very strange look.

"Must be due to all the steam I'm giving off," he thought. As he concentrated hard on trying to regulate his temperature, and thus limit the amount of steam he emitted, another thought occurred to him.

"Oh please tell me they haven't found out about the incident with the neighbour's cat," he thought dejectedly. About a month ago, Peter had been out in his garden, just to tidy up, do a little planting and cut the grass, that sort of thing, when he discovered that quite a large area of his lawn at the back of the house had lots of cat poo on it. Now Peter wasn't a particularly keen gardener, but he did like to keep his house and garden looking neat and tidy, much like all the other houses in the street where he lived. So he was quite appalled to see all of this mess all over his lawn, and even more disappointed to have to get amongst it with the mower. Over the next few days, he kept a close eye on the state of his lawn and discovered that the cat belonging to the people two doors away was coming into his garden, doing its business and then returning home. This was happening all times of the night and day, and it made no apparent difference when Peter ran out into the garden to shoo the cat away. In the end he went round to the house the cat belonged to and explained the situation to the people there, expecting them to try to do something about reining their cat in. But the people there just laughed and said cats will be cats and shut the front door in his face. Not much made Peter angry, but as he came away from there he was absolutely fuming, and decided, very un-Peter-like, that he would do something about it. He waited until it started to get dark, later that night, and after having had lots to eat and drink, he crept out into his garden. Adjacent to the lawn, was a small wooden container that held all the recycling material and would be taken out to be emptied every couple of weeks. The men had been to empty it only that morning and now there was just enough room for someone to fit inside. Peter slid in and left the wooden door slightly ajar. With his excellent dragon night vision, he would have no problem spotting anything entering his garden from where he was. As it happened he didn't have long to wait. Slinking its way through a small gap in the fence at the bottom of the garden, the cat sauntered its way across the path and on to the lawn, not six feet from where Peter was hiding. The cat was facing the other way as it started to do its business. "Perfect," Peter thought. Slowly moving the door open to create a slightly bigger gap, Peter drew in a deep breath and concentrated with all his dragon ability. Now it's not impossible for a dragon to breathe fire whilst in human form, but it is very difficult, requiring an immense amount of effort and concentration. It is also very frowned upon by other dragons. At the nursery ring it was taught that it was never appropriate to do such a thing because it was deemed there would never be a situation where a dragon would need to do it, but even so the young dragons practised it anyway. As he felt the warmth run through his body, threatening to engulf him, he couldn't give a stuff about it being frowned upon. Opening his mouth and tilting his head slightly to get the right angle around the door, Peter let rip with a searing stream of fire that hit the cat right on the tail. Although the stream of flame was relatively narrow, the heat was unbelievable and the cat's tail disintegrated almost immediately. The accuracy of the flame was so good that he didn't singe even one blade of grass on his lawn. The howl of terror from the cocky cat was something that to this day still brought a smile to Peter's face even though he knew it shouldn't. On the plus side, his garden had been cat pooh-free since that very day, and the cat now gets mistaken on a regular basis for a Manx cat, much to the disappointment of its owners, Peter had heard.

"Oh God, please don't let that be the reason I'm here," Peter thought, folding his wings over his head in shame. Peeking out from under his wings, Peter noticed the clock was just approaching 5.30. He unfolded his wings and sat up straight just as the clock struck the half hour. The door to Hitch Rosebloom's office opened right on cue and a dragon's head appeared round the door.

"Please come in, Bentwhistle," said Rosebloom politely.

Peter stood up, took a deep breath and walked into the office. Rosebloom indicated a chair to Peter with his wing and Peter promptly sat down. Rosebloom sat shuffling some papers on his desk, keeping Peter in suspense as to the reason he was here. Already nervous enough, Peter tried to calm himself by concentrating on something other than his summons. He took a good look at Rosebloom for the first time and was quite surprised at what he saw. He was quite small by dragon standards and his colouring was nothing special - light green all over, except for a big, white mark that resembled a rose and ran across the whole of his tummy. "Ah, must be where he got his name from," Peter thought. His head though was something else entirely. He had a huge mane of black hair growing from the back of his head and it was tied into a pony tail. As if that wasn't strange enough, he had glittering red jewels running down either side of his nose and he was wearing funky wrap around glasses. Peter had never seen another dragon like him. He knew that some of the top laminium ball players had taken to jewel piercings on their faces, but he'd never heard of a dragon with that much hair, and as for the glasses, well they just looked...... wrong...... like he was trying to be...... hmmmmm......... "hip and trendy", as the humans would say. Peter could start to feel his body temperature rise, due to his anxiety and was so focused on trying to maintain it at a reasonable level that he failed to notice the councillor looking over his funky glasses at him.

"Everything alright Bentwhistle?" asked Rosebloom.

Startled out of his concentration, Peter managed to say,

"Ummm...... sure...... yep...... everything's fine."

"You know why you're here of course...... don't you...... Bentwhistle?" said Rosebloom slyly.

"Well...... not exactly," Peter stuttered nervously.

Rosebloom put down the papers he had been sifting through on his desk and stared intently at Peter.

"I would have thought it was obvious, young man."

Peter sat there under the intense scrutiny of the councillor, imagining that a great big crevice had opened up and swallowed him whole and that he was now tumbling away into oblivion. Unfortunately he was still in the chair, with Rosebloom on the other side of the desk, waiting for some kind of response.

Peter could feel his temperature start to rise again and decided to just admit he had no idea why he had been summoned. Before he could do that though, the councillor began to speak.

"You have been summoned here today due to the untimely death of Mark Hiscock. My understanding is that you are now the highest ranking dragon in the whole of Cropptech. Is that true?"

Peter was so relieved to hear that he was here due to his position at Cropptech and not because of any of the crazy ideas that had been going through his mind beforehand, that he managed in one go to bring his body temperature right down and look calm and composed.

"That's true. I am the highest ranking dragon at Cropptech," Peter agreed, nodding his head.

"Well, as I'm sure you fully appreciate, we take a great deal of interest in Cropptech, mainly due to its extraction and processing of laminium."

Peter continued to nod his head, wondering exactly where this was going.

"Mark Hiscock was always the council's point of contact if we needed to know anything or get anything done, and now that responsibility has fallen to you. So you might find from time to time you get asked to arrange specific orders with Al Garrett as Mark used to or to check some information on mining sites, again as Mark would have done. You can liaise with this office at any time you like and if there are any problems or anything you are unsure of you can contact me directly. I will give you my card on the way out."

Peter sat in the big oversized chair and felt a great weight almost lift right off him. "At last," he thought, "somebody I can turn to and trust about all the things happening at work. Somebody that will know the right thing to do all the time."

Rosebloom leaned across the desk and said,

"Anything you are unsure of or want to ask?"

"Well there is something actually," said Peter, relieved to be passing the burden of Manson and his antics on to somebody else finally. Peter sat an outlined what had been happening at Cropptech, particularly the effect Manson seemed to be having on Al Garrett and the changing state of power at the moment. Much to Peter's delight, Rosebloom sat and listened very carefully to every word that he said and even at one point started to jot down notes on a pad, despite the fact that he too should have perfect memory recall.

"So you see, after the funeral, I spoke at length to Gee Tee and he suggested that we use a mantra to cancel out the toxic effects in Mark's house and......."

"Just hold on one minute, Bentwhistle," said Rosebloom forcefully. "Gee Tee?"

"Yes that's right. My best friend Tank works at his Mantra Emporium in London and that's how I got to know him and he suggested........."

"Enough!" shouted Rosebloom, slamming his wing on to the table, causing all of his papers to fly off wildly in all directions.

Shocked by the outburst he had just provoked, Peter remained seated and wide-eyed as Rosebloom leaned across the table, so close that Peter could feel the heat from his breath tickling his face.

"That old dragon is nothing more than a meddling idiot, with barely any idea about mantras or any other dragon lore that he claims to understand," Rosebloom said menacingly.

Not quite sure what kind of reaction was expected of him, Peter sat stock still and remained silent. The councillor pulled himself back to his side of the desk and bent down to retrieve some of the things that had flown off his desk in the fit of rage that now seemed to have passed. After a few minutes had passed in total silence, Rosebloom had finally returned everything to its rightful place on the desk and, satisfied, turned once again to face a very intimidated Peter.

"Listen very carefully Bentwhistle," Rosebloom said with an edge to his voice, "as I'm only going to tell you this once. I don't want any more of this Gee Tee nonsense. Do you understand?"

Peter started to open his mouth but read the glint in Rosebloom's eyes and decided against it, realising that he was only going to make his predicament worse.

"That dragon is nothing but trouble and if I find out that he is any way involved in events taking place at Cropptech then there will be serious repercussions for you Bentwhistle. Am I making myself clear?"

Peter slumped in the chair and nodded obediently.

"Now get out of my office," said Rosebloom sharply, gesturing to the door with his wing. "And I would suggest that you use your initiative to take care of that Manson fellow. After all he is only human, shouldn't be too much of a challenge even for you," he added unpleasantly.

Peter closed the door to Rosebloom's office very gently and breathed a sigh of relief. He looked at the chairs in the corridor outside Rosebloom's office and thought how inviting they looked. He needed to sit down and sort out his thoughts, but looking over his shoulder at the office he had just come out of made him realise that he needed to get far away from here before he did.

He followed the same route out of the majestic building as he had come in, but this time did not once appreciate his surroundings on the way out. Once he'd reached the exit and made his way down the huge steps, past the lava pools, it suddenly dawned on him that he did not know what to do now. His head was literally buzzing from all the things going on inside it. As he continued walking all he could think about was that he wanted somebody to talk to. But who? Tank, Richie, Gee Tee.................oh he just couldn't decide. He found that he had walked all the way back to the monorail station but instead of boarding a carriage, he picked one of the very few seats on the platform and sat down in it, watching the steady stream of passengers coming and going. The reason he supposed there were very few seats at the station was because generally, unlike some of the train stations on the surface, nobody ever had to wait more than a couple of minutes for a monorail carriage to arrive.

Frustrated, Peter buried his head in his wings, confused and unable to think what to do next. He was so consumed by his own predicament, Peter failed to notice somebody slide into the oversized chair on the platform next to him. After a few minutes of self pity, Peter decided he didn't know what to do, so thought he would go home and get some sleep. He unfurled his wings and as he did so noticed the occupant of the next chair. It was the old man/ dragon - the one that used to visit the nursery ring when he was studying there. The old man was in his human form and looked much the same as Peter remembered, but with slightly longer grey hair and a face that looked even more weary and tired, despite the fact that it was currently flashing Peter a great big smile.

"Peter isn't it?" said the old man.

"That's right. Long time no see. What are you doing here?" said Peter, noticing that the old man was staring intently at the trident hanging around Peter's neck.

The old man managed to tear his gaze away from the trident and looked up into Peter's eyes.

"I have an office close by and was just on my way to catch the monorail when I thought I recognised those markings," the old man replied, while pointing towards the bent whistle marking on Peter's body.

Peter nodded his head, and said,

"So have you been back to the nursery ring recently? I go when I can but it's not as often as I would like."

The old man smiled and a faraway expression came over his face.

"I've not been back for quite some time. Like you, finding the time becomes increasingly difficult."

Peter nodded his head in agreement.

"So anyway young Peter, you look...... troubled," said the old man, in a gravelly voice that seemed to be full of understanding.

"More than you could ever know," Peter replied, flippantly.

The old man stroked the grey stubble on his chin, considering Peter's reply carefully.

"Perhaps it would help to talk about it. I'm a very competent listener you know."

Shaking his head, Peter said,

"I think I've already told too many people as it is, but thanks anyway."

"No problem," said the old man, getting out of the chair to continue his journey. Before he did so, he turned to Peter and added,

"This may not be much help, and I don't know the details of your dilemma, but having witnessed some of your time in the nursery ring, I have little doubt that you will make the right decision in whatever it is that you have to. I've always found that trusting my gut instinct has worked incredibly well, whether it's judging a situation or judging somebody's character. Go with your gut feeling and trust your friends. It will all work out." With that, the old man turned to leave and started to walk down the platform.

Peter was left speechless at what the old man had said. He got up from his seat and bounded after the old man who by now had nearly reached the end of the platform. Peter reached out and put the tip of his wing on the old man's shoulder.

"Who are you?" Peter asked. "I don't even know your name."

The old man smiled and turned his head just slightly.

"Trust me, it's much better that way." And with that he squeezed his way through the closing doors of the carriage that was just about to pull away from the platform.

As the monorail pulled away, Peter locked eyes with the old man through the window and sensed there was much more to him than there seemed. Peter stood stock still on the platform for a few minutes after the old man had departed, pondering an encounter that made him feel more than a little...... uncomfortable. But the more he thought about it, the more the words that the old man had uttered made sense. He regarded himself as a great judge of character and thought that he had the best friends in the world. All of which

made him think that he should go and see Gee Tee, no matter what that......
that ...... berk of a councillor thought.

With a course of action decided upon, Peter startled himself out of his daze and looked around the platform to see where the cross-London monorail would depart from. He gathered the information he required from the nearest LCD display on the wall and noticed how busy it had become on the platform since he had arrived. Monorail carriages were turning up at the station full to bursting with dragons and nearly all of them seemed to be dressed up to the nines in cloaks and hats, some even wearing brightly coloured tights, as if they were attending some sort of ball or formal dinner.

Instead of using the bridge provided, Peter flapped his wings twice and delicately looped over to the other platform, where the next cross-London monorail would depart from in approximately ninety seconds. As he stood waiting for the carriage, he suddenly realised that it being Saturday evening now, the Mantra Emporium would be closed and he had no idea whether Gee Tee lived at that address or not. He could have phoned Tank and asked if he had brought his mobile phone with him, but he hadn't. Much as mobiles were handy pieces of technology, they mainly didn't work underground very well, with only a very few places having transmitters that provided any kind of network. These transmitters were totally illegal and set up by dragon engineers to fool the phone that was being used into thinking that it was on the planet's surface somewhere. He supposed that here was probably one of those places and that if he had brought his phone he would have been able to use it. "Oh well," he thought.

As the lights of the carriage he was expecting appeared in the darkness of the very narrow tunnel, Peter decided that he would go to the Mantra Emporium and see if the shopkeeper was there anyway. It wasn't like he had anything better to do, he thought to himself. He boarded the monorail for the short journey that lasted all of three and a half minutes and that included a stop as well.

Getting off the monorail, he noticed still more people dressed up, boarding the monorail on the other track and heading towards Buckingham Palace. He made his way through the streets towards Gee Tee's, feeling almost claustrophobic in the confined spaces after all the openness and freedom surrounding the councillors' building that he had come from.

Hardly anybody seemed to be about, away from the monorail station, which he thought was odd, as the only other times he had been this way there had always been plenty of dragons about. But not now it seemed. Finally reaching the door to the Mantra Emporium, he knocked and waited. After two minutes of no response, he knocked again. Still no reply. Peter took a few paces back and looked up at the front of the building. A dim light shone out of a small grubby first floor window. Peter gave it one more go and knocked as hard as he dared on the wooden door of the Emporium. After waiting another three minutes with no response again, Peter decided to leave. As he turned to leave, he heard a noise coming from above. The small grubby window creaked open just slightly and Gee Tee's nose poked out.

"Hello. Who's there?" said Gee Tee clearly fumbling about for something.

"It's me Peter. Peter Bentwhistle, Tank's friend," said Peter, trying to be quiet.

Gee Tee's head disappeared and then, after a little more fumbling, reappeared with his glasses firmly attached to his nose. As the old dragon looked down from the window at him, Peter found himself suppressing a laugh, due to the fact that Gee Tee was wearing a red and white stripy night cap and looked like something from a Victorian story.

"Ah young man," said Gee Tee. "Don't you know what time it is?"

"It's five past seven," Peter said hesitantly. "I'm sorry if I've woken you up."

"Five past seven? Really? In the evening?" said Gee Tee.

"Yes," said Peter, nodding vigorously.

"Hey ho," said Gee Tee, as he threw something out of the window towards Peter. Stretching out, Peter caught the object which turned out to be a brass key, much to his surprise.

"Let yourself in and lock the door behind you," said Gee Tee from above. "I'll be down shortly."

Peter put the key in the lock and after about thirty seconds managed to jiggle it so that the door unlocked. He entered the shop, which was now in total darkness and proceeded to try and lock the door, which to his amazement took even longer than it had to open it. Eventually he managed it, by which time a light had appeared at the back of the shop, in an area that Peter had never seen before. Peter could just make out Gee Tee making his way down a steep set of stairs, painfully slowly. Peter weaved his way in and out of the bookcases towards the bottom of the stairs, skilfully avoiding piles and piles of disregarded books, which by now any human would have tripped over many times.

Peter got to the bottom of the stairs and stood watching the old shopkeeper. It was only then that it dawned on him exactly how old and frail Gee Tee really was. Peter was suddenly wracked with guilt about involving Gee Tee in any of this. What had he done? The old shopkeeper should be left alone to get on with his own life. Why couldn't Peter handle things on his own? All of these thoughts ran through his mind as he watched Gee Tee slowly negotiate the last two steps. Gee Tee poked the glasses up his nose and leant forward, so that Peter could feel the breath from the old dragon on his face. The old shopkeeper looked right into his eyes and just stared for what seemed like eternity. Peter felt like he was back at the nursery ring, under the scrutiny of one of the stricter 'tors.

"I'm sorry you have to see me like this, child," whispered Gee Tee, "but I don't need your sympathy or pity."

Peter was shocked. Was Gee Tee reading his mind, he wondered? Before he had a chance to ask, Gee Tee continued.

"Your expression says it all, child. When you've lived as long as I have, you tend to pick up a thing or two."

Peter felt relieved that Gee Tee wasn't reading his mind, but was still concerned that he had got him involved and had woken him up tonight.

"Do you know why I don't need your pity, child?" Gee Tee continued.

Peter shook his head and stared at the wooden floor of the shop.

"I don't need it because I've lived longer already than any other dragon in history my young fellow," Gee Tee said cheerfully. "And I don't intend on getting deep fried in lava just yet," the old shopkeeper added with a smile.

Peter felt the tip of Gee Tee's wing under his chin, pulling his face up from the floor.

"I've had the most wonderful life, child. The most amazing adventures. I wouldn't change a single thing. How many dragons can say that? Eh! And most importantly, if I want to help someone, like I've helped others many times before, then I think that should be my choice. Don't you?"

Peter looked up at the old dragon, lost for words. There was such passion in his face. His eyes seemed full of...... adventure and mystery. He just nodded his head in acknowledgement. As he did so, Gee Tee caught sight of the chain around Peter's neck, on which hung the trident. The old shopkeeper leaned in close and put the tip of his wing under the chain, pulling it taught around Peter's neck.

"Just when I think I've seen everything, something jumps up and bites me in the bum to prove me wrong," said Gee Tee shaking his head.

Without another word, the old dragon relinquished his grip on the chain and turned away, walking over to the counter. Leaning over it he flicked a switch and the room slowly became bathed in light. Hobbling off towards the workshop, the old shopkeeper turned towards Peter.

"Let's see if we can find something to drink and then you can tell me what brings you here at this...... early hour," he said with laughter in his voice.

"Do you want me to boil the kettle?" Peter asked, pointing towards the small kitchen.

"No, no, no, child. We can do much better than that," said Gee Tee, beckoning Peter towards the workshop.

Peter followed Gee Tee into the workshop and took a seat in the chair he was guided to. Gee Tee pulled out a small stool and moved it in front of a very tall bookcase that contained many varieties of parchment and ink. Gee Tee climbed awkwardly onto the stool and started hunting around on top of the bookcase. After much rummaging about, he finally seemed to have retrieved what he was looking for.

"Ah, here it is. Just right for special occasions and times of need," Gee Tee said, stifling a laugh. "And right now I feel the need."

As Gee Tee turned around to step down from the stool, Peter finally caught a glimpse of what he had been searching for. It was a tall metallic flask, covered in dust, through which Peter could just make out some writing that said '12th Century Peruvian Ink (only to be used with 12th century Peruvian parchment)'. Peter wondered what an earth was going on.

Gee Tee held the flask up to examine it, a playful glint in his eye. He blew some of the dust from the flask and twisted off the cap, as Peter sat in the chair, intrigued. Gee Tee held up the flask to his nostrils and inhaled, clearly liking what he smelt. Just as Peter thought it couldn't get any weirder, Gee Tee did the last thing that Peter expected. He took a swig from the flask. Peter sat gobsmacked in the oversized chair, watching as Gee Tee swilled some of the flask's contents around in his mouth. Suddenly, the old shopkeeper turned sharply and blew an almighty stream of searing blue flame across the room, hitting the wall on the other side of the room and leaving the mother of all scorch marks.

"Your friend will have a hissy fit when he comes into work on Monday and sees that on the wall," said Gee Tee, licking his lips.

"What on earth is that stuff?" asked Peter, warily.

Gee Tee gave a huge guffaw and held out the flask.

"Well it's not Peruvian ink, that's for sure." The two dragons both spontaneously burst into laughter, which lasted for what seemed like some time. When Gee Tee finally finished laughing, he held out the flask and offered it to Peter. Unsure of what to do, Peter reluctantly took the flask from the shopkeeper, holding it as if it were a ticking bomb.

"That, my young friend, is the finest, most potent and most enjoyable drink you will ever try."

"Why does it say Peruvian ink on the side?" asked Peter, more than a little confused.

Gee Tee chuckled and smiled at Peter.

"If your best friend found out what it really was, you can bet that would be the last I would see of it. Much as I appreciate his constant fussing over the state of my health, I do like a little treat now and then. And it says 'to be used only with Peruvian parchment' simply because there's no such thing, reducing the chances of anyone opening it by mistake."

"Sneaky," said Peter proudly.

"I sometimes feel that's what I should have been named," said the old shopkeeper, smiling.

Peter smiled, shook his head and held the flask under his nose and sniffed. "Smells like petrol," he said.

"Petrol?" said Gee Tee, confused.

It suddenly dawned on Peter that Gee Tee, having never been to the surface would have absolutely no idea what that was.

"Ah............it's a fuel that the humans use to power their vehicles," Peter said, hoping that would be enough of an explanation.

"Oh," said Gee Tee, nodding his head. "Well anyway, this as I was saying is simply............magnificent. It was a gift to me from the king."

"The king?" said Peter incredulously.

"Oh not the current king, child, although I'm pretty sure he owes me more than a few flasks of this. If he ever remembers, that is."

"If it's not from the current king, how old is this stuff?" said Peter nervously.

Gee Tee shrugged his shoulders and said casually,

"Nearly three hundred years, if my memory serves me correctly. Go ahead, child. Try it."

"I........I.........I couldn't," said Peter, offering the flask back to the shopkeeper.

"I wouldn't offer if I didn't want you to have any, child. You really should try it. That might be the only one of its kind left on the planet. My understanding is that it was a gift to the king of the time, from the nagas of the frozen north. A peace offering I believe," said Gee Tee with a faraway look in his eyes.

"Sounds important," said Peter. "Why did the king give it to you?..... If you don't mind me asking."

Gee Tee turned and looked at Peter, with a special knowing look in his eyes.

"You wouldn't be the first dragon that I've helped, oh no, not the first by a long way. And some of the things that I've been privileged to be involved with, well let's just say that not only have I experienced a lot of history, being as old as I am, but I've helped shape a fair bit of it as well."

Peter looked at the old shopkeeper in amazement at what he had just heard, seeing the old dragon in a completely new light.

"Now stop gawping and start drinking," Gee Tee said, indicating the flask. "Just a small mouthful, and savour the taste. You'll know when it's time for the flame," said the old dragon with a smirk on his face.

Peter lifted the flask up and took a small swig. The thick liquid rolled effortlessly over his huge tongue, leaving a gorgeous sweet, fizzy, tangy, almost indescribable sensation in his mouth. The flavour seemed to penetrate not only his nose but seemed to seep down into his throat and caress the top part of his huge stomach. Peter stood in the middle of the workshop, eyes closed, thinking of nothing other than the amazing experience the drink was producing. It seemed like pure heaven. Never before had he experienced such wonder. Not even the first time he had taken to the air. He began to wonder why he had never heard of such a drink and why it was not widely available to every dragon on the planet. Just as he had that thought, a tingling feeling started to......... erupt in his mouth. Opening his eyes, he saw Gee Tee standing in front of him, grinning from ear to ear. In the split second it took him to open his eyes the tingling had turned to......... burning. But not just any burning: ice cold burning that made every one of his sharp teeth feel like they were being hit individually with a hammer. The feeling in his teeth had masked the sensation in the back of his throat and stomach that was now coming to the fore. It felt like the flesh was being stripped away inside him. With panic starting to consume him, he looked up to see tears of laughter running down Gee Tee's face, sizzling as they came into contact with the heat of his nostrils. Fear and anger threatened to over take him, when all of a sudden he felt his stomach make a giant..........bubble. "Oh my God," he thought, "I'm going to explode."

Turning around in blind panic, the bubble that had started in his stomach had gathered momentum and was making a mad dash for freedom up his throat. Peter clenched his jaw, determined not to let it out for some reason. Not quite what the bubble had in mind. Nothing was about to stop it from leaving Peter's body. Abruptly Peter's jaws shot open, as wide as they possibly could. A resounding 'BUUUUUUURRRRRRRRRRPPPPPPP' emanated from his mouth, followed by a huge blue fireball that crossed the room and hit a grey metal filing cabinet, reducing it to a steaming mass of burning slag. Peter slumped into the oversized chair, relieved that whatever that bubble had been, it no longer existed inside him. Gee Tee had finished laughing and wandered over to stare at the remains of the filing cabinet.

"Well I'm not nearly so concerned about that scorch mark on the wall now," said Gee Tee, teeming with sarcasm. "You're supposed to produce a concentrated stream of fire, not a ball of absolute devastation."

"Sorry," said Peter, feeling a little light headed.

Gee Tee shook his head.

"It's not your fault child. I should have explained a bit more. Anyway, what did you think? Awesome eh?"

Peter let out a long breath, still tasting the after effects of the drink.

"Oh yeah................awesome."

"That's the spirit," said Gee Tee, patting Peter on the back.

Peter surveyed the mess they'd made of the workshop and then asked,

"How are you going to explain all of this to Tank?"

Gee Tee smiled and looked thoughtful for a few seconds before replying,

"I'll just tell him I was rooting about and found some old mantras that I didn't recognise and decided to try them out. If he asks where they are, I'll just point to that," said Gee Tee pointing to the steaming molten mess that was the filing cabinet. "Like I said before....................sneaky."

Peter chuckled under his breath and thought to himself, "What a way to spend a Saturday night." It was only then that he realised that he didn't mean it sarcastically, and in actual fact he had been having a really great time just talking and mucking about with the old shopkeeper.

"Anyway, I haven't asked you what you're doing here tonight. Much as I enjoy your company, it's an odd time for a social call," Gee Tee said, sitting down in the other dragon sized chair in the workshop.

Peter recalled all the events of today that had led him to being here and once again felt the weight of the world on his shoulders. He began to tell Gee Tee about his trip to the council chambers, but got only as far as mentioning Hitch Rosebloom's name, before the old shopkeeper interrupted.

"Bloody Hitch Rosebloom, the bane of my life," said Gee Tee, clearly annoyed. "Let me guess what happened. You started telling him all about the events at Cropptech and then unwittingly dropped my name into the conversation and he probably went into one. Would that be about right?"

"Pretty much," said Peter, surprised.

"That dragon should be frozen in ice and left there for a thousand years to rot," said Gee Tee with venom in his raised voice. "I'm sorry child," said the old shopkeeper, noticing the worried look on Peter's face. "It's just, as you may have guessed, we have a little bit of........................... history."

Peter just nodded, waiting to see if the old dragon would expand on what he had just said.

Gee Tee began to pace up and down the workshop, wings swishing about behind him, totally oblivious to the still smoking molten scraps of metal that littered the floor.

"Of all the councillors that could have responsibility for Cropptech, it would have to be him, wouldn't it," Gee Tee mumbled to no one in particular. After a few more minutes of pacing and much more muttering, the old shopkeeper suddenly pulled the other chair across the room, plonked it down in front of Peter and sat down in it.

"I'm sorry if you've got it in the scales from him, but I'm glad you came and sought me out, particularly after whatever bad things he's said about me," Gee Tee said, smiling at Peter.

Smiling back, Peter was pretty sure his gut feeling about Gee Tee was right, no matter what the crazy councillor had said.

"It all started a very long time ago," said the old shopkeeper. "Long before you were hatched. Although it doesn't look it, this shop used to be incredibly busy. At our peak, nobody else in the world could match us for mantras, whether it was new mantras or everyday mantras. We always created and sold the best. Our healing mantras were on average between fifteen and twenty per cent more effective than anyone else's, purely because of the quality materials we used. Dragons knew if they came to Gee Tee's Mantra Emporium they were getting top quality merchandise. We even had the King's Council's Seal of Approval.

"All in all, business was booming. The shop itself already had a staff of ten, not including the five dragons employed in the workshop doing repairs, research and development, which incidentally is where I spent a great deal of my time. Even with all the current staff, things were spiralling out of control, and I decided that I really needed someone to help me with the research and development side of things. So I put an advert in the Daily Telepath for an assistant. How I wish I'd never done that, for oh so many reasons. Anyway, the response from the advert was overwhelming. The Daily Telepath was the only paper available at that time and nearly every dragon family in the world saw it at some point. Combined with the prestige of the company and the fact that it was a position working right alongside me, well let's just say that things went berserk. If my memory serves me correctly we had nearly five thousand applicants. I was absolutely gobsmacked at the time. It never occurred to me that it would be a sought after post, but it appeared that indeed that's what it was. I spent weeks whittling down the candidates, which of course meant the shop was getting busier because - yes that's right - I was sifting through five thousand applications. Eventually I managed to get it down to a manageable twenty dragons, which was no mean feat I assure you."

Peter nodded, riveted by the thought of the shop being so busy and successful.

"Anyway, I proceeded to interview the candidates and finally managed to cull it down to four outstanding dragons, all of which were nearly straight out of their nursery rings. One of the four was a particularly arrogant young dragon called..........yes, you've guessed it, Hitch Rosebloom."

Peter was starting to see what Gee Tee meant when he said that he and Rosebloom had history.

"Well, I agonized long and hard about the four prospective candidates. It was, to this day, one of the hardest decisions I have ever had to make. Needless to say, the very pleasant Hitch Rosebloom wasn't the candidate that I choose. At the time I didn't think very much of it. The job went to an outstanding, clever and shy young dragon called Cat. Ahhh..........Cat. She was wonderful in every sense. Oh, in case you're wondering, Cat was short for Catfish, as that was what the marking sprayed across the back of her neck resembled.

"Anyway, she came to work for me and I let all the others that had an interview know that they hadn't got the job, and thought nothing more. Well it appeared that the boy Rosebloom was more than a little offended that he didn't get the job. Not only that but so were his family, a family very well connected by the way, if you know what I mean. I had a few visits from some of his family's ....associates, trying to persuade me to relent and give Rosebloom the job, but meanwhile Cat had excelled in the few weeks that she had been with me. Never having given in to bullies before, I wasn't about to now so I told these so called associates of Rosebloom's family quite what they could do."

At the mere mention of bullies, Peter's stomach started doing a loop the loop and all he could think of was Fisher, Casey and Theobald. A shudder ran the entire length of his body at the thought of the three of them. Concentrating hard, he turned his attention back to Gee Tee, who momentarily looked lost in thought.

"At the time it seemed like the right thing to do, and looking back with hindsight, it probably still was. But what I didn't realise was the extent of the power Rosebloom's family actually had, and quite how vindictive they would be. Anyway to cut a long story short, through manipulation and their contacts they managed to get the King's Council's Seal of Approval taken away from the shop, on some trumped up reason and things went rapidly downhill from there. The family's influence persuaded important customers to take their business elsewhere, and I ended up laying off most of my staff including the delightful Cat I'm afraid to say. My fortunes went from bad to worse, unlike that weasel Rosebloom, who through his family contacts managed not only to get selected as a councillor but the youngest one in dragon history."

Gee Tee got up and paced about a bit more, shaking his head and looking thoroughly angry. Peter was amazed to think that any one dragon could be so vindictive, to totally destroy something just because he didn't get selected for a job.

"If anyone tells you that dragons are not like humans at all child, or that dragons are better than humans, think again. This story, along with others just like it, should always remind you how much we have in common with our so-called 'barbaric' charges on the surface.

"Anyway, where was I? Oh yes, the delightful Rosebloom. You might have thought that ruining my business and becoming the youngest councillor in the history of dragonkind would be enough for the delightful young dragon, because I clearly did. But not so.

"About a year after he became a councillor I had a visit from a troop of the King's Guard, supposedly looking for illegal mantras and artefacts of all kinds. When I questioned their commander, he stated that the search had arisen from a tip-off from a highly placed source. Of course they didn't find anything but they managed to totally trash the place in the process. To this day I still get a visit from the King's Guards, every six months or so, looking for the same thing. Luckily for me, I've helped their new commander out a number of times, so whenever the orders come down from above, he brings a few trusted men and they come and join me for hot charcoal and stories for a few hours, before reporting back that the place has been thoroughly searched and nothing found."

Peter felt numb at the thought that one dragon could be so petty and horrible to another. Surely any resentment would fade over that period of time, he thought to himself.

"So there you have it child, the reason why the beloved councillor and I don't quite see eye to eye," said Gee Tee, much more calmly.

"That's something of an understatement isn't it?" said Peter, still stunned at the old shopkeeper's revelations.

"Now," said Gee Tee, "why don't you tell me about that interesting little trinket round your neck, child?"

"It was left to me by Mark Hiscock, in his will," said Peter, twirling the trident around on the end of its chain with the tip of his wing.

"Really," said Gee Tee, poking his large square spectacles as far up his nose as they would go. "Do you know what you have there, child?"

Peter smiled and looked up from the trident.

"A cool piece of bling, as they would say on the surface."

The old shopkeeper looked completely confused at Peter's description.

"Never mind," said Peter. "I don't really understand what it means either, and I'm supposed to be young and hip. By the interest you're showing in it though, I would assume that there's more to it than just a great looking piece of jewellery."

"Very much so, if I'm not mistaken," said Gee Tee, a sparkle in his eye. "Would you take it off so that I can have a better look?"

"Sure," said Peter, unhooking the clasp of the chain and handing it all over to the old shopkeeper.

Gee Tee shoved a few books aside on one of the workshop's benches and switched on a light overhead so that he could see a little better. Both he and Peter hunched over the desk, studying the trident.

"I've never seen one quite like this," said Gee Tee with awe in his voice.

"One what?" said Peter, gazing down at it.

"What you have there, child, is known as an 'alea', which roughly translated means 'gamble' or 'last chance'," said Gee Tee, wide-eyed.

Peter looked at Gee Tee with a blank expression, still not knowing what it was.

"It's a mantra, child, a mantra," said Gee Tee. "Not just any mantra either. An extremely powerful mantra to be used only as it says as a............. last chance, a last roll of the dice."

"I'm sorry I still don't understand," said Peter, feeling more than a little stupid.

Gee Tee sat down in a chair and beckoned Peter to do the same.

"Let me try and explain from the beginning then. My understanding is that the Aztec dragons were the first to develop *aleas*. If I remember correctly, a group of dark dragons tried to take over a large part of South America, and as a result the Aztec dragons had little choice but to try and bring them back into line. That didn't happen and as a result a small but very bloody war broke out over there. The dragons on each side became extremely proficient at killing each other, in all sorts of clever ways. Anyhow, the dragon in charge of the

167

light warriors..........his name eludes me at the moment.... fed up with losing so many dragons, asked his mantra specialists to come up with something that would turn the tide of this small but very nasty episode.

"I believe he was hoping for something on a bit of a larger scale, but this is what his specialists came up with, the *alea*. Of course at that time the *aleas* were a lot cruder than what you have here, but the principle was very much the same. A piece of jewellery that had a mantra embedded within it.

"Now the only problem with doing this, as the Aztecs were the first to find out, is that when you try and imbue something physical with any kind of mantra, the physical element more often than not alters the very nature of the mantra. The bits and pieces that I've read on the subject start to get a bit vague at this point but it seems that the very first *aleas* had shield mantras imbued into them. They were supposed to, at the very last minute, provide a powerful shield that would allow the dragon to fend off multiple attacks and make a successful escape, when said dragon used the mantra and broke the particular piece of jewellery. Perfect, if you've just been caught up in an ambush. You live to fight again another day.

"The first couple of times they were used they worked as intended. A shield sprang up around the dragon and enabled it to escape and report back that the *alea* worked perfectly. Not so, however. The more the war raged on, the more desperate encounters there were. Dragons with *aleas* were found dead, when they should have escaped, some even taking whole groups of enemies with them. Others reported that instead of a shield appearing when used, the *aleas* produced powerful streams of lightning that struck all those around them, killing them instantly, no mean feat where dragons are involved.

"The Aztec specialists tried and tried to work out what was going wrong but to no avail. They did eventually manage to win the war and bring the dark dragons under control, but only after a large loss of life, both to dragons and humans. The *aleas* proved something of an enigma to all concerned. The Aztecs gave up totally on the concept, believing them to be too unreliable and dangerous.

"That, however, is not where things ended. Different groups of dragons throughout history have sought to emulate the *aleas*, all having about as much success as the Aztecs first did. Oh, they would all claim to have solved the stability problem, but alas nobody to my knowledge ever came close to producing a stable and reliable *alea* that worked as it should all the time."

Peter sat in the chair, hooked on every word the shopkeeper was saying.

"You should come and teach at the nursery ring. That was absolutely fascinating," said Peter in awe. "Why don't they mention that in the nursery ring? I've never heard anything like that at all."

"Ah that, child, is a good question. Why do you think they don't teach it?"

Peter scratched his chin with the tip of his wing, pondering the question.

"I suppose they don't want people tinkering, trying to make their own *aleas* what with the instability and everything."

Gee Tee nodded in agreement and said,

"That, and the fact that it might encourage some sort of rogue movement, like the dark dragons the Aztecs had to deal with. Things like that have started over a lot less in the past."

"Really?" said Peter.

"Oh yes," replied Gee Tee. "It might sound unlikely, but I assure you it's a possibility. Evil is always around. You may not see it, but it lurks in the shadows just waiting for an opportunity to exert itself. The king and the council are fully aware of all of this, and that would be my guess why things like this aren't taught to young dragons."

Peter felt like his head was going to explode with all the new information he had learned today. He also felt a small pang of envy that Tank was working day in and day out with Gee Tee. "What must it be like to work here full time and learn everything that he knows and has experienced?" wondered Peter. The two dragons sat there in silence for a few minutes, just looking at the *alea* hanging off the chain on the workshop bench. Finally Peter broke the silence.

"Can I ask how you use it?" he said cautiously.

"You really want to know after everything I've told you?" said Gee Tee suspiciously, peering intently over his large square glasses.

"I'm not going to use it," stuttered Peter unconvincingly.

"You'd have to be either incredibly brave or unbelievably stupid to use it. Makes no difference to me whether you are or not." Gee Tee picked up the trident and turned it around with the tip of his wing. As he did so, the purple glow surrounding the trident left a kind of trail in the air that took a few seconds to dissipate.

"If you look carefully, past the purple glow, child, you should be able to make out words, running down the length of the main shaft and also on each part of the fork," said Gee Tee, holding the *alea* up in front of his face.

Peter put his head close to the trident and squinted hard, trying his best to see the writing that was microscopic at best.

"Come on, child, if an old dragon of over six hundred can see it, surely you must be able to."

Peter used all of his dragon ability and really concentrated on the tiny sides of the trident's shaft and the prongs. After a few seconds the letters swirled into focus and Peter could just make out small words beneath the purple glow. "*Amplificare..............Magicus................Nunc,*" said Peter finally.

"That's right," said Gee Tee. "And that means..............?"

Peter knew that was coming and silently cursed the fact that Latin was easily his worst language in the nursery ring. He thought hard and tried to imagine his language 'tor, standing in front of him with the answer. Eventually it came to him but by now he was feeling unusually hot and more than a little stressed, particularly as the old shopkeeper had been staring at him intently all this time.

"Amplify Magic Now," said Peter, mentally exhausted.

"Nursery rings have sure dropped their standards since I was last there, that's for sure," said Gee Tee. "Anyway, 'Amplify Magic Now'. It's a bit vague isn't it? It could mean absolutely anything. Anyhow you wanted to know how to use it."

Peter nodded, not sure quite what he was letting himself in for.

"Like any normal mantra, you can either say the words out loud, or project them in your head, but the difference here is that at the same time you must use all your strength and break the trident."

"Break it?" said Peter, surprised.

"Of course," said Gee Tee. "How else do you think you would release the power that it has imbued in it? Well as I said before, brave or stupid. I wouldn't recommend it. Even if it was more specific as to what it did, I still wouldn't recommend it, so............. think really carefully before using it."

"I really have no intention of using it.............honest," said Peter.

"Whatever you say child, but don't say you haven't been warned," said Gee Tee wearily. "If you end up with five ears, no nose and a tongue long enough to lick your own tail, you can be sure that I will say............... 'I told you so'."

"I know, and thank you for your advice. It's much appreciated," replied Peter, smiling at the thought of being able to lick his own tail.

"So is there anything else that an old dragon can help you with? I confess to feeling more than a little tired now, but don't fret child, I've had a very enjoyable evening," said the old shopkeeper, more than a little drained.

Peter felt a wave of guilt roll over him again at having worn out the old shopkeeper. Nevertheless he decided to press on, knowing that he really needed some guidance in what to do next.

"I don't know what to do about the situation at Cropptech," he said quietly. "Rosebloom was no help whatsoever and.........I just don't know what to do next."

Gee Tee scratched his chin and fiddled with his glasses, thinking about what to tell his young friend.

"Well it's clear from what you've said that the mantra used at Mark's house was successful which would lead us to conclude that it might rid Garrett's office in much the same way. The problem there would be that even if you managed to get into the office and use it, there's nothing stopping Manson coming back in and starting all over again, because I very much doubt that Garrett would be cured instantly; it would only be the first step on his road to recovery."

Peter nodded in agreement.

"That makes sense," he said.

"So with that out of the question, the only thing I can think you can do is to bide your time and try and find some evidence against Manson or something that indicates what his eventual goal is, be that taking over the company, stealing something or whatever else."

Peter could see now the toll the night's events had taken on the old shopkeeper. He looked worn out and kept yawning between each sentence.

"That's good advice, thanks. I think I'll do just that. Thank you for an unforgettable evening. I won't keep you any longer," said Peter, meaning every word.

"You're welcome child," said Gee Tee, showing Peter out of the workshop and back to the front door. "Go careful now child, and don't forget you're welcome anytime, but daylight hours are always best," said Gee Tee, chuckling.

Peter moved out into the street, waving the old shopkeeper goodbye and waited to make sure he could hear the key turn in the lock. Once Peter was sure that the door had been properly locked, he made his way through the now deserted streets back towards the monorail station, feeling a lot happier than he had in a very long time.

11

Holly Jockey Sticks

Peter woke full of energy. Normally on a Sunday he was bleary eyed and not at all keen on getting up, but the previous night's events had made him feel hugely optimistic about everything in his life. Also he had received a text message on his phone reminding him that hockey training started that Tuesday, signalling the start of the hockey season, something Peter found he had been missing like crazy all over the summer.

It was, of course, Richie that had got him into playing hockey after he had been complaining to her about a lack of interest in his life apart from his work. Richie had taken up playing lacrosse some time ago, something that most dragons couldn't really see the point in. Yes, dragons had begun to infiltrate many popular sports at all levels, mainly professional sport, particularly because the power and adoration that most of them commanded, enabled them to influence all levels of society and guide the humans in the right direction. To assume human form and participate in a human sport just for fun, without using your dragon abilities seemed................unthinkable to just about every dragon. There had even been stories written in the dragon press about Richie playing lacrosse purely for pleasure, none of which cast her in a very good light, most indeed questioning at the very least her sanity. But as far as Peter could see it was lava off a dragon's tail as far as she was concerned.

So, after hearing him complain about lacking something in his life, Richie took Peter to the sports club in Salisbridge one busy Saturday afternoon. He spent all afternoon wandering around the ground, marvelling at the sheer enjoyment all the humans seemed to be getting from being part of a team sport. He'd never really taken much notice of any of it before, either on the television or anywhere else, and like most other dragons, couldn't really see the point, but to see these games up close, was just………..unbelievable. The passion with which the players pursued their sport, the bonding that seemed to go on in each side, the ferocity of the challenges being made against the opposition…..it was all truly a wonder to behold.

That afternoon Peter had watched Richie play a whole game of lacrosse for the first time and was absolutely agog. Most of the comments in the dragon press referring to Richie almost always maintained that it was impossible for her to play without using her dragon abilities. This seemed to be the most contentious part of the complaints levelled against her, with most dragons just unable to comprehend why she would bother in the first place. But as Peter sat in a cold and wet dugout adjacent to the pitch and watched Richie play, he got a glimpse of something very special. Not only could Peter tell that Richie didn't use her abilities throughout the whole of the match (something that even Peter had had reservations about secretly, even though Richie had given her word on more than one occasion that she didn't use her dragon powers) but also it was blatantly obvious to Peter, who had known her nearly her whole life, that she was happier playing lacrosse than Peter had possibly ever seen her. And that included the moments she would dazzle everybody with her amazing aerial acrobatics, something every dragon loved more than just about anything else.

"How could this running around with sticks, chasing a little ball produce so much pleasure?" Peter wondered for days afterwards. He talked to Tank about it and he couldn't explain it either. In fact Tank was so taken aback at what Peter had said that he had to see for himself the pleasure that Richie was so obviously getting out of playing in a team sport alongside other humans. The two friends attended every one of Richie's home games for a couple of months hoping to find the secret to Richie's happiness, but to no avail. However hard they tried they just couldn't seem to hit the nail on the head as to what was so captivating about playing in a team. After a few months Peter and Tank sat down with Richie and asked her to explain it to them. After laughing at the pair of them for what seemed like an eternity and then jokingly banging their heads together, she told them the only way to find out what they were missing out on, was to try it.

Tank and Peter were more than a little unsure, but they didn't want to let their friend down, so both agreed to go and train for a few weeks at different sports. Peter chose hockey and Tank rugby. His bigger, stronger build they thought would be better suited to that particular sport, even though both had wanted to try lacrosse at first. Richie had told them to try something different and said that they could swap sports after going to a few training sessions.

Peter could vividly remember turning up to his first hockey training session on a cold and wet Tuesday night. Richie came along and introduced him to the coach, and then turned around and left him there..........on his own, well.......... not exactly on his own, as there were forty other players around him, but that's how it felt. Richie had shown him the previous night how to hold a stick and how to strike a ball, in the back garden of Peter's house.

He joined in with the players as they did a brief but effective warm up in the cold November weather. As he did so he noticed that even though there was no game going on, they weren't even holding their hockey sticks for goodness' sake, there was an incredible amount of ....banter. Everyone from the smallest to the biggest, oldest to the youngest were all chatting, making jokes and just..............bonding. Peter had thought previously that the bonding must have just been a game kind of thing but on that cold wet windy night he wasn't so sure.

The brief warm up finished and the players started to partake in exercises with a stick and a ball. Peter joined in, and although he wasn't anywhere near the best, strangely he wasn't quite the worst, even though he wasn't using any of his dragon abilities. The banter continued, as did the exercises, and still Peter was no nearer discovering Richie's magic secret of happiness. The exercises were okay, but it sure didn't set Peter's world alight. The night progressed and it got colder and wetter, but all of the people training didn't seem to mind one bit. "Very strange," Peter thought more than once. Just when Peter thought about calling it a night, the coach blew his whistle and called everyone in. The group was divided into two, each given blue and red bibs respectively, and a game started.

Now while Richie had been showing him the night before how to hold a stick, she had also been explaining the rules and how to play. Peter had listened dutifully but hadn't really taken it all in. Now the training game had started, he wished he had paid more attention to his friend the previous night. Things were moving so quickly. The ball was almost a blur. Tackles were being made left, right and centre. People were calling for passes and screaming for others to close down the player with the ball. Peter could feel his heart pounding and his temperature rising, no mean feat in the cold and rain of a November evening. He moved about, trying desperately to get in the right place to receive a pass from one of his team mates. Unfortunately someone on the opposition had picked him out and decided to mark him rather tightly, making a pass seem more and more unlikely as the game went on. Peter ran around, trying to lose his marker, but to no avail. Just when he thought his chance at getting in on the action had passed, the guy who had been marking him received the ball from one of his team mates and looked like he meant to dribble straight past Peter down the wing.

By now Peter was fully engrossed in all the excitement and adrenaline of the match. More than a little disappointed that he hadn't seen the ball yet, he was determined to take it from the opponent now heading straight at him at quite a pace. Having seen how some of the better players at the training session had been tackling, Peter knew just what to do. He waited until his opponent was nearly on top of him, and moved his stick to the open side, knowing full well his opponent would perform a 'dummy' and take it down his so called 'weaker' side. The 'dummy' came and just at the last split second, Peter flipped his stick over and laid it flat on the Astroturf, as strong as he could with a one handed grip, taking the ball off the opponent with an amazing reverse stick tackle that anyone there would have been proud of.

Having made the tackle, he could feel the excitement pumping through his body, he fought the impulse to try anything else clever, but instead played a very simple pass to one of his team mates. Within seconds he was getting words of encouragement from everybody and even the odd pat on the back. The feeling was absolutely amazing; it was like nothing else he had ever experienced. At that point Peter became aware that he had found Richie's secret. He knew that the smile on his face just then, easily matched the one that Richie wore during the whole of a lacrosse match. "It was so simple," he thought. "I just had to join in."

The training match continued for a little while longer, during which time Peter made another couple of tackles and a few more passes. As the session came to an end, Peter received more pats on the back and got on the end of some of the 'banter'. One of the captains came to take Peter's details on his way out of the Astroturf and the rest, as they say, is history; Peter was well and truly hooked.

It was pretty much the same scenario with Tank, except that he didn't get that lightning bolt of excitement until he played his first game of rugby on a Saturday. After that, he too was hooked in very much the same way as Peter and Richie. For the three friends, the thought of not joining the humans to participate in team sport was just unfathomable, something alas most dragons could not comprehend, more's the pity.

Peter was really excited at the thought of going training on Tuesday and wondered if he would be selected for one of the sides to play on Saturday. With it being September, there were usually two or three friendly or inter-club games before the league season started, normally in the second week in October. Peter's thoughts turned to Tank, who had resumed training many weeks ago and would be participating in his first league game this coming Saturday. "Perhaps I'll get to watch some of his game and get to play a game of hockey as well this Saturday," he thought.

With renewed optimism and a generally brighter outlook, Peter wolfed down his breakfast, whizzed through the housework that he had made a mental note to do, and then settled down in front of his computer. Much as he wanted to log on and play his latest MMO, he needed to sort some things out beforehand. He was determined to design a spreadsheet that could be easily filled in with all the information that he was gathering about Manson's movements at work. His previous effort of writing things down in the suede covered book had gone a bit awry, with the information being very hard to understand once it had been written down. He thought that by designing a spreadsheet and collating all the information in a clear and concise manner, he might be better able to see where it was all leading to, if that was at all possible. Also, a plan had developed in Peter's brain about designing a computer program that would collect all the data from Manson's computer at work if, that is, he could somehow find a way of downloading it onto his computer in the first place. Computer programming wasn't Peter's strong suit by any means but all dragons had a strong grasp of computer basics thanks to their teaching at the nursery ring.

Peter cleared his mind and began to focus on the job at hand. It didn't take long to create the spreadsheet, although it was quite time consuming putting all of the previous data from the suede fronted notebook into it. The main problem was that Peter couldn't read his own writing. "Clearly I'm qualified to be a doctor or maybe even a teacher," he thought to himself, as he squinted at the pages of the book. "On second thoughts even my writing's not illegible enough to be a teacher's, and I'll be damned if I'm wearing one of those crazy jackets with the patches on the arms," he thought with a smile on his face. "Human teachers seem to have the worst fashion sense on the whole planet. Fact!" Or at least it was to most dragons, anyway.

After a couple of hours, Peter had finished the spreadsheet and transferred all of his previous data on to it. He sat staring at it, trying desperately to see some sort of pattern, something, anything, but after half an hour he gave up.

Peter made himself a ham sandwich, all the time thinking about the data. The conclusion he came to after munching through his sandwich, two apples and a banana, was that more data was needed before any sort of recognisable pattern would reveal itself. So, determined to find as much data as possible, starting the next morning when he returned to work, Peter now sat back down in front of his computer to try and develop a program that he could put on to Manson's computer at work.

This proved to be a lot harder than Peter thought it would be. After nearly three hours sitting in front of the computer, Peter had only got as far as downloading three different types of software that might allow him to create the program that he wanted. In searching the internet he had to be extremely careful in what it was he searched for. It wouldn't be very prudent to type in the search engine 'wanted computer spy program, Trojan or virus', particularly if he didn't want anyone to know what it was he was up to. Peter's head felt like the hard drive on his computer sounded..........in need of a rest. He'd spent over five hours sitting at the computer so far today and it was only mid afternoon.

He closed down the computer to give the whirring hard drive a break and then went through to the living room and sat down. Taking one look at the television, he dismissed it out of hand and instead thought about catching up with the dragon news. Sprawling out on the sofa, he closed his eyes and let go of his consciousness, just giving it a little prod now and then to guide it in the right direction. In a very short space of time, it had returned with a copy of the Daily Telepath and unbelievably it contained the scores from the Global Cup Quarter final games which had been played last night. Peter was astonished. He had been so caught up in the events of yesterday that he had totally forgotten about the Indigo Warriors playing one of their most important matches in recent history. Glancing down the back page, his heart racing, he noted with relief that the Indigo Warriors had won and made it through to the semi finals. He saw that an in depth match report was further inside the paper.

Peter opened his eyes and stretched his entire body, almost off the end of the sofa. "That was pure bliss," he thought to himself. "Well, nearly anyway. The only thing better would have been to be at the match itself. It's a pity Tank couldn't get any tickets, but nevertheless, being through to the semi finals.................................FANTASTIC."

Peter sat up sharply and got a bit of a head rush from having been lying down so long. He stood up and felt in his pockets for his mobile phone. "Hmmmm not there," he thought. "Now where did I put it?" This was quite a common occurrence with Peter. He was smart, intelligent, some even said witty. But he was always a bit ......dizzy, absent minded, forgetful, all of the above. And more often than not it was usually his keys (car and front door) or more likely his mobile phone that was mislaid.

After searching for nearly five minutes, he eventually found it, on the table beside his wardrobe in his bedroom. He couldn't even remember taking it upstairs, let alone putting it there. He quickly fired off a text to Tank asking if he knew any good laminium ball teams and could he try for some tickets to the semi finals. Tank replied a few minutes later saying that he was just off to do some rugby coaching and that he would check for some tickets that evening. Peter rubbed his hands together in celebration on seeing Tank's response. Seeing the Indigo Warriors in the semi final of the Global Cup was beyond his wildest dreams, but in fact it was so close he could almost set it alight with his breath.

Peter had fully intended to go back to the computer to try to make a start on developing a program on the software that he had downloaded earlier, but he was so excited after reading the paper that he forgot all about that and started playing on his latest MMO, and didn't finish until well into the early hours of the following day.

Peter went into work the next day, exhausted from being up most of the night playing on the computer. Although extremely tired, he was still on a high from learning about the Indigo Warriors and couldn't help but check his mobile phone regularly to see if Tank had sent him a text message. Peter didn't know exactly how Tank got hold of tickets to the good laminium ball matches, particularly since demand always considerably outstripped supply, but Peter knew that the contacts Tank used usually dealt in days rather than hours, and that more than likely he would have to wait until later in the week to see if his dream of going to the semi final was going to come true.

In the meantime he focused all his attention on trying to account for all of Manson's movements to see if he could determine some kind of goal that his nemesis was working towards. Now you would think with access to all of the security systems (CCTV, web cams, computer access and one or two trusted allies) that logging Manson's whereabouts at any one time wouldn't be too much of a challenge, but things were quite the opposite in reality. When Manson did leave the upper floor of the building, he managed to avoid detection all too often. Whether by luck or skill, he always seemed somehow to slip past the security cameras and turn up in some part of the complex without it being clear how he got there. Peter would scrutinise the bank of monitors in his office and when Manson left Al Garrett's office he would try and follow where he went. It shouldn't actually have been that hard, as all routes out of Garrett's office were covered by security cameras at some point and Peter had often checked that there were no 'blind spots'. That said, Manson seemed to have a 'knack' of somehow getting past these, either to go out or to come back into Al Garrett's office. Peter had no idea how Manson was achieving this, even after checking the system for faults and making sure all of the cameras were giving off live feeds. The more Peter tried to work it out, the more puzzled he became. Peter had ordered the maintenance crews to strip down all the cameras in the main building and give them a thorough overhaul, on the grounds of routine maintenance. The crews were also ordered to check for anything suspicious and report directly back to Peter. The crews spent two days taking apart the various cameras and checking them rigorously. After all had been examined, the crew chief made his way to Peter's office to report his findings.

The crew chief was a tall, pale skinned, gangly man named Alastair. Peter had dealt with him many times before and had found him very competent and extremely knowledgeable on any technical subject. Alastair knocked on the door to Peter's office and then entered. Peter liked to keep things as informal as possible, and actively encouraged those that he dealt with on a regular basis to just knock and go straight in. He found that people were just a little more receptive to small touches like that. Alastair wandered round the bank of security monitors, clutching a huge pile of paperwork and sat down in the chair opposite Peter.

"Hi Alistair, how's it going?"

"Good thanks Peter. We've finished the maintenance," said Alistair, plonking the pile of papers down on the desk. "No problems to report. One or two of the cameras in the stairwells had got a significant amount of dust in them, which if left for much longer may well have caused a problem, but other than that, nothing else untoward."

Peter nodded, while picking up the top sheet of paperwork and studying it.

"So does that mean that it would be prudent to decrease the maintenance interval of all the cameras in stairwells across the entire complex?"

"Already done Peter," said Alastair, sitting back in his chair proudly. "We've adjusted the schedule on the computer system to flag the stairwell cameras every nine months for routine checks, as opposed to every year and a half for the cameras elsewhere."

Peter leaned across the desk to shake Alastair's hand.

"Great work, as always. Thanks for fitting us in at such short notice."

"Anytime for you Peter. We value the security of this place almost as much as you do, so adjusting our schedule isn't that much of a problem. I have to ask though... it sounded when we first spoke two days ago as though you were looking for something specific. Clearly we didn't find it. Is it something that I should be concerned about?"

Peter's brow creased as he thought for a split second about telling Alastair how Manson was managing to avoid the cameras regularly. He was sure he could trust the man and didn't doubt for a second that he was sincere in valuing the security of the complex, but he just couldn't bring himself to do it.

"No it's nothing to be concerned about. I just..........well.........I've just been working hard and have had a few late nights. I must have imagined the odd glitch on one of the monitors and wanted to be safe rather than sorry," Peter lied.

"Well I know the feeling about working too hard. Try and catch up on your sleep. You're no good if you're nodding off in front of the monitors. And don't worry, your secret's safe with me. We've all done it at some point." With that the two men shook hands and Alastair turned and headed towards the door. Before he left, Peter called out,

"Don't forget to thank your team for me, for doing such a good job and all that."

"Of course," said Alastair, opening the door and disappearing down the corridor.

Peter sat back in his chair, more frustrated and puzzled than ever, now that each and every camera had been checked. He also felt guilty about lying to Alastair about the reason he wanted the cameras checked in the first place, but knew deep down that it was probably best not to get anyone else involved, particularly as he didn't know exactly what it was he was getting himself involved in.

The day dragged on, with Peter mainly staying in his office, catching up on emails, filing and phone calls, all the while keeping a close eye on the bank of security monitors in front of him. The only thing keeping him going during the afternoon was the thought of going to the first session of hockey training tonight.

With only an hour to go until it was time to leave, Peter's mobile phone gave a high pitched warble from his jacket pocket, which was hanging up on the back of the office door instead of the wooden stand, indicating that it had just received a text message. After finishing the sentence he was typing, he got up and retrieved the phone from his jacket. Sitting back down at his desk, his heart skipped a beat with excitement as the phone's display showed the message was from Tank. "He's got the tickets......yippee!" thought Peter. Pressing the button to open the message on his phone, Peter's joy soon turned to sadness. The message read:

'Sorry couldn't get tickets to the game. However, may still be able to watch it. Will be in touch soon regards'. Peter let out a long sigh, disappointed that Tank hadn't managed to get the tickets. "The biggest match of my life and I don't get to go," thought Peter. "I wonder what he meant by 'may still be able to watch it'?.....hmmmm."

Peter saved the email he was working on, closed down his workstation and grabbed his jacket before leaving. Although slightly earlier than he normally left, he decided he'd had enough for today and, taking advantage once again of all his accrued flexi-time wasn't such a bad idea anyway. As he was about to get in his car to leave, he noticed that Manson's Mercedes wasn't parked anywhere in the car park. Peter had been watching the security monitors vigilantly all afternoon, or so he thought, and Manson had still managed to slip out of Garrett's office without being seen. Peter felt like banging his head against the roof of the car in frustration, but didn't. "How does he do it?" he thought, before getting in and driving home.

On arriving home Peter made himself some beans on toast, not wanting to have a big meal before going training. After eating he had more than an hour to kill before he had to leave for hockey, so decided to boot up his computer and have a look at the software that he had downloaded on Sunday. He started to experiment with it to see what he could create in a short period of time, knowing that the kind of program he needed would take a lot longer to put together, but having a good understanding of what the software could do would no doubt save him time later in the process. After forty-five minutes he was quite pleased with what he had achieved. While nothing special, it would, if it worked, tell how many times a certain application on a computer was being used and the times of day that application was being accessed. He realised he didn't have time to install and test it now, so saved it onto his hard drive and ran upstairs to change into his hockey kit. Two minutes later he charged down the stairs and headed into the kitchen. Grabbing his water bottle from the cupboard under the sink, he filled it at the tap and put it in his stick bag, which was leaning against the coat stand in the hall. He retrieved his astro trainers from the cupboard under the stairs, noting that they were covered in sand from the last time he had played hockey some months earlier. (The Astroturf hockey pitch at the sports club is sand-based, meaning it has a light covering of sand on it at all times, so most people that use it usually end up with sand in their shoes and socks to some degree when they've finished playing.) He opened the front door and banged them against the wall outside the house to get rid of as much sand as possible. He quickly did up the laces to his astro trainers and grabbed his stick bag. Just as he had walked through the front door and was about to slam it shut, he realised in a panic that he didn't have his keys or his phone. As he sprinted upstairs to retrieve these items from his work jacket pocket he thought, "Blimey that was lucky. I would have spent the night sitting on the doorstep instead of training.

Why do I keep forgetting all the time?" With keys, phone and wallet firmly about his person, Peter picked up his stick bag, closed the front door and got into his car to head to the sports club.

On arriving at the sports club, Peter was surprised by the sheer number of cars in the car park. The place was nearly full and that hardly ever happened on a busy Saturday, let alone in the week. After finding one of the few remaining spaces, Peter got out of his car and headed to the Astroturf pitch. On his way he noted that not only was it hockey training tonight, but the men's and ladies' lacrosse teams seemed to be here to train as well as the entire rugby club by the look of things. As he watched the rugby players come out of their dedicated dressing room, he spotted Tank trotting out onto the rugby pitch. His friend must have sensed this, as he turned his head and gave Peter a little wave, which Peter duly returned. As well as all the sports, there seemed to be some sort of function going on in the clubhouse, with lots of well-dressed people going in carrying gifts and flowers. "No wonder it's so busy," he thought. As he got closer to the gate into the Astroturf he had to join a queue to get in.

"Wow, I've never had to queue to get into training before. Lots of new faces and old ones. Everyone seems to be here, they must have missed it as much as I have over the summer," he thought.

At precisely seven o'clock, the two groups of footballers that were using the pitch finished and the queuing hockey players made their way out on to it. As Peter made his way through the crowd, he nodded and exchanged words with friends and team mates. The number of people here just for training was staggering, particularly as all of the first team players were missing as their training was separate and didn't start until eight thirty, directly after this session finished.

The sensation of being back on a hockey pitch with all of these people was awesome. It was only now dawning on Peter now just how much he had missed the hockey and just how much it meant to him. The training started with some light fitness work and then split men and ladies into groups to work on their basic skills. As the evening wore on, the exercises became more complicated and eventually led into a series of mini games for everyone. The coaches wrapped things up at eight thirty, allowing the first team men and ladies respectively to come on to the pitch and have a half each.

Peter trudged over to the sideline to find his stick bag and a drink, sweat running off his forehead and dribbling down his back after all the running about in the mini games they had played at the end. As he did so he noticed a familiar, smug face, looking with contempt at those coming off the pitch amongst those of the first team.........Manson! Peter kept his head down amongst the crowd of players leaving the pitch and made his way to his stick bag, unzipping the side pocket and pulling out his water bottle which he promptly drained dry.

Keeping his back to the first team players on the pitch, for fear of being confronted by Manson, Peter made his way off the Astroturf and back to his car. Putting his stick bag into the car, he grabbed his wallet from the glove compartment and headed for the bar in the hope that Richie and Tank would be there as both the lacrosse and rugby training had finished at the same time as his session.

Walking into the club house, Peter was surprised to find the bar wasn't nearly as busy as he had thought it would be. The private function was being held in the room upstairs that had its own bar, keeping the large main bar free downstairs for those club members that had just finished their training sessions. Peter queued patiently at the large bar; even though it wasn't that busy downstairs clearly some of the bar staff were serving upstairs.

Eventually getting served, he turned around and scanned the room for his friends. Richie was sitting at the far end with a gaggle of lacrosse girls all chatting and making far too much noise for Peter's liking. Looking through the mass of rugby players, Peter could just make out Tank having a very animated discussion with two other rugby players about tactics or a game or something, waving his hands all over the place to emphasise his point. Peter thought that he would just prop up the bar rather than interrupt Tank's heated conversation, and was way too intimidated by all the gorgeous looking lacrosse girls to even think about approaching Richie at the moment. Shuffling along the bar, he started paying attention to the rather competitive doubles pool match that was taking place in the corner between four of the rugby boys. Just then Peter felt a hand on his shoulder. He turned ready to confront Manson.........only to find it was the second team captain, Andy, who was clearly disturbed by the look on Peter's face.

"Sorry Andy. I thought you were someone else," Peter said, breaking into a great big toothy smile.

"That's quite alright Peter. Good to see you at training. How was your summer?"

"Well quite lazy really, didn't do very much. Missed playing hockey like crazy though."

"Good to hear it," said Andy, producing a notebook and pen. "Are you available for Saturday?"

"Sure am. In fact, barring injury, I'm available every weekend throughout the season."

"Good man," said Andy, slapping Peter on the back playfully. "Well, we've got friendly games for the next three weeks and then the league starts, so hopefully we can kick on from last year's mid table position and aim to finish in the top two and gain promotion. There were a few new faces out there tonight that might fit in nicely and bolster the squad from last year. The only people we won't have from last year are Ben and Matt who have both been posted abroad during the summer, but apart from that the squad should remain pretty much the same, with the addition of some of the new faces from tonight. Anyway Pete, I've got to catch up with some of the others before they slope off, so I'll see you on Saturday, two o'clock for a two thirty start. Okay?"

"Sure thing Andy, see you Saturday," said Peter, raising his pint glass as Andy disappeared into a mass of hockey players. "Fantastic, I'm in the side," he thought as he spotted Tank making his way towards him through the dwindling number of rugby players.

"Good training?" said Tank, leaning over the bar trying to attract some service.

"Yeah, it was good to be back playing again. Why are you training twice a week now?"

"Well," said Tank, "we do light work and tactics on a Tuesday, and the more physical work on a Wednesday."

"How was it?" asked Peter.

"It was okay, but as you probably know we had our first game on Saturday and got our arses handed to us on a plate," said Tank, shaking his head.

Peter had seen the result and the match report in the local paper only that morning and was surprised that Tank hadn't mentioned it before. Not that Peter would have been that much help, he didn't really understand fully the rules of rugby, so anything more complicated such as tactics or formations would go straight over his head.

"Any reason why you lost?" said Peter, not really sure he wanted to hear the answer.

"Hmmm.........lots. The coach and I have very differing opinions on that, let's just say."

"That explains the rather frantic debate I saw you having a little while ago, you know, with all the arm waving. I thought you were gonna take off at one point," said Peter, trying to lighten the tone.

"Very good," said Tank sarcastically. "I don't think it was quite that bad. Anyway, how would you feel if your hockey team was going tits up and you knew how to put some of the bad things right, but the important people refused to listen to what you had to say? Wouldn't be so funny then, would it?"

Peter could see his friend in real distress over this. "It means so much to him, just like the hockey means so much to me," he thought, looking at his friend finishing his drink.

"I'm sorry. I understand how much it means, I really do. Perhaps you need to change the way you approach the problem. You've done all the coaching courses and you coach the youngsters on a Sunday. Is there nothing there that you can use to help you?"

Tank thought about that for a few seconds as he let the last mouthful of beer slip from the pint glass and glide down the length of his throat.

"Well maybe I could..................yeah that might just work."

Peter looked at him blankly.

"I could simplify some of the tactics and get the kids to use them on a Sunday. The result should be the same, maybe not as dynamic and full on but just maybe those narrow minded idiots might just get the idea .... uh.............not the kids you understand Peter, the coaches."

Peter nodded and smiled.

"Yes I know what you mean. Anyway, on an entirely different sporting matter...............your message said something about watching the game even though you couldn't get any tickets. What's that all about?"

This got Tank's full attention.

"Well I've been working on a little something in my spare time. Something that should allow us to........." Tank looked around to make sure there was no one within ear shot, and leant in close to Peter. "Should allow us to watch the game through a television."

Peter was gobsmacked.

"Through a television? Are you mad? How the hell do you think you can do that?"

Tank put his arm around his friend to calm him down and try to limit the attention he seemed to be attracting with his little outburst.

"Well, it's not as hard as perhaps you would think, Peter. Would you like me to explain the details to you?"

Peter thought for a moment, slightly unsure, because Tank had that 'be careful what you wish for' look in his eyes. After a moment, still unsure, Peter decided he did want to know a little more about it.

"Go on then."

"Well you know how you access the ... papers?"

"Yes," said Peter carefully, fully understanding Tank's meaning.

"Well it's kind of like that. You see, what happens is that the game is transmitted out to the papers and then the papers select the images from the game that they require to go with their stories for the next day. The whole game remains in a giant buffer for a few more days, until it is no longer needed and then it is purged because it takes up an incredible amount of space. The reason they don't transmit the whole game out to every dragon who wants it is that most dragons wouldn't be able to cope with that level of information coming in to them and sort it out in the right way. Also there aren't the facilities to broadcast something of that magnitude to everyone. It's broadcast to the papers and that's it. I've developed a crystal node that can access the information from the node at the paper's headquarters via the local node and then display it in digital form hopefully on a television."

"Hopefully?"

"Well.........it's not fully functional just yet. But it will be by the time of the big match. I just need to buy a new television to test it on, that's all."

"What happened to that nice big fifty inch flat screen that you had?"

"I .....um ....hooked up the crystal to it and...........um didn't regulate the power properly and it............um.........kind of...........exploded.......
um a bit anyway."

"IT EXPLODED??!!!!!!!" said Peter. "How can it explode a bit?"

"It exploded a bit," said Tank, putting his arm around Peter, "because there was some of the screen left intact, alright," said Tank, wishing that he hadn't gone into detail with his friend.

"Right," said Peter nodding his head.

"I don't suppose…….." Tank started to say.

"NO," said Peter firmly.

"It's just that it would speed things up while I wait for a new television to be delivered."

"I like my television just how it is, thanks," said Peter, finishing the last of his diet Pepsi.

All of a sudden there was a loud 'BOO' from behind them. Peter's glass jumped from his hand, as if it had a mind of its own and twirled in the air. Time seemed to slow down, with the glass spinning violently as it headed swiftly towards the floor………………..before being expertly caught by…………. Richie, once again.

"Crikey, you guys are jumpy," said Richie, offering the glass back to Peter.

Peter gave Richie one of his best 'I'm more grown up than you' looks, took the glass from her and returned it to the bar.

"So, what's going on guys?" said Richie with a huge grin on her face.

"I was just explaining to Peter how we might all watch the Indigo Warriors in the Global Cup together," said Tank quietly.

"You've got tickets…….fantastic!" said Richie, breaking into a little dance.

"Not exactly," said Tank, trying to curb Richie's rather premature celebrations.

"Oh…..how are we going to watch it then?"

"On a television," said Peter, rolling his eyes. "It's something Tank's been………… working on."

"For a second there I thought we might actually get to see the game," Richie said to Peter, knowing all about Tank's 'little projects'.

"Hey, that's not fair. I know I've had a bit of bad luck in the past, but this has a real chance of working. I just need Peter to let me use his television to test the thing on. Please Peter, I know I can get this to work…………. honest. And once I do, we can all watch the match together, doesn't that sound great?"

Peter had to admit to himself that the thought of watching the match together, the three of them, did sound great, but Tank's track record on succeeding in these little projects was practically zero. Still, he did find it very hard to turn down his friend, particularly when he thought about all that Tank had done for him in the past.

"Okaaayyy........what do you need?" asked Peter reluctantly.

Tank lurched forward and gave his friend a big hug.

"You won't regret it, I promise."

Peter looked over Tank's shoulder at Richie and rolled his eyes again.

"I just need to come round and use your television a couple of times between now and the game, that's all," said Tank innocently. "That's all. Nothing will go wrong........honest."

"Sure Tank, whatever you say. Come round whenever you like and use the television," said Peter.

And that was that. The friends chatted for a few more minutes, catching up on their respective sports and training routines. Just as Peter thought it was time for him to think about leaving, the main doors to the bar opened and the first team hockey players started to file in.

"Oh crap," thought Peter. He had hoped to leave before Manson had finished training, to avoid bumping into him. Richie caught Peter looking nervously at the entrance just as Manson came in.

"It's alright Peter, he's just here playing hockey. Just ignore him," said Richie confidently.

"So that's the slimy rat I've been hearing about," said Tank. "I was just about to leave anyway Peter. Why don't we all go out together?" Tank gestured at Richie.

"Good idea," agreed Richie.

The three friends made their way through the very quiet bar area. Other than themselves, there were no more than twenty people remaining, a dozen or so of whom were the men's first hockey team who had just come in from the Astroturf. Peter strode down the length of the bar, flanked by Tank and Richie. He kept his eyes looking down at the floor, not wanting to make eye contact with Manson and hoping that he could leave without being noticed. No such luck. About six feet from the end of the massive bar, just as Peter thought he had made it out without being spotted, a body moved out in front of the three of them.

"Ahhh ………if it isn't my little underling. I didn't realise you had any friends."

Peter looked up into Manson's smug round face and noticed for the first time that his eyes were nearly totally black. He fought down the urge to lose his temper, knowing that whatever happened his friends would back him up, but realising that if something happened here, Manson would no doubt exact some sort of retribution back at Cropptech. So in a split second, Peter decided that he would take a leaf out of Richie's book and be diplomatic and polite.

"Good evening Mr Manson. Did you have a good training session?" said Peter, with just the tiniest hint of sarcasm.

"Yes I certainly did. It was very physical and tactically demanding. I would explain it but someone from the lower echelons of hockey like you would be hard pushed to understand it," said Manson, trying to provoke Peter.

With every atom in his body wanting to jump up and spank Manson, Peter used all his self control and just smiled.

"See you back at work," he said, stepping around Manson and heading swiftly towards the door. With his friends at his side, Peter had got no further than five paces before he heard Manson's voice.

"Good work with the maintenance of the security cameras. Find anything useful?"

Peter turned around to see Manson, hands on hips, smug as ever. As Peter looked deep into Manson's eyes from six feet away, everything suddenly became crystal clear to Peter. Manson knew that Peter was trying unsuccessfully to track him by using the cameras. He also knew that this moment had changed the entire situation. The moment seemed to Peter to last forever. Manson wasn't just a plain criminal of some sort trying to make material gain or exact revenge for some wrongdoing. He was far more than that. Far more than a human being, Peter suspected, even though there were no obvious signs, not even to a dragon.

Peter broke eye contact, turned slowly, and made his way out of the main entrance with Richie and Tank hot on his heels. The slightly chilly air rushed over him, cooling down his overly warm body and bringing his temper back in line at the same time. Tank and Richie walked next to him in silence as he made his way across the near deserted car park to his car, even though their cars were in a totally different place to his.

As they all reached his car, Peter turned and faced his friends.

"Well?" he demanded, expecting them to have had the same kind of epiphany about Manson that he had just had.

"Well what?" asked Richie.

"Well, did you not see what just happened?" snapped Peter sharply.

"Yes, the nasty man tried to get a rise out of you," replied Richie sarcastically.

Peter's temperature rocketed, so much so that steam was literally coming off him in waves in the chilly evening air.

"The whole thing, Rich, not just him provoking me."

"Yes I can see now that he's a bit of a git, something I hadn't seen before, but that's all. Get over it," said Richie turning her back and marching across to her car.

Peter took a step forward to follow her and continue the argument but a huge arm came out to block him.

"I don't think that's very wise, do you?" said Tank quietly.

Peter took a deep breath and ran his hands through his hair.

"Did you notice anything?" Peter said to Tank, not really wanting to hear the response. Tank pondered the question for what seemed like and age to Peter.

"As Richie said, he is certainly a first class git."

Peter's head dropped, knowing that his friend was once again going to side with Richie.

Tank continued.

"I tried using all of my dragon senses on him as he stood there, but I sensed......... nothing. Just a plain old human being, albeit a git, but a human git."

"There it is," thought Peter. "Again he's sided with Richie. Why can't they see what's happening?"

"Despite sensing nothing other than human, there was something else," Tank said, screwing up his face in concentration. "A feeling of ....oh it's so difficult to explain. Like the whitest cold it's possible to have. Pure, calculated.............. malevolence. I don't really understand what it is or where it came from. It didn't really seem to come from him, but it was just...........out there."

Peter knew exactly what Tank was talking about, but was surprised to hear that he hadn't felt it radiating off Manson like he had. It was however, Peter thought, 'a start'.

Tank and Peter said goodbye, with Tank adding that he would be in touch about coming round to use the television. While they were doing this, Richie's car had sped out of the car park like something out of a Formula One race.

12

A Member of the Magic Circle?

The rest of September seemed to positively fly by from Peter's perspective. With the start of the hockey season he was happier than ever, despite the obvious ongoing tensions at work with Manson and the fact that Richie hadn't spoken to him since their argument after the first night's hockey training. She had been avoiding him at work ever since.

The hockey though, was great. Peter had been to two more training sessions and played in two more games. The games were just friendlies at the moment, with the league games commencing in two Saturdays' time. The second team had won all of their friendly games so far, the last by eight goals to nil. The players in the squad were playing much better than last season and the three new additions had only strengthened things further. At this rate, Peter thought, they weren't far off the standard of the first team.

Another reason for the month going so fast was that Peter had spent his evenings at home sitting in front of the computer trying to develop the spyware program that he hoped to load at Cropptech, with the aim of detecting what Manson was up to. Peter knew, of course, that even if he managed to perfect his program and get it uploaded onto the Cropptech mainframe, there was still no guarantee that anything would come of it.

Tonight was going to be another night in front of the computer for Peter. He hoped to test his program for the first time, with a view to uploading it sometime within the next week. Having just finished his tea, Peter headed for the living room, plopping down in his great big black swivel chair in front of the computer monitor. As he did so, the doorbell rang. Peter exhaled sharply before getting up to answer the door. "Let me guess," Peter thought, "someone who wants me to change energy supplier no doubt, because there have only been three of those already this month."

As Peter wandered into the hallway, he could see the silhouette of someone tall through the semicircle of triangular windows at the top of the wooden door. Peter psyched himself up to be brutally rude to whatever sort of salesman it was, knowing full well that he was normally a bit of a soft touch for this sort of thing. He put on a steely face and opened the door sharply to find..............Tank grinning inanely at him.

"Wotcha guv'nor, I've come to fix your telly," Tank said in a comedy voice, as he squeezed by into the narrow hallway carrying a huge tool case.

"Come in, why don't you," said Peter to Tank's wide back, which was quickly vanishing up the hallway.

Tank made his way into the living room and proceeded to open his tool case on the floor and pull the television out from the wall so that he could get to the back of it. Peter stood over him, trying to get some idea of exactly what he would be doing.

"So......heard from Richie at all?" Tank enquired, while using his magnetic screwdriver to take some black screws from the back cover of the television.

"Nope.......you?"

"Well I tried ringing her mobile, but there was no answer and it didn't even go to the answer phone so that I could leave a message," said Tank, sliding a long thin flat-bladed screwdriver behind the back panel, trying to lever it out.

Peter stood over Tank, wincing and waiting for the television to explode into a million pieces. He could see the huge muscles in Tank's arms straining at the effort he was putting in to trying to lever out the panel, and with the television looking so.......... delicate, he just knew that a busted set was the only possible outcome.

Suddenly there was a tiny little 'pop' and the panel came away from one side in Tank's enormous hands. Tank repeated the feat on the other side of the panel, and much to Peter's amazement it came away in one piece, exposing the inner workings of the television. As Tank propped the panel against the wall, out of the way, he turned to look at Peter.

"Surprised?"

"Not at all," said Peter. "Just curious, that's all."

"You're such a terrible liar Peter. I could see your reflection in the blade of my screwdriver; you were just waiting for something awful to happen."

"Yes, yes I know, I'll leave you alone to get on. Can I get you a drink or anything?"

"No I'm fine thanks," said Tank, once again buried in the back of the television.

Peter moved across the room to his computer and slumped into his chair, hoping to successfully test the program he had developed. The two friends worked in silence, with Peter occasionally glancing across the room to see how his friend was getting on.

As the evening wore on, Peter became more and more frustrated. The program just wouldn't do what it was supposed to do, and however much he altered it, he still couldn't make it work. Tank on the other hand seemed to be getting on a lot better, much to Peter's surprise. Well I say a lot better, the television was in a thousand different parts, but............they all seemed to be laid out on the living room floor in a clear and logical manner and they all seemed to be ....undamaged. Seemingly satisfied with his progress, Tank got up from the floor and made his way to the hallway and out to his car. Intent on getting the computer program to work, Peter didn't even notice his friend was missing. When Tank came back in, a few minutes later, Peter was swearing and cursing like a Premiership footballer, most unusual for him.

"What's the matter bud?" enquired Tank.

Peter explained to his friend what he was trying to do and why, also adding the fact that he couldn't make the program work, despite his best efforts. Tank told him he would have a look at it when he had finished his work on the television, and that perhaps he should take a break for a while. Peter did what his friend had suggested and took a seat on the sofa, secretly relieved that Tank was going to take a look, knowing full well that Tank was way better with computers than he would ever be.

As Peter sat watching his friend's progress from the sofa, Tank unwrapped a large object from a very flowery old towel that he had retrieved from his car. As Tank removed more of the towel, the shape of a pyramid became more apparent. Peter sat transfixed as his friend removed the final part of the covering. From out of the old towel, Tank pulled a very bright and shiny translucent crystal pyramid, with a cable running out of the centre of it.

Tank held up the crystal for Peter to see and said,

"This, my friend, is the clever bit."

"What does it do?"

"This is what allows us to pick up the feed and also converts it into a digital format so that the television can display it......hopefully."

Tank sat the crystal on its base and ran the cable carefully up to the back of the television. Carefully he plugged the cable in and started to put some of the components back in their correct places. Peter could see that his friend was concentrating very hard, so remained completely silent and out of the way on the sofa. After about fifteen minutes Tank let out a visible sigh of relief and looked over towards Peter.

"Want to give it a try?" said Tank with a manic grin on his face.

"What can we expect to see?" asked Peter nervously.

"Dunno. Depends what's in the buffer at the other end. Whatever it is, it will be in tomorrow's newspapers, that's for sure."

Sceptical as he was, Peter knew that he had no chance of getting out of what was to come, so he put on a little smile for his friend and said,

"Sure, let's do it."

Tank plugged in the mains lead of the television and switched the set on. The pyramid seemed to glow slightly from within, a sign, Peter was sure, that indicated something bad was about to happen. Tank held the remote control and started the manual tuning sequence for the television. As the static-filled screen scrolled through the different settings, Peter noticed the look of absolute confidence on Tank's face. Just then the static started to form itself into a black and white picture. It took the two friends a few seconds to make out what exactly it was they were looking at, as Tank fine-tuned the picture with the buttons on the remote control. The two friends were looking at a mass of sand dunes in a desert by the look of things. That's all they could see..........sand everywhere.

"Nice picture. Not very exciting though," said Peter.

"Give it a minute," said Tank, squinting hard at the picture.

The two friends studied the vivid picture on the screen. Peter was impressed that his friend had managed to get the television to work with the crystal, but couldn't understand for the life of him why they were staring at sand dunes in a desert. As this thought crossed Peter's mind, a small dark shape could be seen far away in the distance, just above the dunes. At first, Peter thought it was a bird swooping down low, but the more they watched, the more it became apparent that it wasn't. Whatever the shape was, it was clear it was moving at quite a speed, and was quite a way off. So much so, that its down-draught was producing an amazing spray of sand beneath it. And that was the giveaway.

"SANDSKIMMING!" the friends cried in unison.

"That must be the new course in the Sahara," said Tank in awe.

"I didn't think it was supposed to be ready for at least another six months," said Peter.

"Cool though eh?" said Tank.

"Oh God, yes."

Sandskimming was another dragon thing. Not so much a sport as a relaxing pastime. The idea was to fly low to the ground, doing a timed lap. The lap or circuit would be created by the first dragon, due to them flying so low the down-force would produce a pattern in the sand, a pattern that looked very much like a road or route. The next dragons to do their timed laps would have to follow this pattern in the sand. The winner would be the dragon whose timed lap was the fastest. Sand was the ideal surface for this game to be played over.

Sandskimming had started off as a younglings game but had managed to capture the imagination of older dragons everywhere and, although not as popular as laminium ball (what was?), every dragon knew about sandskimming and most had tried it out at some point in their life.

It had started when dragons in the nursery ring had on occasion been taken on field trips to different parts of the world and whenever they went somewhere exotic and out of the way, usually a desert, young dragons would take to playing this game. However, the last fifty years or so have seen the development of dragon holiday camps and it is there that sandskimming has really taken off as a form of relaxation.

Dragon holiday camps first came about in 1956 as the brainchild of a dragon called Firesworn. Firesworn was a respected scientist who had been working on supplementing the worldwide dragon monorail with solar power. He was very committed to his study of solar power and once his work underground had exhausted all its theoretical possibilities, he then had to find an area on the surface to continue his experiments. His exploration and development of solar power took him to the Kalahari Desert in Southern Africa. He was based there primarily because of its remoteness and the fact that contact with any humans was unlikely, which meant that he could put all of his equipment out in the open as well as maintain his dragon form without fear of discovery.

Firesworn found that he really loved being in his dragon form above the surface, soaking up the rays of the sun and flying around the hot arid desert, in between working on his solar power project.

Now most dragons in Firesworn's position would occasionally return underground to visit their family and friends. But Firesworn got so caught up in his work and living on the surface in his dragon form that the last thing he wanted to do was to go back underground. So instead he got his family to come and visit him on the surface. Once there, they too were captivated by the desert and the sheer exhilaration of spending all of their time in dragon form. Once it was time for Firesworn's family to return, they did so grudgingly and once back underground they told all their friends and neighbours about the experience.

Soon Firesworn was inundated with dragons wanting to visit him or help him with his project. At about this time Firesworn's passion seemed to be less concerned with solar power and more with developing a place where dragons could rest and relax on the surface, while still maintaining their privacy and keeping any knowledge of their existence a secret. After nearly two years of work and an incredible amount of help from his family and friends, Firesworn came up with the answer......... the first dragon holiday camp.

The camp was based in the same place he had been conducting his research, the Kalahari Desert. An area of around five hundred square miles was set aside for the camp when it was first fashioned. That sounds a lot, but when you consider the Kalahari covers an area in excess of one hundred thousand square miles, it was really only a grain in a sandcastle. The camp itself was, at that time, rather basic. The only feature of any real note was a large oasis situated almost exactly in the middle of the camp. Firesworn and his team extended the oasis, from a very small and rather badly formed watering hole, into a superheated swimming pool for dragons that was over five square miles in size.

To ensure that the visiting dragons weren't accidentally discovered, lookout dragons were placed along the perimeter at ten mile intervals. The lookouts' tasks were simple: to use their telepathic powers to persuade animals, and in particular humans, to change their course if they looked at all like they might be heading in the direction of the dragon holiday camp, an easy feat really for a dragon with enhanced telepathic abilities.

However, at first this wasn't as easy as it should have been. While animals were relatively easy to dissuade, some of the human tribes of the area were rather harder to convince. The lookouts soon found the easiest way of convincing the humans was to show the area of the camp as rather treacherous terrain while at the same time offering up mirages of watering holes or oases in other directions away from the camp. This combination seemed to be a huge success and still plays its part in some of the modern day dragon vacation camps that exist in remote areas across the globe.

Before long, Firesworn didn't know what had hit him. Dragons were coming from all over the planet to sample the delight of simply relaxing in the sun on the surface in their dragon forms. With popularity going through the roof, the camp was increased in size, provided with underground access and an easy link to the developing monorail and better facilities, such as restaurants, sleeping areas and entertainment areas. More lookouts were provided as the camp expanded and special designated lookouts had the task of making sure the camp wasn't spotted from the air from any stray aircraft that might be passing.

Firesworn's solar power project had been totally replaced by his obsession for creating the ultimate in dragon relaxation and he had more than achieved that. Over the coming years that original camp expanded even more and became the blueprint for many more camps to come. Today major dragon vacation/recreational camps can be found all around the globe in such places as The Great Basin in North America, The Namib in Southern Africa, The Gobi Desert in China, and the Gibson Desert and Great Victoria Desert, both in Australia.

The very latest undertaking, and the one Peter and Tank were viewing through their television at that very moment, is very special indeed. This camp had been over ten years in the making, quite a feat in a dragon timescale. It dwarfs anything else like it on the planet. It sits proudly in the middle of the Sahara Desert about one hundred and fifty miles south of Adrar in Algeria. The camp itself is just north of the Tropic of Cancer and just west of the Prime Meridian. Its location had been subject to much planning and apart from the fact that it needed to be remote and in a suitable climate, its current location had the added bonus that it was on the main southern monorail route out of London which follows the Prime Meridian all the way to Accra, and then splits into two, with one heading Southwest to Rio and the other heading Southeast towards South Africa.

The camp itself covers an area of nearly a thousand square miles, which sounds a lot again, but is merely a needle in a haystack when it comes to the size of the Sahara itself. Every conceivable dragon luxury has been catered for, from lava pools with giant flumes, to a la carte charcoal dining, to death defying sandskimming courses. Everything under one roof so to speak, or not as the case may be.

The lookouts have spent years being trained to make sure they are the best that they can be at their jobs to try and do everything to minimise the risk of discovery by the outside world. Everything that can be done has been done to make it as hard as possible to be discovered. The only eventuality that the dragons in charge seem to think presents any sort of risk is the scenario of a passenger plane crashing down and landing smack bang in the middle of the camp with lots of survivors, and that, they say, is so unbelievably unlikely that the odds can't even begin to be calculated.

So with that in mind the camp is nearly ready to be opened and announced to the dragon population. The images that Tank and Peter could see are the few privileged members of the dragon media trying out the facilities so that they can then tell the world, well some of it anyway, about the most amazing getaway resort ever.

Tank and Peter sat in the living room for another twenty minutes watching the television as the images changed from different dragons flying over the sandskimming course to views of the giant lava pools, to watching charcoal being prepared in various new and exotic ways (which made both of the young friends' stomachs rumble repeatedly) for the consumption of the expected guests.

"Well we know it works," said Tank, beaming.

"I never doubted you."

"Yeah...........right," said Tank, punching Peter in the arm playfully.

"Well........maybe just a little," said Peter, rolling away and standing up.

"Anyway, doesn't matter. We can watch the match.............. Yipppeeeeeeeeeee! Now all you have to do is tell Richie," said Tank awkwardly.

"Oh good," sighed Peter.

"I'll do it if you want?" offered Tank.

"No it's all right, it should be me. I'll do it tomorrow at work."

"Want me to look at that program on the computer for you?" said Tank as he began putting the television back to its former state.

"That would be great if you've got time."

"Sure...........no problem."

Two hours later, having fixed Peter's computer program, Tank and his huge tool case made their way back through the front door and into his car. Peter walked down the garden path in the crisp night air to see his friend off.

"Thanks for fixing the program," Peter said, his breath freezing as it came out of his mouth.

"No problem mate," said Tank, switching the car's so-called heating system on to full blast to clear the windscreen of all the condensation that was on it. "Don't forget, talk to Richie tomorrow.......tell her the good news about the game."

"Will do. Safe journey back."

And with that, Tank pulled away from Peter's house, hunched down in the front seat, due to only being able to see past the condensation through a hole the size of a pea that had cleared on the windscreen. Peter smiled as he made his way up the garden path, weaving his way in and out of the snails which were in such great numbers that they could start a military engagement by the look of things.

The next day at work, Peter found himself scanning the bank of security monitors in his office once again, only this time not for the ever elusive Manson, but for his friend Richie. "What did I do with my time before I became hooked on these?" Peter thought to himself, looking across the rows of monitors.

Richie proved as elusive as Manson, at least until lunchtime when Peter spotted her heading for the canteen. Having waited for this chance all morning, Peter grabbed his coat and broke into a sprint, knowing full well that if he got a move on he could time his entrance to the canteen to match that of Richie's. As he rounded the last corner, he slowed to a walk and was rewarded with the sight of his friend right in front of him as he got to the canteen's double entrance doors.

"Hi," said Peter, holding one of the doors open for Richie.

Richie stood hands on hips, refusing to go through the door that Peter was so gallantly holding open.

"Taken up running have we?" said Richie, so that everybody in the now developing queue to go into the canteen, could hear.

Peter could feel himself start to blush. Clearly Richie had no intention of forgiving him. "DAMN! This is going to go badly," he thought to himself.

Suddenly Richie grabbed him by his tie and yanked him through the double doors, much to the amusement of the gathering queue.

"Could you be any easier?"

"Probably not......no," said Peter, not quite sure what was going on.

The two friends joined the queue for lunch and it soon became obvious to Peter that he had in fact been forgiven.

"How did you know I'd run all the way?"

Richie sighed and shook her head. Leaning forward so no one could overhear, she whispered,

"You may be a prim and proper dragon, only using your senses when told you're allowed to, but me.........not so much. Heightened heart rate, perspiring badly and most obvious............your tie was flying back over your shoulder," she said, smiling.

"You're way too clever for me."

"I know," said Richie, nodding her head.

The two friends went on to have an enjoyable lunch, with Richie telling Peter about all the gossip from her department and Peter telling Richie about Tank and the television and the fact that they could all watch the big game together. For once Richie seemed genuinely surprised, something Peter could barely remember happening before. As the pair cleared their plates away after finishing lunch, they agreed that they would meet in the bar at the sports club on Saturday after their respective lacrosse and hockey matches before going back to Peter's house to watch the Global Cup on the rigged up television. Peter went back to work a happy man or dragon, depending on how you looked at things.

Peter's good mood continued throughout the week, particularly at the prospect of a fantastic Saturday to come, which he hoped would include a home hockey win in the last friendly before the league games started, followed by a rousing night in watching the Indigo Warriors with Tank and Richie.

Hockey training on Tuesday night was fantastic and the whole of the second team squad was there, for the first time ever. Peter knew this season's league campaign could be their best yet, with promotion there for the taking. With just one more friendly game to go, this Saturday, he just knew they couldn't fail to get off to a cracking start.

Saturday morning was normally quite a relaxing time for Peter. Generally he fell out of bed quite late, had a bite to eat and then went and played hockey. Not this Saturday. He was awake at just gone six o'clock and that almost never happened. After half an hour of trying to go back to sleep without any success at all, he gave up and decided to get up. After brushing his teeth and having some breakfast he came to the conclusion that, like a little child at Christmas, he was too excited to sleep. "What a sad fool," he thought to himself.

Peter wasn't due to leave the house to drive to hockey until three o'clock, with the game itself starting at four. Even though he attempted to keep himself busy, the time really dragged. By midday Peter was going up the wall. All he could think about was hockey, hockey, hockey. How he would play, how the team would perform, who would be playing for the opposition, would they have a strong team out or a relatively weak one?

Eventually two fifty arrived and Peter, not being able to wait any longer, picked up his kit and sticks from the hallway, which had been packed and ready since eight thirty that morning, and headed out to his car. He drove to the sports club and upon his arrival in the car park was greeted by Andy the second team captain.

"Hi Pete," said Andy. "Looking forward to the game?"

"Sure am," replied Peter, trying desperately not to sound like an excited little kid.

"There's been a bit of a change of plan I'm afraid," said Andy, rummaging through his kit bag.

"Oh?" said Peter inquisitively.

Andy kept on rummaging as he talked.

"The opposition cried off late last night. Half the team have flu or some sort of virus. Anyway all is not lost. The same thing seems to have happened to their first team as well and they were due to play our first team, so we're going to be playing against our first team, which as it happens is not a bad warm up for our first league game next Saturday," Andy said, grinning.

Peter was crestfallen. "Oh my God," he thought. "I'm going to have to play against Manson."

"You okay?"

"Ahh……….. yeah……….. fine."

"You just look all………………….pale that's all," said Andy, having found what he was looking for in his kit bag.

"No……..no…….. I'm fine."

"Okay, I'll see you in the changing room in a while," said Andy, heading off towards the entrance to the club house.

Peter leant on his car and put his head in his hands. It felt like his world had ended. Of all the things to happen. "I'd rather face a team of drunken, diseased, ravaging Vikings on a hockey pitch than Manson," he thought. Peter took some deep breaths to calm down and brought his head out from under his hands, just in time to see Manson's black Mercedes pull into the car park. One word and one word only popped into Peter's head…………PANTS! Manson got out of his car and headed towards the changing rooms with some of his team mates, who had gathered in the car park. Halfway across the car park, Manson gave a sly glance across his shoulder at Peter and made a mock salute. What was supposed to be an absolutely brilliant afternoon had started in the worst possible way. Peter knew he had to focus on what a good evening he was going to have and not to worry about the hockey match too much. "Easier said than done," he thought.

Peter made his way towards the changing rooms to join his team mates after taking as long as he could to retrieve his kit from the car. About halfway across the car park he changed his mind and instead headed into the bar. He just couldn't face going to get ready just at the moment. Hearing that he would be facing Manson on a hockey pitch this afternoon had really knocked him for six. The bar itself was relatively empty, with only a few players from earlier hockey matches on the Astroturf gathered around tables at the far end. He walked the length of the deserted bar, and on reaching the end, plonked his kit and stick bag down on the well worn carpet. Looking out through the spacious windows he could see that both the rugby and lacrosse matches were in full flow. Squinting a little because of the bright sun streaming in his direction, Peter could just make out his friends competing in their separate matches. Richie was screaming down the wing at full pelt, holding her stick high above her, in possession of the ball, heading for the opposition's goal. Tank on the other hand had just that second been buried beneath half a dozen huge rugby players. Peter watched, just a little concerned, as the play continued. His worries turned out to be misplaced as only a few seconds later his giant friend stood up, covered from head to toe in mud, holding the ball aloft, players from both teams tumbling off him like rag dolls. Peter smiled. A light tap on his shoulder startled Peter out of his thoughts. He turned to see one of the bar staff smiling at him. He struggled to remember her name.

"It's Janice isn't it?" he asked.

"That's right," she replied in a very bubbly sort of way. Her beaming smile and enthusiasm brought a smile to Peter's face despite the fact that he felt thoroughly miserable. Not only that, but as he gazed across the bar at her he couldn't help but think how beautiful she was.

"Umm.... you couldn't do me a little favour could you?" she asked.

"Sure, what can I do?"

"I need some more cartons of orange juice from upstairs and I can't leave the bar unattended. I wondered if you could just nip up and grab a couple of boxes for me," she said, beaming her best grin.

"Of course," said Peter, captivated.

"The boxes are on the right, just inside the stock cupboard on the floor. The cupboard's open, they just need bringing down to the bar."

Peter flashed his best smile and said, "Back in two tweaks of a dragon's nose," as he headed towards the stairs at the end of the bar. Peter bounded up the stairs towards the upper floor. It wasn't just the stock cupboard that was located on the top floor. There was a private function room with its own small bar, a tiny balcony overlooking the sports pitches and the chairman of the sports club's private office which was only accessible through the function room. Peter reached the top of the stairs, and strolled purposefully along the corridor to the stock cupboard. He pushed gently on the door and it slowly swung open. Without switching the light on, Peter could see the boxes of orange cartons on the floor just where Janice had said they would be. Peter used one foot to prop open the door while he bent down to lift up the boxes. As he turned round to take the boxes down to the bar, he caught a glimpse of the function room, through the door opposite. The hairs on the back of Peter's neck stood to attention faster than Usain Bolt rushing for the last of the chicken nuggets. Peter could see the chairman of the sports club stood outside his office, having a heated conversation with... Manson. The chairman did not look at all happy. Peter slipped back into the dark stock cupboard and closed the door as much as he could, while still being able to see what was going on. Manson had his back to Peter, so it was only really the chairman's face that Peter had a view of. The heated discussion went on for another couple of minutes, with the chairman looking more and more disappointed.

Suddenly the chairman's face turned paler than a ghost. Manson had pulled something out of a bag on the floor. Peter couldn't see what it was, but it was heavy and the chairman clearly didn't want to take it from Manson. The chairman seemed scared, nervous, petrified. Even from as far away as Peter was he could see the sweat pouring down the man's neck and face. Manson leaned closer to the chairman and whispered something in his ear. The chairman stood stock still, barely able to move, just shaking his head from side to side. After thirty seconds of this, the chairman reached out and took the object from Manson. Taking it very carefully, almost as if it were going to explode, the chairman walked into his office, put down the parcel and then came out and locked up the office. The two men then turned towards the door and headed out of the function room, towards the corridor where the stock cupboard was. Peter gently closed the door right up and stood as still as he could. He heard the footsteps of the two men head off down the corridor towards the top of the stairs. Not being able to resist one last look, Peter opened the door up a little, just enough for him to see out. All he saw was the two of them going down the top flight of stairs, Manson clapping the chairman on the back, the chairman looking as though someone had just told him he had one day left to live. Leaving it for two minutes, Peter picked up the two boxes of orange juice cartons and headed back down to the bar. A beaming Janice was there to greet him.

"I was just about to send out a search party for you," she said with that gorgeous smile.

Peter smiled back as he plonked the boxes on top of the bar.

"The lock on the door jammed just as I was coming out. Don't worry I managed to fix it. It's fine now."

"Well thank you very much," said Janice as she started putting the cartons from the boxes on to the shelves behind the bar. "Perhaps I'll see you after you've finished your game," she said, all bubbly again.

Peter was lost for words as he realised that he really should be heading for the changing room. He gave Janice a quick wave and scooted out of the back entrance of the bar and straight into the changing rooms. His team were in the changing room adjacent to the first team and could hear all the banter and confidence through the very thin separating walls. Although the second team should have been on a high from all of their previous results, the changing room seemed to have an air of negativity about it. Peter was unusually quiet with good reason, but then he was never really the life and soul of the banter and chat that went on anyway, so that shouldn't have made a whole lot of difference. It was almost as if a spell had been cast on them.

The changing room took on the feeling of a morgue as the first team passed as a group on their way to the pitch, joking around and slapping each other playfully, full of spirit, the exact opposite of their opponents. Andy, the second team captain, gave his normal rousing team talk without it having the usual motivating success. It was almost as if the passion had been sucked out of the team. Reluctantly the Seconds headed for the Astroturf pitch to do battle with the First XI.

The current match on the Astroturf finished and both teams made their way on to complete warming up. The first team were wearing the club's normal home strip of orange tops and white shorts, while the second eleven, Peter included, all wore light, bright blue tops with dark blue shorts. As Peter knocked a ball back and forth with one of his team mates, he noticed from the distant cheers that the rugby and lacrosse matches being played were just finishing. His thoughts turned to his friends, hoping that they had enjoyed their afternoons much more than he expected he would, and hoping that it would suddenly be this evening, so he could be with his friends and watch the Indigo Warriors.

A match umpire blew his whistle to indicate that the game would start in one minute. The players from each team quickly finished stripping off their tracksuits and assumed their corresponding positions on the pitch. After having removed his tracksuit top, Peter trotted from the sideline to his position as sweeper, the last line of defence except the goal keeper. He turned and saw that Manson was playing in the centre forward role for the first team. That pretty much meant that he would be facing him all match. Taking a deep breath and tapping the soles of his shoes with his hockey stick, something of a ritual he had developed just as games were about to start, he focused his concentration on the game ahead.

With that, the two umpires checked both goalkeepers were ready and then blew their whistles to start the match. The second team had push back and managed to retain possession for seven or eight passes before being hounded off the ball by the first team. When the first team had possession they surged forward with unbelievable pace. The accuracy of their passes wasn't bad either, Peter thought to himself as one of the first team midfielders slipped a ball through their opponents' defence for their forwards to run on to.

In the blink of an eye Peter found himself faced with two opponents running at him at full pace, the one without the ball being Manson, with only the goalkeeper behind him. Instinct took over as he approached the player with the ball. Manson was running on Peter's left as he closed in on the player, so with a deep breath, Peter offered his stick out to the right and then...... at the very last split second, flipped it over and laid it down flat, reverse stick on the Astroturf.

Much to Peter's relief, the player had taken the bait and had tried to pass it around Peter to the onrushing Manson, only to find Peter's interception timed to perfection. With the ball on the end of his stick, Peter pulled it round to his open side and passed it wide to his right back, who had, along with the rest of the defence, been 'busting a gut' to get back to help out after the defence-splitting pass had exploited their weakness. The Seconds went back on the offensive, and as they did, Peter looked round to see if any immediate threat presented itself, knowing full well that it was his responsibility to rally his defenders and make sure they pick up their assigned players, preferably goal side.

As he did this, he noticed Manson growling some very harsh words at his team mate from the previous attack, the one whose pass Peter had intercepted. Peter turned away from the two players, with a slight smirk on his face, hoping that the first team's team negative spirit remained that way throughout the game, as that just might give the second team some sort of chance of getting a result.

The game proceeded at a lightning pace, with both teams winning short corners and having very good scoring chances but for last gasp interventions from brave defenders. The closer it got to half time, the more dominant the first team became, with their superior fitness showing. However, Peter's thought about team spirit seemed to echo more and more as the game wore on. With each new onslaught that the first team created, that more often than not ended with a missed chance to take the lead, frustration seemed to boil off the players and take the form of some sort of verbal backlash towards a team mate, with Manson being the main culprit. It seemed every three or four minutes he was berating one of his own players for a sloppy pass or just general bad play. With the second team being run ragged, the umpires finally put them out of their misery and blew for half time and a much needed break, with the score remaining level at 0-0.

The second team players plodded over to their stick and kit bags to take on some welcome water before joining their captain in the goal mouth at the opposite end of the pitch to the one that they had been defending in the first half. As the players gathered round, Peter noted how exhausted they all looked. Each and every one had given nothing short of one hundred per cent, and although tired, most had a smile on their face.

As Peter stood with the other players and watched, Andy the captain gave one of his highly motivating and successful speeches, the gist of which was that they were playing out of their skins and that the first team should be beating them by a rugby score really, bearing in mind the different leagues that the two teams played in.

With everyone suitably pumped up, Andy asked if anyone else had anything to add to his rapturous speech. This happened every week and normally one or two of the more experienced players might add something that they had noticed on a tactical level, or mention some potential weakness that they thought could be exploited. Peter had never had the courage or felt the need to speak up before now, what with him being incredibly shy and also relatively inexperienced compared with the others. He had after all only been playing hockey for just over a season. But something about the game today had just ……… got under his skin, or scales if you like. Peter raised his hand nervously and felt his temperature rising as the whole team gazed in his direction.

"Peter, this is a surprise. It's not often we hear from you……..go ahead," said Andy.

With all eyes watching him, Peter suddenly wished he'd kept his mouth shut. Forcing a smile to his face and trying desperately to ignore the fact that his stomach was doing somersaults he forged on.

"Well I …..ah……….um………totally agree with everything you've said," he stuttered. "The ……..um……..um one thing I would add is that……… well………that I think we can use their lack of team spirit against them."

A few of the team members nodded their heads in agreement.

"The longer it stays 0-0, the more volatile they'll become. Anything we can do to enhance that, we should," added Peter, more confidently. "Laugh at them, mock them, ignore them - anything that gets them riled will only benefit us and, I believe, give us enough of an advantage to win the game."

"Who knew we had our own sports psychologist in the team?" said Andy.

Peter could feel his temperature rising rapidly, making his face start to turn a rather dark shade of crimson.

The umpires blew their whistles to signal the teams to get underway. Before the players turned to walk back to the positions, Andy said,

"You heard the man," pointing to Peter. "Do as he says, make them lose their tempers and we can celebrate a stunning victory in the bar afterwards."

Andy waved them towards the pitch, and the team duly obliged, taking up their normal positions. Peter felt like he'd never felt before. It couldn't be the adrenaline, as he was a dragon and although his DNA had been manipulated to nearly the same atomic level as that of a normal human, he had none, but the feeling was………hmmmm, so hard to describe. It felt like opening up a promotional packet of anything and winning a huge expensive prize. It felt like…….opening a door and finding limitless amounts of all of your favourite foods and some new ones as well.

Peter was suddenly jolted out of his foody thoughts by the umpire's whistle starting the game. As he took in his surroundings, looking to make sure the other defenders were picking up their players, he spotted Tank and Richie wandering into the watching area beside the pitch, both with plastic pint glasses full of beer, which they raised when they'd seen he had spotted them.

As the game progressed it didn't take long for Peter to realise that the whole nature of the game had changed quite dramatically. There was far more urgency in everything the first team players did. Their tackling, movement and passing was way better than it had been in the first half, not to mention that some of the tackles flying in were on the hospital side of dangerous. The stakes had definitely changed; clearly the first team had got a rollicking at half time from someone, and Peter thought he knew who.

Peter and his team found themselves defending for their lives for the first ten minutes of the second half, barely getting out of their own half and giving away numerous short corners. In Peter's mind it seemed only a matter of time before they would concede a goal and then the floodgates would probably open up. Even Peter's idea about exploiting their lack of team spirit seemed dead, as they were playing so well they didn't seem to have anything to argue about.

As the second team lost the ball once again in midfield, the first team forwards came hurtling towards Peter, for what seemed like the thousandth time in only a few minutes. Peter held his concentration and, very much as with the first tackle he had made in the match, he dummied to go one way and went the other way at the last second, again finding the ball on the end of his stick.

Momentarily relieved to have gained possession of the ball, Peter looked up to play a simple pass to one of his team mates. His first thought was that things looked pretty grim for him. Not only was there not an obvious simple pass to a team mate, but more worrying was the fact that three of the opposition were heading his way really quickly.

Ever since Peter had taken up playing hockey it had become quite apparent what type of player he was. He certainly wasn't an attacking player, that's for sure. His dribbling skills were erratic at best and he lacked the confidence to run at people and take them on, nearly always preferring to play the simple pass to get himself out of trouble. If anything could be said to be his best quality on a hockey pitch, then it would have to be his tackling which seemed to get better and better each time he played. It was as if he could tackle and stop a ball instinctively.

With this in mind, his current situation didn't bode at all well. Time had seemed to slow for Peter; even so, the only apparent options seemed to involve Peter dribbling around at least two opponents. Not a great idea, particularly at the top of his own 'D', he thought.

All this zipped through his mind in milliseconds. As Peter scanned the scene in front of him, his eyes suddenly caught the movement of one of his own players through the oncoming mass of orange shirted opponents. The only problem was that the team mate Peter could see was at least fifty yards away, with an opponent in the way, easily able to intercept his pass. Or was he, Peter suddenly wondered. The last couple of training sessions had involved practising flicking the ball. A difficult skill to master, being able to flick the ball and produce an aerial pass was very rare at this level of hockey but it was something that Peter hadn't done too badly at during training. His mind made up, Peter totally changed the shape of his body and angled his stick under the ball. With the opponents getting closer and closer, Peter knew it was now or never as the incoming players would be too close to make an aerial pass safely in just a few seconds. Watching the ball intently and twisting his wrist with all his might, he flicked the ball into the air. Fully expecting the ball to roll about two inches in front of him, Peter was stunned as it left his stick and safely travelled over the heads of the incoming opponents and continued on towards his team mate on the forward line. All of this took place in about three and a half seconds from the time that Peter picked up the ball.

Those few moments would be permanently engraved into Peter's memory, particularly the looks on the faces of the onrushing opponents as the ball sailed over their heads. As the ball landed from Peter's pass, his team mate picked it up on the run and after a great sequence of five passes in a row, the second team found themselves one nil up, much to the disappointment of their opponents.

Two or three of Peter's team mates congratulated him on the fabulous pass that set up the goal, while their opponents seemed to be having an inquisition as to who was responsible for letting the goal in. Peter wasn't quite sure how it would play out from here on in, and in fact it took only a few moments for him to get some idea, as a sloppy bit of play from the first team allowed the Seconds in on goal again, only for them to blast the shot wide. The first team's composure seemed shot to ribbons, with players openly arguing and blaming each other left, right and centre. For the first time since the match started, Peter actually started to believe that the second team could win.

With the breakdown of any sort of team spirit in the first team, the match had started to become much more even and the game seemed to be almost wholly played in the midfield area of the pitch. Peter found that he was constantly marshalling his defenders and thought at one point he might even be about to lose his voice. Every now and then he would look over to his friends, watching the game from the sideline. When he did, both his friends would give him terrific smiles and thumbs up signs, while at the same time carefully avoiding spilling their beer. As the midfield struggle continued, the intensity of the tackles increased and predictably ended up with the umpire cautioning two first team players and a second team player in the space of only a few minutes.

With the game becoming very scrappy now, Peter pushed further up the pitch to help his team mates in the midfield area, all the time wary of the space left behind him, as in hockey there is now no offside rule. The first team's defence seemed to be doing the same thing, making the middle of the pitch a frantic battlefield with foul after foul being committed by both sides. As Peter feared the umpires might start to get fed up with the constant series of fouls and send someone off with a yellow card, the second team skipper, Andy, intercepted a pass and went on a gung-ho run straight at the opposition's goal. Because all of the defenders had pushed up, Andy found himself in acres of space after beating two opponents and used a quick burst of speed to put himself through on goal. Once again time seemed to slow right down and Peter, even from his relatively far away position could see everything that happened. The goal keeper had started to come out from the goal to narrow the angle, while at the same time a defender had run his socks off to try and get round the keeper to the goal line to provide cover. By this time Andy had reached the top of the 'D' and upon crossing the line had let rip with a fearsome shot. The first team goalie (Greener) had a reputation as an excellent shot stopper, which on this occasion was well deserved, as he managed to get a heavily gloved fingertip to the ball, taking all the pace off it. The ball ended up right by the penalty spot, about half way between Andy and the defender on the line. Instinctively the pair of them raced for the ball with the grounded goalkeeper unable to make any difference to the outcome of the situation.

With both players racing towards the ball at full pelt, the rest of the players looked on in anticipation. Unfortunately two strides into his run, the defender slipped on the sandy Astroturf and skidded to his knees. Andy, the second team captain, raced onto the ball and slipped it past the flailing defender and into the back of the net. The second team had gone two nil up.

"Amazing," thought Peter, waving his stick in the air.

The whole team was jubilant about scoring a second goal, some celebrating victory already, something that Andy the captain tried to contain by motioning with his arms for everybody to calm down as he made his way back to the halfway line after scoring.

While this was happening at one end, a meltdown of epic proportions was taking place at the other. Pushing, shoving, finger pointing and all sorts of recriminations were going on amongst the members of the first team. It got so bad that the umpire had to blow his whistle and tell the first team captain to calm his players down before the restart could take place. One of Peter's team mates asked the nearest umpire how long until the end of the game.

"Eleven minutes," he replied.

"All we have to do is hold on for eleven minutes," Peter thought promisingly. "With the first team all bickering like babies, we might just be able to do it."

As the teams lined up against one another once again, Peter caught sight of Manson taking up his forward position, ready for the restart. As Peter watched his menacing adversary he noticed that Manson was doing something very strange with his hands. Shielding them with his body so that most people on or around the pitch couldn't see what he was doing, Manson was making small intricate patterns with them, patterns that seem to Peter to............ almost come alive. Peter found himself mesmerised by the complex patterns, that is until Manson looked up.......directly into his face. Peter froze in terror. The look on Manson's face was one of pure unadulterated hate. Peter felt his legs turn to lead, his arms to jelly. He was having trouble focusing and standing upright. Subconsciously he heard a noise, a sharp shrill noise. In his peripheral vision he could make out movement..........shapes getting bigger and bigger. It took a few seconds for Peter's brain to register what was happening...............the match had restarted and the opposition had started to attack again.

With this revelation the fogginess clouding his brain began to clear, albeit rather slowly. By the time Peter had any real idea of what was going on, attackers were on either side of him, just about to enter the 'D' and have a shot at goal. Peter waved his stick frantically in an unconvincing effort to intercept the ball as it flew past him from one attacker to the next. His pathetic effort had been in vain and, as he turned to give chase to the ball, he noted that most of his team mates seemed to be as confused and perplexed as he was, some in fact a lot worse off. Completing his turn he willed his heavy legs to move towards the attacker on the ball and although they did move, it felt to him like running through treacle. Nevertheless he continued, his mind concentrating on nothing other than ploughing on towards the ball, but was abruptly brought back down to earth by the sound of a sharp whistle and sounds of people cheering. Peter blinked and looked around. The first team had scored, straight from the restart!!! Not only that, but most of the second team were swaying about in a daze. It didn't look as though anyone from the Seconds had even tried to stop them.

Richie was just taking the last swig of her beer on the sideline when the whistle blew to restart the game. She'd been standing talking to Tank and watching Peter for the best part of twenty minutes now. Just before the restart Tank had wandered back towards the clubhouse to chat to one of his rugby team mates about something. Richie was blown away by what she saw as she pulled the empty plastic pint glass away from her lips. Nearly the whole of the first team surged forward in one big wave of players, passing it from one side of the pitch to the other. That wasn't what blew her away. It was the fact that they were allowed to surge forward relatively unhindered. One or two second team players half heartedly waved their sticks about, but most just stood, seemingly swaying on the spot. Even Peter seemed rooted to the spot, right up until the last second by which time it was too late to do anything. Richie couldn't believe her eyes.

"Perhaps," she thought, "that is the answer."

When dragons take on human form, generally they take on a lot of human characteristics. They seemingly have a human heart with a pulse, their blood becomes red instead of the usual green, and things like fingernails, toenails and hair grow of their own accord, unlike in dragon form where once a dragon reaches maturity, nothing else will grow, no extra scales, talons stay the same length, nothing. As well as all of this, when a dragon takes on human form, its vision will also take on human form. Primarily, when in its natural form, a dragon can see in a lot of different ways by, if you like, scrolling through different modes of vision. It can see normally, as would a human; it can see in the infrared spectrum; it can see the different effects of mantras and such; it has a limited heat sense, where it can convert the things that it sees into different temperature ranges, slightly different to infrared, and it has an enhanced night vision. When a dragon takes human form, its default mode is the human vision. While it still has access to those other forms of vision, it isn't easy to use them in human form and it certainly isn't the norm. No dragon in human form would ever normally go round looking in anything other than human vision.

For whatever reason, whether it was instinct, suspicion or just plain curiosity, Richie closed her eyes, took a deep breath and let her mind slowly alter her physiology. After a few seconds, she opened them again. This time she took in the sight of the hockey pitch and everything within it with the benefit of her, if you like, mantra vision. She gasped at what she saw. The scene before her bore little or no resemblance to the one she had witnessed only moments ago with her human vision.

Every member of the second team was shrouded in a swirling cloud of black mist, which seemed to coil around each of them like a snake, apart from Peter. His cloud seemed to be dissipating slowly.

"What on Earth...?" Richie thought. Suddenly a hand touched her shoulder. Unusually for her, she jumped, startled.

"Whoa..........sorry Rich," said Tank. "Didn't mean to startle you."

Richie pulled him closer to the small fence, from which they were watching the game and lowered her voice.

"Look at the pitch and tell me what you see."

Not sure what was going on, but assuming it was one of Richie's renowned practical jokes, Tank reluctantly looked at the pitch, waiting for the punch line.

"Well?" said Richie quietly.

"A game of hockey?"

Richie leaned in close and whispered in Tank's ear.

"Now use the vision you would use if you were experimenting with a mantra."

Tank, confused and surprised by Richie's comment, managed to stutter a "What??"

"Just humour me....................pleeeeeeeeeease."

Putting his near empty glass on the ground, Tank closed his eyes momentarily and focused on changing his vision. The look of disbelief when he opened his eyes easily matched Richie's from a few minutes earlier.

"Twist my tail and call me a polar bear," said Tank loudly.

Richie clamped her hand quickly over Tank's mouth, much to the amusement of other nearby spectators.

Quietly, Tank whispered,

"What's going on Rich?"

Richie swiftly brought Tank up to speed, while on the pitch the game seemed to have paused.

Peter gradually came to his senses, albeit too late to prevent the first team from scoring. He felt like he had just woken up from the longest sleep in his entire life. Looking around it was obvious something very odd was going on with the rest of the members of his team. What was also obvious was the fact that neither the umpires nor the first team were either aware of this or if they were, they clearly weren't going to stop the game for it. He needed to buy some time, and he needed to do it very quickly. Jogging over to his goalkeeper, who was just standing on the goal line in a daze, Peter reached behind his right leg and in the blink of an eye undid the straps on his kicker and forced the kicker off over the shoe he was wearing. Nobody spotted him doing this as everyone else was busy trying to get the woozy second team forwards to restart the game. With the keeper's kicker dangling right off the end of his shoe Peter shouted and waved to the nearest umpire to indicate something was wrong. Raising his eyebrows and shaking his head at another enforced interruption, the umpire reluctantly blew his whistle to stop time and halt the match. The umpire ran over to where Peter was squatting in front of the rather bewildered goalkeeper.

"What's wrong?" asked the umpire.

"Straps on the kickers are broken," replied Peter, fiddling around with the perfectly good kicker and its straps. "Give me a few minutes and I think I can fix it."

"Well, try and make it snappy. We've had enough stoppages to last the whole season in this one game," said the umpire haughtily.

Peter knew he had only bought himself a couple of minutes at best. He had to figure out what was wrong with everyone.

Meanwhile, Richie had just finished telling Tank about the first team's goal on the sideline.

"It looks like someone's stunned them all using some kind of mantra," said Tank, frowning.

"Well," whispered Richie, "you're the mantra expert……..do something."

"Like what?"

"Like use a mantra to get rid of it," hissed Richie, starting to lose her temper.

"You know we're not supposed to use mantras out in the open like that. What happens if the council finds out?"

"When has that ever bothered you before?" Shaking her head, Richie turned away and looked out on to the pitch, where Peter appeared to be fiddling about with part of the goalkeeper's kit. Abruptly turning back towards Tank and getting right up close to his face Richie said,

"Whatever that is out there Tank, it's not a natural phenomenon. You have a duty to get rid of it if you can. If you won't do it for me, do it for Peter. Ultimately he's the one that's being affected by this the most. He's out there now trying to figure out what's going on and by the time he does it will be way too late."

Tank knew he'd already lost, and for once wished that it was possible to win an argument with Richie.

"If I had access to the mantra emporium, getting rid of whatever that is would be a piece of toasted charcoal," he thought. Limited by the number of mantras that he knew by heart, he quickly wracked his brain to find one that might help.

Peter had run out of time. Both umpires had run out of patience and had told him that unless the kicker was fixed immediately, they were going to award the game as a win to the first team. Not knowing what else to do, Peter reattached the kicker and moved gingerly back to his position. Looking around, he could see quite clearly that unlike himself, none of the others had shrugged off whatever it was that was affecting them all.

Tank thought he knew what pressure was, with some of the things that Gee Tee had got him to do since he had been working there. Although he thought the world of the old dragon, at times he could be a really harsh taskmaster. That, however, paled in comparison to what he felt now with Richie standing over him; well, not exactly over him, more staring up at him from chest height, hands on hips.

"She could intimidate the king himself," he thought, feeling small beads of sweat running down the back of his neck, which was quite something in the cold October air.

Then...............he had it. Of course, why hadn't he thought of it sooner.......? The Tornados. Not two weeks after joining Gee Tee's mantra emporium, Tank had been given the mundane task of filing away some old mantras. The key, he had been told, was to keep his mind totally blank while doing this because sometimes a mantra can respond to just being thought about in a dragon's mind. At first things went well, if the task was a little boring. The filing got done at quite a rate. However, as time progressed, Tank became more and more fascinated by the language and the words being used in the mantras he was filing. They were so unusual and Tank had never seen anything like them. Unfortunately his fascination had accidentally set one of the mantras off, unleashing a plague of magical monkeys throughout the emporium. They were everywhere, turning over bookcases, eating scrolls, playing chase and, the thing that most of the staff that day will remember, they were peeing off the rafters in the ceiling into a giant vat of mantra ink that Gee Tee had spent two weeks making. When he came downstairs to see what all the noise was about, he went absolutely ballistic, particularly about the ink. What he did do, however, was cast a mantra that created a series of small tornados that sucked up anything magical and had made short work of getting rid of all of the monkeys. Tank had been too amazed by the mantra that Gee Tee had cast, to be afraid of the consequences of his mistake. So amazed and in awe of what the mantra achieved in fact, that he committed that mantra to memory. That was what he needed now. The tornados could easily get rid of everything out there, but he needed to make sure it was the powerful rhyming version of the mantra that he cast. Noting that the umpires were just about to restart the game and Richie standing next to him, glaring, he closed his eyes and searched his memory for the words he needed. Putting the full force of his mind behind it, he whispered very carefully:

"Round and round and round you go,

Tall and powerful you must grow,

Suck up magic in your path,

Don't hold back, let loose your wrath."

Opening his eyes, he stood transfixed with Richie and watched with his mantra vision as four waist height tornados zoomed through the fence in front of them and headed on to the Astroturf pitch. The tornados zigzagged back and forth, taking in the whole pitch. The leaves and sand littering the pitch didn't move an inch, but the black vapour surrounding the second team players was sucked up into the tornados as they tore past them. With the vapour removed, the players started to come back to their senses, just in time for the game to restart once again. Tank turned to Richie, winked and smiled.

"Not bad huh?"

Richie patted her friend on the back as they both stood and watched the tornados, which had all now grown as tall as Tank, finish cleansing the pitch, knowing that they were the only ones that had seen anything at all.

Out of the corner of his eye, Peter had caught sight of his friends, watching the game behind the fence. He'd sorted out the kicker rather quickly after the threat from the umpires to award the game to the first team, and as he stood waiting for the inevitable assault from the first team forward line, willing to battle them on his own, he had the peculiar feeling that his friends were............ up to something. It wasn't anything obvious, well not to anyone else anyway, it was just that they looked as if they were conspiring. "Conspiring about what?" was the million dollar question running through Peter's head. Those two conspiring together could mean anything from human police arriving, to the dragon council punishing all three of them. For what? He didn't know but was sure he would find out later.

As these thoughts weaved through his muddled brain, his team mates for no apparent reason started to.........act normally. The swaying stopped and the blank looks were replaced by puzzled ones, just momentarily until they realised where they were and what was going on. Peter's feeling of doom turned to elation, realising his friends were back to their normal selves and that he wouldn't have to face the opposition on his own. He shouted across to the nearest defender.

"We let a goal in. It's two one now. Tell everyone else!" The message travelled throughout the team like wildfire, with nobody seemingly being able to remember letting the goal in, but all accepting Peter's word that it had happened.

The game restarted with the second team pushing back; however the first team soon regained possession of the ball and began another overwhelming attack. With the second team players still shaking off their heavy legs, Peter knew the rest of the match was going to be hard fought if they were going to get anything from it. Peter and his team managed to weather the next three attacks mainly due to luck rather than judgement. But with every minute the game went on, the second team played more like themselves and Peter started to hold out hope that not only would they get something from the game, but that in fact they could hold on and win it.

The game was much more of an even affair now with the second team even going on the attack once, forcing the first team to get players behind the ball. As Peter rallied his defenders, making sure they were goal side of the players they were marking, he noticed the umpires signal that there were only two minutes of the game remaining. Knowing that they only had to last two more minutes, Peter became even more vocal, encouraging all of his team and urging them on to greater things. Everything looked fine until a foul by a first team player wasn't spotted by either umpire, thus giving possession of the ball and rather a big advantage to the first team. They surged forward and with a couple of clinical passes had carved open the second team defence. Peter himself had been beaten by a nifty dummy and was now duly sprinting back into the 'D', hoping to get round behind the onrushing goal keeper and provide cover on the goal line. The approaching forward got to the top of the 'D' as the second team keeper came rushing out to meet him. Peter would have bet his tail that the player in question would choose to take on the keeper but, much to his amazement, the player slipped the ball square to Manson, and in doing so totally took the goalkeeper out of the game. Manson picked up the ball on his open side and stepped into the 'D'. Peter now stood squarely in the middle of the goal, two footsteps in front of the goal line. He could see other defenders from his team racing back to help, but knew that no one would get to Manson before he could unleash a shot. It was just Peter versus Manson!

Surprisingly, as all of this flickered through Peter's clumsily organised brain, rather than it producing a reaction of fear, he realised he was rather looking forward to the next few seconds and in a way knew that he had every chance of thwarting Manson. Normally not exactly having an over-abundance of confidence, Peter had in his short hockey playing career made some excellent goal line saves. Diving saves, one handed saves, reverse stick saves, even saves that, had he not stopped the ball, the ball would either have taken off his head or in one rather noticeable case something far more precious, his.............. well let's just call them his..........ears. Yes that's it, his ears. Ears were very important to a dragon, much as certain parts of the anatomy were important to humans, in particular human males.

Peter knew what to do when it came to goal line saves and he was going to do it here and now to stop Manson. It all seemed once again to happen in slow motion. Manson was five feet into the 'D' now and drawing his stick back to hit the ball at goal. As he did so, Peter tightened the grip on his stick, making sure his hands were apart, ready to stop the ball. Still moving forward, Manson's stick started to move down to strike the ball.

Concentrating only on the ball, Peter could see in his peripheral vision Manson mutter something as he was hitting the ball. Manson's stick made contact with the ball and it flew towards the goal at an amazing velocity. Not once had Peter taken his eye off its trajectory and he knew with every molecule in his being that he was going to stop the ball going into the net. Lining his stick up, he loosened his lower hand slightly so that he would stop the ball cleanly and not let it bounce away from his stick. He knew then that it would just be a matter of playing the ball wide to one of his players who could clear it up field and wait for the whistle to blow for the end of the game.

With the ball only a split second from the end of his stick, Peter felt all warm inside knowing that this was HIS victory over Manson. All the things that had gone on over the previous months, all the bullying, silent threats, the treatment of Al Garrett, this, Peter knew, was the start of his fight back. It started here and would end with Manson's imprisonment and a healthy Al Garrett and Cropptech back to the way it was supposed to be.

Peter looked down at his stick, waiting expectantly for the impact of the ball, knowing that its course would put it right on the end of his stick; he was ready to pass it out of harm's way to one of his defenders. To his utter amazement, just as the ball was about to hit the end of his stick, it disappeared and then reappeared six inches to the right of where it was supposed to be, still travelling at the same cracking speed. Instantly, Peter's hands moved his stick to try and get a touch, anything at all, on it. But by now it was way too late. It had happened in the blink of an eye. There was a resounding THUD as the ball hit the backboard in the goal and as he caught sight of Manson wheeling around, stick in the air celebrating his goal, a massive cheer went up from the entire first team.

Peter went over the events again in his mind. He'd watched the ball all the way. It should have arrived on the end of his stick. At the last instant it just......... moved over to the right. Manson had been saying something as he was about to hit the ball. What the hell?! Peter felt an arm go round his shoulder.

"It's alright Pete. It's not your fault," said Phil the goalkeeper.

Peter was still in a daze. He looked over to his friends on the sideline, hoping that maybe they'd seen something, but they just shrugged their shoulders.

"You must have seen what happened?" he said to Phil.

"It was just a good shot mate, one of those things. Don't beat yourself up about it."

"But the ball, it changed places, you must've seen it?"

"Don't worry Pete, a draw for us today is as good as a victory. Head up."

Shaking his head, Peter caught sight of Manson on the halfway line, getting ready for the restart. The smug, arrogant sneer on his face told Peter all he needed to know. Somehow Manson had power, magic, something. In that single moment on the goal line, everything Peter had feared and suspected had been confirmed. Not only that, but Manson had risked revealing it just to take Peter down a peg or two in a hockey match.

"What on earth is going to happen when we get back to work?" Peter thought. Manson now knew that Peter knew. What did it all mean?

The umpires restarted the game, only to blow their whistles to end the match some ten seconds later. Each team gave the other three cheers and players shook each others' hands, including the umpires. For the first time in a hockey match, Peter reluctantly shook his opponents' hands. He had often thought that the sportsmanship side of hockey had been one of the keys to luring him into the sport, and before today he had never had any qualms about shaking an opponent's hand, but all of that seemed to have gone out of the window in the last seventy minutes. Aimlessly shaking the first team players' hands, another was thrust in his direction from the side. Reaching out for the hand he looked up into the face of Manson. Peter's hand shot back faster than a man peeing against an electric fence. Manson walked right up to Peter and stood head to head. The two just gazed into each other's eyes for what seemed like the lifespan of a new universe.

"Not very sporting," said Manson, grinning.

Peter continued looking into his face, unmoved by the attempt to provoke him.

Manson moved his head in even closer to Peter's face, so much so that Peter could feel the hot breath on his cheeks and nose.

"You and your kind have had your day. Looking down your superior noses at everything else, judging, manipulating. WELL NO MORE. There's a new force to be reckoned with, one that won't bend to your will as easily as everything else. Your pitiful existence will soon be put into perspective for you," said Manson darkly.

Peter had closed his eyes and, while trying to ignore the knot in his stomach and the fear running through his arms and legs, had opened himself to all of his dragon senses, letting them flow out and explore this solid pillar of hate that stood before him. With Manson's hot breath cloying at his face, Peter tried with all his might to find something, anything, to explain what gave Manson his powers. But even though Manson stood only a few inches away from him, Peter could find nothing, not even a hint of magic or dragon or anything to explain what he knew in his heart of hearts. Manson came out smelling of roses and seeming to be nothing more than an ordinary human being. Opening his eyes, Peter noticed that players from both sides were staring at the two of them, wondering what was going on between them. Looking into Manson's dark maelstrom eyes, Peter tried hard to think of something dramatic and frightening to say. But try as he might, nothing came to mind. Anyway Manson had just beaten him to it.

Barely a whisper came out of Manson's mouth, designed so that Peter was the only one that could hear his words.

"Enjoy your victory with all the other little people," Manson waved his arms to indicate everyone else on the pitch. "If you think you've had a tough time at work so far, you wait until Monday. I will personally crush you like the insignificant insect that you are." With that, he dramatically turned away, head held high, waving his hockey stick above his head.

Peter turned his head as a voice from behind said,

"What was that all about?" Andy the second team captain had a worried expression on his face.

Peter shrugged his shoulders.

"Dunno. Just sore about not beating us I suppose."

"Well don't let it bother you. The whole team did really well today and I can't believe I'm gonna say this, but the first round of drinks in the bar is on me," said Andy.

And with that the two players joined the rest of the team in the showers and then headed off to the bar to celebrate their well deserved draw. Once in the bar, the celebrations began properly with Andy buying the first round of drinks for his team, who were for the most part in very high spirits.

After being in the bar for about fifteen minutes, it became very apparent that something odd was going on. Normally both teams from the Astroturf would have a shower and then come in and have a drink and some food. But Peter wasn't the only one to notice that only two members of the first team had come in. Just as it struck him as being a bit odd, Andy walked over to the two first teamers, who were having a quiet drink at one of the tables at the end of the bar and asked them what was going on. From where Peter was standing he couldn't quite make out what was being said, but from what he could see, Andy had clearly taken offence at what the two players had reluctantly told him. Peter looked away from the rapidly developing disagreement and noticed his two friends sitting at a table in the corner. They waved him over but Peter was interested to see what the two first team players had said to Andy, so he held up five fingers and mouthed that he would be over in five minutes. The two friends nodded and went back to their conversation. In the meantime Andy had left the two first teamers and was heading back across the bar with a look of thunder on his face.

"What's going on?" Peter asked as Andy rejoined the group. The highly spirited second team players had all gone quiet, waiting for the response to Peter's question.

"Well apparently all of the first team players have gone off to one of the pubs in town to get drunk, according to those two," said Andy, indicating the two first team players with a shrug of his head.

"Why the hell have they done that?" said one of the players.

"Bad losers," somebody muttered, to the sound of much sniggering from the rest of the team.

"All I know," said Andy "is that they were all persuaded to go by that Manson bloke who plays up front for them. The two over there," again Andy shrugged his head in the direction of the two first team players, "are as embarrassed and shocked about it as we are, so don't give them a hard time," he said, waving a finger in front of all the second team players.

The players all at the same time got their team spirit back, with some breaking into song, while others made for the pool table and a couple headed for the games machines. With it being so late, the huge bar was probably the quietest it had been all day and would almost certainly be empty if not for the players who had played in that Firsts versus Seconds game. With everybody dispersing to various corners of the bar, Peter headed over to his friends.

"Can I get you both a drink?" he said to Richie and Tank as he approached the table.

Tank looked at his watch thoughtfully.

"Just got time for one more," he said, raising his eyebrows and winking at the same time.

"You've had a big day. Congratulations by the way. That was a fantastic result, well done," said Richie, gulping down the last of her drink and handing the empty glass to Peter.

"Yeah, well done," said Tank. "On that subject we've got something we really need to talk to you about."

"Tank, I thought we agreed we'd tell him later."

"Oh yeah, sorry Rich."

"What's going on?" said Peter, intrigued.

"Grab the drinks and we'll tell you."

Peter sauntered off to the bar to get fresh drinks for his friends, carrying their empty glasses. As he approached the relatively quiet bar, he saw Janice slip round to the front of the bar from somewhere behind. With her friendly smile beaming at him, he nearly dropped the glasses, instead of putting them on the bar; only his swift dragon reflexes saved him.

"Did you win?" asked Janice in her infectious, bubbly way.

"Umm......it was a draw, but it certainly felt like a win," Peter managed to stammer back, unused to any sort of attention from someone so pretty.

"Oh look," Janice said, suddenly waving, "your friends are waving at us."

Peter turned round to look. Tank and Richie had both recognised that Peter had a newfound friend and were doing their very best to embarrass him. Some of the things that Richie was mouthing to him were very rude indeed. He just hoped Janice couldn't lip read as well as he could. He turned back to face the smiling barmaid, pretending to ignore his friends and hoping against hope that anyone from his hockey side didn't catch on to what was happening or he'd be in a lot more trouble than he was now.

"What can I get for you?" said Janice politely.

"Can I have a pint of bitter, a diet Pepsi with ice and ....a traffic light, please," said Peter, slightly embarrassed about ordering Richie her traffic light cocktail.

"Oh, who's the traffic light for?"

"It's for my friend Richie, the one who was waving and trying to whistle."

"Ahhh," sighed Janice, as she started to get the drinks. "Is she your girlfriend?"

Peter started to feel the heat within his body build. He was sure that within seconds he would be giving off more steam than a dozen kettles.

"No, no, nothing like that. She's just a friend, one of my best friends in fact. We've known each other since.............................school." Peter's nervousness had nearly caused him to say nursery ring.

"That," he thought, "would have just about finished things. God I'm hopeless at this."

"Oh," said Janice intently, "that's really nice. I think it shows a lot of maturity to have a member of the opposite sex as a best friend."

Peter nodded in agreement, as he handed over a ten pound note for the drinks. Janice quickly returned with his change.

"Perhaps I'll see you on Tuesday after training?" she said with a big smile, as Peter picked up the drinks and headed towards his friends. He turned over his shoulder and managed to get out, "I hope so," before he staggered out of range. He placed the drinks on the table and flopped down into the chair opposite his friends.

"Welllllllll look at you, you............................human women attractor!" slurred Richie as she picked up her drink.

Tank, who was in mid gulp of his fresh pint of bitter couldn't contain his laughter, and covered his friends as the top of his drink went everywhere.

Peter gave both his friends The Look! The one that said "NO MORE PLEASSSSSSEEEE!" Richie and Tank seemed to take the hint, but Peter knew for certain that he would hear more about this from Richie at some point soon.

"Well.............?" said Peter.

His two friends looked back at him, puzzled.

"You had something you were going to tell me."

"Ahhh," they both said, nodding their heads.

With nobody anywhere near the three of them, Tank and Richie started to tell Peter about everything they'd spotted at the match: the strange mist that led to the entire second team not responding to the goal, and the way Tank used the mantra to get rid of it. Peter in turn told his friends about how he noticed Manson chanting something before the restart, the ball moving on the goal line, and about the threats he'd made at the end of the game. Richie looked stunned about the whole episode and, while she didn't actually offer up an apology, Peter got the distinct impression that despite the fact that alcohol was taking its toll on her, she did feel sorry about ever siding with that slime ball Manson. The three friends agreed to rally behind Peter and use all of the resources available to them to try and find out exactly what Manson was up to.

Tank glanced down at his watch, shocked at how long the three of them had been talking. Looking at his two friends he tapped the face of his watch and mouthed the words, "Laminium ball match." From the look of shock that developed on Peter's face, it was clear to the other two that he'd forgotten all about the match. Peter stood up and pulled out his car keys, ready to head home for the match straight away. Tank followed suit, leaving Richie languishing in her comfortable chair.

"C'mon Rich," said Peter. "Finish up your drink, it's time to go."

Richie wobbled to her feet, much to Tank's delight and Peter's frustration. Squinting and swaying just slightly, she moved closer to Peter and slurred,

"For now, hockey player," she said poking him in the chest, "you are driving me and the huge one to your ....house as both me ......hic.....and the huge one......hic...... have had waaaaaaaay too much beer."

"Yes the big one has had a lot of beer but unlike the little one, has chosen not to let it affect him in any way," said Tank clearly, flashing his best smile.

"Spoilsport," slurred Richie.

The three friends made their way back through the bar towards the exit, with Peter saying goodbye to his team mates while guiding the slightly intoxicated Richie around the maze of chairs and tables. As they got out into the cold October air, Peter let go of Richie, who had been leaning on him all the way out of the front of the clubhouse, where she promptly fell onto the cold hard pavement.

"Heeeeeyyyyy!" said Richie looking up at Peter. "That's not very friendly."

Peter leaned down really close and whispered in her ear.

"You know full well Rich, that with one click of your fingers, so to speak, you could purge all of the alcohol in your system. Your dragon physiology allows you not to be affected by its influence but every now and then you feel you have to 'experience' its effects. Well the next time you want to 'experience' its effects, get someone else to carry you through the bar." With that Peter turned round and stomped off towards his car which was parked over the far side of the car park.

Rolling her eyes, Richie lay spread-eagled where Peter had dropped her. "Grumpy teetotaller!" she shouted after Peter. "Tank.............do you mind?"

Tank had been watching the situation with much embarrassment, hoping to avoid getting involved. "Too late now," he thought as he picked Richie up and threw her over one of his gigantic shoulders and carried her to Peter's car. Once at the car, Tank threw Richie into the back seats and before getting in whispered to Peter.

"Just be thankful that she just gets a little bit silly when she's drunk. Can you imagine what would happen if she got a little bit feisty? We'd have to get the dragon guard in to contain her."

After a short drive in complete silence, the three friends arrived at Peter's house. Peter and Tank got out first while Richie lounged across both back seats. Peter stood with his hands on his hips, glaring down at Richie.

"All right, all right I'm doing it." With that, Richie closed her eyes momentarily and.........bam. Simple as that, sober as a judge.

"Happy now?" asked Richie, as the three friends walked up the garden path to Peter's house.

"Much better," replied Peter.

"You really should try it."

"Why on earth would I want to do that? Can you remember the last time we went to the cinema? I seem to recall it was a Saturday night and the film finished at eleven pm. We decided to walk back to your place, if I remember correctly. Salisbridge High Street looked like the aftermath of some sort of war. People lying in the gutter, others throwing up, some urinating in shop doorways. And that's the best that you could say about it. There were groups of girls fighting amongst themselves, three blokes having an argument with a taxi driver, passengers being thrown off buses, not to mention the two gangs of youths having a running battle at the end of the street, watched by a van full of police, too afraid to get out and get involved. All of that and it was only eleven pm. What's it like at two am? You know full well that it's all fuelled by alcohol. It's the same discussion that we've had time and again Richie. You accuse me of being dull and unadventurous. But you should just take a look at the results of the binge drinking and the alcoholics. Salisbridge is only a tiny little city. This happens throughout the country every night and frankly it's out of control. If I was on the dragon council it's one of the first things I would try and change. I'm all for guiding the human race and letting them fulfil their potential, but on some issues we take a back seat when we know how damaging they are, and this, I believe, is one of them."

Peter stood on his doorstep, looking at his friends, both of whom carried expressions of complete and utter shock.

"Sorry, I didn't mean to go off on one...............it's just that........ ah......never mind. Let's just say it's something I have extremely strong views about and leave it at that. Forgiven?"

Tank and Richie nodded in agreement, much to Peter's relief. The three friends went inside the house, excited about watching their team compete in the semi finals of the Global Cup.

13

Nursing a Semi (Final, that is)

Once inside the house, Tank got straight to work on the television, connecting the crystal and tuning it in. Peter and Richie headed into the kitchen to prepare some dips that Peter had bought. With Peter's rant over, the two friends soon started larking about, which culminated in Peter throwing carrots, cucumbers and then celery at Richie, which she duly caught and chopped at incredible speed into edible slices to serve with the dips. Halfway through the chopping, Richie stopped abruptly, wandered up to Peter and pulled his shirt wide open at the neck. She gazed intently at the gently swaying *alea* that hung round Peter's neck. Carefully putting her hand between Peter's skin and the *alea*, she moved her head in closer for a better look. It wasn't often that Richie was gobsmacked, but as she gazed at Peter's chest, it seemed she was just that. After a silence that almost bordered on uncomfortable, Richie finally spoke.

"What is it?" she whispered longingly, gently caressing it with her index finger.

Peter looked anxiously at the door to the living room, hoping that Tank wouldn't come.

"It's called an *alea*," he replied, smiling down at his friend.

"It's so...............................captivating."

Peter nodded.

"Yes it is."

"What does it do?" asked Richie quietly.

Over the course of the next few minutes Peter explained how he had inherited it from Mark Hiscock, how Gee Tee had told him what it was and in particular how Tank had no idea that Peter had been to see the old shopkeeper on that very memorable night, while all the time Richie didn't take her eyes off it, not once.

"Name your price?"

"Huh?"

"Whatever you want, just name it."

Gently drawing Richie's fingers away from the *alea*, a very staggered Peter looked her straight in the eyes.

"I'm really sorry Rich," he said, meaning every word, "but I just don't want to part with it."

An angry scowl crossed Richie's face for a millisecond and then disappeared.

"I understand," she said softly.

And then everything returned to normal. Richie threw two sticks of celery in the air, and in a dazzling display of dexterity proceeded to cut them into bite sized strips in mid air. Peter joined in and the kitchen turned into a bizarre experiment that looked like someone had crossed two Gordon Ramsays with a circus act as knives and vegetables flew across the kitchen in a blur.

Just as the two vegetable jugglers had run out of ammunition and were using the last carrot and cucumber as swords to fight like pirates, they heard Tank's voice from the living room, urging them to look at something. Sword fighting their way to the living room, (Peter's carrot had by this time definitely seen better days), the two friends entered to find Tank cross legged on the floor in front of the large LCD television gazing intently at the picture.

"It's even better than I imagined it would be," said Tank, dreamily.

Peter and Richie stopped fighting and moved closer to the television. The screen had been split in two, with a view of the giant arena on the top half of the screen and a close up picture of one of the goal mouths on the lower half of the screen.

"Is that live?" asked Richie.

Tank pulled his attention from the screen and turned to Richie, frowning at the battered and bruised cucumber in her hand.

"Sure is."

"The quality of the picture is incredible, despite the fact that it's in black and white."

"I think they must have integrated some of the latest human cameras into their broadcasting equipment."

"It does look fantastic."

As the three looked on, the images changed. The top image zoomed out to show the whole stadium, the roof and the surface of the lava lake. The lower image changed to show a view of a rocky overhang on one side of the stadium. The three concentrated on the lower view, anticipating what would happen next. With no sound coming from the television, only the breathing of the three friends could be heard. Suddenly, triangular portions of the rock face peeled back to reveal a hexagonal entrance with bright white light streaming out of it. Moments later, out flew the two teams, the Gipsy Kings with their players surrounded by dark auras, and the Indigo Warriors surrounded by lighter auras. The three friends cheered excitedly on seeing their team enter the stadium.

* * *

As the three friends sat, engrossed in the laminium ball match, across town it was a very different story. Manson sat at the bar of 'Ye Old Ale House', high up on a cherry red bar stool. Behind him, fellow first team players were playing a very silly drinking game about bunnies. Most of the team members who had opted to go with Manson into town rather than stay at the clubhouse were now very drunk indeed. Manson was not. That's not to say that he hadn't been drinking, because, oh, he had. It was just that the drink, much like for Tank, had absolutely no effect on him.

He had, up until five minutes ago joined in all the different drinking games, but now sat, elbows propped on the dark wooden veneer of the bar itself, nursing a tankard of ale, consumed by anger and hate. As he mulled over events in his mind, blocking out the rowdy revelry that ensued behind him, hatred seemed to roll off him like an angry sea in a violent storm.

"That sap Bentwhistle has no idea what I am. No idea at all. His friends are just as clueless. 'Ohh look at us, we're really useful little dragons doing just as the council demand. Ohh we're untouchable because we're smarter than all the humans. Ohh the humans are our little pets, we must look after them, for the future of the planet.' Huh. Boy are you all gonna be in for a big shock.

Yes that's right, not everything's gonna go your ever-so-laid-out dragon way. When the time comes you're gonna be punished for what you did, ohh and after that your little human pets are gonna suffer like they've never suffered before while you all stand by, helpless to intervene, you…….smug………. self righteous……….sanctimonious …….spineless ………lackeys."

Manson looked up from the beer-stained bar and into the terrified face of the bartender. He couldn't understand why the idiot of a man had such an expression on his face. He was sure he hadn't blurted any of that out loud. Looking down at his hands he soon realised why. The metal tankard that he had been drinking from looked like a child had crafted it from play-doh. In his rage, his hands had quite literally squeezed it into something unrecognisable. Reaching into his pocket he pulled out a fifty pound note and tossed it on to the bar, in the direction of the tender.

"Sorry about that, don't realise my own strength sometimes." The man nervously took the note and moved swiftly off to the other end of the bar to continue polishing glasses. Manson shook his head and sneered as he did so.

Looking around, he could see the drunken antics of the pesky humans he called team mates were becoming more out of hand with each minute that passed. He even heard the word 'curry' being used and knew then that it was time to make his excuses and leave. Dropping down off his stool, he added a slight wobble as he walked to the nearest corner beside the dart board and dropped his misshapen tankard into the filthy looking bin. It made a resounding thud as it skittered through all the crisp packets and hit the bottom.

Turning round, he added a slight stagger to his limp and carried on over to his team mates, walking stick in hand. Feigning a smile, he told his team mates he had to go, using his age as his excuse for not being able to keep up. While everybody jeered and made sarcastic comments, nobody thought anything more about it as he was the oldest member of the team by a few years. After slurring his goodbyes, he gingerly walked to the door and headed out into the cold air. He turned left outside the main entrance to the pub and walked along the badly paved footpath past the windows, all the time exchanging rude gestures to his so called team mates and putting on another bout of staggering.

Once he was clear of the pub, he straightened up and walked briskly to the adjacent car park where he promptly jumped into his black Mercedes. As he tossed his walking stick on to the back seat and settled back against the soft leather of the seats he thought about what a day it had been. Deep down he knew he shouldn't have risked revealing himself like that to that berk Bentwhistle, but Manson was pretty sure he would end up dealing with him one way or another whatever happened, and wasn't about to let a jumped up jerk like that get the better of him at hockey. It wasn't just the fact that he couldn't have Bentwhistle, a bloody dragon, getting the better of him, he also needed to keep up the appearance of being a prolific hockey player for the other part of the plan to fall into place.

Turning the key in the ignition, it was only now that he realised how risky today had been and as he switched on the car lights, vowed next time to be more.............clinical and not let his emotions get in the way. What would the others say if they knew how........rashly he had acted?

"Oh well, it's not like they're going to find out anytime soon," he thought, as he sped out of the car park.

* * *

Back at Peter's house, the friends were glued excitedly to the mute television with an intriguing mixture of food and drink spread out on the living room floor. The dips that Peter and Richie had prepared were strewn all over the place accompanied by an assortment of bizarre additions. A large bottle of ketchup was standing upside down in the middle, from which Tank periodically covered a carrot, stick of cucumber or massive stalk of celery and wolfed down the whole thing much to the others' disgust. As well as the ketchup, there were jars of mayonnaise, coleslaw, pickled onions, strawberry jam, marmalade, chocolate spread and a large jug of very cold gravy. Young dragons like to experiment with an array of tastes and these three were no exception, especially in the privacy of Peter's home. As well as the vegetables being dipped, there were also sponge fingers (Peter's favourite), bread sticks, iced buns, marshmallows and, I kid you not...........pencils. Oh yes pencils, a dragon's staple snack when no humans are looking. Most tend to like the 2B or 3B variety on account of the darkness making it taste so much more.........tangy.

You may think that the food was odd, but only as much as the drinks the three young friends were consuming. Peter had developed a taste for lime cordial. Neat lime cordial, straight out of the bottle. Richie was on her third Baileys and lime, which it has to be said was much more like a meal rather than a drink, while Tank was being the most conventional of the three and drinking a 'Mississippi Mud Pie' or orange juice, lemonade and coke to you and me.

Normally Peter would go berserk if any part of his house looked like his living room currently did, but he was far too interested in the match to care about anything else. They all were. The two split views on the television had just changed to one, and both teams were performing their fly pasts for the excited crowd. The teams were flying around the edge of the massive subterranean stadium, in opposite directions: the Indigo Warriors clockwise, the Gipsy Kings anticlockwise. They were both at exactly the same height and when their rotations met, one team would fly above the other at the very last second, much to the rapturous applause of the crowd.

After two more laps, the teams broke off and headed towards the roof, directly in the middle of the stadium.

"Come on Warriors!" shouted Tank at the silent television.

"Kick their scaly asses!" yelled Peter.

Tank and Richie looked at each other in shock.

"Who rattled your cage?" asked Richie.

"Just getting into the spirit of things," replied Peter.

Tank gave a great big belly laugh. All three returned their attention to the game. The view on the television had changed from both teams of dragons hovering midair, to showing the ten glowing crystals over one of the goal mouths. As the three watched, one crystal winked out and all at once the three said,

"Nine." One by one the crystals winked out and the friends continued their countdown knowing that everyone in the giant stadium was doing the exact same thing.

"Four...................three......................two.....................
one."

As the last crystal winked out, the view on the television returned to both teams hovering in midair. The metallic laminium ball shot out of a concealed hole in the roof, bouncing off the chest of one of the Gipsy Kings players, winding him momentarily. With the ball in play, mayhem ensued. Peter,

Richie and Tank all inched closer to the television, trying to make out what was going on in the crowd of players, and who had the laminium ball. The camera angles were changing, but both teams were still in the same area they had been when the ball had shot out of the roof, and the action seemed to be frantic with tackles, talons, tails and fiery breath raging within such a relatively small area.

Suddenly one of the Gipsy Kings players broke free, making a headlong dive for the lava and only pulling out at the last possible moment to zoom inches above the surface heading towards the Indigo Warriors' goal mouth. Players from both sides of the congested pack gave chase, with Gipsy Kings players holding off Indigo Warriors, and one even dumping Barf unceremoniously into the lava.

The Gipsy Kings players had done a reasonable job of holding off their opponents, much to the dismay of the three friends watching at home, and had given the player now hurtling towards the goal with the laminium ball nestled on the end of his tail, a free run at the Indigo Warriors' goal mouth. Although this was a good thing, certainly as far as the Gipsy Kings were concerned, it was by no means a sure thing. Because standing in the players' way was a certain Silverbonce, the oldest player in the game and, most fans and players alike would say, the craftiest and one of the most talented to grace the game in living memory.

As the Gipsy Kings player rose from the surface of the bubbling lava, he slowed his ascent, trying to get in the right position for a good shot. As he did so, Silverbonce came out of the mouth to narrow the angle. Only it appeared to everyone, including the player with the ball, that the old mouth guard had got the angles 'all wrong'. A huge gap had opened up down Silverbonce's right hand side leaving an easy shot for the eager Gipsy Kings player. Grinning with the thought of the easiest goal he had scored in a long time, the player with the ball threw all of his momentum downwards and at the same time hurled the ball with his tail into the great big gap left by Silverbonce. Not waiting to see what happened next, the relatively young dragon turned towards the fans, opened his wings, as if to say "How great am I?" and waited for the inevitable applause.

It was a real shame he had turned away from the goal mouth, because if he hadn't, he would have seen a real master at work. As the ball had left the young dragon's tail, bound for the goal mouth in the gap that Silverbonce had deliberately left, the cunning old mouth guard had let out the most amazing jet of flame from his old jaws, with such precise timing that it hit the ball almost square on and deflected it well away from the mouth and into the side of the cavern, after which he coolly gathered it up with his tail and played a sublime pass out wide right to Flamer, who was just picking it up with his tail. Meanwhile the young Gipsy Kings forward, puzzled by the lack of applause, was still trying to get his head round the fact that the whole mouth was still intact and that his team mates were expressing a reasonable amount of displeasure with him right at this very moment.

Flamer, having gathered the ball in, had taken flight heading towards the lower right of the massive stadium. Cheese and Barf were speedily heading in the same direction to help him. Steel, meanwhile, had sneakily lost his marker and was flying along the upper left cavern wall, trying hard to be inconspicuous. The Gipsy Kings, with the exception of the young forward were rallying their defence, getting players between the laminium ball and the goal mouth.

Peter, Tank and Richie all sat on the living room floor, munching on various combinations of food, guzzling down drinks, but not once taking their eyes off the action on the television screen in front of them.

One of the Gipsy Kings' defenders thundered towards Flamer, talons out, clearly hoping to dislodge the ball and inflict injury at the same time, but Flamer was having none of it. At the very last second, a quick flick of his tail was enough to send the ball flying surely into the path of Cheese, who took it on the move and headed up towards the mouth accompanied by Barf. Two more Gipsy Kings players hovered in their way, with the mouth guard anxiously moving from side to side behind them. Still nobody had spotted Steel, who was by now only a few metres out from the mouth, but way out on the left hand side. The two Gipsy Kings players looked at each other and nodded, and then both drove towards Cheese and Barf at full speed. Cheese and Barf only had a couple of seconds to react, but that was all they needed. Both knew where Steel was, it was just going to be a matter of getting the ball to him. Cheese feinted right and then flew left and went into a sharp dive. As he entered the dive, he gave a flick of his powerful tail and pushed the ball through the air as hard as he could towards Barf.

In the meantime, Barf wasn't quite as happy as he could be. He'd tried hard to lose the Gipsy Kings player, but had only managed to gain a few metres on him, rather than shed him altogether. Spotting the ball steaming towards him on one side and the player steaming towards him on the other, Barf realised there was only one thing to do. He put on a small burst of speed towards the ball, knowing that this would get him there a fraction of a second before the player got to him. As he reached the fast travelling ball, he just brushed it lightly with the back of his right wing. The fans in the stadium let out a collective gasp at the fact that Barf had failed to gather in the ball. The Gipsy Kings player continued on his course and ploughed into Barf, sending him spiralling out of control towards the lava. All this happened in a split second; the only dragon in the stadium to have any idea of what had really happened was Steel.

You see, Steel was hovering in the same unmarked position he had been for about thirty seconds now, and as the ball rocketed towards him he knew that it was all that Barf could do to deflect the ball in his direction because of the onrushing player. Steel gave one great flap of his wings and sailed to meet the ball as it flew straight into his path. Because none of the Gipsy Kings had realised he was there, or that that was where the ball was heading, the mouth was totally unguarded on the left side, leaving Steel with a clear shot. Not even bothering to collect the ball, even though he had plenty of time, Steel hit the ball first time with his tail and the ball smashed into one of the teeth in the middle of the mouth. A resounding roar went up across the stadium from all of the Indigo Warrior fans. Flamer, Cheese and Barf all flew across the cavern to congratulate Steel, while Silverbonce remained guarding the mouth, but even he was pumping his wings in delight, trying to stir up the crowd.

Back at Peter's house, the three friends had gone absolutely wild. Jumping up, Tank had knocked over his drink, Richie was roaring in delight, while Peter was using some very colourful language indeed, most unlike him.

"That was the best goal ever!" shouted Tank.

"Did you see what Steel did?" said Peter to no one in particular. "He was amazing sneaking up like that. No one else could have done that. He is a GOD!!"

"Well................he's alright I suppose," said Richie, grinning. "But I could take him."

240

The three friends burst into a fit of laughter, and, it was only the sight of the restart taking place on the television some thirty seconds later that brought them out of it.

"Come on Warriors, make it to the final........Pleeeeeaaaaaasssssssee!" shouted Tank at the top of his voice, as the action got underway.

The restart resembled the beginning of the match to a great degree, with punches and streams of flame being thrown in a very confined area, until, that is, the Gipsy Kings once again took possession and pressed the attack. Unlike their previous attack, this one led to them scoring a goal, and it was the young forward who failed so spectacularly last time that got it. He scored from a long way out, after a double tailed attack (very illegal) on Silverbonce, which the referee failed to spot, left the Indigo Warriors' mouth wide open. The players were up in wings about it, all hovering around the ref, blowing smoke at him, the whole lot. But clearly he had no intention of changing his mind about the decision, so the game continued. 1-1.

If Peter's language had been colourful before, it was nothing to what Tank's was now. It was all Richie and Peter could do to get him to sit back down and watch the game restart once again. Peter looked over at Tank waving his oversized fist at the television, threatening the referee and wondered how someone as sensitive and caring as his friend, with not a selfish thought in his body, could get so worked up about something like this.

"The humans," he thought. "We're all becoming more human. Hah."

The teams gathered in the centre of the stadium once again, waiting for the laminium ball to come shooting out of the roof. From the concentration on the faces of the Indigo Warriors players, it was clear they were discussing tactics telepathically. The young Gipsy Kings forward, pleased at having just scored the equaliser, was trying desperately to taunt the Indigo Warriors, but they sensibly were ignoring him, or maybe they were just too busy planning their next attack.

As the ball shot out of the ceiling, the Indigo Warriors, with the exception of Silverbonce, all grouped together and made for the ball. A Gipsy Kings player reached it first, but a split second after getting control of the ball he was hit with the amazing force of four dragons travelling at full tilt. The Indigo players gained possession of the ball, while the surprised Gipsy Kings player tumbled, stunned, towards the surface of the lava, eventually hitting it head first. As the injured dragon floated on the surface, clearly unconscious, a small passageway opened in the middle of one side of the cavern right above the lava. Out shot two medic dragons, dragging behind them a giant green net. The two medics headed straight for the injured dragon as the game above them continued at a frantic pace.

The group of Indigo players had the ball and were lining up for a run at the Gipsy Kings' mouth. The Gipsy Kings players, a dragon down, had got themselves between the opposition and the mouth but were a little unorganised. As the group of Indigo players swooped towards the mouth, one by one Gipsy Kings players hurled themselves at the group. Although this tactic seemed to be born of desperation, it was also quite effective as it did take out at least one of the Indigo players each time it happened.

With all of this going on, the two medics had scooped the unconscious Gipsy Kings dragon up in the net and were now flying with him between them towards the opening that they had came from. Now that the injured player had left the stadium, the Gipsy Kings were finally able to bring on their substitute, albeit a little late to help with the current action that they were having to defend. All the Gipsy Kings players, with the exception of their mouth guard, had hurled themselves at the travelling group of opponents. Only Barf from the Warriors was left flying, with the ball. As he zoomed towards the mouth, with only the guard in the way, he looped the ball up and over the mouth guard, while at the same time blasting him with a sustained stream of flame from his giant jaws. The mouth guard was momentarily disorientated, giving Barf the chance to zip around behind him, gather in the ball and shoot at the undefended mouth.

With the crowd on the edge of their seats, and Barf seemingly having all the time in the world, the Indigo player unleashed his shot. It was for all intents and purposes one of the easiest shots Barf was ever likely to have. With the whole mouth to choose from, probably the hardest part was picking which of the teeth to aim at.

Inexplicably though, Barf had got all his bearings totally wrong, whether from over confidence or perhaps from nerves because of the importance of the occasion. His shot sailed well wide of the undefended mouth, only to be picked up by the covering Gipsy Kings substitute out in the corner of the stadium. The crowd roared in disbelief. Some of the Gipsy Kings fans chanted wildly, with some hurling abuse at the distraught Barf.

The three friends sat on the floor, shocked at what they had just seen. It was Tank that broke the deafening silence.

"I've seen unhatched eggs that could have put that away," he said, angrily.

Peter buried his head in his hands, hoping that somehow everything he'd just seen on the television had been a mistake, a poorly set camera or the telepathic thoughts of a Gipsy Kings fan interfering with the reception.

"Clearly ....Barf is not a big game player," said Richie solemnly, looking up from her drink. "I say substitute him and get Zip on."

"Huh! Like Zip's gonna do a better job," moaned Tank.

After a few seconds of feeling down, Peter picked himself up with a deep breath, determined that tonight was going to go his way.

"Come on guys, we can still win. So Barf made a mistake. So what? The Warriors can still do it. We just need to believe. It's not like we're even losing - it's only a draw and there's plenty of time left yet."

"Well.........I hope they start pulling their wingtips out, that's all I can say," said Tank, slowly picking up on Peter's optimism.

"I still say we need to bring on Zip...........but I'm pretty sure we can still win," said Richie, sipping her drink.

Back at the game, the Indigo Warriors poured their thoughts into the telepathic collectiveness that they used to communicate to tell Barf that his miss didn't matter, but it didn't seem to do the trick. He looked utterly inconsolable as he flapped his wings dejectedly on his way back to defend.

Meanwhile the Gipsy Kings had retained possession of the ball and had strung one or two great passes together. The Warriors, as well as trying to raise Barf's confidence, were all chasing the ball frantically. Not with a great deal of success it could be said. The movement and co-ordination of the Gipsy Kings players on this particular attack was very much reminiscent of how they had played two seasons ago when they won the league title for the second time in succession, so much so that the Warriors were barely able to get near the ball, let alone intercept it.

As the Gipsy Kings closed in on the Warriors' mouth, Steel made a last ditch attempt at a tackle but missed quite spectacularly and went tumbling into the side of the cavern, clearly injuring himself in the process. The Gipsy Kings player with the ball was wide on the right, at about mouth height, and had two players in the middle to pass the ball to. Silverbonce, unusually for him, didn't know whether to come out to the wide player or stay back and defend the mouth. Just as Silverbonce decided to come out to meet the player, the wide player thrashed the ball across the middle towards his two waiting team mates. With amazing speed and agility, that nobody would have thought possible, Silverbonce changed direction and was almost on top of the closest Gipsy Kings player in a flash. All of which would have been great if it weren't for the fact that this player, in all his wisdom, dummied the ball and let it fly right through the middle of his wings to his team mate behind him. Again it was the young forward who, calmly as you like, gathered in the ball with his tail and smashed it aggressively into the mouth, knocking out one of the teeth at the end.

As the teams headed back to the middle of the cavern to await yet another restart, the Warriors appeared to be in total disarray. Barf looked like someone who just wanted to be somewhere else, lonely and dejected. Cheese and Silverbonce were arguing over some aspect of the previous attack that had led to the goal, while Steel just looked on, a cold, reflective expression on his face.

The mood back in Salisbridge at Peter's house wasn't that much better. Whereas only moments ago it was all noisy, optimistic, and full of hope with regard to the Warriors winning the game and reaching the final, now you could hear a pin drop. The three friends studied the images on the screen, willing their team to buck up their ideas and go on to give the Gipsy Kings a damn good thrashing, but even to the three friends, it would seem you would get better odds on winning the lottery than that occurring. And much as the three friends hoped they would, the Warriors never really seemed to recover from that particular moment. The Gipsy Kings scored another goal quite quickly after the restart, once again shattering any small amount of confidence that the Warriors retained. Shortly after that, Barf was substituted, much to Richie's delight, but even though Zip had lots of energy when he came on, it didn't really impact on the game that much.

And so it was that with five minutes to go, a determined Steel had made a conscious decision to retrieve the ball and make a run on goal in one last concerted effort. The Gipsy Kings players were playing the ball around for fun almost, knowing that at 3-1 and with the Warriors looking so disorganised, all they had to do was keep possession and the match would be theirs.

Steel, like his team mates, had spent most of the last half hour chasing the ball without much success and was quite frankly getting more than a little fed up. But unlike the others, he believed implicitly that they could turn the game around and get through to the final. All they had to do was to get two goals and they would go through, because in cup matches of laminium ball, whoever scores first will win the game should the match be drawn. As the Warriors scored the opening goal, they would win if the match were 3-3 at full time, something Steel thought the Gipsy Kings should realise and know that they were not quite as safe as they evidently thought they were, showboating it around like it was a training match.

Steel, while flying around chasing the ball, had hit on an idea to get it back from the Gipsy Kings. The young forward had taken up a position low down just above the surface of the lava, roughly in the centre of the stadium. Every sixth or seventh pass would go to him and he would just keep hold of the ball until one of the Warriors closed him down. If nobody from the Warriors managed that, he would just hover there keeping possession and running down the clock. Steel knew he had to act quickly for his plan to work. Feigning an injured wing, he hovered down to a low ledge away from the main action and started to rotate his wing and act as if he were in a fair amount of pain. At the same time he sent out a message to his team mates to tell them not to close the young forward down, but to just stand off and be ready to attack the mouth.

Cheese and Zip were covering an enormous amount of air, chasing and harrying the opponents who were more than happy to keep hold of the ball. While the Gipsy Kings had noted Steel flying down to the ledge, supposedly injured, they didn't think much of it because they had already used their one substitute by taking Barf off. They continued much in the same vein that they had done, making Cheese and Zip follow the ball round the cavern at top speed. Meanwhile, if anyone had been paying attention, which they weren't, they would have noticed that Steel was no longer on the ledge, or for that matter anywhere to be seen.

Back at Peter's house, the friends had all but given up on winning the game and going through to the final. The view from the television was focused solely on the ball and the players it was travelling between. Because there was no commentary, the three friends had no idea that Steel had even feigned injury, let alone that he was on his way in a daring attempt to put things right.

The clock was ticking down now. Four minutes remained for the Indigo

Warriors to score two goals and get themselves through to the final of the Global Cup for the first time in their history. The Gipsy Kings confidently passed the ball from player to player; some, it would seem from the look on their faces, were planning what they were going to do in the final. That's how confident they were that this game was already wrapped up. Cheese and Zip continued to whizz after the ball, that is until.................the ball was passed to the young forward, hovering just above the lava.

From the look on his face, not only was he planning his moves in the final, but also what he was going to say when he lifted the Global Cup high in the air after having won it. As the young forward controlled the ball with his tail, Cheese and Zip both slowed to a stop in mid air. Cheese wiped his brow, in mock exhaustion. Zip shook his head as if to give up. The cocky smile on the young forward's face grew tenfold as he realised his opponents had already chucked in the towel. His team mates were roaring for him to just keep the ball and waste as much time as possible. He was happy to oblige. Zip and Cheese gave each other a worried look from thirty feet away. Something must have gone wrong. Whatever Steel had planned had not come into effect, and here they were just watching the opposition hold the ball and gloat. Even through their telepathic link, they could not sense him anywhere, which could only mean one thing. He was under the lava, well under for them not to be able to sense him. The thing about diving beneath the lava in a laminium ball match is that generally the lava in question is the hottest and most volatile found outside of the Earth's core. Even a dragon's highly impervious scales can be susceptible to exceptionally high temperatures for a prolonged period of time. Because of this, dragons in a laminium ball match struggle to last any longer than about ten seconds beneath the surface. Steel had been missing for over thirty.

The clock ticked down to three minutes. The Gipsy Kings players hovered in their positions, knowing that they had won the match. The ball remained with the young forward, who held his position just above the lava, as the whole stadium looked on. Beneath the forward the orange lava swirled around in mesmerising patterns as great plumes of steam rose into the humid air. Small bubbles broke the surface unnoticed. The rising panic that was asserting itself in the telepathic collective of the Indigo Warriors suddenly turned to relief as all the players could once again sense the presence of Steel, heading upwards from beneath the lava at a great speed. The small bubbles underneath the young forward had turned into much bigger ones that were spluttering and bursting like a miniature firework display. The crowd, unlike the young forward, were just becoming aware that something was about to happen. Before any of his team mates could warn the young forward with the ball……….happen it did.

Steel burst through the surface of the lava, like a fiery phoenix erupting from the sun. Giant flares of the dazzling orange liquid exploded all around him. His normally shiny scales were all dull, some even black and apparently on fire. He had appeared directly beneath the young forward with the ball and flew straight into him, making sure to gather the ball on the way. The sound of dragon bones cracking and breaking as the inevitable collision took place echoed around the stadium. As Steel came away with the ball, the young, wounded dragon fell unceremoniously into the lava with a giant 'plop'. It was no surprise for any of the crowd to see the two medic dragons shoot out of the hole in the wall towards the spot where the young dragon had sunk beneath the lava.

In the meantime, Steel, having taken everyone by surprise, was winging his way towards the Gipsy Kings' mouth, smoke and lava still pouring off his ravaged looking body. The clock showed two and a half minutes remained.

With almost every player caught by surprise at Steel's audacious move, only one Gipsy Kings player was likely to intercept Steel before he reached the mouth and the very nervous looking mouth guard. In Steel's mind, there was no question of what had to happen. He knew that only about two minutes remained and that he had to score immediately and hope that some miracle opportunity presented itself to get the ball and score once again after the restart. He cursed the fact that it had taken him so long to find the young forward from under the lava. He'd been under different types of lava lots of times before, some for even longer periods of time, but none had felt quite like this. Once under, he felt like a blanket of ice had encased him. A few metres below the surface the lava had lost its warm kiss, only to be replaced by a kind of needle sharp darkness that had enveloped everything. He knew at the time that he would get only one shot at what he had planned and that if he broke the surface at all it would totally give the game away. It took every ounce of courage and bravery that he possessed to stay under so long and find the right route up to the surface to appear beneath the player with the ball. But he couldn't help but wonder now if, having taken so long, it would all be for nothing.

Terror and alarm pulsed through the Gipsy Kings' telepathic bond, where only moments before calm, joy and a sense of victory had existed, even though they were still two goals ahead. As Steel closed in on the terrified Gipsy Kings mouth guard, the unthinkable happened. The only Gipsy Kings player close enough to get to Steel in time had done so, but had clearly been affected by the desperation and alarm from his team mates, telepathically. Instead of trying fairly to take the ball from Steel or even slow him down or anything like that, he had in fact used his jaws to grab Steel by the throat. The crowd roared in disgust, even the Gipsy Kings fans. This was practically the worst kind of foul that could be committed by any player in laminium ball. Not only that, but it was also something that was really taboo in the wider sense of the dragon community. One dragon did not put its jaws anywhere near another dragon's throat EVER. In the meantime the referee had stopped the match. The whole of the Indigo Warriors team were gathered around Steel, to see if he was all right.

Even from their not so great view on the television, the three friends could see that the Warriors captain was in a pretty bad shape. As well as the half dozen puncture wounds on his neck oozing blood, about twenty per cent of his body's scales were as black as night, smouldering away. The trip under the lava looked like it had really taken its toll.

"They should ban him for life for that!" shouted Tank at the television. "It's bloody disgraceful."

"You're right of course," said Richie shaking her head. "But it was a bloody clever move on his part."

"Whaaaaaaaaaaaat?!" screeched Peter.

"Think about it for a second. If you were in his position and you knew that you could totally take out Steel, run down the clock and win the game for your team, and that all it would cost you would be a ban for the next game - wouldn't you do it?"

"No I bloody wouldn't!" said Peter furiously. "I can't believe you would even say such a thing."

"Calm down Peter. I'm not condoning what happened, only saying that from his perspective he did the right thing to win his team the game."

"Yeah, well it's not over yet is it," spluttered Peter, trying to control his temper.

"Oh that's right. How are the Warriors possibly gonna win now?" replied Richie.

Peter turned away and returned his attention to the television, knowing in his heart of hearts that she was right, it was all over. He just.......................... didn't want it to be, that's all. Turning back to the television, the three friends watched as the ref sent the Gipsy Kings player out of the arena, issuing him with a one match ban at the same time.

The three friends wouldn't have known, but the crowd roared approval as the player was ejected and banned, which for him would have meant missing the final, supposedly.

Steel looked in slightly better shape than he had a few moments before, thanks in the main to his team mates. As he recovered after the brutal tackle, his team mates took part in licking his wounds, quite literally in fact. Flamer, Cheese and Silverbonce all attended to the smouldering scales, dabbing them with their own wings, and giving them a good lick once they were fully extinguished. As the others did this, Zip attended to the puncture wounds on Steel's neck that had been inflicted by the Gipsy Kings player. He carefully licked Steel's neck, making sure to leave a thick coating of saliva. This may sound kind of gross, but dragon saliva contains a whole host of antibiotics, and acts much quicker than any kind of tablets available for humans. Even in human form, dragon saliva still provides a potent form of healing, curing a wide range of ailments.

With Steel now upright, the ref informed both the teams that he had awarded a penalty to the Indigo Warriors. Cheers rose from the crowd, but only from the Gipsy Kings fans. They knew that with the clock almost run down, this would almost certainly be the last action of the game, meaning that the best the Warriors would be able to do was to lose 3-2. Steel and his team mates also realised this and looked as dejected as was dragonly possible. Except for Silverbonce, who looked..............like he was up to something. Steel was the team's assigned penalty taker, so it was he who hovered, ready to take said penalty.

The referee hadn't yet restarted the play, so when Silverbonce asked if he could just recheck Steel's wounds to make sure he was fit to take the penalty, the ref gave a resounding yes. Silverbonce flew over to Steel, slowly circling him, making it look as if he was checking him over. Steel had absolutely no idea what was going on, but the wily old mouth guard was clearly pitching an idea to the captain. This went on for a couple of minutes, the two Warriors players clearly quite animated in their discussion. By now the ref had cottoned on to the idea that whatever was going on, it had absolutely nothing to do with Steel's injuries. Calling both players over, the ref gave them both a verbal warning for time wasting and made it clear in no uncertain terms that he expected the penalty to be taken as soon as he restarted play.

Nobody had any idea what had gone on between the two players, but because Silverbonce was involved, the Gipsy Kings players were looking more than a little agitated, even though they knew it was impossible for the Warriors to win the match. The ball could only score one 'pure' hit. Even if the ball was played in such a way as to hit one tooth and then rebound and hit another, the second hit wouldn't count because rebounded shots don't count towards the goal tally. The Gipsy Kings players, with the exception of the mouth guard, all had to be in the Indigo Warriors' half, when a penalty was taken. They all were. Between them and the penalty area, hovered Flamer, Cheese and Zip.

The referee hovered just outside the area, ready to signal play to restart. Unusually, Silverbonce remained by Steel's side as he prepared to take the penalty. There was no rule that said he couldn't do that, it was just.........unheard of.

Peter, Tank and Richie were all glued to the television. The last few minutes had been amazing. Even though they knew with their heads that the game had already been decided, the involvement of Silverbonce gave them some sort of hope. They too, just like the Gipsy Kings players, couldn't see how the Warriors could possibly win, but the very fact that the Warriors' mouth guard was getting involved gave them some sort of false hope.

As everyone in the stadium and the three friends at home looked on, the referee restarted play. Steel drew back his tail, with the ball nestled on the very end, looking as though he were about to shoot. The Gipsy Kings mouth guard tensed, ready to try and save whatever was thrown at him. Steel brought his tail forward quickly and just as he was about to release the ball, he slowed his tail right down and flipped the ball right up in the air in front of Silverbonce.

The whole stadium was deathly quiet with almost everyone wondering what the hell was going on. Now that the ball had been played, the Gipsy Kings players on the halfway point of the stadium surged forward to try and get back and make a difference. The ball had reached the apex of its trajectory and had now started to fall. As it did so, Silverbonce had started to do a forwards roll, bringing his tail over the top of him to make contact with the ball. It looked for all intents and purposes like he was going to slam the ball straight down into the lava below.

Just a split second before the flat open side of Silverbonce's tail made contact with the ball, the cunning old mouth guard rolled his tail round, bringing the full force of the serrated edge down on to the middle of the laminium ball. The shiny silver ball split neatly in half, showing the many layers inside that had gone into producing it.

While the two halves of the ball were falling apart, Silverbonce had ducked out of the way of the onrushing tail of Steel, which even though he couldn't see it, he knew would be rushing towards the broken ball. A resounding 'THWACK' echoed around the stadium as Steel's tail made contact with the two halves, sending them spinning towards the Gipsy Kings' mouth. The bemused Gipsy Kings mouth guard stood rooted to the spot as the laminium ball halves flew past either side of him, each hitting the outer tooth on either side of the goal mouth.

The giant scoreboard signalled two goals for the Indigo Warriors making the score '3-3' flash up on the side of the rocky wall. The game was a draw. The Indigo Warriors had won.

The stadium was deathly silent. Spectators and players alike could not believe what they had just witnessed. As a few seconds passed, some of the Warrior fans in the crowd started to take in just what had happened and the fact that their team had made it through to the final. A muted round of applause and a little shouting started off in one corner of the stadium, slowly gathering momentum and making its way to every part after about ten seconds. The atmosphere grew so loud that the rocky ceiling of the huge cavern started to shake and drop small rocks that plunged into the lava at high speed. Cheese, Flamer and Zip belted over to Steel and Silverbonce to celebrate the unlikeliest of victories. The Gipsy Kings players had surrounded the ref, pushing and shoving him, complaining that the goal should not have stood. The referee was taking no notice of the players and was clearly, from the distant expression on his face, having another conversation with the match arbiter, who remained hidden behind the rock of the stadium somewhere.

The noise in the stadium died down as both sets of fans and players became aware that the ref had not given the signal to end the game. The referee will always signal the end of the game by crossing his wings in front of his body and then sharply open them out and point to the expired clock in the wall. At the moment he had most certainly not done this, and all could see that he was clearly discussing telepathically with the arbiter whether the result should stand. Both teams hovered in separate huddles, waiting for what seemed like an eternity but was actually more like forty seconds, to discover their fate. The referee finally returned his attention to the present and found that the eyes of all the players and most of the seventy thousand crowd were firmly fixed on him. Looking closely at him, it was possible to see steam rising from nearly every part of his body as well as an expansion and constriction in the scales on his neck which seemed to indicate a massive 'GULP' on his part. With an expression on his face that said he had finally realised that half the crowd was going to love him and half the crowd was going to want to lynch him, the referee turned towards both sets of players, crossed his wings in front of his body and pointed towards the clock. The double goal had stood.

A mixture of 'boos' and 'roars' resounded around the stadium. The Indigo Warriors went mental. Flamer leapt backwards into the air, doing a continuous loop the loop that seemed to go on forever. Cheese and Zip hurled themselves at each other, bouncing off the other one's chest high up in the air. Steel grabbed Silverbonce's wing with his own and raised it aloft for the fans. The cheers and applause quadrupled as he did so. Even the Gipsy Kings fans were in awe of what they had seen and knew that they had all witnessed something that would go down in the history of laminium ball matches. The Gipsy Kings players had grudgingly accepted the referee's decision and had very slowly flown off to the exit tunnel that was now wide open and filled with journalists and photographers from all the telepathic papers. The Warriors, now joined by the ecstatic Barf, continued to enjoy their moment of glory, circling the stadium in a flying formation, waving with their wings and shooting huge streams of fire from their mouths as they did so.

Back in Salisbridge, Peter's house was quite literally rocking from the noise the three friends were making, celebrating the Indigo Warriors' progression to the final. Tank had been jumping up and down, using the full force of his very sizeable bulk, Richie had been screaming in a very high pitched way, that is until Peter and Tank both gave her quizzical looks, and then she realised she had been doing it and stopped abruptly and began blowing intricate smoke rings with her mouth. Peter, when he had seen the referee signal that the Warriors had won, had just pumped his arms in the air, mouthing the word 'yes,' over and over again. The three friends were about as happy as they had ever been, with Tank vowing to get tickets to the final at all costs, even if he had to sell his own tail. As they watched the Warriors circling the stadium, the television picture suddenly turned to static. Peter and Richie turned to Tank hopefully.

"I think that's all we're going to get," said Tank quietly. "To be honest I'm surprised they broadcast that much. I expected it to end as soon as the game had finished. My best guess is that because of how it finished they decided to keep transmitting, but that's all we're gonna get. Looks like we'll have to wait for the papers in the morning to see anything else."

Peter sighed long and hard.

"That was one of the best nights of my entire life."

Tank and Richie nodded in agreement. After that the three friends started going over the game again, re-living all the best bits and in particular THAT PENALTY. They stayed at Peter's house well into the early hours of the morning, celebrating.

14

A Sprinkling of Magic

When Peter eventually awoke, it was nearly lunchtime. His stomach was rumbling, not only from being hungry but almost certainly complaining from the near fatal combinations of food and drink. Combinations that had produced while he was sleeping, cosmic amounts of what can only be described as aroma, challenged clouds of a gaseous nature, that with a will of their own had floated throughout the house of their own accord, as he was now finding out.

Sitting down at the breakfast table with a bowl of cornflakes, eyeing two of the aforementioned clouds that hovered menacingly in the far corner, giving off a strange........pink glow, Peter sent out his subconscious and broke the habit of a lifetime by commanding it to return with more than one paper. After only a few more mouthfuls of cornflakes, Peter found he had access to four of the most popular telepathic tabloids. Scanning the front and the last pages really quickly, headlines such as 'Greatest Game Ever' and 'Controversial Penalty Sends Shockwaves Through the Sport' made him feel warm inside. Crunching through his cornflakes, Peter spent the next hour engrossed in the various descriptions of the previous night's match.

The rest of the day seemed to pass really slowly. Peter spent most of the afternoon cleaning his home, not something he looked forward to doing; however, it had to be said that he was something of a stickler for things being tidy and clean, so it would sometimes get to the point where Peter could no longer look away from the dirty carpets and the dust gathering in out-of-the-way places that only he knew were there, such as it was now.

After making the house tolerable, (only to himself, most others would have found it quite acceptable) Peter decided that he fancied going for a walk. Wracking his mind for ten minutes, unusually he couldn't come up with anywhere he fancied going, so after further consideration he decided to go below ground to the dragon world.

As he made his way through the secret underground route from his house, he realised that it had never occurred to him before just to take a walk for no reason at all in the dragon domain. He made his way to the monorail station, having decided, on the way through the house, to catch the first monorail he saw and head off to its destination and take a walk there. As he ambled into the station he walked straight on to the first silver carriage that presented itself on the platform, without even looking up at the giant displays to see where it was headed. After thirty seconds or so of watching different rock formations pass by at high speed, Peter stifled a grin, knowing that he was in fact heading towards Purbeck Peninsula. Not six minutes later, Peter stood facing out of the carriage as it pulled into the terminus at Purbeck. As the doors of the monorail carriage quietly slid aside, Peter felt the warm air from the concourse wash over him. Making his way through the surprisingly busy plaza, Peter caught the scent of something.............ummm, delicious. Stopping in his tracks, he slowly turned trying to identify the tantalising smell that was assaulting his nose. Looking around, first he ruled out the doughnuts, then the pancakes, then most of the other stalls that he could see. Just when he thought he must be imagining things, he caught sight of a tiny little alcove, off to one side, which housed a vendor he was quite sure he had never seen before. Pushing his way through a whole host of people who were heading for the main exit, Peter eventually reached the secluded vendor.

"That smells amazing," said Peter to the vendor, licking his lips.

A dark blue dragon, with the most amazing mottled effect Peter had ever seen, looked up from a sizzling hot griddle.

"Can I interest you in one, Sir?"

"What are they?" enquired Peter.

"I call them 'Charcoal Surprise'," said the vendor with a big toothy smile.

"And?" said Peter.

"That's all I'm saying."

Peter shook his head, wondering if it was some kind of scam. The vendor

255

looked genuine, he thought, but it wouldn't be the first time some unscrupulous dragon had come in from elsewhere, selling something dubious. The 'Charcoal Surprise' did smell absolutely fantastic though and Peter hadn't had anything to eat since his cereal earlier.

"Sure, I'll try one."

"You won't be disappointed I assure you, Sir," replied the vendor, boosting the heat of the griddle with a quick spurt of flame from his jaws.

Peter watched intently as the vendor started to make the 'Charcoal Surprise', keen to know exactly what it was he had purchased. Next to the griddle was a small clay oven that Peter had neglected to notice. The vendor took off its lid, tested the temperature and then blew a stream of flame into it to warm it up a little. Finding it to his liking, the vendor pulled out a big lump of what looked like dough from back to one side of him. Placing the dough on the table next to the griddle, the vendor started to knead and shape the dough. As he did so, he took a small container from under the counter and sprinkled out small dark lumps of something all over the dough.

Peter smiled. "Hmmmm, there's the charcoal," he thought.

The vendor continued to knead the dough, now speckled with charcoal, finishing off by using the backs of his wings to roll the dough flat. The dough was then cast into the oven, sticking to the side of it from what Peter saw briefly before the vendor hurriedly put the lid back into place. With the griddle now sizzling away nicely, again the vendor reached under the counter and pulled out two pink juicy fruits.

"Oh my God," said Peter absolutely astonished. "Are those what I think they are...... giant lau laus?"

The vendor gave a deep throated chuckle.

"I suppose you thought the sprinkles of charcoal were the surprise?"

Peter gave the vendor a lopsided grin and said sheepishly,

"Maybe."

The vendor expertly sliced the giant lau laus as he continued to talk to Peter.

"Don't worry, most dragons are the same. Most are suspicious and used to the same old things. Pancakes with charcoal, doughnuts with charcoal, fajitas with charcoal. No offence to any of that, but it's all a bit bland for my liking. When I describe something I'm selling as 'Surprise', then I genuinely mean 'surprise'."

"But giant lau laus? They're a delicacy and so limited in supply. Where on earth did you get them? If you.............um ....um don't mind me asking."

The sliced giant lau laus had been thrown on to the griddle by now, eliciting an unbelievable aroma. The vendor had been adding pineapple, strawberries and bananas to the mix and squirting what appeared to be two halves of a giant lime on to the sizzling concoction.

"It's okay to ask. It's no big deal, not to me anyway. My grandfather owns and runs one of the biggest plantations in the South Pacific. He always supplies me with enough to be going on with. He's one of the most down to earth and well grounded dragons anyone could meet and while you are right when you say the giant lau laus are now considered something of a delicacy, in times gone by they were available to the likes of you and me. My grandfather keeps me supplied for that very reason, knowing that I can let ordinary dragons get a taste of these delightful fruits."

"Sounds like a top dragon, your grandfather."

A faraway look came across the vendor's face as he tossed and turned the sizzling fruity mixture on the griddle.

"A top dragon, yes, that's what he is indeed," agreed the vendor.

Taking a quick peek in the oven, the vendor plainly realised the bready mixture had finished cooking. He pulled it out and expertly sliced a big hole in the middle. Peter thought the bread looked very similar to naan bread that he had tasted on many outings with Richie and Tank to their favourite Indian restaurant in Salisbridge. Using the bread itself, the vendor scooped the fruity mixture into the hole inside and then proceeded to pour a white dressing all over it.

"There you go Sir. Hope you enjoy."

Peter could feel the heat of the bread and its contents almost burning his hands, but was only interested in the fastest way to get it into his stomach.

"Thank you very much. I hope to see you again," said Peter, looking up momentarily from the gorgeous smelling snack.

The vendor gave Peter another big toothy grin and a short bow as he started to clean the griddle for the next customer.

Walking across the plaza, weaving in and out of commuters, Peter used his hands to lift the bread towards his mouth and gobble furiously on its contents.

The 'Charcoal Surprise' was easily the most amazing thing he had ever tasted. The fruit was sweet and tangy, cooked to perfection, while the bread melted in his mouth as the occasional fizz of charcoal laid waste to his tongue, causing an almost perfect combination. Passersby in both forms were craning their small human and enormous dragon necks around to give him very curious looks. Peter imagined he looked a sight right at the moment, but cared not one iota. It felt as if his eyes were circling his head at a great speed; perhaps this explained the strange stares from those around him.

After leaving the monorail station plaza, Peter headed towards the centre of Purbeck Peninsula. About halfway there, he stopped and sat on a seat carved into the dark brown rock. Expecting the feeling of cold rock on his human shaped bottom, it came as something of a surprise to get a surge of heat passed on to him by the seat. Peter examined the rock closely, to find tiny rivulets of molten lava running just beneath the surface and little plumes of steam rising from the entire length of the seat, that he hadn't spotted before he had sat down.

"Wow," he thought. "Some fancy pants has designed the seats with built in heat from the lava running beneath the city. It's just one pleasant surprise after another today."

Taking ten minutes or so to let his stomach soak up the delightful snack that he had so greedily gobbled down, and to make the most of the very comfortably warm seat that just seemed to ooze away all his worries, eventually Peter reluctantly got up and continued walking into Purbeck. With his stomach contented, his thoughts turned to where he should head to next. He'd already had a great time and didn't really have a destination in mind.

While he was trying to decide he spotted a dragon information terminal on one side of the path up ahead. He strolled purposefully over to it and began to look at the display. Information terminals can be found dotted around the dragon community all over the world. They're free, and can be used for very simple tasks such as looking up a dragon's address or getting directions, or for more complex tasks such as contacting council officials, checking on the latest construction work anywhere in the world, or boosting a mobile phone so that it can connect to one of the topside networks. Information terminals are mainly found in and around the more modern parts of the dragon community. Station plazas and the centre of towns and cities would have dozens, if not hundreds, while somewhere like the area that Gee Tee lived in would probably be miles away from the nearest one.

Looking at the different headings on the LCD touch screen, Peter stumbled across one entitled 'Purbeck and Surrounding Area Covert Entrances'. He scrolled down the screen and looked at the information available. It was basically a list of all the surface access points to Purbeck Peninsula and the local area. When dragons are in the nursery ring they learn all about how to access the surface discreetly and how to enter the dragon domain from any number of concealed entrances. While they aren't given the exact details of all the entrances to the dragon community, they do have access to anything they want to know, either via the information terminals, the dragon library or telepathically.

Peter started to develop a big grin on his face. When this part of the curriculum hit Peter's nursery ring, he, Richie and Tank had developed a game that they had played for some weeks. It was all such a long time ago, but Peter could remember it so vividly. The idea of the game was to ultimately find and use all the covert entrances in and around Purbeck, and the winner would be the one who found either the most fun one to use, or the most bizarre. Tank and Peter had spent days at the library, unusually for Peter, not so much for Tank, looking up all the access points. All their hard work, however, turned out to be in vain. As was normally the case, Richie was way ahead of them both. Not only did she find the most bizarre entrance, but two others that were so much fun, the three of them constantly used them over and over again.

The bizarre entrance was located topside at a children's park in Swanage itself. Peter could remember Richie taking him and Tank there in the dead of night, in the middle of August. Most entrances to the dragon domain that Peter had come across up until that point had seemed relatively simple to him, so consequently he thought that they would all be like that. But his opinion changed forever after that particular night. The three friends sneaked into the park, easy really, with just a three foot fence surrounding it. After that Richie showed them the sequence for unlocking the entrance. At the time Peter couldn't believe what he was seeing. The petals of four separate flowers in three separate flower beds all had to be folded so that they pointed down towards the ground. Finding the flowers in the dark would have been impossible, or so Peter thought. Richie managed to find them all first time without damaging

259

any of the nearby blooms, even though they were all surrounded by hundreds of flowers that looked exactly the same.

Next, the three small children's sprung mounted rides all had to be twisted around to face a northerly direction. As if that wasn't all enough, the next stage of the operation was time dependant. The children's roundabout had to be spun at more than twenty revolutions a minute. After that it would then be a case of sprinting to the far end of the playground to the giant yellow enclosed spiral slide. With the flowers and sprung mounted rides all in position, a small gap would open up about halfway down the enclosed slide just where a wide metal support held it in place, for as long as the roundabout managed to stay turning faster than twenty revolutions a minute. Richie led the way up the yellow ladder and leapt into the slide, feet first. Tank followed next, his big frame only just fitting inside the yellow tube of the slide. Peter knew he had to hurry, because the roundabout would be slowing down all the time. Grabbing the rail above his head, Peter hurled himself down into the dark after his friends. As he turned one of the sharp corners in the dark, he suddenly felt the surface underneath him disappear. He felt like screaming, but fought against the urge, seeing as his friends before him had made no noise at all. Almost as soon as the sensation of falling had started, it stopped with a very wet 'THUMP'.

In the pitch black, even with his enhanced dragon vision, Peter could still not see his friends, who he assumed were still somewhere in front of him. Sitting up to his tummy in freezing cold, flowing water, Peter started to be carried along by it. The water behind him began to build up more and more, making him move faster and faster along the underground stream. Twice Peter banged his head on the ceiling as he was carried along. Just as he was about to call out to his friends, to make sure he was still travelling in the right direction, again the world beneath him fell away and he found himself falling in a shower of cold water in the pitch black. Abruptly he began to tumble as he fell and noticed that he was now in a small cavern with a body of water rushing up to meet him. With a great big splash he found himself unceremoniously dumped into a small, shallow lake. As he sat up, roars of laughter echoed around the small cavern. Shaking themselves dry on the water's edge were Richie and Tank, curled up with mirth. Peter got to his feet and waded over to his friends. The smile on their faces made him laugh, which in turn made the other two laugh again. The three must have looked a sight, soaking wet, freezing cold and bursting with laughter. Peter couldn't recall that incident without laughing out loud himself. To this day, that was still the most bizarre entrance to the dragon kingdom that Peter had ever used.

Of the two fun entrances, one was a sinkhole a little offshore from one of the beaches at Sandbanks, just East of Swanage. Hardly ever used as far as Peter could remember, it was mostly accessed from a boat, but it was possible to swim there as it was about three hundred yards off shore. The point of the sinkhole was marked by a discoloured old buoy. Had any humans dived in that particular area, all they would have found was the wreck of a small ship, with absolutely no defining features. Something utterly uninteresting. However, a dragon would know that the sinkhole lies directly beneath the small wreck. Peter remembered fondly Richie once again leading him and Tank out in the dark. Much like the park in Swanage, this one had to be done at night simply because there would be way too many people about in the day time. Three swimmers going out that far and then not returning would definitely arouse suspicion in the day time on the usually crowded beach. Under the cover of darkness the three had a leisurely swim out to the wreck, changing into their dragon forms halfway, diving down to the bottom on occasion on the way, to swim amongst the seahorses and other marine life. Once at the wreck, Richie found an old steel bar, lying on the bottom and used it to lever the wreck from beneath. As she did so, water and sand started to disappear into a gap beneath the wreck at a tremendous speed. Richie indicated to Tank and Peter that they should dive through the narrow gap which she held open with the steel bar. Tank didn't need a second invitation and dived through, once again just making it through with his oversized frame. Reluctant to throw himself into the darkness, Peter closed his eyes and propelled himself forward anyway, knowing that Richie was becoming more and more impatient. Using his enhanced dragon senses, just like Richie and Tank, Peter was capable of holding his breath for more than half an hour, something he concentrated on now more than ever. Peter found himself surrounded by a dizzying array of bubbles after disappearing down the sinkhole. Suddenly something hard smashed into his shoulder, sending him tumbling head over tail. It was all he could do to hold his breath as Richie's slim form fell past him in a very ungainly manner. She sent him a short apology for bumping into him and just managed a short wave with her left wing as a stream of large bubbles sent her further out of control. For someone who was used to doing acrobatics, normally the aerial kind of course, Peter found himself having a great deal of trouble controlling his urge to throw up. It was as if he was caught in a giant underwater vortex, being spun round and around at a positively dizzying rate. Imagine, if you like, the biggest, most amazing waterslide, only underwater and at the speed of a racing car. That's the only way to describe what Peter found himself going through. As Peter tumbled wildly out of control, concentrating on holding his breath and not throwing up, (which in his mind only added to the building sense of panic he was feeling, as he assumed that if he opened his mouth to throw up then he would probably drown), he could just make out Tank in the distance, being tossed and thrown around like a rag doll. He looked like he was loving it. Richie, by now, had turned her uncontrollable descent into something of an art. She had stopped tumbling and had made her slim dragon form resemble a kind of torpedo shape, and was currently zooming in and out of the giant plumes of bubbles at a jaw dropping angle that seemed to go on forever. As Peter watched his friends, it dawned on him that he was approaching his journey all wrong. "Perhaps trying to enjoy the experience is the key to surviving it," he thought. With this in mind, he spread out both his wings in an attempt to control his ungainly drop. The feeling of the rushing water and bubbles against the membranes of his wings made him want to............giggle. It tickled. It really, really tickled.

Peter couldn't tell if things had just got better or worse. On the plus side he'd forgotten about throwing up, but he just wanted to laugh out loud, so bad was the sensation of the water and bubbles on his wings and that made him think that if he opened his mouth to laugh he would once again drown. The panic started to rise once again from the pit of his stomach, but before he had a chance to do anything about it, he found himself tangled up in a mass of dark green sea weed. The weed was everywhere, preventing him from moving or getting untangled. He looked around for his friends, but they were nowhere in his line of vision. All of a sudden, the seaweed contracted, nearly making him open his mouth. With a good grip on him, the weed spun him round and hurled him towards an oversized orange starfish, which as he approached used one of its arms to bat him away in another direction. Peter found himself hurtling through the water towards the open mouth of a giant clam. Looking back on it, he could certainly see how funny it seemed now, but at the time he had no idea if this was what was supposed to be happening or not. He hit the inside of the giant clam at a considerable speed. As he did so, its massive structure closed up, leaving him dark and alone. Lying trapped in the clam, concentrating on holding his breath, Peter could feel the clam moving......... upwards, he thought. After what seemed like an hour, but was more probably only a couple of minutes, the clam opened up, revealing the surface of a well lit chamber. Peter swam gently out of the clam's mouth and broke the surface, once again to be greeted by his friends' laughter. Richie and Tank were desperate to go again, and come to think of it, now that Peter knew what to expect, so was he.

"The other fun entrance, well that's......that's.........hmmm. That is only a short walk away," Peter thought, consulting the map on the terminal in front of him. Indecision set in, well at least for a split second. It was a bit childish to want to use the entrance just for the fun of it, wasn't it? Especially as he was on his own.

"What the hell," he thought, and headed off in the direction of the nearest way to the surface.

It turned out the nearest access point was only a few minutes' walk away and would bring him out in one of the arcades on the seafront at Swanage. This worked out quite well because the entrance that he was planning to use was only a little further along the seafront, in the guise of a beach hut.

Peter turned off the main walkway that he had been on since the monorail station and headed up a steep flight of rocky stairs. Climbing roughly three storeys, Peter turned a corner and found himself in a small circular chamber, all carved out of rock. In the middle of the chamber was a round glass cage with a circular metal pad at the base of it. Warning signs were plastered on either side of the cage's door. White writing on a red background warned 'ONLY USE IN HUMAN FORM' and 'NARROW IRIS IN USE. DRAGON BODIES WILL NOT FIT'.

Peter slid the glass door aside and stepped on to the metal pad. A tinny voice came out of a small speaker beside his head.

"Keep your body within the circumference of the pad. Be prepared for human interaction."

The glass door in front of him closed automatically, enclosing him fully.

Peter bent his knees slightly, preparing to be shot upwards at high speed. The lights in the chamber dimmed and then a staggeringly loud 'WHOOSH' sent him straight up into the air, through a hole in the top of the chamber and up into the darkness. Still crouched slightly, Peter could see the rock face all around him whizz by only a few inches from his face. The noise at the start of the ascent was starting to die off. The pad was starting to slow, ever so slightly. Peter craned his neck to look above him. He knew at some point soon he would see the hexagonal shaped iris above him, ready to open and let him through. Sure enough, Peter could just make out the metallic surface of the iris and just see where the hexagonal shapes would split apart to let him through. The pad had decreased speed quite rapidly now and was probably only moving silently at about a metre a second.

Peter's eyes were suddenly dazzled by bright light shining through the now open iris. The sounds of an arcade could be heard all around him as he came to rest in the middle of a group of fruit machines. The pad had stopped moving now, and looked just like any other part of the floor in the arcade. Peter had ducked down on coming through the iris, and was now looking out for the opportunity to sneak through the very narrow gap between two of the machines. Right on cue, one of the two penny machines down the far end of the arcade made a loud paying out kind of sound, followed by the ching-ching-ching of money falling out of the bottom of it. As it did so, Peter squeezed through the gap and stood up nonchalantly.

Nobody in the arcade had noticed what had happened, with the exception of the woman behind the change counter. A seemingly middle aged woman with long, dark hair, part of which was tied back with a kind of stripy bandana. She gave Peter a long stare, then broke into a smile and gave him a big wink with her right eye. Peter smiled and winked back before casually leaving the arcade by the seafront entrance.

The lady (or dragon) behind the counter was known as Madame Ladybird. She was renowned in the dragon community for the charity work that she carried out amongst the humans. As well as working in the arcade, she was also its owner and had been for many decades.

On leaving the arcade, Peter found himself looking out across Swanage Bay, a sight he never got tired of looking at, even on a chilly day like today. Much as the heat and warmth of the underground world that he called home felt wonderful, there was something mesmerising about the sea and this view, in particular, that he found intoxicating. Whether it was the golden sand, the gentle sound of the waves lapping against the shore, just the right number of boats in the bay, the view of the Isle of Wight and the Needles or the tummy-rumbling smell of fish and chips, he just didn't know, but Peter felt that this could well be his spiritual home, if such a thing existed.

He turned and headed east along the seafront and past the three storey houses that were successfully rented out as holiday homes throughout the year. In the distance he could hear the shrill whistle of one of the steam trains that ran regularly on the celebrated railway. He continued walking towards the main stretch of beach, looking at the waves rolling in and crashing on the sand only a few feet away. "The tide," he thought, "seems to be neither in nor out."

He continued walking, past two bars and a couple of shops that sold all sorts of holiday stuff: inflatable boats, beach balls, boogie boards, towels, swimwear, that kind of thing. He made it on to the road that ran behind the main stretch of beach and walked past another arcade, a fish and chip shop, information centre and antiquated toilet block. Set back from the road, past the aforementioned facilities, was a row of brightly coloured beach huts.

Peter bent down on the pavement, pretending to tie the laces on his grubby white trainers. As he did so, he looked along the beach front to see if anyone was acting suspiciously or paying him any undue attention. He saw several couples with young children, two gatherings of youths, numerous old aged pensioners, but nobody looking at him. Still keeping his wits about him, he wandered down in front of all the beach huts. As it was the end of October, none of them was in use. It was probably luck more than anything, as he was sure he had been here later in the year than this and found huts with their doors open and people sitting down taking in the sights.

Eventually finding the hut that he was looking for, he very carefully placed one finger on the tip of a rusty old nail that was poking out from the door frame and using two fingers on the other hand he pulled out a small fragment of wood from the side of the hut, just a few inches. With the fragment of wood pulled out as far as it would go, he pushed hard on the tip of the nail and heard a satisfying 'click' as the door unlocked. All this happened in a split second. Peter gave a quick check in the reflection of the hut's window as he squeezed in and quickly shut the door. Once inside he looked out through the white, musty, net curtain to once again check that nobody had paid him any attention. Satisfied that he wasn't being watched, he turned his gaze to the interior of the hut. It was just as he remembered, right down to the ancient white gas stove that stood in the back right hand corner and the blue and white striped deck chair placed right in the middle of the floor. There were half deflated beach balls and inflatable boats propped up in the other corner, along with mismatched oars to heaven knew what sort of boats. An old metallic white fridge stood at waist height next to the stove, with a brown electric kettle that looked like it had been transported straight from the 1970's. Peter wrinkled his nose as he took a step further into the hut. It smelt of old carpet and.... strangely, candy floss, he thought. He rubbed his hand along the worktop that the old brown kettle stood on and was rewarded with the thickest layer of dust he had ever seen in his life accumulating on the side of his fingers.

"Just as I remember it," he thought, ignoring the tidying instinct that was trying to overwhelm his body.

Jolted out of his daydreaming by the sound of small children running and laughing, Peter knew better than to hang around a place like this for no apparent reason. He needed to get on and activate the entrance, as soon as possible. Wracking his brains, for this was another puzzle activation just like the children's park, which ironically was only a stone's throw from the hut that he was standing in, he thought long and hard about what he had to do. First, he took the lid off the dark brown kettle, checking to make sure it was plugged into the mains. After that he opened the door to the fridge. The light inside stuttered and flickered on, looking like it was on its last legs. Inside the fridge, in the door, were three ancient bottles of lemonade. Carefully taking the first bottle, Peter poured its entire contents into the kettle. He then put the lid on and flicked the switch on to boil, whilst at the same time putting the empty bottle back in the fridge and shutting the door. All he had to do now, he knew, was to sit in the deck chair and wait for the kettle to boil. He slumped down in the deck chair and looked at his watch. The whole thing, he seemed to recall, would take less than three minutes. He looked around at all the old junk, desperately trying to fight the overwhelming urge that had overcome him. It was no good he knew. He just had to look. Standing up, he took a pace over to the fridge and opened the door. Sure enough there were again three full bottles of lemonade in the door. "How do they do that?" he wondered. "Must be some sort of self replicating mantra. I bet Gee Tee would know." He made a mental note to ask the old shopkeeper when next their paths crossed.

The sound of the kettle bubbling made him leap back into the deck chair, ready for his journey below. He just had time to notice through the dirty net curtains that covered the window of the beach hut that a rainbow had appeared across the bay, looking stunning in the grey autumn sky. Abruptly, the floor beneath Peter's deck chair opened up and the chair slid into the dark below. Had anyone been in the hut after Peter had disappeared down below, they would have seen a whole section of the dusty old floor revolve through one hundred and eighty degrees, with a new deck chair, this one red striped, appearing again in the middle of the hut.

Meanwhile Peter found himself zooming down a steep rocky slope in the dark, occasionally lit by tiny patches of lava that he either zoomed over or noticed to the side of the deck chair's crazy trajectory. Sparks flew from the bottom of the chair, which had been fitted with tiny metal feet on each of its long wooden legs, feet that constantly remained in contact with the rocky path Peter found himself on. The screeching ride was nothing short of exhilarating, with its sharp turns left and right in the near dark, combined with sometimes steeper drops and then wicked hairpin bends. The speed at which the chair descended was positively unbelievable. Peter guessed it had to be in excess of ninety miles per hour. Something he had never been able to work out, in all the times he had used this particular entrance, was whether he actually had any control over his journey or not. It always seemed to him that he could affect the course of the chair by throwing his weight into it and changing direction ever so slightly, but he always got the impression that the chair was almost.....................humouring him, if such a thing were possible.

Without warning, the angle of descent increased dramatically, and along with it the speed. Peter was forced back into the chair as the screeching of metal on rock got louder and the sparks from the metal feet got wilder. Gripping the sides of the chair for all he was worth, Peter prepared himself for what was to come.

Sure enough it came. The sudden drop changed in a split second, being replaced by the feeling of going up a slope and then aaaahhhhhhhhhhhh! Even though he had known what to expect, he was still caught by surprise

267

at the viciousness of the manoeuvre. After his first ever use of this entrance, with Tank and Richie, it had been explained to him that this individual section of the so-called track he was on, was what can only be described as a 'loop the loop'. Being used to 'G' forces of varying intensities was nothing new for dragons who, when flying, were used to pulling more Gs than most fighter pilots. This 'loop the loop' though was something else, thought Peter. Not sure if it was because the darkness didn't allow you to anticipate what was coming next, just the sheer speed, the enclosed space, or maybe a combination of them all, the only thing that Peter knew was that going through that 'loop the loop' was like nothing else he had ever experienced. It combined fear and excitement in equal measures, which certainly got his blood pumping.

Once through the 'loop the loop', Peter found himself back on a relatively gentle slope in the deck chair, but rather than face forwards and travel down the slope, the deckchair was turning in circles as it negotiated the slope, much like the Waltzers in the fair that, every year, comes to Salisbridge market square.

Just as Peter was starting to regret eating the scrummy 'Charcoal Surprise' earlier, the chair stopped doing circles and slowed right down. As Peter looked around, the faint light of the occasional slither of lava showed him that he had come to a complete stop at a dead end. A solid rock face stood no more than three metres away. Peter sat tangled in the chair, puzzled. For the life of him he couldn't remember this particular part of the journey. As far as he could remember, the chair was supposed to cross paths with two underground streams, travelling down one for a short period, before hitting a tight spiral slope and ending up just on the outskirts of Purbeck Peninsula.

Grabbing the armrests of the chair to lift himself up, Peter decided to get up and look around. Halfway to a standing position the chair folded up on him and disappeared into a very small opening that had appeared from somewhere beneath him. Peter couldn't move, with his knees touching his chin. He couldn't force the chair any wider apart, no matter how much strength and effort he put in. Changing forms was out of the question as the chair had a seemingly vice-like grip on him. All he knew was that he and the chair were falling fast now, very fast. Trying desperately to lever himself out of the chair, Peter could make out rock and tiny slithers of lava flashing by as he travelled straight down at a great speed. All sorts of thoughts were whizzing through his head, none of them very pleasant. "This definitely isn't supposed to happen," was the most prevalent.

Abruptly, the speeding 'V' shaped deck chair, with Peter sandwiched in the middle, tore through a mass of roots and leaves and shot out into a gigantic well lit cavern. Craning his neck to look down the side of the chair, Peter could make out dragons in natural and human form walking along a well worn path hundreds of metres below. "Don't they realise I'm flying to my doom?" he thought, preparing to scream at the top of his voice, in the hope that someone would fly to his aid. Opening his mouth to scream, he suddenly realised that his descent had started to slow. It was then that he noticed the roots of the plant which he had shot through on entering the cavern, had in fact attached themselves to the deck chair and were slowing the fall of the chair itself. The roots seemed to have an almost elastic quality to them, which Peter could see as he looked up towards the roof of the cavern.

Peter was still sandwiched in the 'V' shape of the deck chair, but was now falling towards the surface at a very sedate pace, if falling was what you could call it at all. Half a metre from the ground, the roots let go of the chair and it sprung fully open, landing with the 'click' of metal on rock as it hit the ground. As Peter forced himself up out of the chair, numerous dragons around him were smirking and laughing, giving him a round of applause. Trying hard to look casual, Peter stepped through the gap in the short wall and on to the busy path. Casual didn't really come off, as Peter's legs felt like rubber. Momentarily sitting down on the stone wall to recover his composure, Peter felt a giant hand slap him on the shoulder.

"Shook you up a bit did it son?"

Peter turned round to find a tall, mature, spindly-looking dragon, munching a stick of charcoal, looking down at him.

"It just wasn't quite as I remembered it," stammered Peter.

The dragon let out a high pitched giggle, combined with some kind of splutter, as a lump of charcoal seemed to stick in his jaws.

"It's okay son, they only changed it last week. The repair teams had to close off the main shaft because part of it collapsed when a small tremor hit about ten days ago."

"Ahh," Peter thought. "It all makes sense now. Emergency repair teams often come up with some ingenious solutions to problems, which would explain the giant plant and all its roots."

Peter gave the tall dragon a reluctant smile.

"Well thanks for letting me know. I was starting to feel more than a little stupid."

"That's okay son. Most of the people walking along here are only doing so in the hope of seeing some unsuspecting traveller get a bit more than they bargained for. If you stick around long enough, someone else will come on down."

With that, the dragon patted Peter on the shoulder, turned around and walked slowly away. Peter stayed sitting on the squat stone wall, getting nods and smiles from those dragons walking along the path, in light of his extraordinary entrance to the cavern. As he sat there, he felt his mobile phone vibrating in his pocket. Bemused, he took the phone out and had a look. At some point he'd received a text message. "Must have happened while I was at the surface briefly," he thought. Scrolling through the menus, he reached the text message and opened it up. It was from Tank. The message read:

Pete, what a night last night. Still can't believe it. Trying my best to get tickets for final. Also got something for you from my boss. Will pop round on Tuesday night if that's okay. Let me know. Tank.

"What on earth can he have from Gee Tee?" thought Peter, as he started to reply to Tank's text message. About half way through, Peter heard an echoing scream from high up above him. The dragons around him on the path were all gazing up at the top of the cavern where the thick rooted plant had taken hold. A small dark gap appeared in the middle of it, followed shortly by another unsuspecting victim sandwiched in the middle of a deck chair, rocketing towards the ground. Peter smiled and shook his head as the plant's long roots locked around the chair and gradually splayed out, slowing the fall and bringing the rather stricken-looking old lady to a gradual halt, only metres away from him.

Peter finished his text to Tank, remembering to tell him about the 'Charcoal Surprise', knowing full well his friend would like it as much as he did.

After sending the text message to Tank and the surprise of having any kind of signal on his phone, Peter headed for home, having had enough excitement for one day, but constantly thinking about what it was that Tank had for him from Gee Tee. Tuesday evening couldn't come round fast enough, as far as Peter was concerned.

Work on Monday and Tuesday was fairly routine for Peter, with absolutely no sign whatsoever of Manson. He didn't even appear to be in the grounds of Cropptech and no one had seen hide nor hair of his black Mercedes. Still his armed guards, or as Peter liked to think of them, gun toting goons, patrolled certain areas of the facility, making Peter uncomfortable, but without Al Garrett's help, there was absolutely no way to remove them.

Peter used up a little of his flexitime and finished an hour early on Tuesday, keen to see what Tank was bringing him. He didn't have to wait long before the doorbell of his house rang. Opening the door, Peter was greeted by his friend's big toothy smile.

"Evening!" said Tank, squeezing past Peter into the narrow hallway.

"Come on in, why don't you?" replied Peter jokingly, as Tank already had.

The two made their way into the living room and sat down opposite each other.

Peter couldn't contain his eagerness any longer.

"Well.........what have you got for me from Gee Tee?" he asked excitedly.

"First things first," said Tank. "Guess what I managed to get hold of?"

Peter just wanted whatever it was that Gee Tee had sent Tank to deliver. He really wasn't in the mood to play guessing games.

"I don't know. Please can I have whatever it is that Gee Tee's sent?"

Tank waved a finger at Peter, admonishing him for being so impatient.

"I have something way better than whatever the old dragon's sent you. Three things in fact," he said, raising his eyebrows.

Peter became suspicious.

"Three things," he thought. "Hmmmmm." Then it dawned on him. "No way, you...................you.................haven't, have you?"

"Yep," said Tank, pulling three large golden tickets from the inside of his coat pocket. "Three tickets to the Grand final of the Global Cup, to be held in Australia on Sunday the 6th of November."

Peter was staggered. He took one of the three tickets from Tank's mighty hand and gazed lovingly at it. It was genuine, all there in gold and white, tickets to the final of the Global Cup between the Flaming Fire Crackers and the Indigo Warriors. After a few seconds of worshipping the ticket, Peter

271

leapt up in the air to celebrate and then grabbed his friend's hand. Shaking it furiously, not the one with the other two tickets in it, Peter said,

"You are the absolute best, man. I can't thank you enough. What do I owe you for the ticket?"

Tank shrugged off Peter's pretty feeble grip and smiled.

"You don't owe me anything. The tickets are on me. Let's just all three of us go to the game and watch the Warriors become champions of the world."

"Agreed," said Peter, handing back his ticket to Tank. "Perhaps you'd better keep all of the tickets together, for safekeeping."

"Sure thing," said Tank, taking the ticket and putting all three back in the inside pocket of his jacket. Once the tickets were tucked safely away, Tank pulled out a leather bound parcel wrapped in a delicate twine, that was about the size of his fist. Gently, he passed it over to Peter. Holding it with both hands, Peter asked Tank,

"What is it?"

"Typically, I don't know. You'll have to open it and see. Gee Tee said that it would help you to wrestle back control of Cropptech."

Peter carefully untied the twine, and then slowly unfolded the creased green leather. Inside lay a black fabric pouch, tied at the top, with a crinkled up note in the old dragon's handwriting beneath it. Peter held up the pouch and looked at it with one hand, while picking up the note and reading it with the other.

Dear Peter

    Having applied my considerable knowledge to your current predicament, I have used all the resources available to me to create a broad based multiadaptive cure for the poison that you believe currently affects the owner of Cropptech based on the success of the mantra used to cleanse the house of the now deceased Mark Hiscock. The powder in the pouch stems from an ancient Egyptian antidote to an airborne plague. Combined with the mantra at the bottom of this sheet, the resulting effect should be an almost immediate reversal of the poison's effects. The powder has to be in the immediate vicinity of the individual concerned, i.e. on their clothes, hair, etc. Once the powder is dispersed the mantra should be chanted as powerfully as possible, out loud. As previously mentioned the reversal should be almost immediate. Please don't let this information fall into the wrong hands, as this powerful mantra is only known to a handful of dragons still in existence. Good luck with your task. Your friend

> *Gee Tee*

Poison and evil, out you shall seep,
The infections you caused while good people did sleep.
Purification, is nature's good way
Of making sure, that gone you will stay.

Peter handed Tank the note, as he continued to study the fabric pouch, knowing that Gee Tee wouldn't mind Tank seeing the note; in fact he was sure that the old shopkeeper would realise that Peter would show it to his friend.

Tank clasped one of his huge hands onto Peter's shoulder, not quite surprising him enough to drop the fabric pouch he was still holding up.

"Well my friend, looks like all your problems could be solved by this," Tank said holding up the letter from Gee Tee. "Douse Al Garrett with the powder, use the mantra and BANG, things are back to normal, Garrett can get rid of Manson and you'll be a big hero."

Peter took the letter back from Tank and carefully put it and the fabric pouch into the top drawer of the old wooden sideboard that stood along one side of the room, while considering Tank's remark carefully.

"The last thing I want to be is a hero, as you well know," said Peter, clipping his friend playfully round the ear as he returned to his seat. "I just hope it's as simple as you make out. Nothing would make me happier than curing Garrett and getting Cropptech back to the way it should be. Guards running around toting machine guns should be reserved for Hollywood, not Salisbridge."

"Perhaps you're letting your imagination run away with you, and just perhaps it will be as simple as all of that," said Tank, getting up out of his chair. "Anyway I have to go, I've got to pick up some coaching kit from the sports club as I'm coaching at one of the local schools tomorrow afternoon."

Peter shook his friend's hand on the way out and they agreed to catch up later in the week.

Drifting off to sleep that night, Peter's mind kept going over and over using the mantra and the powder on Garrett. Each time ended with success, and a fit and well Garrett once again controlling Cropptech, with Manson nowhere to be seen. It was all going to be soooooooooooo easy... at least in Peter's dreams.

Peter awoke the next morning, rested, more so than he had been in a little while. He remembered vague snippets of his dreams, all of which centred on curing Garrett of the poison that inflicted him so. During his breakfast, he toyed with the idea of taking Gee Tee's cure with him to work and keeping it in his office, so that it was there if an opportunity presented itself to get to Al Garrett while he was on his own. After much consideration, Peter decided that it was too risky to keep the valued cure at work and that he must somehow find a way to track Manson's movements so that he could approach Garrett without fear of Manson getting in the way. So far he'd had little luck with the computer program that he'd developed, with Cropptech's mighty mainframe rebuffing it at every opportunity, but just maybe he could apply it in a different way to try and help him keep tabs on the dreaded Manson.

Over the next few days Peter worked furiously to try and find a way to get to Garrett with Manson out of the way. Using the CCTV surveillance system seemed to be utterly useless, as his previous investigations had found out, and seemed no better at the moment with Manson popping up in places that he shouldn't have been able to, seemingly bypassing some cameras, while being caught by others. Peter also spoke to the secretary in charge of the whole top floor and asked for a copy of Al Garrett's schedule, something he used to be given on a regular basis before Manson arrived, but was told in no uncertain terms that he didn't have access to that particular information, as it was for authorised personnel only.

The break Peter was looking for only came late on Friday afternoon. He'd phoned across to the guard room to ask one of the managers for some information regarding next week's duty roster, only to be told by the lady that answered the phone that said manager was off the premises attending a meeting. She stated that had Peter checked the scheduling software that the company used on its main computer he would have known that to be the case. That's when it hit Peter: the scheduling software was the answer!

Happy as Larry, he apologised to the person on the end of the phone and thanked her immensely for helping him solve a much bigger problem.

Bemused, she said, "You're welcome," and hung up. For the next hour Peter busied himself on his computer. He went through the scheduling software with a fine toothcomb and came to the conclusion that his program just might work, with a little bit of reconfiguration. Unlocking the drawer to his desk, Peter picked up the dark blue memory stick that contained his computer program and attached it to his key ring. Picking up his lunch box and grabbing his jacket from the hook on the back of the door, he headed home.

Friday night was never anything particularly special as far as Peter was concerned. Very rarely he would go out with either Tank, Richie or both, but more often than not he found himself at home, playing online games on the computer or crashing out in front of the television. Tonight though, he was working hard on his computer program, hoping to put the finishing touches to it that would enable it to scour the software at Cropptech and provide him with a chance to either get Manson out of the way or meet with Al Garrett somewhere other than Cropptech.

Peter found working on the software very hard indeed. Don't get me wrong, being a dragon meant that the technical abilities required were well within his grasp, it was just that when it came to computers he was more adept and took great pleasure in building them, rather than from sifting through what seemed like endless files, altering this and tweaking that. Working well into the night, eventually he came up with a program that he thought would do the job for him. Only time would tell. Coming out of the programs he had been using, it crossed his mind to log on to one of the half dozen or so online role playing games that he liked to play regularly. "One thirty am," he thought. "That's only just getting started." Toying with the idea for thirty seconds or so, he eventually decided on bed and being fresh for his away game of hockey the next morning.

The weekend didn't pan out at all the way Peter had hoped. He played like a drain at hockey, with his side losing away 4-1, their worst defeat of the season so far. Sunday didn't get any better for him, as his washing machine broke spectacularly. It couldn't have happened at a worse time, as the pile of dirty clothes in his bathroom was nearly three feet high. Two journeys in the car to the launderette in the centre of town just about finished his weekend. "Boy, I'm looking forward to going back to work tomorrow," he thought on the journey home.

Monday morning came and as Peter drove through the security gate into Cropptech, he couldn't help but feel a little guilty about the program he had developed, that sat lurking on the memory stick attached to his key ring, even though he knew that what he was doing was in the best interests of everyone, particularly the company.

Once in his office, Peter got on with all the relatively boring tasks he had come to associate with his job. Responding to emails, checking the weekend log book, checking the CCTV system and its backups, were just a few of them. By late morning, with most of the mundane tasks out of the way, he carefully loaded his program onto the computer system. Almost instantly he knew it was going to work. The mainframe computer hadn't blocked it in any way, shape or form, because unlike his other attempts, this program was only designed to attach itself to the scheduling software that the company used, something the mainframe clearly considered little or no threat at all.

Feeling more than a little pleased with himself, Peter decided to treat himself to lunch in the staff canteen, something that had become rarer and rarer since his little run in with Manson's gun toting maniacs.

Logging out of his workstation, he made sure to lock his office door and walked round to the other side of the building, to see what was on offer for lunch. As soon as he saw the decorative coloured writing on the giant chalk board, outlining all the lunch options, Peter knew exactly what he was going to have. "Steak fajitas uuuuummmmmmmmmmmmm," he thought as he joined the back of the short queue. His stomach rumbled and gurgled with anticipation as he waited, hearing the sizzling of the steak, onions and peppers being served to the people at the front of the queue. Eventually it was his turn. Smiling as the friendly staff gave him the fajitas and the sizzling hot skillet, Peter knew he'd made the right decision to come to the canteen. So pleased was he with his lunch, that he'd forgotten all about the program running back on his computer. Peter left the canteen some forty five minutes later, by which time it was absolutely heaving with people. Taking a roundabout route back to his office, he hoped he might bump into Richie, but was wary of meeting Manson. As it happened he didn't meet either, but ended up having a leisurely stroll through the site, burning off just a little of his delicious lunch. Upon entering his office, his thoughts turned to the computer, which he quickly logged back on to.

He couldn't believe his eyes. "Success!" he thought. The program had searched the entire database of the scheduling software and had found just what Peter was looking for. On Friday the 4th of November, just a little over three weeks away, Manson was scheduled to attend the Annual Security Awards of the Year dinner, on behalf of Cropptech, at a hotel in London. The event was supposed to start mid morning and go on well into the evening. It was ideal. "Maybe just a little too ideal," Peter thought suspiciously.

He spent the next ten minutes on the internet checking that the awards ceremony was genuine and was to take place when it said in the scheduling software. After some quick checks, all did indeed appear genuine. "Come to think of it," Peter mused, "I think I can remember Mark Hiscock attending the corresponding event last year, before he started to get sick."

Peter spent the next half hour erasing all evidence of his program, before putting the memory stick back on his key ring to take home. The rest of the afternoon seemed to whizz by for Peter who was happy that, by the looks of things, everything would be cleared up and better within the month. The only thing that played on his mind was the fact that he had to wait for so long to put his plan into action. He had everything that he needed, he just lacked the opportunity for three more weeks. Frustrated as he was, the more he pondered, the more it seemed clear that the best thing was to wait until the 4th of November when Manson wouldn't be in a position to ruin things.

* * *

He listened to the guards surrounding his truck bark out orders in a language he didn't understand. Despite not being able to speak Russian, he knew from his many trips here that everyone was agitated. All of the guards were alert and most had at least one hand on the machine guns that they wore over their shoulders. None was smoking at the moment. That, he thought, was a tell-tale sign that the tension was higher than normal.

Ice was once again starting to form on the inside of the windscreen. He reached over to turn the fan on full, hoping to keep the ice at bay. This was the part of his job he hated the most. The waiting, in this most foreign of foreign places. It wasn't just cold, it was absolutely freezing. When you mention Siberia to anyone, they immediately think of cold, snow, ice. But until you've actually been there you can't imagine how cold, desolate and bleak it really is. In some ways it's almost like being on another planet.

A glimpse in the side mirrors showed the forklift trucks, with their orange flashing lights loading the cargo carefully into the back of his lorry. Soon, he told himself, soon he would be able to go. At least he would be away from these damn guards. They all seemed to regard him with some degree of suspicion, even though he had done this dozens of times, so in theory they should all recognise him. He, on the other hand, thought that they all looked the same, steely jawed, lean with just a hint of stubble, all seemingly smokers.

A sharp knock on the window jolted him out of his reverie. A guard waved a clipboard with some documents on it at him. Instinctively he depressed the button to operate the electric window on the cab's door, but of course it did nothing. "Damn cold," he thought.

Pulling the hood up on his jacket, he opened the cab door and grabbed the clipboard from the guard. The cold assaulted the inside of the cab, forcing all of the hot air out within a few seconds. He quickly checked the documents and signed in the relevant places, waiting for the guard to give him his copy of the relevant forms. Reluctantly the guard did so. He quickly shut the cab door, all the time watching the ice re-form at quite a rate on the inside of the windscreen. Finally he heard the double doors of the container being slammed shut. Looking in his side mirrors he could see the forklift trucks retreat back into the warehouse, their jobs done. Once again the guard slammed his fist on the window of the cab door, but this time indicated with a wave that he should get moving. Not needing to be told twice, he engaged first gear and began crawling forward very slowly in the fresh snow. About halfway to the main gate of the facility, just when the heater had once again started to win the battle with the ice on the inside of the windscreen, his escorts appeared on either side of the snow laden track he found himself on. Nothing unusual there, apart from the fact that on previous trips there had only ever been one or two top of the line Range Rovers accompanying him. This time there were four, each full to the sunroof with guards. "Wow," he thought. "Something must be going on."

Holding the steering wheel with one hand, he flicked on the interior light and pulled his copy of the documents out of his top jacket pocket and gave it a closer inspection. Eventually he found what he was looking for. Once again he was transporting 'laminium' whatever that was. The only difference he could find this time was the fact that there seemed to be more than four times the amount than on any of his previous trips. "Come to think of it," he thought, "they were a long time loading up," and the normally responsive truck he was driving did seem more than a little sluggish.

By now the first Range Rover had reached the security barrier at the main entrance and the driver was showing his papers to the guards. The driver was waved through quite quickly, by Russian standards that is (about five minutes), and he headed out with two Range Rovers in front and two behind. Like the previous trips, the Range Rovers would shadow him from Magadan (his current location) through Siberia, beyond Moscow, leaving only at the Russian border with Belarus. From there another security contingent would join him and accompany him through Belarus, Poland, the Czech Republic and on to Germany and France before the final leg into England and back to the processing plant at Salisbridge. All in all, the journey should take about three weeks, depending mainly on what sort of weather he encountered in Siberia. "Oh well," he thought, as the snow started to pepper his windscreen. "It may not be the Caribbean, but with the sort of money that Cropptech are paying me, at least I'll be able to afford to retire there." The convoy disappeared into the snowy wilderness, carrying their rare and valuable cargo towards its destination.

*　*　*

Back in Salisbridge, Peter was busy keeping his head down and doing his job and just trying to look as ordinary as ever. Secretly he couldn't wait for Friday the 4th of November to come round so that he could implement his plan to cure Al Garrett and return Cropptech to normality. Currently he was trying just to look normal and not arouse anyone's suspicion. He didn't want to do anything that would cause Manson to change his plans and not attend the awards ceremony that he was supposed to be going to. He had come to the conclusion that the best way was to do his job as efficiently as possible, avoid contact with Manson whenever possible and just act as though he was resigned to all the changes that had occurred within the company. He had been doing this for the best part of a week now and was quite sure he had perfected his 'I'm disappointed with the situation but resigned to it' face. It was, he was sure, the same face that about ninety per cent of the workforce had as they wandered about the complex during the day. Only a few people ever smiled in the complex, mostly visitors Peter thought, or those gun toting maniacs armed with machine guns who patrolled certain parts of the facility. Theirs was more a psychotic grin than a smile though, as if they would really and truly love to open fire on someone breaking in. "Anyway," he thought, "all I have to do is blend in with all the other unhappy workers for just over two more weeks and then it will all be over and everything will be back to normal."

Later that week, as Peter sat at the table in his kitchen, he sent out his consciousness to get the latest edition of the Daily Telepath as he hadn't looked at an issue in a while and had no idea what was really going on in the world below him. With his body on autopilot, continuing to munch on the mini Weetabix in front of him on the table, his consciousness reached its destination and began to search for today's issue of the paper. As it did so, Peter became aware of a message that was flagging itself up to draw his attention to it. Finding the paper, Peter grasped hold of the message and commanded them both to return. As soon as they did, Peter stored the Daily Telepath to read later and immediately took a look at the message. It was from Councillor Rosebloom, asking for an update on what was happening at Cropptech. Caught up in everything that was happening at the moment, Peter had totally forgotten to keep in touch with the councillor about what was happening. "Damn!" he thought.

As he ran the message over and over again, cursing the fact that he'd virtually forgotten all about Rosebloom, he noticed that instead of the basic usual message, this was one of the fancy new ones that he'd read about in the paper. The message had an attachment to it that would allow the person who'd received it to return a reply automatically, much like the corresponding facility on an email. Knowing that Rosebloom would know when Peter had picked the message up, he decided to make use of the new automatic return facility and send a reply immediately, even if it meant being a few minutes late for work. Taking a few minutes to compose what he thought was a proper reply, Peter then added it to the message and checked it over one last time. The message read :

Councillor Rosebloom,

Thank you for your brief message. Rest assured I have been working tirelessly to resolve the issue at Cropptech that I mentioned to you when we met at your office. All is going well and on track. The whole issue should be resolved to a satisfying conclusion on the 4th of November and I would hope that Cropptech itself would be restored to its former glory very shortly after that. Regards,

Peter Bentwhistle

Satisfied that it contained just the right amount of information, Peter used the automatic reply and kept an eye on it until it was out of range. Chucking his empty bowl in the sink, he grabbed his sandwiches and raced off to work, hoping his lateness wouldn't attract any unwanted attention.

Time passed relatively slowly for Peter over the coming weeks. All he could think about was making it to the 4th of November and curing Al Garrett and making everything better. For him it became something of an obsession. He couldn't concentrate on anything else. Not the Global Cup final, for which the three friends had tickets, thanks to Tank. Not the firework display which was taking place at the sports club on Saturday the 5th of November, for which Richie had got all three of them tickets. The event itself sounded great, with a barbecue, fairground amusements and a spectacular firework display. Normally he would be looking forward to it a great deal. But nothing could distract him from this most important of tasks. Everything he had been through in the previous months all culminated in curing Garrett and returning the company to its previous state.

Eventually Thursday the 3rd arrived. Peter kept a low profile at work, as he had been doing for weeks now. Nothing extraordinary happened. Peter kept thinking that he would be found out. The nerves were getting to him, which in itself was unusual. It was the first time that he'd ever really felt under pressure. I mean real pressure. The first time he'd had to blend in with humans on his own, felt ....scary, but it wasn't really pressure. After all, he'd been training in the nursery ring for nearly fifty years practising holding human form under all sorts of circumstances, so you see that wasn't really pressure.

He had to keep telling himself that everything was going to go as planned and that nobody was watching him. Once or twice during the day he caught glimpses of Manson on the security cameras in his office. He studied the pictures intensely, but no matter how hard he tried, nothing seemed to be out of the ordinary. Manson seemed to be going about his business as he would on any other day. As well as the security footage, Peter also kept checking the scheduling software to make sure that Manson's appointment at the awards dinner wasn't cancelled or changed. Before he left work, Peter checked once again, to find, surprise, surprise that yes, Manson was still booked to attend and leave the next morning. Peter left at the usual time of five thirty to head home. As he drove his car under the barrier of the security check point and waved casually to the guard on duty, sweat poured down the back of his neck. He'd be glad when this was all over, and by this time tomorrow night, hopefully it would be.

After eating his tea and doing the ironing, Peter packed the dust that he needed to work the mantra into his jacket pocket, to make sure he took it to work in the morning. He was as restless as he'd ever been, and not even sitting down at his computer to play one of the online games that he enjoyed so much seemed to cure him of it. Unable to concentrate, he quit the game and tried reading a book, with about the same amount of success. Finally he switched on the sports news and watched that for about an hour before finally retiring to bed. He drifted off to sleep much as he normally would, but his dreams were far from pleasant. They all featured him trying to cure Garrett and failing miserably, whether it was because he was late, or had lost the dust, or used the dust and muttered the wrong mantra. All his dreams pointed to failure, and when he awoke the next morning he was more tired than he could ever believe possible. As he sat bleary eyed, eating his breakfast, he kept telling himself that they were only dreams and that they meant nothing. Nothing at all.

After double checking everything, he set off for work earlier than usual. He was aiming to get there just before seven thirty, just before the first shift change of the day. Nobody would think it odd, as sometimes he was called in at that time anyway. He wanted to get there early to keep an eye on Manson's car and make sure it left on time to get to the awards ceremony. Once it had gone, he knew that he'd be safe to approach Al Garrett and administer the cure. He reached Cropptech at exactly twenty past seven and after driving under the security barrier he parked in a very empty looking car park. Of the five hundred spaces available in this particular car park, he guessed that fewer than forty were currently occupied, due to the early hour.

The reason he had chosen this car park was because this was the one that Manson always chose to park his black Mercedes in. And just as Peter had predicted, there, not sixty yards away, was said Mercedes, parked all on its own with just a solitary street light illuminating it on this dark and frosty morning.

Peter shivered as he crossed the car park and headed for his office. His breath froze as he exhaled, sending shivers down his back and along the tail he so often thought he had in his human form. Once there, his office was toasty warm, so much so that he was able to take his jacket off and leave it hanging on the back of the door, aware that the cure for Al Garrett was sitting in its inside pocket, along with his mobile phone and the *alea* which he had taken to keeping in a pocket or his car rather than wear round his neck. After taking a few minutes to warm up completely, Peter sat down and started to get on with some work, while all the time keeping an eye on the security monitor that flicked between the different car parks, hoping to see the exact moment that Manson would leave. By Peter's estimation, Manson would have to leave no later than half past ten to give himself enough time to get to the awards venue. Only when he was sure that Manson was out of the way would Peter put his plan into action.

The morning went by with Peter clock watching furiously. By ten o'clock, the Mercedes was still in the car park, according to the security cameras which switched between car parks roughly every ninety seconds or so. Despair started to well up inside Peter. What if Manson didn't go? What if Al Garrett went with him? What if Al Garrett was already off site somewhere? All of these thoughts kept going round and round in Peter's head as he sat at his desk and waited for the monitor to flick round to the appropriate car park. He'd pinned all his hopes on this one opportunity. When the hell would he get another chance to get Garrett alone, without Manson anywhere to be seen?

Just as Peter's hopes of Manson leaving the Cropptech site looked to have been shattered, the security monitor flicked back to the car park that held Peter and Manson's cars. Peter leant in close to the monitor. The driver's door of Manson's black Mercedes was just slamming shut as the camera tuned into the car park. A small puff of smoke was just visible from the exhaust of the car as it speedily exited the car park. Peter stood up from the bank of monitors in his office and headed to the window. Carefully peeking through the blinds, he watched as the black Mercedes approached the security barrier. The guard on duty stood up straight, noticing it was Manson's car. After a few seconds the barrier was raised and the Mercedes shot off, turning out into the main road at speed, paying little attention to oncoming traffic from either direction. Peter let out a long sigh of relief. Everything, it seemed, was back on track, he thought to himself smugly.

He'd decided days ago that it would be prudent to wait at least half an hour to make sure that Manson didn't come back. This he did, mainly staring out of the blinds at the main security gate, hoping not to see that black Mercedes ever again. Every now and then he would look at the clock on his computer, checking to see how much time had elapsed since Manson had left. He dialled down the control setting on the radiator as he could feel himself getting hotter and hotter, the anxiety of the situation starting to get to him. After half an hour had gone by, Peter checked that he had the antidote, checked that he knew the corresponding mantra in his head, and leaving his jacket with his phone and the *alea* hanging on the back of his office door, he started out towards the top floor.

With nothing to lose now, he took the most direct route to Al Garrett's office. Once in the lift, he looked at his reflection in the mirrors surrounding him. He was sweating profusely under his arms, around his neck and although he couldn't see it, he could feel the beads of sweat running down his back, just like they were having a race to see which could reach the waist of his trousers first.

With a 'ding', the door to the lift opened on the top floor. Peter stepped out on to the plush carpet. Al Garrett's personal secretary now sat at a desk in the opulent corridor. She reacted with surprise at seeing Peter stepping out of the lift. As Peter approached her, the expression on her face turned from surprise to outrage.

"I'm afraid Mr Garrett isn't available at the moment," she said snootily. "My understanding is that you are not allowed on this floor, Mr Bentwhistle," she added.

Peter was prepared for this and thrust a handful of papers in her direction.

"I'm afraid there's been some sort of error in the payroll department," he said calmly. "My department's overtime for last month hasn't been sanctioned due to some kind of mistake on their part. I've spent all morning redoing all the paperwork and it just needs to be authorised so that I can get it down to payroll before midday. If it misses the deadline, my staff would have to wait another month before they can get their money. Not something most of them can afford to do in this financial climate, as I'm sure you can appreciate."

As Peter stood stock still, waiting patiently with a smile on his face, the secretary's face grew into a suspicious kind of frown, with her eyebrows doing what looked to be some kind of caterpillar mating ritual.

"I really am under strict instructions that Mr Garrett is not to be disturbed for the rest of the day," she said with a hint of genuine regret in her voice.

Peter let out a long sigh.

"All I need is Mr Garrett's signature on these papers. I won't be more than sixty seconds." Peter could see the secretary wavering and thought to himself, "Gotcha!"

"And think of all those loyal Cropptech staff who would be short of money if this isn't done by midday today." He leaned in close to the secretary, almost being overwhelmed by the sickly smell of her overbearing perfume. "I'm sure you wouldn't want it known by the staff that it was your fault that they had to wait an extra month for their money," he said with an air of menace.

Peter could see the conflicting emotions play across the secretary's pale face. He was sure he had done just enough to get to see Garrett. After a few seconds the pale face turned into a snarl. "Oh no, I've misjudged," he thought.

"You've got two minutes. Get his signature and get out," she said forcefully, pointing her thumb towards the entrance to Al Garrett's office.

Peter nodded and smiled politely.

"Thank you," he said as he walked past her desk. She muttered something under her breath that even with his enhanced senses he still couldn't quite pick up.

Reaching the solid oak door, Peter gave a short knock and then went in. Once again the room was very dark. The overpowering smell of . . . . evil assaulted his nostrils in waves that made him feel physically sick. He knew there and then that it had to end now. And that it would, in just a few more moments.

Peter stepped forward towards Garrett's desk. He was sitting in his high backed black leather chair, taking little notice of anything going on around him. Peter shook his head. "No one should be put through this," he thought.

"I was willing to let Manson go his own way, but the more I see, the more I think he should be locked up for a very long time."

Reaching the desk, he leant over towards Garrett. His boss's bloodshot eyes didn't move at all. Peter waved his hand in front of Garrett's face. Again, no reaction. Seeing Garrett like this sent spikes of anger surging up Peter's spine. "How could anyone do this to another human being?" he thought. "Well, no more. It ends now, once and for all."

Peter walked around the desk until he stood behind Al Garrett's high backed chair. Slowly he took the pouch containing the powder out of his trouser pocket. "It will soon be all back to normal," he thought as he held the pouch in his hands.

"Well, well, well what do we have here?" came a voice from the far corner of the room.

Peter nearly jumped out of his skin he was so startled. He gripped the pouch in one hand tightly as he turned towards the dark corner. From out of the darkness stepped.................Manson, cane in one hand, drink in the other.

"What the hell....?" thought Peter. "I could have sworn there was no one else in the room."

Garrett's head swivelled at the sound of Manson's voice, the first discernable sign of movement since Peter had entered the office.

Peter could feel his pulse racing. All the questions went through his mind about what Manson was doing here. He tried his best to push them out of the way and concentrate on what needed to be done. "Manson is still over ten feet away," he thought. "All I have to do is cover Garrett in the powder and recite the mantra and it's over."

Poised to act, Peter took a deep breath. Suddenly there was the sound of a faint 'click' over the other side of the office. The huge book shelf that covered all of one wall silently slid back to reveal two of Manson's smirking guards, both toting machine guns in Peter's direction. "Oh crap!" Peter thought.

"No sudden moves now, Bentwhistle," whispered Manson in a tone of pure evil. "It would be a crying shame if we had to fill you with holes."

Having quickly reassessed his situation with the emergence of the two guards, Peter knew he had no choice but to comply with Manson, at least for the time being. Even with his enhanced dragon abilities, he knew he would stand very little chance against two machine guns: maybe in dragon form he might fare better, but that was something that really wasn't going to happen, possibly ever again if he didn't keep his cool. So he stood totally and completely still behind Al Garrett's chair, holding the pouch with the antidote in it, in one of his outstretched hands.

"Now you see, Mr Garrett, what has really been going on here. I told you I would get to the bottom of things and this I think you'll find is as far down the bottom as you can get with all the scum and the slime that never see the light of day."

Manson walked over and put his drink down on Garrett's desk. The old man's head followed his every movement. Peter remained stock still, aware not only of the machine guns levelled at him but also of the sweat once again racing down his back. Abruptly Manson slammed his hand down on the desk, causing even the very sedated Garrett to jump just slightly in his chair. Peter stood motionless.

"This is the reason why you feel so ill," said Manson, leaning down and addressing Garrett, while at the same time pointing at Peter. "This... degenerate.....is the reason you feel so overwhelmingly bad. He's been sneaking in here and poisoning you, making you worse every day."

Peter wanted to protest. He wanted to grab Garrett by his sagging shoulders and shake him until he could see what was really happening. But the two guards were starting to look rather anxious and they still very much had their weapons trained on him. Manson continued.

"You still don't really trust me, do you Alan?" he said in a very mocking tone. "Still in your poor health you think I have something to do with all of this." Manson slammed his fist down on the desk once again.

Peter closed his eyes, praying that the sudden shock wouldn't cause one of the two maniacs with the guns to open fire accidentally. "Manson seems really out of it," he thought. "Not so much drunk, as....................unbelievably angry and obsessed about something."

Manson grabbed Garrett's chin and forced the old man to look him in the eyes. "I can prove it you know. I can prove that it was this little worm that's been making you ill."

Still with a million things running through his head, Peter wondered exactly what Manson had in mind.

Manson stomped angrily around the desk until he stood directly in front of Peter. Swiftly he grabbed the pouch from Peter's outstretched hand. All Peter could think was, "Oh boy am I gonna get it for wasting Gee Tee's precious powder."

Manson waved the pouch in front of Garrett's remarkably unresponsive face. "This is what he was poisoning you with. And I shall prove it."

Peter let out a very silent breath of air. "At least this won't catch me out," he thought. "The powder should be totally benign without the mantra, so Manson can do what he likes, but nothing will prove his theory."

Manson stomped over to the unoccupied area between Garrett's desk and the door. Standing in the middle of the room he fingered the pouch, pulling the drawstring loose. Suddenly he cast its contents in the air and to Peter's utter amazement muttered the exact mantra that Peter had memorised. The benign powder lit up like tiny fire flies as it wriggled around in the air, shimmering and sparkling in all different colours. The effect was hypnotic. It only lasted a few seconds, but that was enough. The damage had been done. Garrett's weary face, with the two bloodshot eyes turned and looked up at Peter with a look of resentment and disbelief. The guards had also looked a little sceptical before the powder show, but now looked meaner than Peter could ever have thought possible.

Peter just couldn't get his head round what was happening. How did Manson know the mantra? What the hell did this mean for him? Nothing good, he concluded. He needed help, and he needed it now. Richie, of course, that was it. He could contact Richie telepathically and let her know what was going on. At the very least he could get her to come up here and interrupt things.

Clearing his mind, he focused intently on his surroundings. He reached out with his mind, looking for one mind among the hundreds belonging to all the workers in Cropptech. Abruptly, panic overwhelmed him. Not only could he not sense Richie, but he couldn't sense anyone outside this room. He knew that Garrett's personal secretary was sitting only twenty five feet away in the corridor, he knew that forty or fifty staff worked on this level, let alone the hundreds or so that worked on the other levels, but he couldn't get a sense of any of them. He concentrated again, feeling the minds of the two guards, alert and deadly, having no hesitation about shooting him should he warrant it. He sensed Garrett, weary, dejected and ....dying. He let his mind drift towards Manson but there was just a void. A void filled with anger, despair, revenge and destruction. But he could sense nothing outside of Garrett's office. Now he knew he was in trouble.

As the remains of the powder floated down on to the thick carpet, the shimmering finally fizzling out, Manson strode over to the front of Garrett's desk and looked straight into the old man's bloodshot eyes.

"You see............it's true. He came here to poison you. What else could it be?"

Once again Peter found himself biting his tongue, desperately resisting the urge to try and tell Garrett everything he knew about Manson. Garrett looked up into Manson's face and gave a small but telling nod in his direction. Things, it seemed, were just about to get a lot worse for Peter.

Manson twirled round, arms open wide, a deeply disturbing smile upon his face.

"So now it would seem that everybody knows exactly what's been going on, what on earth are we going to do with you?" he said looking in Peter's direction. Manson scratched his chin for effect.

Peter knew better than to reply to Manson's rhetorical question. Whatever Manson had in mind, he was sure his fate had already been decided and he wasn't about to give the two goons an excuse to open fire.

Manson walked around Garrett's desk once more and opened the top drawer. From it he pulled some plastic binders, very much like big white cable ties, which he proceeded to wrap around Peter's wrists, after forcing his hands behind his back. Peter had no choice but to comply, with the machine guns firmly focused in his direction. He waited for an opportunity, which he hoped would come.

"There, that's better," said Manson merrily. He turned to address the guards with the machine guns. "Escort our ex employee off the premises immediately. Do not stop for anyone and only at the main gate can you cut the binders from him. Do not, and I repeat do not, take him to his office, do not linger. Take him to the main gate by the most direct route. Get one of the plods from security to fetch his car."

"Yes sir," the guards said in unison, whilst both nodding at the same time.

The meaner looking of the two grabbed the binders behind Peter's back and thrust him forward towards the office door. Peter stumbled and nearly fell, just managing to regain his balance at the last moment.

"Well..........it's been fun, let's do this again sometime," Manson said cheerily from behind Peter, as the other guard opened the door, revealing the corridor leading to the lift and a very startled looking secretary who wasn't particularly surprised to see Peter, but was surprised to see him in restraints and frogmarched out by two armed guards.

Peter looked straight ahead as he walked past the secretary at her desk. He stopped in front of the silver lift doors as one of the guards pressed the button for the ground floor. Despite everything that had gone on in the previous few minutes, despite the dismal failure of what he was trying to do and the fact that he had wasted Gee Tee's precious antidote and discovered the fact that Manson was way more than he seemed, the only thing on Peter's mind at this very second was hoping beyond hope that he wasn't frogmarched by these armed goons past Richie at any point in the next few minutes. He didn't think he could face the shame of seeing his friend from this position.

The doors to the lift silently slid open. Peter stepped in, with the guards hot on his heels. As the lift travelled to the ground floor, Peter noted the guards' expressions in the mirrored surround. "They are enjoying this way too much," he thought to himself.

The lift doors opened on the ground floor to reveal a large open plan office that was part accounts department and part marketing department. Peter stepped out, wrists bound behind his back, followed closely by the two guards who both had their machine guns pointed firmly into the small of his back. Peter looked down at the floor for the first few silent steps. He wondered how long it would take people to realise what was going on. As it happened, not long, not long at all. About five paces into his walk through the open plan office he heard the first 'gasp'. It was quickly followed by a few more and then a whole lot of chattering and whispering.

"Keep moving," grunted one of the guards, while at the same time slapping Peter in the back with the butt of his machine gun. Clearly wanting to demonstrate his power, the move had the desired effect, as the whole office fell silent. "You could hear two brain cells rubbing together," Peter thought. "Oh well, that counts either of these two muppets out," he thought, trying to keep his spirits up and spying the guards in the reflection of a water cooler.

Looking straight ahead, he saw many faces that he knew and some he had come to think of as friends in the silent office. The expressions he saw ripped his heart to shreds. The looks of disgust and hatred seemed to penetrate his entire being. "Please, please don't let Richie see me like this, pleeeaaasee," he thought as he reached the other side of the office and exited into one of the main corridors.

The corridors that led towards the security gate were busy thoroughfares, and this morning was no different. Again Peter saw people he knew, and again their faces registered much the same expressions as the people before them. As Peter was ushered outside into the cold November air he was just glad that he had avoided bumping into Richie. Crossing the road Peter looked all around him. On all floors of the main building that was now behind him, Peter could see people crowded at the windows, peeking through the blinds, looking to see what was going on. The same seemed to be going on at the security gate, where people who he'd been responsible for were scrabbling for a view through the vertically slanted blinds. The two guards on gate duty looked horrified as Peter was frogmarched over to them, machine guns pointed into his back. Peter shook his head trying to warn the men, who he knew reasonably well, not to make a fuss and just do as the goons asked.

"You," said one of the goons behind Peter. "Get his car keys from his pocket and bring his car round.................NOW."

"What the hell is going on?" demanded the guard on the gate who had just been spoken to.

Peter took a deep breath and spoke just before the goons could provoke the gate guards any more.

"It's okay. Just do as he says. My keys are in my left trouser pocket."

Reluctantly the guard came over to Peter and took his keys out of his pocket.

"It's parked in car park B," said Peter calmly.

The guard nodded an acknowledgement and headed slowly off towards said car park. Peter could see the other gate guard, a burly man called Owen, who Peter had known since he had started at Cropptech, was starting to get anxious. He mouthed to him to just to keep calm and not make a fuss, hoping the goons, who were standing behind him, wouldn't notice.

"Raise the security barrier," one of the goons said bluntly to Owen, the remaining gate guard.

"Raise the security barrier................PLEASE," said Owen sarcastically.

It was all Peter could do not to laugh, despite the seriousness of the situation.

"Do it now!" demanded the other goon, waving his machine gun from side to side clearly for effect.

Owen just stood there and crossed his arms. In that moment, Peter gained a new respect for his friend and colleague and vowed to himself, that should things ever get back to the way they were meant to be, i.e. with Garrett back in charge and Peter returned to his old position, he would definitely make sure Owen got a well deserved promotion. The tension of the situation was unbelievable, but eventually the goons decided, probably because just about everyone on the site was watching, that they would have to accede to Owen's request.

"Raise the security barrier... please," said one of the goons, smiling falsely.

After much consideration, Owen looked inside the gatehouse and gave the sign for the barrier to be raised. As the red and white striped barrier began its ascent, Peter was shoved forward so that he was the other side of the barrier. Just then Peter's car came around the corner with the other gate guard at the wheel. It slowed to a halt right beside Peter and the gate guard switched off the engine and got out, leaving the keys in the ignition. In one swift movement, one of the gun toting goons reached down into his boot and pulled out a rather vicious looking knife. Putting his hand on the back of Peter's neck, the guard bent Peter forward and then in one fluid motion cut the binders on his wrists, letting them drop to the floor in the middle of the road. He then shoved Peter with his foot in the small of Peter's back, hurling him towards his car door.

"Don't come back if you know what's good for you," the goon spat as he and his mate turned and headed back towards the main building.

Peter felt the gaze of hundreds of people on him, all at once. Looking up though, only one person caught his attention. There at the top of the building was Manson gazing down at him, looking oh, so pleased with himself. Peter turned away to get into his car. As he did so, he kept that picture of Manson in his mind.

"It's not over," he told himself. "It's sooooo not over."

15

Fawking Hell!!!!!

It was raining, blowing a gale and even in the cab of his lorry, his breath was freezing as he exhaled. But by goodness it was great to be back in England, even on this bleak November day. His truck trundled over the bumps in the ramp as he departed the ferry at Dover. The journey so far had taken over three weeks and even though he had done the same trip at least a dozen times before, this one was by far the most arduous. The weather in Siberia had been unbelievably bad, even by Russian standards, which was really saying something. It was the first time he'd been thankful for the military style escort that he'd been given, as the guards in the convoy that accompanied him had had to dig his truck out on more than one occasion during the trek across Russia. As he headed out of Dover on the A20, he flicked the radio on to his favourite station, Radio 2, and looked forward to spending some quality time with his wife and two children. All he had to do now was negotiate the M20, M25, M3 and A303 and then he would be back at the Cropptech site in Salisbridge. With any luck he would be back there by six o'clock, an hour or so to unload his valuable cargo, and then he would be home in time to read his children a bedtime story. He couldn't wait.

*   *   *

Peter turned the key in his front door and dejectedly walked through the hall and into the living room. He slumped down on the sofa, feeling more than a little sorry for himself. He couldn't even remember driving home. Oh, he knew that he'd done it, he was here of course, and he could recall tiny snippets of the journey, but it had all been done on autopilot so to speak. He held his head in his hands, wondering where it had all gone wrong. He'd lost his job, blown the chance to restore Cropptech to its former glory, and wasted Gee Tee's rare and valuable antidote. "At least things can't get any worse," he thought.

After a few minutes, it might even have been half an hour, as time seemed to have lost its significance, Peter turned on the television and tuned into the sports news channel, hoping to take his mind off things. Information on the television seemed a distant blur to him as he remained slumped on the sofa. Unhappiness and the lack of a decent night's sleep the night before seemed to both hit at the same time like a giant bulldozer. Before he knew it, he'd fallen asleep, television still going on in the background, grey dreary daylight shining through the window.

He woke up in a room only lit by the images from the television. It took him a few seconds to clear his head. "Oh pants," he thought. "It wasn't just a bad dream after all."

The muscles in his neck and back sent waves of pain down his spine as he sat up. "Falling asleep on the sofa wasn't the best way to catch up on sleep," he thought as he forced his body to get up and turn the lights on. As he pulled the curtains shut, the day's events came flooding back to him, in a moment of crystal clarity. Shuffling into the kitchen, he shut the blinds on the window and tried hard to ignore the grumbling noises his stomach was making. How could he eat at a time like this? With the events at Cropptech stuck in his head, like pins in a pin cushion, he suddenly wondered why he hadn't heard from Richie. She was, after all, bound to have heard what had happened even if she hadn't witnessed it firsthand. "Odd," he thought. Then it dawned on him. "Crap!!! I've left my jacket there. It's got my phone and the *alea* in it. Oh this is so bad." No wonder he hadn't heard from Richie. She almost certainly would have tried to contact him on his mobile. This was sooooooo not good, he thought miserably.

He went back into the living room, and instead of sitting down, he paced around the coffee table trying to think of what to do. He could ask Richie to get it back for him, but then she might get into trouble, or worse, with Manson on the loose. He could phone up and ask for it to be dropped back to him. "Hmmm, that just draws attention to it, not something I really want to do, especially with the *alea* in the pocket of the jacket. I could always go

294

back there myself. Yes, that would be incredibly bright. Go back there myself, particularly after today's events."

He sat down on the sofa and leant forward, theatrically banging his head on the coffee table for effect. After a few seconds of intense pain and nothing becoming clearer, he sat up and thought, "I really need a clear head before I decide how to get it back. Hmm, time for something nice to eat methinks."

With that, Peter went to a drawer in the kitchen and did something he only did every couple of months or so. He pulled out the takeaway menu for the local Indian restaurant. Peter loved Indian food, something that he had developed a taste for before taking up hockey, but had become so much more appealing since. Nearly every other Saturday, one group or other from the sports club could be found heading for the local Indian restaurant for a curry. Peter had ended up tagging along on more than one occasion and had found the experience................well, memorable for more than a few reasons. The witty banter and drunken antics had opened his eyes quite a lot the first few times. Although Peter was over fifty years old, most of that had been spent in the dragon domain, i.e. underground, hence he was still quite naïve when it came to some of the more social aspects of human culture. The post sport curry was something that he seemed to really enjoy. He'd never really gotten into going around all the different pubs and clubs just drinking until you fell over. That, to Peter, seemed a complete waste of time. But there was just something about sitting down and having a meal with your friends, no matter how intoxicated they were, that just really appealed to him. The last time he'd got dragged along for a curry, he'd been surprised to see Tank and Richie at the restaurant when he and his team mates entered. Tank was there with his rugby team, and Richie, having nothing better to do, had gotten in on the action. Something that happened on quite a regular basis, he'd subsequently found out.

That night had turned out to be one of the most memorable of his life. The hockey team had joined tables with the rugby lads, and they plus Richie had spent the entire night swapping drunken anecdotes and playing silly drinking games at the restaurant. Looking back on it, the night itself was great, but what really made it special was the fact that he had managed to share it with his two best friends.

Anyway, every couple or months or so he would treat himself to a takeaway.

It wasn't generally any more often than that because Peter was quite frugal with money, but tonight he considered an emergency. As he dialled the number for the restaurant, he thought that a curry would be just what he needed to settle his stomach and help him think of a way out of the mess that he was in.

Forty minutes later, Peter opened the front door and paid the delivery man for the steaming hot food that had arrived. Peter smiled and said, "Thank you," as the delivery man jumped in his car and sped off at rather an excessive speed. Shaking his head, Peter shut the door, double locked it and wandered up to the kitchen, all the while inhaling deep breaths of the delicious smelling cuisine he carried.

Unlike most of the people from the sports club who he occasionally went for a curry with, Peter found that his preferred options from the menu were usually those dishes without very much sauce. In particular, anything with Tandoori in the description. Tonight he'd ordered chicken tikka, onion bhajis, keema naan with poppadoms and onion salad. As he spooned it all on to one very large plate, his stomach gurgled in anticipation. As it turned out, one plate wasn't enough for the enormous feast that he'd ordered, and he ended up precariously balancing two plates and a drink on his way into the living room. For the next hour, he sat in front of the sports news, slowly eating all of the wonderful things he'd ordered. This, to him, was a great way to spend a night in. If he wasn't in the company of Tank or Richie, or both, then this is what he liked to do.

Later that evening he sat, bloated, on the sofa, full to the brim with delicious Indian food, contemplating what he should do next. Watching the sports news, he started to wonder how someone else would handle things if they were in his position. Looking back, he felt that he'd been a bit of a pushover. He'd never really confronted Manson, when maybe he should have. Maybe Manson was just like a schoolboy bully and just needed to be confronted, or to have his bluff called. Anyway it was too late for that now. But maybe it wasn't too late to stop being a pushover. As he turned off the lights in the living room, and silently berated himself for not having washed up all the dirty plates from his takeaway, he decided that he most definitely would stop being a pushover. And with that thought roaming its way around his head, he went to bed, hoping that a solution would present itself in the clear light of morning.

Peter woke up early, just after six, which was really unusual for him.

Amazingly, he felt bright, awake and full of energy. Normally he would be sleepy, reluctant to get up and grumpy, particularly at the weekend. Perhaps subconsciously his body knew it was November 5th because for weeks he had been looking forward to going to the firework display at the hockey club with Tank and Richie. He shot downstairs and switched all the lights on, deciding to keep the curtains closed as it was still dark and cold outside on this famous November morning. He switched the news on and began clearing away the plates and mess from his takeaway last night, all of the time thinking about the situation at Cropptech. He hadn't woken up with a solution buzzing around his brain, but things did seem a little bit clearer. He no longer felt the pressure or the loneliness that had seemed to consume him before. Until now, he hadn't even realised that it had been affecting him that much. But only now did he see things clearly. He also felt renewed, invigorated and full of self confidence. His decision last night to not be pushed around anymore must have had some deep down psychological effect.

Halfway through clearing the plates away, the weather forecast appeared on the television. Peter stopped what he was doing and paid attention. Normally he wouldn't have cared, but the fact that he was playing hockey later and the firework display was being staged at the sports club, piqued his interest.

He watched the much talked about new graphics the weather man was using to assist in his forecast, much as a child would watch its favourite television programme. After a couple of minutes it became clear that the weatherman was stringing things out and despite a ground frost being forecast for the next week or so, no rain, sleet or snow was due for the whole country for at least four or five days. "Good news for the firework display," he thought cheerily, as he continued to tidy away.

Peter focused his mind on what to do about losing his job and getting his phone and the *alea* back from the Cropptech site. He was also aware that he was due to play hockey this afternoon at the sports club and then meet up with Richie and Tank at the fireworks, later in the evening. In the back of his mind he knew also that he should contact Councillor Rosebloom and let him know that he'd been sacked, but that was something that he wished to avoid for as long as dragonly possible. He had a bad habit of putting off anything like that for as long as possible, usually causing more trouble by doing so he realised, but even so, it was something he just did.

By the time he'd finished crunching his way through his cornflakes, Peter had decided what he was going to do today. He knew that if the right people were on gate duty this morning, then getting his jacket back from his office, or ex office as it was now, would be relatively straightforward. Unfortunately it would be very difficult to find out who would be manning the main security gate without actually going there. So, he'd decided that the best course of action would be to drive his car and park it on the nearby housing estate, and then, in his running gear, go for a run along the main road that runs straight past Cropptech's main entrance. If he wore a hooded top, nobody should know that it was him running, and hopefully he would be able to get a good look at who was on gate duty.

He sat down and downloaded today's Daily Telepath, carefully reading all of the stories on the front page:

The Daily Telepath

Britain's Oldest Telepathic Newspaper   Issue No 252314

Plane Disaster Averted

By Beth Coil

A transatlantic plane flight had a lucky escape yesterday thanks to the actions of a heroic dragon passenger. Miranda Mower was travelling on the flight in her human guise, when an electrical fault caused the plane's computers to fail, some thirty miles off of the coast of Britain. An emergency was declared on board the flight and in the ensuing panic, Miranda managed to slip out of one of the auxiliary exits where she quickly transformed into her true form. While cloaking herself in an invisibility mantra, she managed to help glide the plane down for an emergency landing on an isolated farm in Cornwall. The Council would like to stress that under no circumstances should inexperienced or young dragons attempt to imitate what Miranda Mower did. She is a trained professional and has had over ten years of experience in the dragon guard. The human authorities are still looking in to the cause of the problem with the plane's computers. The British authorities seem puzzled by such an astonishing landing. Long may it continue.

Air Support Team Help Contain Wildfires

By Bertram Boat

The wildfires currently spreading across Northern Australia at the moment have been partially contained due to dragon intervention. The Tenth Southern Hemisphere Covert Operations Team stepped in around midnight local time yesterday. Under the cover of darkness the covert team burnt away large areas of scrubland in a bid to contain the fires and give the human firefighters a chance to resolve the crisis relatively quickly. The team also managed to shepherd a whole host of wildlife to safety while putting their own lives at risk. Our thanks, thoughts and best wishes go out to all the dragons throughout the world who constantly put themselves in danger on our behalf....bravo.

Dragon Census Download Ready

By Rory Key

The 1510 dragon census is now available for download from the government crystal node in London. The information available from this census totally eclipses the 1010 census, which was limited to say the least. No time restrictions are being placed on the download at the moment, although that may change depending on the usage. A small fee is applicable. The Dragon Council will soon be starting their recruitment drive for special enumerator dragons for the next census. Any one interested can find more details on the London crystal node.

Dragons Cause Credit Crunch?

By Omen Pliers

The council are looking in to reports that claim rogue elements in the dragon community may have deliberately manipulated events to ensure the start of the economic meltdown in the human world. When asked, all Councillors declined to comment.

South Pole Expedition Underway

By Amy Atlantis

Councillor D'Zone has sent an expedition of five top scientists to the South Pole to further investigate the global warming phenomenon. The group hope to arrive in the next couple of days, having travelled all the way by air. They hope to be set up and working within a day or two and will spend a further three months investigating before reporting back to the Council with their findings. The eyes of the dragon domain as a whole will be watching in anticipation for the results.

Choir Wins Yet Again

By Angela Crab

Dragon's Rage the famous pop choir and winner of this year's Telepathic Times Best New Entertainment Artist, have won another prestigious award. At last night's dragon entertainment awards in below ground Los Angeles, the stunning pop choir picked up the award for best newcomer in the overall music category. Choir Master Dev Ford was quoted as saying "This is the pinnacle for all of us. The award is a testament to everyone involved with the choir. Long may our success continue." The group have many new offers open to them, including a chance to appear on 'Dragon Factor'.

After half an hour he went upstairs and changed into his running gear, making sure to pick up his hooded top. With a new found confidence, he walked down the stairs in his shorts and running shoes, picked up his car keys from the table in the hallway and walked out to his car. With his hooded top on the passenger seat, he drove leisurely to the housing estate that backed on to the Cropptech facility, all the while listening to Radio 1. For the first time in as long as he could remember, Peter felt carefree and .... happy.

Parking in one of the estate's small car parks, Peter made sure he hadn't left any valuables on view in the car, as the estate itself had a bit of a reputation. Pulling on the hooded top, Peter did a few calf stretches and then set off at a light jog towards the main road. After a couple of minutes, Peter had left the estate and found himself running alongside the main road on a narrow strip of tarmac with grass and weeds either side of him, most coming nearly up to his knees. "Hmmm," he thought, "only a madman would choose this route to go for a run. Oh well, with any luck nobody should know it's me and I can be back at the car in ten or fifteen minutes with my jacket and its contents."

Peter focused desperately hard on the tarmac in front of him, convinced that if he lost concentration for even a moment it would mean a twisted ankle or worse, something he could definitely do without. Before he knew it, the turning into Cropptech came into view, and as he got closer and got a better view around the trees that separated the housing estate from the Cropptech site, he could see the security gatehouse, with the red and white barrier sitting across the road. Peter glanced down at his watch, pretending to be concerned about his running time as he approached the entrance. "Odd," he thought as he got nearly to the road. "Nobody manning the gate on the outside and although I can't be totally sure, it doesn't look as though there's anyone on the inside either."

Peter's pulse was racing and it wasn't anything to do with the running that he'd done. He stood about fifteen yards away from the gatehouse, his face masked by the grey hooded top that he wore, pretending to catch his breath and stretch out the muscles in his calf. His mind was overflowing with questions. "It could be a trap. But nobody knows I'm here," he thought. "Why would nobody be manning the gatehouse? In all my time it's never been unmanned and even if there's an emergency in another part of the facility, it still should under no circumstances be left unattended."

His new found confidence was wavering just a little. Thinking back to his vow last night not to be a pushover anymore, he reluctantly straightened up and walked briskly towards the open window of the gatehouse, which was adjacent to the security barrier. Looking around the outside to check whether anyone was about, he casually stood on tiptoes and peeked into the open window. He could see most of the open plan part of the inside, and nobody appeared to be there. It didn't mean that no one was in there of course. Someone could be in either of the toilets or the storage bay right at the back, all of which he couldn't see from where he was. But it was odd, he thought once again as a violent shiver raced up his invisible tail and made him shudder. Still worried that it might be a trap, but not really being able to see how, Peter opened the white double glazed door to the inside of the building. The corridor leading to the open plan office part was deserted apart from the water cooler and the hefty photocopier.

"Hello, is there anyone here?" he called out in the friendliest voice he could muster, not wanting to startle anyone.

Nothing, not a sausage. He tried again, this time a little louder.

"Hello, is there anyone here?"

Still no response. He cautiously edged his way down the corridor. As he passed the two toilets he gently pushed the doors in on themselves. Both doors opened, revealing nobody inside either. He carried on along the corridor, until it widened out into the office. There was definitely nobody here. None of the computers were even booted up, likewise printers and there was a full load of received faxes in the tray of the fax machine that should have been dealt with immediately. Peter walked through the open plan office until he got to a large metal door on the far side. The door led to the security bay, the only other place anyone could be in here, without Peter having come across them by now. Reluctantly he knocked and once again asked,

"Is anybody here?"

Still there was no reply. Gingerly he turned the handle of the door, and to his surprise, it opened. This in itself was enough to make the hairs on the back of Peter's neck stand up. This door was always kept locked. Always! Something was desperately wrong here. He just didn't know what. He walked into the security bay, looking at the bank of lockers on one side, spare uniforms truncheons and handcuffs on the other side. The whole place was like a ghost town, he thought. What should he do?

Coming out of the storage bay, he decided he would head over to the main building and see if anyone was over there. If they were he could let them know about the situation here, even, he supposed, if it meant revealing his identity to them. "The security of this site is way more important than that," he thought as he started back up the corridor towards the outside. Just then, through the open window, he heard a vehicle pull up outside the gatehouse. "Oh great," he thought. "How am I going to explain this away?"

Through the window, Peter heard the vehicle switch off its engine. Prepared to go and meet the driver and try and explain the situation, Peter suddenly heard voices from outside. His blood, which in its true form was green, abruptly ran cold.

"Oh please no, anything but this," he thought as panic surged throughout his body. It was Manson!

Standing halfway along the corridor, Peter froze, not knowing what to do, only able to listen to the voices coming from outside.

"You're late!" barked Manson.

"Only a few minutes," came the disinterested reply.

"I don't pay you the kind of money you're earning to be late," blustered Manson, with an edge to his voice.

"Hey, lighten up will ya."

"I'll lighten up when our business is concluded. I strongly suggest you concentrate on what you're paid for, or I'll make sure that you don't see the remaining fifty per cent of your payment," said Manson, angrily.

"Okay, okay, no need to get all silly about things," came the reply from beyond the door. "We'll just do what you say. No problem."

"Make sure you do," said Manson with venom in his voice.

"I'll raise the barrier. Take the trucks round to the loading bay. I want everything to run like clockwork. Just think, in a matter of hours you'll have been paid and I'll be long gone."

With that, Peter heard footsteps on the concrete outside, heading his way. Stuck halfway along the corridor, with few options open to him, Peter slid into the nearest toilet, letting the door gently close behind him. As he did so, he heard the familiar sound of the double glazed door opening up.

As he stood cornered in the tiny toilet, he tried to think of anything that would help his situation. In a flash, it came to him. Quickly he put down the lid on the toilet itself and clambered on top of it. Reaching up, he slid one of the polystyrene ceiling tiles out of position. Through the gap where the tile had been, just as he suspected, ran a series of thick pipes. Knowing that he was running out of time and probably had only one shot, Peter closed his eyes, bent his knees, and with just a hint of extra dragon strength, launched himself up towards the pipes. He got both hands around the largest and swiftly pulled himself up, so that he was crouching on a group of pipes. He leant over and pushed the polystyrene tile back into place. Just as it fell into place, Peter caught a glimpse through the diminishing gap of somebody opening the door from the corridor. Peter remained totally still, in the now pitch black hidey hole that he had found himself. Whoever it was, they were still there, he thought as sweat poured down his back and neck, while he tried to remain silent.

Abruptly a voice echoed down the corridor.

"What's the hold up? You alright in there?"

The toilet door swung closed. Peter could hear Manson on the other side of the door.

"No hold up. Just checking the place is totally empty," he told the impatient truck driver. "I'm just raising the barrier now."

From his hidden position in the ceiling, Peter could just make out the sound of two trucks starting their engines and then carefully moving off. A minute or so after that, he heard the outside door once again open and close. He hoped with all his heart that Manson had now left the gatehouse, but having been deceived before, Peter was in no hurry to get down from where he was, just in case. As he remained precariously crouched on the pipework, a small smile crossed his face, despite his rather dire predicament.

The reason he knew about the pipes running above the toilets was because of an incident that happened shortly after he joined Cropptech. To this day, he remembered it quite vividly. At the time, it was the talk of the security department. One of the most popular security guards was on a nightshift during the week. This particular guard was renowned for his pranks. Nothing malicious, just stuff to put a smile on people's faces. As nearly all the security staff had a decent sense of humour, the guard found himself to be quite popular and people generally appreciated the stuff that he got up to. Anyway, this particular night, the prank playing guard found himself on duty with a colleague he had worked with for years, and a trainee that had only started two weeks previously. As the night wore on, the prank playing guard plied his longstanding colleague with as much tea and coffee as he could. Just as he could see that his colleague was busting to use the toilet, the prankster disappeared, supposedly to do his 'rounds'. What he actually did was dive into the gents toilet, and do exactly what Peter had done. He removed the polystyrene ceiling tiles and hid above the toilet, waiting to surprise his friend. He knew it was just a matter of time before his friend would need the loo, so he waited patiently in his concealed spot. He didn't have to wait very long at all, as it turned out. Within a few minutes the toilet door opened and somebody entered. The cubicle door to the toilet then closed and the sound of the lock sliding shut could be heard. It was all the prankster could do to contain his laughter at this point. Hearing his friend below start his ablutions, the prankster slid back the tile and shouted "BOO!" as loud as he could. The shock couldn't have been greater for both of them. It wasn't his friend that jumped in fright from the toilet seat, but the newly employed trainee. He had quite literally, ... himself, a fact that everybody found amazingly funny when recounting the tale, some days later. Unfortunately for the prankster, the trainee had absolutely no sense of humour whatsoever, and ended up leaving Cropptech quite quickly after that, but not before making sure he got some compensation for his trouble. This in turn led to a company policy of no pranks, something it was rumoured that displeased Al Garrett greatly, although he apparently had little choice in the matter. The prankster was never the same again after that and left to take up a new job some six months later.

As Peter crouched in the same spot in the dark, he found it hard not to laugh at the poor trainee being surprised. Just a shame it couldn't be marketed as a laxative, he thought, grinning to himself.

Nearly an hour passed as Peter crouched for all he was worth on top of the array of pipes, in the ceiling above the toilet cubicle. He could tell it was nearly an hour because he kept on switching on the night light on his watch. Despite his dragon abilities, Peter's legs had started to get cramp, which was proving to be particularly difficult in such a tight space.

Most young dragons start out by thinking that when they assume human form, they will be immune to such simple things as cramp, but it just simply isn't so. To create the kind of form that will withstand time and everything the above world has to throw at it, dragons have to manipulate their DNA to such an extreme, that it is very difficult on first inspection to detect that they are anything but human. Only a very experienced surgeon or a series of blood tests would confirm that the subject is something other than a human being, and even then it would give no clue to what they actually are. Some dragons have even been able to manipulate their DNA to fool all known tests, blood and others. So, although Peter was struggling with his cramp, it wasn't the first time he had suffered from it, and he was pretty sure it wouldn't be the last.

"Hmmm," he thought as the muscles in his legs convulsed with pain once again. "Whatever's waiting for me, whether a trap by Manson or an empty building, now's the time to find out." He pulled back the ceiling tile carefully and swung his legs over towards the pipes. The pain from the cramp increased tenfold. He jumped down on to the lid of the toilet, trying to make as little noise as possible, at the same time expecting a dozen armed guards to burst through the door and open fire on him. Needless to say, this didn't happen, and after a few minutes of stretching, he was feeling a lot more confident about his chances of getting out in one piece.

Cautiously, he opened the door into the corridor. A wave of relief swept over him as he saw that it was as deserted as when he had arrived. His first instinct was to make a bolt for the door and then run back to his car so that he could get help. But what kind of help would he get? If he called the police, what would he tell them? That he was trespassing on private property and had seen the head of security letting two lorries into the site. "Oh yes, very suspicious," he thought, sarcastically. He couldn't go to the authorities, he couldn't go to Garrett and even if he knew exactly who to turn to in the dragon world, the chances were that Manson would be long gone by the time help arrived. What really didn't help matters in Peter's mind was the fact that nobody knew where he was and he didn't even have his phone so that he could let Tank or Richie know what was going on, not that they'd necessarily believe him, of course. For all intents and purposes, he was on his own. As he strolled back into the open plan office to find a working bank of security monitors, he thought to himself, "If it means being on my own to take Manson down, then so be it."

After two or three minutes of rooting around, it became clear that all of the monitors had been disabled. Peter tried everything that he knew to get them back up and running but very little seemed to work. After ten minutes, a very nervous ten minutes, Peter had only managed to get the car park cameras back online, and they were scrolling through the different views every ninety seconds or so. Peter watched carefully, not seeing anything out of the ordinary at first. By the third rotation, it became apparent that something was going on at the distribution depot. There were people driving fork lift trucks around, when on a Saturday none of that should be happening. Also, the whole area was littered with Manson's guards, the thugs with machine guns. Things, Peter thought, had just got a lot more serious.

Going back into the security bay at the back of the building, Peter picked up three pairs of handcuffs, all he could fit in the pockets of his running shorts, and took a truncheon as well. Not that it would do much good against a machine gun, he thought as he poked it in the pocket of his hooded top, but you never knew when it might come in handy.

As he walked back across the open plan office, he stopped at the nearest desk. He lifted up the handset on the desk's phone and pressed the button for an outside line. Just as he suspected, there was no dial tone, just a long constant buzz. "Oh well, figured as much," he told himself, "but it was worth a try. At least Richie and Tank would have known where I was."

Peter walked out of the gatehouse and headed for the entrance to the main building. He was careful to circumvent the car park security cameras, knowing that if he avoided them, then the chance of anyone detecting him was remote at best, because the other cameras had been sabotaged. Once at the main entrance he tried the doors but unsurprisingly they were locked. He carefully skirted the building and arrived at the door he would normally have used to enter when walking between the gatehouse and his office. That too remained firmly locked, but Peter thought it worth a try, if only to get his phone and the *alea* back. With options running out, Peter had little choice but to head for the distribution depot. He headed the long way round, hoping that any security he encountered might be a little less stringent than he'd witnessed on the security cameras.

Avoiding the car park cameras proved more of a challenge than Peter would have thought, but thanks to some diving over ornamental hedgerows and a very long crawl underneath two portacabins, he found himself overlooking the back of the distribution depot in no time at all. The much smaller car park at the back of the depot was deserted, apart from an unmarked white van which stood alone almost in the middle, with its tailgate down. From what little Peter had gathered from the security cameras it appeared that the two large trucks were around the other side, having something loaded into them by the fork lift trucks inside the warehouse.

Peter had hoped to sneak in through the back entrance with a view to seeing exactly what was going on, but this van was parked directly between him and the back entrance. He decided to wait and see if anyone was actually in the back of the van, something he couldn't see from his current position, or if anyone was coming out of the back entrance to load it up regularly. He was going to have to cross the expansive car park in order to get to the back entrance of the depot and if anybody at all was about, they would spot him immediately.

He waited just over ten minutes before deciding it was as clear as it was going to get. He just hoped his luck held out. Starting out at a sprint, Peter zipped across the car park and stopped at the side of the van, putting it between him and the back entrance. He listened carefully for any noises coming from the inside of the van, but it was totally quiet. Gingerly he slipped along the side, until he stood right next to the tailgate. Very slowly he peeked around the corner and peered into the back of the van. Lying on the floor of the van was a massive... what could only be described as a harness. The harness itself looked as though it had been insulated against the cold, like a giant parka coat. Attached to the harness on either side were two giant nets, all folded up and instead of being made of rope, they were made from some sort of pliable metal. Peter looked on in astonishment. What the hell could carry a harness like that, he thought.

His thoughts were abruptly interrupted by two figures appearing from the other side of the van.

"Well...........look who it isn't."

Peter's stomach felt as if he had just jumped off the Empire State Building. His temperature was rising rapidly and his head felt like it was spinning faster than a fart in a hurricane. There, not three feet away, were two of the bullies from his nursery ring: Theobald and Fisher.

"So Benty, what would you be doing here on this cold winter's day?" said Theobald, grinning.

Peter tried desperately hard to focus his mind. What was he going to tell them? Would they even believe him? Had some help arrived, even if it was in this most unusual of forms? He felt so confused, so very light headed and confused. He had to get them to help him; it was his only chance of bringing Manson to justice.

Peter turned towards Theobald and Fisher and, opening his arms in a show of friendship and to signify that he meant no harm, he appealed to them.

"Guys, let's just put our differences aside for a while. There's something much more important going on here," he pleaded.

Theobald and Fisher both frowned at the same time.

"Such as?" said Fisher.

Peter put his arms around the shoulders of them both and drew them back out of sight of the back entrance to the distribution depot. Pulling them in close, he lowered his voice to a whisper.

"Something really bad is going on here. I'm not exactly sure what, and what I do know would take too long to explain, but I really need your help, both of you."

Fisher and Theobald both looked at each other, confused expressions marking their faces.

"This is really, really big guys. I'm sure the dragon council would be very grateful for your help. Very grateful," Peter said, hopefully appealing to their selfishness, knowing that if they helped him and thwarted whatever it was that Manson was up to, the council would almost certainly reward their efforts in some way shape or form.

"The............the council know you're here?" stammered Fisher nervously.

"Oh no," replied Peter without thinking. "Nobody knows I'm here. All I was saying is that once the council find out how much you've helped me, I'm sure they'll honour you or reward you or both."

As he was speaking a strange, menacing look was forming on Theobald's face. Just a split second too late, Peter realised what he'd just told them. That nobody knew he was here, especially anyone from the dragon council. Peter stepped back from the two of them, convinced he'd just made one of the biggest mistakes of his relatively short life. Theobald and Fisher both glared at him with evil intent. Peter prepared to turn and run. Without warning, a sharp pain blossomed in his head and, as he started to fall to the floor, his last memory was the image of Theobald and Fisher both laughing, before he lost consciousness.

* * *

The first thing he noticed was the cold. He was so cold it hurt. Summoning up every ounce of strength in his body, he rolled over onto his side. Slivers of light illuminated the dark space that he found himself lying in. Trying to push the excruciating pain to one side, Peter attempted to recall what had happened. After a few seconds, it all came flooding back to him. Miserably, he let out a long breath, which immediately condensed in front of him. He tried, against the pain, to sit up, and it was only then that he realised his hands had been bound behind his back, presumably, he thought, with one of the pairs of handcuffs he had taken from the security bay of the gatehouse.

As he wriggled around, eventually getting in a sitting position, still with his hands behind his back, he took stock of his situation. He was almost certain he was in the back of the white van that was in the rear car park of the distribution depot. He deduced this partly from the fact that he was definitely in a van of some sort, but also because, lying on the floor at the other end of where he was sitting, was the harness that he'd noticed when he first looked into the back of that white van. Apart from that, the insides, lit only from the light shining through the tiny gaps in the rear doors, were totally and utterly bare. His head throbbed really badly from whatever had hit him. "Almost certainly Casey," Peter thought to himself.

It was unusual to start with that it was just Theobald and Fisher. Peter couldn't think of a time when it hadn't been the three of them. "That would also explain why I didn't sense the presence of anyone. A human, I would have sensed, a dragon, well..................... I should have sensed them, but maybe like Manson they were using a mantra or something."

He was suddenly overcome with a feeling of complete failure. He felt so stupid. It seemed so obvious looking back at it now. Of course Theobald, Fisher and Casey were in league with Manson. It made sense on so many different levels. Those three idiots were always after a fast buck. It would also explain how Manson was able to perform some of his so called 'tricks'. It wasn't him doing them, Peter thought. It was Theobald, Fisher and Casey.

Manson himself must be just some low life devious human criminal, who had just employed the three stooges to help out.

Although this moment of clarity about what had really happened had washed away the feeling of failure, the physical pain Peter was starting to experience was becoming unbearable. He tried in earnest to break free of the handcuffs, something which in normal circumstances would take little or no effort, even for a young dragon. The cold was affecting him deeply. He looked down and studied his legs. He was still dressed in the same shorts and hooded top that he had been wearing before being knocked out. To his horror, he could just see his legs turning a pale shade of blue with cold, in the very dim light. He hadn't been put in a freezer or anything, just dumped in here by the look of things. If that was the case, the cold he was feeling was just due to the fact that it was a cold November day, and he was in shorts and a very thin top. All of which must mean that he'd been here for a fair few hours.

He looked round to try and check his watch, but only succeeded in seeing that it had been removed from his wrist. "That's how cold I am," he thought. "I can't even feel whether I'm wearing a watch or not."

Peter sat back against the inside of the van and tried to think warm thoughts in the hope that it would clear his head, even a little. The problem was the cold. There was just no way he could use any of his dragon abilities while he was feeling this cold, so in effect he was stuck and at the mercy of either Manson, his nursery ring bullies, or both. Not a pleasant thought, either way. Desperately not wanting to give up, he forced himself to topple over on to his back, so that his head was facing the harness. Slowly, he used his feet to scoot along in its direction. It was only eight or so feet away, but it felt like an eternity as his cold wrists and back dragged against the dirty, freezing floor of the van.

Eventually after two or three minutes, he reached the edge of the harness. Pushing himself up against the side of the van once more, he leaned forward to have a good look at the harness and all its fittings. The netting appeared to be made of some sort of very tough, flexible, metal filaments. The straps and linkages of the harness were made of the highest quality leather by the looks of things. And underneath all of the leather straps was a giant insulated cocoon-like enclosure, made from what looked like a dozen different high quality thermal jackets. It looked like a giant patchwork of very desirable arctic protection gear. "I'm not sure I want to meet whoever knitted that thing, or more importantly, who or what it was intended for," Peter thought to himself, as he tried keenly to rub back some heat into his wrists.

He now had some kind of goal, something to aim for. He figured that if he could open up the cocoon enough, he could snuggle up inside, and hopefully get warm enough for some of his dragon abilities to become available, all providing of course that he remained 'bad guy free'. As he managed to wiggle across the metal netting, once again causing a great deal of pain to his hands and wrists, he noticed that the small slivers of light coming into the van from outside were getting dimmer. "Oh great, it's getting dark outside." The only consolation was that at least now he had some idea of what time it was and how long he'd been unconscious for. Knowing that it was starting to get dark made Peter think about the firework display that was due to start at the sports club, in about two hours time. At this precise moment, he'd have given anything at all to be there with Tank and Richie.

After what seemed like about three hours, but his best guess told him it was probably more like half an hour, (for he had no way to know with the light having totally faded, and his enhanced dragon abilities all but a distant memory), he had managed to rip enough of the thermal material to create a gap big enough for him to wriggle inside. Of course, getting in there was a whole different matter. After another twenty minutes of trial and error in the dark, Peter had managed to get as much of his body in the cocoon as he was going to get. As he curled up against the material, he tried again to think warm thoughts, in the hope that it would speed the whole process along. The temptation now was to fall asleep, something he was concentrating very hard on avoiding. The moment he had enough strength to break out of the handcuffs, he wanted to be free from all of this. He planned to get out of here as soon as was physically possible, with a view to leaving whatever was going on at Cropptech firmly to the dragon council.

Trying to keep track of time proved of little success, but after a while he was sure he was starting to warm up. He was starting to feel sleepy and could almost feel the metal of the handcuffs chafing his wrists. In the haziness of his mind, Peter started to imagine he could hear voices. Voices that were gradually getting louder, or closer.

Startled fully awake, he realised it wasn't his imagination. The voices were coming from somewhere outside of the van and disappointingly they were most definitely getting closer. Concentrating with everything that he had, he tried to channel his dragon abilities into his cold and frail human shaped body. Flexing his arms, he tried for all that he was worth to break the handcuffs holding his arms in place behind his back. After a few seconds, it was clear that he was still too cold. Silently, he swore to himself as he waited for whoever the voices belonged to, to open the van's tailgate.

The voices were close now. Peter couldn't make out the exact words, but it sounded as though someone was in a rush. The sound of two doors opening, one after the other, became clear, quickly followed by them closing again shortly afterward. The van's engine started with a lacklustre rumble. "We're going somewhere," Peter thought to himself. "I've still got a chance, as long as the journey's a reasonably long one."

Peter snuggled himself up as much as he could in the giant patchwork cocoon, hoping that the journey, wherever they were headed, would give him enough time to warm up. By now he was getting just a little bit mad about the whole situation that he found himself in. So much so that he was even contemplating turning into his dragon form, if he ever got warm enough to do so. Very unlike Peter, but he kept telling himself that desperate times called for desperate measures and that the dragon council would fully understand, once they found out the full circumstances; well, just maybe they would.

As the van started to twist and turn, Peter tried to imagine where they were headed. He tried to visualise every left and right turn, but truth be told he was probably lost long before they actually left the Cropptech facility.

He tried feverishly to warm himself up, not knowing when the unexpected journey would end. He tried to rub his hands together but the handcuffs would only allow him to rub his fingers against each other as he slid about in the back. He rubbed his knees and legs together while at the same time massaging both of his feet. "Another hour like this," he thought, "and things will most certainly be looking up."

But did he have another hour? All too shortly he would find out.

* * *

At the sports club, the evening's festivities were just getting started. Outside, a third of the massive car park had been cordoned off and attractions of different sorts were just finishing setting up. Small fairground rides stood alongside candyfloss stalls, hook a duck stalls, tombolas and all sorts of food stalls, from hot dogs to hog roasts. All of the sport had finished, with every home side, rugby, hockey and lacrosse all, amazingly, having won.

The atmosphere in the bar and the clubhouse itself had been fantastic all afternoon. Some of the sports players from the various sections still remained from the afternoon's exertions, propping up the bar and watching the football results on the giant plasma screen television. Most, however, had gone home to pick up the rest of their family and bring them back for the firework display, and were just starting to return in dribs and drabs. Tank stood at the bar with Richie, mobile phone held firmly to his ear. After a few moments he returned the phone to the right pocket of his jeans and turned to face Richie, with a worried expression on his face.

"Still no response. All I get is his answer phone and I've left about a dozen messages already."

Richie moved in closer to her friend, primarily to make sure that they couldn't be overheard.

"I've left messages for him as well. I'd like to think that he's just sulking, but I have to say I'm really not sure now. It's so out of character for him to miss a hockey match, unheard of in fact. And I think however much he's sulking, I'm pretty sure he'd have the decency to phone that captain guy up and tell him he couldn't play, even if he had to lie and say he was ill or something."

Tank nodded in agreement, while at the same time taking a giant slurp of his drink.

"I went round to his house on the way to the game today, but nobody was there. The curtains were all open, but there was no sign of his car. I just thought he'd left early to go to hockey and that we'd meet up here after the game. But since you told me about him being sacked yesterday, I'm not sure what the hell is going on now."

"I only found out this morning when I ran into one of my training staff in town while I was shopping," said Richie, waving past Tank to one of her lacrosse teammates who had just come in with her husband and two children, both of whom were carrying the biggest sticks of pink and blue candyfloss that Richie had ever seen. "I've been away at our Guildford site doing some

313

in house training for two days. I'm absolutely shocked at what's gone on. I couldn't believe it when Sarah told me, in town this morning."

Tank shook his head, taking the final swig of his drink. He bent down low and put his head beside Richie's.

"I've even searched for him telepathically," he whispered, "using one of Gee Tee's old mantras that can treble the range, but still no luck."

"I don't know what else to do at the moment, Rich. There's still time for him to turn up tonight. Maybe you're right and he's just been sulking. Wouldn't be too much of a surprise would it?"

The two friends parted heads and nodded, looking at their empty glasses.

"More?" said Tank, raising his empty pint glass in Richie's direction.

"Ohh, go on then," said Richie rolling her eyes. "Just one more." As Tank caught the eye of one of the bar staff, the two friends laughed, hoping that Peter would at some point walk through the door and complete their evening by coming to watch the much hyped firework display.

*   *   *

Although Peter had no idea where he was, he knew for certain that the van he was in had just turned off the main road and was now negotiating a very bumpy track full of potholes, and he could feel each and every one. "This," he thought, "does not bode well." A track off the main road almost certainly meant he was very near his final destination and he was not nearly warm enough yet. Once again he tugged frantically at the handcuffs holding his hands together behind his back, but he knew before he did it, what the result would be. Still he hadn't recovered enough to break free.

After a short while the van stopped. Peter lay wrapped in all the layers, as frightened as he'd ever been. He could hear voices outside once again. They seemed impatient, edgy almost. He found a deep-down rage burning inside him. He wanted to take on dragon form and go and destroy these, these..................criminals. How dare they imprison him! Even with the help of Theobald, Casey and Fisher, he should not find himself in this situation. He found himself thinking of all the things he could do to these men, if he managed to change into his dragon form. He could trash the van he was in with one powerful swipe of his wings. He could scare the living daylights out of these humans so much, that however much therapy they received in prison, it would not be nearly enough.

Another sound jolted him out of his wishful thinking. Another vehicle was arriving. No, make that two other vehicles. He heard more voices alongside the van and he waited for the doors to open. As the seconds turned into minutes the doors didn't open. A tiny ray of hope shone from the pit of Peter's stomach. All he needed was a bit more time. Clearly these humans knew nothing, otherwise they would have dealt with him while he was at his coldest or when he was unconscious. Peter heard more talking and then a kind of loud squeaking noise, a bit like a rusty gate creaking open. One by one, all of the vehicles started up their engines, including the van that Peter was in. Once again Peter found himself thinking of his friends, who by now would be waiting to see the fireworks at the sports club. He would have given anything to be with them now.

The van started to move off, swaying from side to side as it dipped in and out of a few more potholes. Then, to Peter's surprise, the van went back to being on a perfectly flat surface once again. If they were back on a main road, which clearly didn't make any sense at all, but if they were, that could only be a good thing, he thought optimistically. His newfound hope was shattered only a few seconds later as the van came to a stop and once again turned off its engine. Peter could hear doors being opened and closed again, but the sound that terrified him the most was the tailgate of the other vehicles being lowered.

"This is it," he thought. He mustered all of his concentration and thought of his friends, hoping that this might help him in some way. "Damn, still nothing," he thought. He was so close he knew. He could feel his dragon powers, just beneath the surface, sooooo very close, but agonisingly out of reach. "Just a few more minutes, please let them ignore me for a few more minutes. That just might be enough," he thought, breathing hard from the exertion of trying.

With the darkness surrounding him, he rubbed together every bit of his body that he could, knowing that even a few seconds might make the difference. The voices he could hear could only be ten or twenty feet away. It sounded to Peter like there were at least six or seven of them. While he was listening intently, trying to glean anything that would help him later, he could hear.............something in the background. It sounded like a ....concert or something but, try as he might, he couldn't make out the exact content of what was going on.

*   *   *

Tank and Richie finished their drinks in the now near empty bar. Hundreds of people packed the patio area and the viewing area of the lacrosse pitch directly outside the window of the bar, waiting in anticipation for the bonfire to be lit and the fireworks to start. The two friends grabbed their jackets off their respective bar stools and headed for the open doors that led outside from the bar area.

As they did so, the reflection of dozens of different coloured sparklers twinkled off the adjoining windows. The children, Richie noted as she stepped outside just in front of Tank, were all having a whale of a time, creating different patterns and laughing their little socks off. Richie felt a pang of sorrow sweep across her, which came as something of a surprise to her. As she slipped her coat over her shoulders to protect herself from the cold, something she and Tank were more aware of than most here, she tried to understand what it was that stirred such powerful feelings inside her.

They stood at the back of the crowd, gazing over people's heads, waiting for it all to start. Children were on their parents' shoulders, rubbing their hands excitedly, dressed in all sorts of colourful attire. Richie had been searching inside herself for some answers to her sudden onslaught of emotion, when suddenly in a moment of clarity, it all became clear. It was because of the children. It was so obvious now that she thought about it. It was like a startling revelation. Richie, she realised envied all of the humans, because of their....................... children. She wanted what they had. "Oh my God," she thought, "as if it isn't bad enough that I play lacrosse, spend nearly all my time amongst humans, engage in arm wrestling contests, but now I want to have children." She could just see all the members of the dragon council toppling over one by one as it was announced to them that a certain female dragon wanted to have children, just as humans did, and raise them that way. A huge grin crossed her face, as she cuddled up to Tank for some extra warmth.

They stood and waited patiently for the proceedings to begin. By the look of things, the chairman of the sports club would be taking hold of the microphone to kick things off just after the music piped through the PA system finished. The pair continued to gaze out over the darkened lacrosse pitch to the barely visible bonfire beyond that was about to be lit. To either side of the lacrosse pitch lay the rugby pitch with its big flood lights, now turned off. The giant H shaped posts could just be seen if you looked carefully in the dark. On the other side of the lacrosse pitch sat the now deserted Astroturf hockey pitch. Just like the rugby pitch, the flood lights were of course switched off, to give everyone a better view of the fireworks. Although the hockey pitch was only fifty or so yards away, because of the absolute darkness that enveloped it, it might as well have been on a different planet.

* * *

The handle to the tailgate of the van squeaked as it turned. Terror raced fear up Peter's spine to see which one would win. The doors whooshed open, letting in a different kind of darkness to the one that Peter had experienced in the last few hours.

"Aaaaahhhhhh look, he's cuddled up like a little fluffy bunny," said a voice sarcastically, as the light of a torch played across Peter's face.

Two pairs of hands appeared and began pulling the metal nets which were attached to the cocoon that Peter was in.

"Sorry Fluffy," said the sarcastic voice once again, "but we can't have you missing the big show. Boss's orders I'm afraid."

As Peter lay in the cocoon, slowly sliding towards the open door at the back of the van and goodness knows what kind of fate, he made one last concerted effort to free his hands from the restraints. Much to his amazement, it worked. His hands were free, and more importantly, nobody else would know. He decided he would bide his time and wait for the right opportunity to present itself.

The last part of Peter's exit from the van was particularly unpleasant. The two large pairs of hands gave a huge yank on the netting; Peter sped up and, as he reached the tailgate, received a huge 'thump' in his stomach that knocked the wind totally out of him, before being unceremoniously dumped on the floor. As Peter tried to adjust his eyes to his new environment, somewhere outside was all he could tell at the moment, the sound of his nice snuggly cocoon being ripped from him assaulted his frozen ears. He moved around and acted as frightened as he could, so no one would realise that his hands were free. "The longer no one else suspects," he thought, "the more time it buys me to find the right opportunity."

As he was pulled free from the last shredded fragments of the cocoon, a large hand grabbed his shoulder and sent him tumbling towards the floor, face first. Midway through his fall, Peter managed to spectacularly roll around, so that he landed on his back, still concealing the fact that his hands were free. Landing with a huge bump, his hands took the brunt of the impact. Pain rolled up both of his arms, causing him to let out a little squeal. However, it wasn't the pain travelling up his arms that caused him the most concern. It was the fact that the skin on the back of both of his hands had been burnt off quite badly as he landed. He recognised the sensation immediately, after all he'd been experiencing it for nearly two years now on a regular basis. He was on an Astroturf pitch. What the hell was going on he wondered, through the pain and the cold biting at his body.

He wouldn't have to wait very long to find out.

*   *   *

Meanwhile, not a million miles away, Richie and Tank cuddled up to each other in their big thick coats, watching as the chairman of the sports club thanked the usual people over the PA system for their help in making the display possible. The smell of cooked food drifted over the crowd from the stalls at the front of the building. The stars lit up the sky like diamonds atop a black velvet cloak. There wasn't a cloud in the sky, making it a very chilly November night indeed. Everybody's breath froze as they exhaled, with most of the young children absolutely fascinated by it. For a dragon, this was not a very nice experience. Even though Tank and Richie were wrapped up in warm clothes, every time they pulled in a deep breath, it was like inhaling a swarm of hungry insects that chewed on your very insides as the breath travelled in, and scraped away anything remaining on the way out. Dragons, you have to remember, are comfortable with exceedingly high temperatures. The average temperature of a normal dragon when it exhales with a flame is in excess of 800 degrees, so by comparison it's quite understandable that a temperature in minus figures would cause very different effects in different dragons. Some can withstand the cold, suffering only a slight irritability, while others suffer extreme pain, in some cases passing out all together. Tank and Richie seemed to be somewhere between the two extremes.

The chairman started the count down from ten, on his microphone. The children were all screaming the numbers as loud as they could. As the numbers approached five, more adults started to join in. 4................3................2.....
...........1.......

The bonfire sprang into life, clearly enhanced by something very flammable, other than the wood that formed its main frame. A dreamy look crossed the two friends' faces at exactly the same time, as they both gazed lovingly at the flames dancing and swirling in the distance.

*   *   *

As Peter's eyes adjusted to the darkness he knew, however unlikely it was, that he was on the Astroturf pitch at the sports club. The noise that he hadn't been able to identify before, he now knew was someone speaking through a PA system not very far away, even though he struggled to make out the exact words. As he was pulled roughly to his feet, he tried desperately to keep his hands hidden, while at the same time having a big long look around to see exactly where he was. Dragged forward by two burly blokes, each holding one of his biceps, Peter counted the number of people he could see on the Astroturf, by the number of torch beams he could see. "Six," he thought, "plus the two either side of me. Not as bad as it could be. I think I might have half a chance, now that my hands are free."

After a sneaky look round, Peter came to the conclusion that it was most definitely the Astroturf at Salisbridge that he was on. He could just make out the side of the clubhouse, which seemed to be obscured slightly by some kind of misty barrier. As if his suspicions needed confirmation, a giant bonfire blazed to life about three hundred yards away. "My god, the firework display," he thought. "I really am here. Tank and Richie must be just over there. All I have to do is attract their attention. Things most certainly are looking up."

A short sharp punch in the back quickly brought Peter back to the reality of the situation. His knees started to buckle. It was all he could do to remain

319

standing and keep his hands together as if still handcuffed. Two of the torch lights broke off from the others and headed towards Peter and the two henchmen. It was very hard to make out any detail in the near total darkness, but as the torches got closer, Peter could just make out two maniacal grins. "Theobald and Casey," he thought.

"Ahhh there he is,"

"Not getting a bit cold are you Benty?"

Peter shook his head in disgust, as he stood in the freezing cold in just his shorts and hooded top.

"There's still time you know. I'll even speak up to the council on your behalf if you stop all this now and come peacefully."

Theobald and Casey both doubled up with laughter.

"Tell me Benty, do you really think you're in any position to speak to the council?" said Casey, in between bursts of laughter.

"They'll find out. You know as well as I do that they will."

"Maybe so, Benty. But do we look like we give any sort of a damn?" snarled Theobald menacingly, with all signs of the laughter disappeared.

A chill ran down Peter's spine, despite the fact that he was barely dressed, on a freezing Astroturf pitch on one of the coldest November evenings in living memory. It wasn't so much what they said, he thought as he faced the two bullies, it was the offhand manner in which they said it, almost as if the outcome of the evening had already been decided, with Peter having absolutely no say in it at all.

Looking beyond his two tormentors, Peter could just make out two other vans, on what he guessed was about the middle of the synthetic pitch. With his eyesight adjusting all the time, he could now see that the tailgates to the vans were open and the figures with the torches were unloading something from the vans onto the pitch. It was, however, impossible to see exactly what it was they were unloading from where he was standing. All he could gather was that it looked heavy and there seemed to be a lot of it.

"Taking an interest in our little operation, eh Benty?" said Theobald sarcastically, having caught Peter looking over at the vans.

Peter remained silent, no longer sure he could hold his temper and wait for the right opportunity. With every second that passed he was getting colder, and with that, weaker and further away from using his dragon powers. Unlike both Casey and Theobald who were wrapped up in very flash looking outdoor weather gear. "They could probably access their powers in an instant," Peter thought, "and tear me apart, no trouble at all."

"Cat got your tongue, Bentttyyyyyy?"

"Yeah, come on Benty, give your old nursery ring mates a smile will ya?"

The two humans holding onto Peter's biceps swapped confused expressions with one another at the mention of nursery rings. In fact much of the night's activities seemed very much beyond them. All they really knew was that they were being paid an awful lot of money for one night's work.

Peter still remained silent.

"Ahh well, perhaps you'll be more talkative for the boss," said Theobald. Casey just stood there and sniggered.

"And look, here he comes now."

*   *   *

With the bonfire blazing in all its glory, the crowd, including Tank and Richie, were on their second countdown of the night, once again being led by the chairman of the sports club, who it had to be said, looked totally out of sorts. Despite missing Peter and the pain of breathing caused by the extreme cold, both Tank and Richie took great comfort in the giant bonfire, even though it was some distance away. Nobody seemed bored with yet another countdown, in fact the children seemed more excited this time round, if anything.

"6...5...4...3...2...1..."

The squeal of rockets zooming into the air surrounded the crowd. That special firework smell that can only mean it's bonfire night, hung in the air. As the rockets reached the optimum point in their flight, they exploded into an array of colours, lighting up the sky in front of the lacrosse pitch and the bonfire on the ground beyond it. The crowd cheered as one. More fireworks continued to be fired into the sky.

*   *   *

Peter froze, as the fireworks beyond the Astroturf pitch lit up the entire sky. It wasn't because he was so close to his friends that he could almost call out, no. It was because the stunning colours and bright lights in the sky had backlit the foreboding figure of Manson, stick in hand, skulking towards him. While the sight of Manson was cause for alarm in Peter's mind, he kept telling himself that he was just a human and that there was nothing to fear. "He may be running things," he thought, "but there's no way that Casey and Theobald would murder me, another dragon. And that's what it would take." Manson, for all his show, was just a human, alright a pretty scary one at that, but still just a human. On his best day he couldn't hurt Peter, he would need the help of the bullies and although Peter despised them, he knew full well that they wouldn't be party to murder. So, as Manson approached, Peter felt confident enough to give him a big toothy smile and jut out his jaw in defiance.

Manson rubbed his chin with his thumb and forefinger, inspecting the grinning Bentwhistle. He turned to Casey and Theobald.

"When you said you had a little surprise for me, I had no idea it would be this good," he crowed. "Where exactly did our cold little friend come from?"

Theobald took a step forward.

"He was sneaking around the distribution centre earlier on. We took the liberty of capturing him, after he told us he was on his own and that nobody knew where he was."

Manson nodded, while walking around Peter as if inspecting him like a piece of meat.

"Very good, the two of you, very good indeed." Turning away from Peter, Manson pointed his walking stick at Theobald and said,

"Just out of interest, I've seen no sign of Fisher tonight. Why is that? I thought the three of you were in this together."

Peter watched carefully as fear passed across the faces of the two bullies, and.........something else.

Casey seemed too frightened to talk. He could barely look Manson in the eyes. It was Theobald that spoke up, albeit reluctantly.

"He um, he um, kind of had a change of heart about things," he stammered, looking in Peter's direction.

"A change of heart?" growled Manson.

Theobald stammered on, while looking directly down at the floor.

"Yes, a change of heart. After we, after we captured...........HIM," he spat, pointing at Peter, "Fisher began having second thoughts, wanting us all just to go to the council and tell them everything."

"Did he now?" said Manson with a menacing glint in his eyes.

"He did."

"So where is Fisher now? Has he run off to warn the council?"

Peter watched with interest and more than a little hope. If Fisher had warned the council, the dragons could be here at any second to free him.

Theobald, head hunched over, staring at the ground, started to shake noticeably as he began to reply to Manson.

"We took care of him," he stuttered quietly.

Manson opened his eyes wide and raised his eyebrows.

"Do tell," he said in his rather feigned posh accent.

Every cell in Peter's body screamed for him to make a run towards the crowd, to get away from the evil that currently surrounded him. Instead he just remained, rooted to the spot, a tear creeping slowly down his cheek from the far side of his right eye.

Manson waited for the panic stricken Theobald to continue. Although the air was filled with Whooshes and Bangs, Whizzes and Crackles, from the fireworks above them, the silence surrounding the beings gathered on the synthetic pitch was overwhelming.

"C...c...c...c...c Casey and I, w...w...w...we ....took care of him, Sire," muttered Theobald, to no one in particular.

"For good?" asked Manson firmly.

"Yes, Sire."

"Sire?" thought Peter, as a steady stream of tears now rolled down his cheek. "What is that all about?"

Manson walked forward towards Theobald and Casey who were standing side by side, shaking from their shoulders downward. He stopped in front of them and pulled their heads up to look him in the eye.

"If I wasn't sure of your loyal support, know this. I am now. It wasn't the fault of either of you that Fisher was so weak and easily led. You did what you had to. You had no other choice."

The two bullies continued to shake, but both nodded emphatically.

Manson grabbed both of them by the shoulder, letting his walking stick drop to the frozen, sand covered pitch, which because of the freezing conditions was rapidly becoming reminiscent of an ice rink.

"When the time comes...............and know this, it will............. both of you will be part of the new order of things. You will have wealth and power such as you can't begin to imagine. The part you've played here will not be forgotten. Now................let's get back to the matter at hand."

Both bullies nodded in agreement, Peter noticed and, as Manson turned away to pick up his stick, Casey sneakily wiped away a tear or two behind his back.

Manson walked right up to Peter and looked him in the eye. Peter matched his gaze, not flinching once. As Peter stared deeply into Manson's dark forbidding eyes, a torrent of doubt rose up inside of him. It did seem to make sense that Manson was a just a normal human criminal, in league with Theobald, Casey and F................... He'd started to think of Fisher. It was true that he'd never liked him very much, mainly because of the intense bullying he had received from the three of them, through pretty much his entire time in the nursery ring. But even Fisher didn't deserve this kind of fate. What on earth was going on that would get one dragon murdered by his friends and two more scared witless by a seemingly unimportant human criminal? Something was wrong. "I'm missing some important piece of the puzzle. Something I don't know, or haven't seen," he thought.

Peter was startled out of his thoughts by Manson spitting in his face. Peter's first reaction was to bring his hands up to wipe his face, but the two brutes still had hold of his biceps, and on thinking about it, Peter decided he would only have revealed that his hands weren't bound, had he succeeded in wiping his face.

"Look at you," growled Manson, only a few centimetres from Peter's face. "You think you're so superior. I bet at this very moment you're planning a way out. A way to contact your friends, just over there." Manson pointed towards where he knew the crowd watching the fireworks would be. He let out a horrid laugh, more of a cross between a laugh and a giant snort, in fact.

Peter just looked straight ahead, trying to ignore the spit running down his face and the cold biting at his entire body.

"It's not going to happen you know. Your friends, I mean. You're not going to be able to reach them. They'll never know how you died, how much pain you suffered and why. Well, they won't know until it's too late, anyway."

Peter's heart (not his real one) was pounding so hard he thought it was going to jump right out of his chest. For the very first time in his life he was scared. Not just a little scared, but genuinely scared that he was going to die. All along he'd thought he had some measure of control over what was happening. He always thought because he was a dragon he was better than most, almost untouchable. Through everything he always treated what was going on with...............contempt. He could see it now, looking back. The death of Mark Hiscock should have been his biggest clue. He'd been to blame. Dragons don't die very easily. He should have taken things more carefully, been more committed, because now, now he found himself at the mercy of someone who quite obviously didn't know the meaning of the word.

Weighing up the whole situation, Peter decided in a split second that it was now or never, although he considered that the odds were not exactly great. Things had gone rapidly downhill ever since he'd arrived on the synthetic pitch. That, combined with the fact that Fisher had been killed by Theobald and Casey and also the odd way that they both referred to Manson as 'Sire'. He firmly believed that Manson believed he wouldn't leave here alive. That in itself was enough. All he had to do was reach the far edge of the Astroturf pitch, right by the surrounding fence. That should put him close enough to the crowd watching the fireworks to attract the attention of nearly everyone, not least Tank and Richie. As he prepared to act, all he could think of was the trouble he'd be in with the dragon council. If his plan worked, the memories of lots of humans would have to be altered just slightly, as well as picking up the bill for maybe a rather messy battle. "Oh well," he thought. "It's not like I've got a whole lot of choice."

As Manson's face hovered close to his, Peter pretended to give up and, in a gesture of submission, pulled his head back with a feigned sigh. When his head was as far back as it could go, Peter focused with everything he had. Pulling in a deep breath, he brought his head forward with as much power as he could.

A thumping "CRACK" sounded as Peter's head butt made contact with Manson's forehead. He went down like a like a sack of potatoes. Knowing he had no time to waste, Peter shrugged off the two men on his arms, hitting them both at the same time with his free hands as he spun round. His real fear in all of this was Theobald and Casey. With their dragon powers they would easily be more of a match for him individually, let alone together. He hoped they would take a few seconds to change into their dragon forms because that might just give Peter enough time to raise the alarm and get help from Tank and Richie, who were more than a match for those two bullies. After dropping the two guards, he turned and, jumping over Manson's writhing body, he ran off into the darkness towards the part of the Astroturf that was nearest the crowd. As he sprinted into the dark, he knew that in only a few more seconds he would know his fate.

He ran for all that he was worth. Out of the corner of his eye, he could see the people with flashlights had stopped unloading and were starting to head in his direction. Pulling in his breath deeply, he gave one last burst of speed. His whole body hurt from being in the van, being in the cold and not having anything to eat or drink for half the day. Wiping the hurt from his mind, he gave everything he had, not looking over his shoulder for fear of what he would find. He imagined that both Theobald and Casey had turned into their dragon forms and were swooping in, talons at the ready to slice him open, carefully followed by Manson and the other humans, all ready to end his life. Two more steps and he was there. He opened his mouth, ready to scream for help and quite possibly, his life. As he did so, he realised something very important. Although he could see all of the people, and the firework display going on through a kind of hazy surround that appeared to encompass the whole pitch, he couldn't actually feel any of them with his dragon senses. Not as he should have been able to do anyway.

Smacking into the inside of the chain link fence that surrounded the pitch, Peter found himself only a few feet from the edge of the crowd watching the firework display. He let out the biggest scream of "HELP" that he could and banged frantically on the fence. To his utter amazement, nobody paid him any attention at all, not even the young children who were standing no more than eight feet away. Once again he banged on the fence with all his might and let out the mother of all screams. Still nothing. "I know the fireworks are loud, but not nearly loud enough to stop them all from hearing me."

From behind him came a great big belly laugh. Scared of what he might find, Peter found the courage to turn around, hoping against hope that it would be nothing like his imagination had pictured it.

The picture that greeted him as he turned around was strangely worse than anything his imagination could ever have come up with. Theobald and Casey hadn't moved at all. The men with the flashlights had resumed their unloading back in the centre of the pitch. Only the enraged figure of Manson, with blood running down the outside of his nose, from the two cuts above each eye, paid him any heed at all. In fact, it was Manson that had produced the giant belly laugh from about twenty yards away.

"So predictable and pathetic," Manson spat angrily, blood seeping down his face.

Peter still couldn't understand why the crowd behind him hadn't reacted to his screams for help. "Surely they must have heard me," he thought.

"Do you really think your annoying friends and these precious humans will come to your aid?" said Manson, wiping some of the blood from his face. "It's almost a shame that they can't. I think I could take great pleasure from killing them all. Hmmmmm, looks like I'll have to make do with just you."

Peter was still puzzled as to what was going on. There were too many things that just didn't add up. How was this misbegotten human in charge of everything, he wondered.

Manson stepped a few places closer, until Peter could see him quite clearly in the reflected light from the firework display.

"It's about time you learned exactly who you're dealing with," he said menacingly.

As the words finished coming out of his mouth, something incredible, unexpected and totally terrifying happened. The blood running down the side of his nose stopped. Not only stopped, but actually started to move back up his nose towards the cuts. Once there, the blood seemed to be taken back in by the cuts, and then the cuts themselves just healed over in an instant. Peter was shocked, and still didn't know what to make of it all. As if that wasn't enough, a vaguely familiar transformation started to occur in Manson's midriff. It was as if his body was folding in on itself, starting with a small part right in the middle of his tummy. Peter had seen this effect dozens of times, but not for many years. In the nursery rings young dragons, on starting to learn how to take human form, were at one stage encouraged to practise in front of a series of mirrors, to try and help perfect their technique and the time it takes to change forms. Peter had done so hundreds of times, and startlingly, the effect when he transformed as viewed from the outside, was very similar to the transition that Manson was going through now.

"Oh crap," Peter thought. "He's a flippin' dragon!"

Time seemed to stand still. Peter could only stand with his back against the cold chain link fence and watch as Manson's transformation continued. The folding in on itself had slowed considerably, Peter noted in horrified fascination. The edges of Manson's form had started to fold out and gain more mass. Although this was all taking place in the space of only a few seconds, Peter noted that the process was still taking longer than in most other dragons that he'd ever seen transform, and the mass that it seemed to be producing appeared to be....................huge. Already he was clearly bigger than Tank was in dragon form, no mean feat in itself, but the really worrying thing for Peter was that there was no sign of it abating.

Peter looked around, thinking about how to get away. His options seemed seriously limited. The hazy mist surrounding the synthetic pitch and its enclosure was clearly designed by Manson, using whatever power he had available to prevent anyone from seeing in, as much as not letting any noise or light out. The entrance that the vans had used to come in on the far side of the pitch from where Peter stood, seemed to be the only way out, as surprisingly it was the only unlocked gate on to the pitch. That particular entrance was used only in an emergency, available to the emergency services via a bumpy track from the main road. What was odd though, was the fact that only two keys to that gate existed: one that was kept behind the bar in the clubhouse, and one that the chairman of sports club looked after.

Peter's wandering mind returned to the scene in front of him, unfortunately for him. The folding out from Manson's middle had all but stopped, with the edges of the giant form just resolving neatly into place. Manson as a dragon was massive. He must have been at least three times the size of Tank, who was the biggest dragon Peter knew personally. The most eye catching thing, apart from the huge size, was the fact that his whole body was a shiny deep black colour, all over. Peter had never seen a fully black dragon, in fact he'd only ever heard of them in stories as myths or make believe characters. Occasionally in the dragon world, you would see a dragon that had some black markings on his or her body, like a black tail, underbelly, stripe on the head or back or something. Those that had these markings were always stared at by other dragons, much in the same way a human might be regarded if they had an unusual birthmark that was visible. But a huge dragon like that, totally black from tail to ear was just........................incredible.

By the looks of things, the transformation had finished. The giant dragon, more like a dinosaur in some respects Peter thought, looked a bit unsteady on its feet. Its enormous head moved from side to side, as if trying to get used to its new surroundings. The tips of its giant wings scraped along the icy Astroturf pitch, slightly disorientated. Peter peered underneath one of its wings and could see Theobald and Casey standing in the same spot they had been all along, not at all surprised at the super imposing dragon that stood before them. "That's why they call him 'Sire'; they've known all along what he was. But why haven't any of us been able to sense him?" Peter thought, as his legs wobbled from fatigue and the piercing cold.

"Not so clever now, are you......................little dragon?" Manson boomed groggily.

The noise from his voice almost knocked Peter off his feet it was so loud. He glanced around at the crowd behind him on the other side of the fence, hoping that someone there might have heard it, but no, they were still hooked on the ongoing firework display. Manson eyed Peter much like a human would an annoying fly, knowing full well he could swat it any time he wanted to. And, Peter knew, Manson was most definitely going to swat him, it was just a matter of time, whether it was seconds or minutes.

Crazy as it may have seemed, Peter started to edge forward from the fence towards Manson. He realised that by standing right up against the fence, he was pretty much a 'sitting duck'. At least if he moved out a little, he might have more room to manoeuvre or run away when the inevitable attack came. He was also on the lookout for Manson's weak spot. He knew if he got close enough, he should in theory be able to see it, not that it was going to help him in any significant way as he had no weapons, was seriously outnumbered, was too weak to turn into his dragon form, and even if he could, Manson would still be way too powerful for him. "Normally," he thought, "I can find something to smile about in just about any situation. Surprisingly, nothing springs to mind now."

Manson's giant jaws opened impossibly wide, giving the effect of a really disturbing smile.

"Coming to attack me, little dragon?" he boomed sarcastically. "Did you really think I didn't know that you had broken free of your handcuffs? I mean really, you are so naïve, even for such a young dragon." Manson dragged one of his giant wings off the floor and pointed it toward Peter. "You've been a constant thorn in my side....................little dragon. Our plans have constantly had to change because of you ....and now......................now you're going to pay the price for your meddling in affairs that don't concern you. Don't worry though, you won't be alone. Your death will be one of many to come. The world below won't know what's hit it until it's way too late. Anyway, little dragon.....................................got any last words?" Manson said with an evil glint in one of his giant bloodshot eyes.

Peter took a breath to try and calm himself. With little alternative, he knew he would have to fight, something he was ill equipped and ill prepared to do. Nothing in the nursery ring he'd been through would prepare him to take on a giant psychopathic dragon, with nothing but murder on his mind. The best he could hope for was to buy himself enough time and hope that some sort, any sort of opportunity would present itself, whether a chance to attack Manson, or to run and escape intact.

Manson opened his jaws, imitating a big cheesy grin. "Here it comes," thought Peter. And, sure enough, it did.

One of Manson's huge black scaly wings came whizzing round at a great speed. Peter desperately willed his body to move. It responded slower than it would normally, due to the cold and fatigue. He jumped back and rolled sideways, feeling the air from the movement of the wing, just above his head. Gingerly, he stood up, knowing he had just burnt the skin off both his knees when he rolled over on the icy, sand encrusted ground.

Manson stamped his feet in frustration, just like a small child not getting his own way. With a snarl on his prehistoric face, Manson opened his mouth and let rip with the biggest stream of flame Peter had ever seen. Peter flung himself once again to the floor, trying to ignore the pain as he rolled along the hard surface. He could feel his shoulder had been caught by the jet of hot air, as a mind numbing pain shot down his arm into his hand, and across his back and up into his neck. He scrambled along the ground, as if completing an army assault course, knowing that ignoring the pain and surviving as long as possible was a matter of life or death. As he came up to a kneeling position, Peter noted that the hired help who had been unloading the vans, had decided enough was enough. Despite what looked like strong threats from Theobald and Casey, the men had all run off towards the van that Peter had been trapped in, the one by the gate that they had entered the Astroturf in, and were now in the process of attempting to drive off at breakneck speed.

Manson, clearly distracted, had stopped heaving flame at Peter. The fleeing men had become more of a priority. Peter knew that he should use this fleeting opportunity to try and escape, but he couldn't see how. Also, some morbid fascination had taken over, and he needed to see what would happen to the fleeing humans who, up until sixty seconds ago had been part of Manson's gang. Kneeling on just one knee, getting his breath back, Peter watched, powerlessly, what he assumed would be the last few seconds of the human conspirators' lives.

Manson hated humans. Not hated them a bit, he really hated them. Hated them with every cell in his superior body. According to him they stood for everything bad in this rotten and wrong world. "Bentwhistle can sweat a bit more, while I take care of these lying, cheating..........................cowards," he thought, as he looked at the human stragglers trying to escape in the white van by the gate. Closing his eyes, he rolled his giant head back as he concentrated on the open gate, for which the van was heading. Feeling power and darkness course through his entire body, he willed the gate to close and stay closed. Like a shot... it did. The gate slammed shut, and seemed mystically welded in place. The van slammed its brakes on, the driver surprised to see the exit suddenly cut off. Confusion and panic seemed to take over inside the van. The men were all arguing over the next course of action.

Manson opened his eyes and in a slow and sure way, gave one flap of his giant wings. He took flight immediately, skimming low across the synthetic pitch. Theobald and Casey stood and watched as their 'master' raced by, heading for the van that was now reversing away from the gate at high speed. The driver of the van slammed the steering wheel round, shooting the van through one hundred and eighty degrees. The driver slammed on the brakes in total and utter fear. Peter could see four of the humans crammed into the van's cab, all peering out of the misty windscreen, terrified. Peter couldn't blame them. Manson was closing in, flying just above the pitch, on a collision course. One of the humans in the middle of the cab overcame his fear briefly, and tried to climb over his stunned friends to get out. He was too late.

Manson's whole body flew straight into the van, and shredded it instantly.

The noise was unbelievable, blocking out the loudest of the fireworks that were going off overhead. Then came the blast. The whole van exploded, with tiny fragments of red hot metal flying everywhere, leaving a smoking, smouldering wreck across the exit through which all of the vans had entered. Out of the smoke and fire trudged Manson, looking very pleased with himself, as he sniffed the air all around him. If Peter hadn't recognised the trouble he was in before, he did now. The casual way with which he'd just taken human life left Peter in little doubt that the same fate was heading his way unless a miracle presented itself.

Peter looked around the shrouded synthetic pitch, partly to try and work out what had been going on, and partly to see if there was anything at all that would help him get out of the predicament he was currently in. The smouldering wreck of the van lay along one side of the pitch, covering the well sealed gate. At one end, roughly in the centre, stood Theobald and Casey, taking in events as they happened, looking more than a little shaky. Right in the middle of the pitch, strewn across the centre circle was another giant harness, much like the one Peter had found in the van he had been trapped in. This one looked to be a little bigger, as it lay flat on the cold, icy surface, with large nets attached to each side. One of the nets had been pulled open, and some of the contents of the two vans which surrounded it had been piled in. Boxes and pallets with boxes on, were all amongst the harness and the vans. The vans were clearly in the middle of being unloaded when the humans had tried to make a run for it. What on earth could be in the boxes, and why were the contents being loaded into the nets attached to the giant harness, Peter wondered in a split second.

Manson, having just stomped out of the wreckage of the van he'd just destroyed, motioned to Theobald and Casey.

"Start loading all of the cargo into the harness, ready for departure," he boomed. As he did so, his breath formed what looked like a massive white cloud in the chilly night air.

As Theobald and Casey headed quickly towards the centre circle, both bowed to the giant dragon as they passed him. Manson, knowing that his harness was being loaded, turned his attention back to Bentwhistle.

Peter watched as the two bullies shuffled quickly past their 'master', heading towards the vans and the harness in the middle of the pitch. "Clearly," he thought, "they have to take up where the humans left off. Whatever contents are being loaded into the harness, they must be very important to Manson."

Manson turned his huge body towards Peter and moved his head from side to side, as if enquiring what Peter was up to.

Peter stood up from his kneeling position, feeling a wave of pain run up his legs as he did so from the burns on his knees. He managed to ignore it, with only a small grimace. Despite the cold, he found that he was starting to warm up. "It must be something to do with the excitement and the situation," he thought. "I'm still a long way off being able to turn into a dragon, or use any of my dragon abilities to help raise the alarm though."

Manson had noted Peter's interest in the harness and its contents.

"Still not clever enough to understand what's going on............little dragon?"

Peter ignored the jibe, knowing full well the giant dragon was trying to bait him. He needed to keep his temper in order to seize that miracle opportunity, should it arise.

"Not even a little interested.... little dragon?"

"Obviously he wants to brag about his plan and feel superior and big. Perhaps I should give him the chance?" Peter thought.

"The dragon council and I know all about your plan," Peter said bravely, hoping his bluff would at least keep Manson a little off balance.

"Haaa haaaaaa haaaaaaaaaaaaa! Then why aren't they here to stop me eh? You know nothing about what's going on here. Even now, your feeble little mind isn't smart enough to put together the pieces of the puzzle. You look at the boxes over there," Manson pointed to the harness that was slowly being filled by Theobald and Casey, "and you have no idea as to their contents."

Peter crossed his arms in front of his chest and put on his most determined expression, which under the circumstances, (standing in the frozen night air in just shorts and a hooded top) seemed utterly ridiculous, but it was all he could think to do. If he could somehow raise some sort of doubt in Manson, then he might consider letting Peter live a little longer.

Manson took a couple of giant strides towards Peter, raking the ice on the top surface of the synthetic pitch as he did so, with his sharp talons.

"I know everything you're thinking................little dragon. You're so predictable, with your plans and schemes of how to get out of this in one piece."

A shudder ran through Peter. Manson didn't appear to be buying any of it. Using all his strength, he maintained the defiant expression, hoping that Manson might give something else away.

"But since you're going to die here anyway, I might as well put you out of your misery." Manson clapped his huge wings together in front of him and then blew out a short jet of flame on to them. Peter wished with all his heart that he could feel the warmth contained within that flame. Manson shot him a sneaky look, knowing full well that Peter was cold and was longing for the heat that Manson so brazenly showed off.

Manson stomped around in a semicircle, some thirty or so feet away from Peter, every now and then blowing out a jet of flame to keep himself warm. As he did so, he turned towards Peter, looking like some kind of prehistoric predator teasing its prey.

"You see, my........associates and I have a rather different long term view of how the planet should be governed. While we've had little choice but to bide our time in the past, now we find ourselves with a real opportunity to bring our plans to fruition, helped in no small part by some resources from Cropptech," Manson said, pointing the tip of one wing towards the boxes and pallets scattered about.

Alarm bells started going off in Peter's head. "Oh my god," he thought. "The only resources from Cropptech that a dragon would be interested in would be the laminium."

A big evil grin crossed Manson's scaly face, his bloodshot eyes focusing intently on Peter.

"At last you've managed to work it out. Where in the world would we as a group find enough laminium for our goals? Where in the world would we find enough laminium, unguarded and free for the taking? Ha ha ha. Here of course. With only a couple of lousy dragons watching over things, one hopelessly inadequate, the other fresh from the nursery ring, with absolutely no idea of how things work in the real world." Manson shook his head as he laughed. "Easier than taking charcoal from a hatchling," he taunted.

Images of what Manson and his friends could do with the laminium flashed through Peter's mind as he stood in the cold, trying desperately to look confident. He pictured a world ruled ruthlessly by dragons. Humans decimated by cruelty and sport for the ruling dragons. Other species totally destroyed by the neglect and misuse of the planet's limited resources. Everything would revert to how the world was thousands of years ago, he thought, terrified at the prospect.

It was the first time that day that his death, a very realistic possibility, was put into perspective. If he didn't stop Manson getting away with all of that laminium then the world might never be the same again. Everything he loved, his friends, Cropptech, the dragon world, Gee Tee, the nursery ring...... hockey. It would all be destroyed. He vowed in his mind not to let Manson leave with the laminium, even if it meant sacrificing his own life. In fact, he would gladly give his life to stop Manson's terrifying plot right now. Things had changed in Peter's mind now. It wasn't so much: how he could survive and even get away? It was more: how could he use his own life to take Manson's and thwart him in the process? Manson's loud growling voice brought Peter back to the present, more determined than ever.

"So you see now, it was never about Garrett or Cropptech. They were just a means to an end so that we could get the laminium," growled Manson loudly, flicking out small streams of flame to keep himself warm.

Peter nodded, finally understanding the overall scheme of things. He'd never even come close to suspecting what it was all about. He'd been too concerned with the people involved, i.e. Hiscock and Garrett, when in fact he should have been making sure the laminium was secure. That was, after all, the primary reason he was put there by dragon society and that should have been his top priority, even if it meant that humans would have paid with their lives. He would have kicked himself if he'd thought his cold, numb legs would have felt it. "Stupid, stupid, stupid," he thought as he gazed across to Manson's smile, that was now becoming more than a little annoying.

Manson glanced over his right shoulder, to see how Theobald and Casey were getting on with loading up the harness. Peter couldn't resist a look and followed Manson's example. Theobald and Casey had, from what Peter could see, loaded nearly all of the contents of the vans into the nets attached to the huge harness. There was so much in each metallic net, that the harness now stood a good four metres off the ground, supported only by the full nets on either side of it. Empty pallets stood scattered either side of the two vans, both of which had their back doors open to reveal almost total emptiness now, as the fireworks exploded overhead.

"Clearly that's how Manson plans to escape," thought Peter as he looked at the giant harness. "It would fit him just right, and if he can reproduce his masking effect that seems to be enclosing this pitch, while flying, he'll get away scot free."

Manson turned his attention back to Peter, now that he was sure the harness was loaded and ready to go.

"I'm afraid it's nearly time for me to depart," he boomed across the pitch, masking the noise from the fireworks that were still going on in the clear night sky. "And that unfortunately means the end of the road for you, although I can't say I'm really that sorry. You've blundered about and got in the way enough to cause me serious disruptions. At least after your death I'll have the satisfaction of knowing all the workers at Cropptech will think you died a traitor, having attempted to poison Al Garrett, only to be stopped at the last minute by me. Think of the irony of it. Even your friends will have their doubts about you."

Peter's temper started to rise within him. He knew he should ignore Manson's jibes, but believing that everybody would think badly of him hurt him more than he thought possible. Peter stepped forward, a rather stupid thing to do under the circumstances.

"You wouldn't know true friendship if it jumped up and bit you on the tail," Peter spouted furiously. "No matter what the situation or circumstances, my friends would never think badly of me. They'd know that whatever I did, however odd it looked, I did it for a good reason. They'd have faith that I would do the right thing, whatever the situation. You probably don't have a real friend in the entire world," Peter spat, letting his temper get the better of him. "The only thing I feel for you is pity. What's it like to be alone, and afraid? I'll take comfort in the fact that when the dragon council catch you, and they will, you'll die all alone with absolutely nobody mourning your death."

Peter evidently hadn't noticed Manson getting angrier as his tirade went on. The huge black dragon had a look of murder in his eyes as his huge head moved from side to side in a deranged sort of fashion.

Peter stood fuming at Manson. It was then that he realised quite how much he'd provoked the dark scaled beast, and the reaction it seemed to have had. The two, a bedraggled looking human, in only shorts, trainers and a grey hooded top, and a menacingly colossal, black-as-the-night-sky dragon stood on the synthetic pitch, staring at each other while fireworks raged overhead and a crowd of hundreds of people stood, not fifty metres away, blissfully unaware of what was going on. The hate and the rage inside Peter was gobbling him up. He wanted to hurt Manson. He didn't know how he'd do it, but, more than anything, he wanted to hurt him ....kill him even. He wanted to do this for Mark Hiscock, who Manson had killed. He wanted to do this for Al Garrett and all the staff at Cropptech who'd been misled. He wanted to do this for the human accomplices of Manson, who had been murdered right in front of his eyes only minutes before. He wanted to do it for Fisher, who had been murdered by Theobald and Casey for not wanting to take part in Manson's scheme any longer. He hated Fisher for being part of the bullying that he had been subjected to at the nursery ring, but nobody, human or dragon, deserved to die like that. Most of all, he wanted to do this for... himself. Manson had made his life a misery for the past seven months and he was planning to change the world beyond recognition. He, Peter decided, deserved to die.

Manson had rolled his head away from Peter. It looked innocent enough, but was in fact designed to lure his prey into a false sense of security. In an instant, he struck. The one thing it wasn't, was subtle. Manson launched himself and flew low over the pitch like a jet plane towards Bentwhistle. Peter reacted instantly, moving off to one side as fast as he could, and then at the last moment, as Manson's oversized talons came zipping towards him, he dived head first as fast as he could, coming up in a forward roll. Peter's tactics had worked, albeit at a cost. He'd got out of the way of Manson and now found himself some thirty or so feet away, with Manson now over by the fence, and himself off to one side. The cost of this became apparent when Peter turned his head to look at his right shoulder, which he thought was throbbing slightly from the impact of the forward roll. It turned out he was mistaken slightly. Manson's talons had caught his shoulder, slicing it open from shoulder to bicep. The torn skin was hanging off, like meat on a butcher's hook.

Manson flashed Peter one of his deranged smiles, as he stood sharpening his talons on the synthetic pitch. Peter lifted his right arm into the air, allowing the flap of skin to sit back down on his arm. He closed his eyes for a split second and, using all his concentration and willpower urged the wound to heal. Under normal conditions, he would have hoped that an injury like this would be fully healed in about an hour; however, these were far from normal conditions. He figured the best he could hope for was for the skin to knit together slightly, and for some of the pain to be taken away. That was assuming that he didn't have to move or receive any other injuries in the immediate future. "Fat chance of that," he thought.

Peter looked up at Manson and out of the corner of his eyes caught sight of Theobald and Casey putting the last of the Cropptech valuables into the cargo nets attached to the giant dragon harness. It looked now as if it was really ready to go. "Somehow," he thought, "I have to stop that cargo from leaving here."

Manson caught Bentwhistle looking at the two bullies putting the finishing touches to loading the cargo. He was done with taunting and insults. He just wanted to get out of this human infested hole and head back south, to the others. Instantly he took in a deep breath and let go with a massive jet of fire that burned blue in the middle. Peter immediately threw himself to the ground once again, but on peering up, had no idea which way to roll to get free of the threat. This was because Manson had turned his head from side to side causing a giant arc of flame above Peter. From Peter's position, it was impossible to gauge just where Manson actually was. Peter had no choice but to gamble. The intense heat was becoming unbearable and he was finding it very hard to breathe. The one positive thing to come out of this was the fact that he had instantaneously become warm enough to access almost all of his dragon abilities, something Manson clearly hadn't bargained on. Putting on a burst of dragon speed, Peter gambled and rolled right, hoping that Manson would have gone the other way. A treble roll later and Peter had his answer. He'd gambled wrong. He bumped into one of Manson's giant legs as he rolled out from under the massive arc of rainbow coloured flame. The huge black dragon had hoped that Peter would appear here, and for the first time in the battle, had got his wish.

Peter knew instinctively that he had to act. He jumped and tried to perform an audacious back flip, throwing in as much dragon power as he could, in the hope that it would get him out of Manson's range. A resounding "SMACK!" boomed across the Astroturf. Every part of Peter's body screamed out in pain as he flew up in the air. His eardrums felt as if they had imploded and horrific pain tore out from the left side of his ribs, which if he were able to turn his aching head to look at, he would have done. After what seemed like months, he landed with a sickening "CRUNCH", his fall broken by something very solid indeed. The awesome pain now assaulted his body in waves, making him feel physically sick. He was now barely clinging on to consciousness. He knew something extremely bad had happened to his ribs; he just couldn't seem to clear his head, or move his tangled body enough to look and see exactly what.

Manson glanced across the icy pitch to the crumpled form of the annoying dragon in human form. There was something about this one that he couldn't quite put his talon on. It was almost as if he preferred being in human form to dragon form, a notion he found almost impossible to comprehend. Humans were weak, feeble and second class. They were imposters, thinking themselves top of the planet's food chain, when very obviously they were not. They shouldn't be allowed to go on deluding themselves. They were about to be put out of their misery in the very near future.

As a thin layer of mist developed just above the surface of the pitch, it was clear to Manson that he'd already won, and completed the mission he was sent here to do. Bentwhistle's body lay smashed against the now ruined green metal fence that would normally separate spectators from the playing surface of the pitch. From where he stood, it was difficult to separate Bentwhistle's body from the twisted wreckage of the sturdy fence, so bad had the damage been. Manson smiled, pleased with himself. "I must have thrown him nearly sixty yards," he thought proudly. "Perhaps we can make this some kind of event, when the new regime begins.................toss a human, it's got a kind of ring to it."

With Manson already celebrating his hard earned victory over one side of the pitch, an altogether different battle was taking place on the other. A battle to stave off the pain, to remain conscious and in the end.................stay alive.

Peter had managed to sit himself up, quite a feat really considering the scale of his injuries. The part of him made to look like human blood was quite literally running on to the pitch, from the injury to his shoulder, but also from the massive wound around his ribs. He was pretty sure he'd broken at least three, and it also felt like some of his internal organs had been badly bruised as well. He tried hard to use his enhanced abilities to heal some of the damage, but realistically he knew that he had neither the time nor the limitless energy required to achieve very much.

The fireworks were going off overhead and, for the first time, he could hear the music from the speakers that accompanied them. From the sounds of it, the spectacle was just reaching the finale. As the pain threatened to overwhelm him, he managed a chuckle at that last thought. "How fitting that our finales seem to be occurring at the same time."

The blood from his wounds congealed on the synthetic pitch, making tiny bright red frozen ponds all around him. He turned his head as much as he could, without passing out or being sick. In his delirious state, he hoped against hope that a wave of dragon guards would come hurtling out of the sky to give Manson the fate that he so deserved. All that he could see though was the clear dark sky, pierced by tiny stars winking at him. At that moment, he finally accepted that he would die here and very soon. Mixed with the pain and the nausea, regret washed over him. His friends would probably never know his true fate. He'd never get to play hockey again, although he thought it was somehow fitting that he should die here on the Astroturf pitch he loved so much. Regret also that he'd never be able to mate, thus ending his birth line. Instantly his thoughts turned to Richie. More than once in his relatively short life span, he'd imagined mating with her. He knew in his heart of hearts that she was way out of his league and that it would never happen in a million years. But it hadn't stopped him thinking about it from time to time. Just recently however he'd found himself thinking more and more about the subject. Oddly enough, whenever he thought about Richie and the idea of mating recently, he somehow got the impression that she would rather mate in her human form, possibly even with a human. He didn't know why he thought that way, as Richie had never spoken to him about the subject in any way shape or form, and since the coupling of dragons and humans was strictly forbidden by the dragon council, it did seem an odd thing to think. But that just seemed to pop into his head whenever his mind wandered that way.

As the cold bit at his body, and the hazy sleep threatened to take him forever, a memory slipped into his mind and shook him awake. "I know where it is," he thought, suddenly alert. The memory was from a split second before Manson hit him halfway across the pitch with his gigantic scaled wing. As the wing bore down on him, Peter vividly remembered seeing a bright yellow patch, covering a couple of Manson's scales protruding from the right hand side of his underbelly. It was his weak spot.

Every dragon has a weak spot: an area or spot visible to other dragons, which if pierced will cause unbelievable pain and often lead to death. The young dragons were taught all about this in the nursery ring and often had to find each other's weak spot and the weak spots of dragons that came to lecture them on various different subjects. Peter's mind wandered to the tale of George and the Dragon, his favourite tale from the nursery ring. George had managed to take down the evil dragon Troydenn by knowing where his weak spot was and hammering a sword into that exact area. As all this crossed his mind, his whole body screamed for him to get up. "We still have a chance," it was telling him. "We know where his weak spot is. We can stop him."

Peter's head was swimming all over the place. He could hear the music to the fireworks and see the amazing rockets shower the sky above him. His body seemed numb and cold all over and he more than anything just wanted to be sick. "Why me?" he thought. "Why has all of this happened to me? I'm simply not cut out to be a hero." He could easily think of several dragons from his nursery ring who had all the attributes of readymade heroes. But not him. He was the last dragon on the planet who should be fighting the forces of evil. He was pretty sure he didn't have a heroic bone in his body (dragon or human). "Why couldn't this have happened to somebody else?" he thought.

As his head flopped back against what was left of the separating fence that had so graciously broken his fall from sixty or so yards away, he noticed something out of the corner of his eye. Only a few metres away from where he found himself propped up, was the olive green light box, containing the controls for the floodlights of the pitch. His thoughts turned briefly to turning the floodlights on. "That," he thought "would surely get the crowd's attention." He immediately dismissed the idea, as the box itself was locked and at the moment, he didn't have the strength to pull a cracker, let alone break into the control box. What did catch his attention though, was a rather large icicle dangling from the underside of the control box. It had to have been there for a few days at least and was more than a foot long, and had a diameter of a couple of inches. The point at the end looked as sharp as one of Gordon Ramsay's cooking knives, he thought with hope welling up inside him.

Gingerly he pulled himself up against the twisted metal of the ruined fence. Fighting off the desire to sleep, he looked across the cold misty pitch. Manson had gone across to the harness and was talking to Theobald and Casey. "Perhaps he thinks I'm already dead," thought Peter. He considered this for a few seconds. If Manson thought Peter dead, he would just strap on the giant harness and fly out of here, in which case Peter had already lost. No, he concluded. It wasn't Manson's style. He would come across and finish the job. "He knows I'm in no condition to go anywhere and that he can take his time. Well, let's see if we can surprise Mister All-Knowing, shall we?"

Peter used his arms to pull himself up into a sitting position and immediately wished he hadn't, when bright spots flashed before his eyes and the pain made him wretch. Gritting his teeth, he tried to stand up. Straight away his legs caved in and he fell back to the icy ground with a "THUD". Standing wasn't going to be an option, he thought as he looked across to make sure Manson wasn't on his way over yet. Sure enough, Manson was still confidently dishing out instructions to Theobald and Casey.

Taking a long, deep breath, Peter plucked up all his courage and put his palms on the freezing cold ground and began to pull his battered body towards the control box for the floodlights. It was slow going, with his hands taking a hell of a beating, not just from the constant icy cold, but from metal shards from the broken fence that constantly pierced the palm of his hand and sliced open his fingers. He did his best to ignore it, telling himself that at least the pain in his hands was taking his mind off his other more serious injuries.

After what seemed like half an hour, but was probably more like ninety seconds, Peter had dragged himself about halfway to the control box. Manson had looked over a couple of times, but had continued speaking to the two bullies, confirming what Peter had suspected, that in fact Manson regarded Peter as no threat and would come over to finish him off in his own time.

Peter continued on, leaving a thick red trail of frozen blood in his wake. The parts of his body that he could feel were generating the most incredible waves of pain imaginable. He tried to focus on his friends, hoping that it would inspire him to drag himself to the control box. He thought back to all the good times they had shared, from the many years in the nursery ring, to their relatively short time above ground in the human world. Images flashed before him as he continued painfully towards his goal. Richie, Tank, Gee Tee, the nursery ring, hockey, laminium ball matches, everything that he'd enjoyed in his scaly and not so scaly life, flew past.

Before he knew it, he had determinedly made it to the control box. With his last ounce of strength he ripped the glittering icicle from the underside of the box with his right hand, gripping it firmly behind his back, while with his left hand he began to desperately scrabble at the locked part of the control box, making it look to Manson as if he was making an attempt to turn the floodlights on. This, interestingly, got the black dragon's attention. He strode away meaningfully from Theobald and Casey, eyeing Bentwhistle with suspicion. Peter fumbled at the locked door to the control box, trying to make it look as though he knew it was his last chance to save himself. He turned to face the approaching Manson and immediately recognised the mad, deranged look in his eyes. "Here he comes," thought Peter as time once again seemed to slow down.

Halfway between the two bullies and Bentwhistle, Manson launched himself forward with one powerful flap of his massive wings. The mist lying low over the pitch shot up into the air, forming a giant silhouette around him as he closed in on Peter.

Peter's face became wracked with fear as the impressive homicidal black dragon zoomed towards him with only one thing on his mind. His grip on the icicle behind his back increased as he prepared to strike. He cleared his mind, urging his body to provide him with the strength he needed for this one last attack, knowing full well that one way or another, the welcome relief of death was not far away. Peter could feel the brush of air wash over his face as Manson approached at full speed. He knew what he had to do. It was now or never.

Manson opened his huge slavering jaws as he approached at high speed the raggedy human form of the irritating pest that was Bentwhistle. He was so close, he could almost feel his razor sharp teeth closing around the battered body in front of him, savouring the delight of flesh and bones crunching in his prehistoric jaw.

Leaving it to the last one hundredth of a second, Peter moved with a speed that betrayed his life threatening injuries. It was the fastest he'd ever moved in his life. He could see straight down Manson's throat, as the open jaws of the fearsome black dragon sped towards him. Horror was still etched on his face as Peter threw himself forward, diving underneath the hungry jaws that looked more frightening than any crocodile or shark he'd ever seen on television. As he dived, he willed his body to turn over in mid flight. Reluctantly it did so, inflicting even more pain, which Peter wouldn't have thought possible. Even so, he maintained his focus and while turning over in flight, below the fast moving scaly body of his nemesis, he brought round the glistening icicle that he was concealing behind his back. In the almost total darkness of the underside of Manson's huge frame, Peter found what he was looking for, an area covering two of the evil dragon's tiny scales. It stood out like a beacon in the darkness, drawing Peter's every action towards it. Having fully turned over in the process of his dive, and knowing that he had caught Manson totally off guard, Peter used every last bit of strength he had to thrust the transparent crystalline form of the icicle into the dragon's heavily shielded body. As the icicle entered Manson, Peter could feel the satisfactory yielding of dragon flesh, followed by what can only be described as the sound of a huge "squelch".

Peter thumped to the hard icy surface on his back, his body now riddled with pain and numbness. As his head cracked back onto the synthetic pitch and he watched the fireworks in the sky, beyond the black body of Manson, relief and regret washed over him one last time. Out of the corner of his eyes, he watched as Manson tried desperately to compensate for overshooting his target, only to be struck by the realisation that he himself had been dealt a fatal blow. The fearsome dragon wheeled round in the air one last time, not knowing what to do at first. Peter watched, captivated, as Manson flapped his wings in panic, and let out the most undragon-like scream he'd ever heard in his entire life.

As he hovered to the ground, one of his legs gave way, causing Manson to topple over to his left. Hitting the ground, the entire Astroturf shook, causing even more ripples of pain up Peter's now useless back.

Tears began to flow like a raging river down Peter's cheek, freezing before they hit his chin. Every emotion that ever existed swirled inside him alongside the pain and numbing of his body. He started to laugh, softly at first and then hysterically for a few seconds. "I've done it," he thought. "I've saved them all." He felt an immeasurable pride well up inside his chest. He knew that he wasn't cut out to be a hero, but when it counted, and in the worst of times, he'd stepped up and given his life to stop Manson and had thwarted his twisted plans for the entire world.

As he lay down, unable to move at all on the bone chillingly cold synthetic pitch, waiting to depart this world, his mind began to wander. "Strange," he thought to himself as he looked towards the edge of the pitch nearest to him, "I'd have thought with Manson's downfall, the mystical haze surrounding the pitch would have dissipated totally. It definitely faded for a split second or so when I thrust the icicle into him, but why hasn't it gone altogether? The crowd should be rushing in from the firework display to see what's been going on."

Over the sound of the very best fireworks launched so far, a soft ringing laughter echoed subtly across the misty pitch. It was the kind of laughter that could freeze another's heart totally. Peter thought he couldn't get any colder. As his goose bumps got goose bumps and the fear inside him threw itself off the nearest tall building in fright, Peter managed to turn his head in the direction of the dreaded laughter.

The sight that greeted him washed away all his hopes and pride. He felt as if the remaining intact bones in his body had all been broken at once as he looked across the pitch. He wet himself straight away, faintly amazed that he hadn't done so before now, with some of the things that had gone on this day. His hope lay shattered, his pride shredded and any dignity he had was long gone. Worst of all was the fact that he knew in the not too distant future his friends' lives would be destroyed and that they might well face the same fate he was facing now.

Manson strode towards the prone Bentwhistle, clutching the icicle he had ripped from his underbelly. He tossed it towards Peter for dramatic effect, not wanting to end things just yet.

"You showed more courage than I ever could have expected............. impressive. It's almost a shame things have to end this way; you might have made a welcome addition to our ....cause."

Peter spat a huge gob full of blood as far as he could in the vile dragon's direction.

"Yes, I thought that would be your response. Shame really, you certainly seem to have more backbone than those two," he said, waving his wing in the direction of Theobald and Casey. "Still.................never mind."

Peter lay on the ground, wondering how the hell Manson wasn't dead, or at least near death. He was sure he'd hit just the right spot and had damn well thrust the icicle in with enough power to finish Manson for good. It just wasn't possible.

Manson watched the helpless Bentwhistle as he lay near death in front of him. He knew exactly what was going through the young dragon's mind.

"Would you like me to put you out of your misery, before I put you out of your misery?"

Once again Peter spat in Manson's direction, but only a tiny globule came out.

Manson chuckled and, turning just slightly, pointed to the spot on his belly where Peter had so carefully thrust the icicle.

"Unlike the poor deluded, weak and pitiful dragon sect that you belong to, I belong to a much stronger, smarter breed of dragon. You all loll round with your weak spots showing to everybody so that they can all see where to deliver a fatal blow. How sporting," he boomed sarcastically. "That will be the undoing of the dragon community as you know it. By the time they realise, it will be much too late. You see, the breed of dragon that I belong to would never dream of showing another dragon its weak spot, not when we can mask our weak spot and replicate it on a much stronger part of our body. You see, much as I admire your one last attempt at winning, you never had any real chance. The spot you saw isn't my weak spot, and when my............associates and I take on the dragon community, in the very near future, they'll find that out the very hard way. Anyway, much as this has been a......................nice little workout," he said flexing the muscles in both wings, "it really is time for me to go. And I'm afraid, for you, it's time to die."

Peter lay on the cold surface, covered in blood and urine, determined to face what was coming, head on. He knew it would be more painful than anything he'd experienced so far this evening, something he found hard to imagine, but he steeled himself to face it. Craning his neck to look at Manson, he waited for the dragon to leap forward and deliver the killer blow. The deranged look crossed Manson's face once more, as he hungrily anticipated delivering death to the already dying body in front of him.

As the muscles in Manson's legs tightened, he prepared to swoop forward and end it all for Peter.

It was only a second or so away now, Peter thought, not caring one bit and just wishing it would end. He thought of his friends one last time, while at the same time looking across at Manson.

As he did so, the most amazing thing in the world happened.

It started to snow. Not just a little bit of snow either. Huge, intricate flakes the size of tennis balls came shooting out of the sky like comets having a race. So dense was the snow that Peter, who couldn't quite believe what he was seeing, looked up and, although he could hear the last of the fireworks going off, he could see nothing but a thick white apron of snowflakes heading his way. The flakes landed all over his broken body, burning as they touched his exposed flesh, of which there was quite a lot. This, however, was nothing to the effect it was having on the supremely confident, homicidal, deranged Manson. Peter knew from the nursery ring that dragons in any form don't like the cold. Normally it's especially bad in dragon form, but the one thing worse than the cold, is...........................the snow. The impact of snow on an unshielded dragon's body had been described by historian dragons down the years as equating to a human being branded with a red hot poker all over, while at the same time being stung by a thousand jellyfish and flogged with a cat o'nine tails. Not very pleasant you could say. Manson at this very moment was proving that the historians were pretty much spot on. Peter had thought that Manson's screams from earlier, which he now knew to be fake, were as bad as anything could sound. Boy was he wrong. The huge evil dragon was screaming and writhing around in absolute agony, trying desperately to bat away the snowflakes as the incredible flurry continued all around.

Despite the burning of the snowflakes, Peter let out a little chuckle at the sight of Manson being in so much pain. Out of the corner of his eye, he noticed the haze that Manson had been projecting around the pitch, starting to flicker. "Manson must be in so much pain that he can't maintain his concentration," Peter thought to himself. Through the occasional gap in the endless stream of snowflakes, he once again caught sight of the floodlight control box, not three metres away. He had nothing left to give. Most of his bodily fluids were strewn across the sand encrusted, icy pitch, which now had about two inches of snow covering it. He really didn't have anything else to give. Honest, at least that's what his body kept saying. His mind, however, had other ideas. With the sound of the very last fireworks and Manson's screams of agony pounding his besieged eardrums, Peter's body made one last heroic attempt at getting to its feet. Peter himself wasn't quite sure how it was happening, but incredibly he had indeed got up, in a very wobbly sort of way. Swaying from side to side, and being pelted at the same time by the torrent of burning snowflakes, Peter shuffled his feet through the deepening snow towards the control box.

His mind screamed out in pain constantly, from the injuries he'd already suffered and from the never ending flurry of snow. As if on some kind of autopilot, his legs continued, shuffling along, determined to get to their destination. The only thoughts fluttering around Peter's nearly insane head now, were ones that welcomed the release that death would bring. But before insanity could take him totally, his mind recognised the object that now stood before him. The green box had a covering of snow, nearly four inches deep, he estimated. It was a thing of beauty he thought, as he stretched out his deeply cut and burned hands. Ignoring the pain and the noise, he gripped the locked panel that covered the front box, and with the strength of someone else, he ripped it off, casually tossing it to one side so that it landed with a "thud" in the soft, thick snow. His vision started to fade, but he knew now that there was no chance of failure. Before him in the box lay four bright red buttons, the buttons that would each turn on a bank of two floodlights. When all were depressed, all eight of the giant lights would burst into life, illuminating the pitch for miles around. He reached out with his right hand and pressed all four in a row. As he did so, his vision started to blur a little, and the pain became too much for him to bear. As his battered legs gave out and he fell gracelessly to the floor, he knew he had switched on the giant lights surrounding the pitch. He just hoped it would be enough.

Slumped below the control box, with his life ebbing away, and the relentless snow burning his body, Peter's mind fed him what limited information it could. Through the flurry of the now illuminated snow, he could just make out two human shaped figures, clambering over the still burning wreckage of the van by the blocked gate on the far side of the synthetic pitch. In the furthest corner of the pitch, it looked as though a giant silhouette of something with wings was trying frantically to take to the sky. That was the last thing he saw, before everything went black.

He dreamed of flying high in the open sky, the radiant yellow sun beating down on his back as he performed loop the loops in the open air. Sometimes he heard voices, some that even sounded like his friends, Richie and Tank. It was difficult to understand exactly what they were saying. He could make out the odd phrase, such as, "Hold on," and "It'll be okay, help's coming," but in the main, it all just seemed like gibberish. He continued with his flying, occasionally feeling the odd burning sensation on his..............hmmm. It felt like his arms, but he had no arms, because he was ....flying. He just had......wings. How odd, he thought, as he continued on, hoping to get ever closer to the sun, and feel its warm radiance embrace him all over.

16

A King Sized Surprise

His eyes fluttered open. A clean, white, bright room swam slowly into view. He combed his memory, searching for any clue as to where he was. Frustrated at coming up empty, he sunk his head into the big squashy pillow and looked up at the bright lights in the ceiling. It was only then that he heard the sound of shallow breathing coming from somewhere off to his right. He moved to sit upright and immediately wished he hadn't, as a wave of what can only be described as 'pain masked by strong medication' washed from his head to his toes. He closed his eyes momentarily, hearing the screech of a chair on the mezzanine floor as he did so. He felt a comforting hand gently squeeze his shoulder.

"Easy son, you've been through a hell of an ordeal," a soft voice whispered in a reassuring manner.

He allowed the hand to guide him back down to a prone position, finding the comfort of the squashy pillow once again as it engulfed his head. After a few seconds he opened his eyes again, staring up at the ceiling, past the bright white lights. White polystyrene tiles, with tiny holes in, covered the whole ceiling. Something deep inside him started to scream. Slowly at first, but it quickly turned into a freight train as his memories returned, triggered by the innocuous ceiling tiles. He distinctly remembered hiding behind similar tiles, not that long ago. The memories came thick and fast, overwhelming him. Fear ran through him, quickly followed by panic. He sat bolt upright, ignoring the drugs coursing through his body, and the pain. He'd felt worse he knew, making it much easier to ignore. Once again the hand landed gently on his shoulder, willing him to lie back. He ignored it, and instead focused on who the hand belonged to. As the man's features materialised through the bright light from the ceiling lights, all he could think to say was, "You!"

The man nodded, offering a sympathetic smile. His long unkempt grey hair, framed a hardened face that looked sad and happy in equal measures, a face that Peter had seen on many different occasions and in many different locations. Never though, had he seem him looking so serious. With his memories now returned, Peter looked the old man in the eyes, and urgently said,

"I need to speak to the council...........................now!"

"It's alright son.....................you are."

"You're part of the council?" Peter said, wide eyed.

The old man's long grey hair bobbed around his shoulders as he nodded his head in reply.

Peter scratched his chin in thought, and for the first time noticed the array of bandages that covered his shoulder and torso.

"You need to know what happened. There was this, this...........dragon............ called Manson. He was, he was.................. after the laminium. Oh god, the laminium. Did he take it? Please tell me he didn't manage to take it."

The old man stood up and walked to the head of the bed, behind Peter. Adjusting the pillows, so that Peter would be propped up properly, he helped Peter shuffle back and become more comfortable. Once Peter was propped up, the old man dragged his seat along the floor to the foot of the bed, and wearily slumped down in it.

"He didn't take the laminium," he said, nodding and smiling at the same time. "Well, not the bulk of it anyway."

Peter frowned, as he sat propped up in the hospital bed.

"Not the bulk of it?"

"There was close to two tonnes of raw laminium stolen from the Cropptech site. The amount recovered from the Astroturf, thanks to your intervention matched that almost exactly. The discrepancy arises because, through intensive research, it appears that before the laminium was loaded into the trucks to take to the Astroturf, a small amount seems to have been taken. As far as we can tell, about fifteen small chunks, roughly ring sized, weighing no more than

350

about six or seven grams each, were cut out of a solid part of the batch, how we don't know. They were then removed from the facility. We believe Manson did this a little while ago with little or no help from anyone else, although he did have full access to the cutting edge technology at Cropptech of course. Still no easy task. Why he did this, we don't yet know. As to where the missing laminium is, we still have no idea either, but we do have agents trying to find out. You interrupted a very sophisticated operation here son."

Peter took in the information, trying to piece it all together. A question popped into his head from nowhere.

"Just how long have I been here?" he croaked, his mouth starting to feel really dry.

The old man got up from his seat and wandered round the bed, heading for the old wooden bedside table. He picked up a jug of water and proceeded to pour some of its contents into a very well worn, clear, plastic glass. He handed Peter the glass and returned to his seat.

"You were in a really bad way when you got here. By all accounts you should have been dead, according to the doctors that treated you when you arrived."

"Just where is here?" Peter interrupted.

"Salisbridge district hospital, where else? You're in one of the advanced treatment rooms in the basement of the hospital. The hospital dragon plan was put into operation as soon as they were aware that you were on your way."

Peter nodded, knowing all about dragon plans from his time at the nursery rings. In time of great emergency, dragon wise, it should be possible in most major facilities to instigate a change of procedure, that in effect moves humans out of the way of what is really happening. In a hospital for example, dragons in their human form should hold posts that would allow them, in an emergency, to change shift patterns unexpectedly and commandeer rooms and equipment without causing suspicion or alarm amongst the humans. Staff, such as nurses, doctors and consultants, who may through their specific training recognise inconsistencies in the medical data from a patient, that looks human but is in actual fact a dragon, would be casually relocated until such a time as the patient can either be found somewhere more private to be treated, in or out of the hospital, or had in fact recovered enough to hide their true identity and return to the dragon realm to be treated. He now knew that he was in the

351

depths of Salisbridge hospital, hidden away, known only to a few people, all of whom were dragons.

The old man continued.

"They say that the only reason you survived, was because someone applied some fancy mantra at the scene, when you were found. The mantra, it appears, was absolutely ancient in its design, but also very effective. It stopped your body bleeding instantly and then slowed down your metabolism, effectively putting you in a coma. If it wasn't for that, all of the physicians say that you would have died."

Peter thought about this carefully, not having any recollection of it happening.

"Do you have any idea who would have done such a thing?"

Peter nodded, knowing instinctively that it could only have been one person.........

"Tank."

"Aahhhh, your friend, the big dragon with a love of plants and animals," said the old man knowingly.

"Yes, that's right," said Peter suspiciously. "How do you know that?"

The old dragon burst into fit of laughter, the first time Peter had seen anything other than seriousness since he'd woken up. When he stopped laughing, the old man turned to look at Peter and said,

"It's my job to know."

Peter just stared, not entirely convinced.

"Anyway, to answer your question. You've been here for six days."

"Six days!" thought Peter. "And I'm still in the state I am."

As if reading his mind, the old dragon chirped in.

"Your injuries were substantial. Also, because they were inflicted by another dragon, they don't seem to be healing as quickly as if you'd been injured by a human. It could be as long as a couple of months before you're fully fit. We also seem to think that the particular dragon that you came up against has some special abilities that might be contributing to how long it's taking you to heal. Perhaps if you're feeling up to it, you could give me a more detailed description of exactly what happened."

Peter nodded and took another small sip of his water.

"Of course," he said. "Where would you like to start?"

"At the beginning of course," replied the old man, settling into his chair and listening intently.

Peter started at the beginning and over the course of nearly two hours, told the old man everything he knew. Occasionally the old man would interrupt him and ask a question, but for the most part, he just sat in his chair and listened as Peter outlined what had happened, only punctuated by Peter sipping his water, or refilling his glass from the jug on the bedside table.

Peter finished reciting his account of how the events of the last few months had panned out. The old man sat silently in his chair at the foot of the bed, clearly taking in everything Peter had said. They sat in silence for a few minutes, Peter getting his strength back, the old man mulling over everything he'd heard, from the overall plot, to the tiniest detail. Eventually he spoke up.

"Thank you for your frank and honest account of what happened. It's pretty much as the council assumed," he told Peter seriously. "There are one or two small details we didn't know, but the bulk of it we'd managed to piece together over the last few days."

Peter nodded in agreement, not wanting to strain his very croaky voice unless he really had to.

"From the look of you, I guess there are questions that you're bursting to have answered?"

Peter nodded eagerly, ready to risk his croaky voice. Before he got the chance, the old man held up his hand to stop him.

"How about I answer as much as I can, and then if you have any questions, you can ask them at the end?"

Peter smiled and nodded, knowing a good compromise when he saw one.

"First things first," said the old man. "You will no doubt be pleased to hear that Al Garrett has made a full recovery, and with the exception of feeling a little fatigued, is back to his normal chirpy self. He's well on his way to reversing everything Manson did at Cropptech while he was there, including re-employing everybody Manson fired."

Peter smiled, as he thought about the old Garrett once again in charge of Cropptech. He could just picture him mixing with the staff, making small talk, jokes and just generally making them feel good about themselves.

"He also knows that it was you who was responsible for taking Manson down, and for getting the stolen laminium back. At the moment everyone thinks you are in intensive care, which in a way you are," smiled the old man. "So I'm sure Garrett and his staff will want to congratulate you when you go back to Cropptech to be reinstated."

Peter raised his eyebrows at this.

"You were always going to get your job back, it's only a matter of when you're fit enough to resume. As far as everyone at Cropptech knows, you had your suspicions about Manson for some time, you just had to bide your time and gather evidence against him. They all know you got hurt badly, while getting the laminium back. As far as they all know, there's a warrant out for Manson's arrest, the human Manson, that is. The humans are also under strict instructions not to approach the human shaped Manson under any circumstances."

A crazy picture of human police officers looking at a wanted picture of a gigantic shiny black dragon ran through Peter's head, causing him to spill some of his water on to his lap.

The old man gave him a curious look.

"The events at the Astroturf have all been resolved successfully as well, mainly due to the quick thinking of the dragons present at the display that night. They managed to alert us to the situation very quickly, and a squad of recovery dragons were able to attend the scene within a matter of minutes. None of the humans who witnessed the aftermath of what happened had left the scene thank goodness. With the recovery squad posing as police officers, a blanket mantra was applied to the whole area, making everyone think they'd witnessed the same thing...... a lightning strike. While the humans were having their memory adjusted, a cleanup squad was hard at work on the synthetic pitch itself. Before daylight the next morning, you'll be pleased to know the Astroturf, its fences and floodlights had all been repaired from the damage caused the night before. It apparently looked as good as new, but with a large smattering of sand over the playing surface; we hope that nobody will be able to tell the difference for quite some time, if ever."

This news pleased Peter as much as hearing that Al Garrett was fully recovered. Strange really, but the pitch itself seemed to be like an old friend to Peter after all the games of hockey he'd played on it. It was hard to explain, as he didn't really understand his feelings about it himself. At least none of his human friends, or more importantly their children, would be scarred by what they would have seen that night. He'd had visions of children seeing a big dragon flying over them in the night sky, or the burning remains of a van full of dead bodies. Although he was one of the many dragons that didn't approve of the use of mantras to adjust human memories as a rule, (something that wasn't done that often anyway, and when it was, it was under strict controls and guidelines), in this instance he was glad it had been done. He felt happy knowing that his friends, teammates and their families had the knowledge that they'd had a nice night watching the firework display and nothing else.

"You will also be pleased to know that your car has been recovered from...." the old man pulled out a sheet of paper from the top pocket of his white linen shirt and studied it. "Ah yes, from the housing estate next to the Cropptech site. It's certainly very handy to have dragons in high places in most of the country's police forces. Your car is now back outside your house. Speaking of which, we have two dragons looking after your house at the moment. They'll remain there as long as it takes for you to heal up. They are posing as your aunt and her best friend. They look very innocuous to the neighbours, who have been more than a little curious, but they are in fact elite members of the King's Guard. We've put them there just in case Manson or one of his associates comes back to try and finish things off. We don't have any reason to believe he will, particularly with the dragon world and the human world on such a high state of alert because of him, but we thought it prudent to do so for at least a few weeks."

Once again Peter nodded, taking it all in. He hadn't really thought that Manson would try and come back for him, but the more he thought about it now, the more uncomfortable he felt about the whole thing.

As if reading Peter's mind once again, the old man interrupted his train of thought.

"Don't worry son, we're having a few modifications made to your house, just in case you should get such a visit. Things undoubtedly will never quite be the same, for either you or dragonkind in general. But the one thing that will happen, mark my words, is that we will all, including you, be prepared."

As the old man said this, a feeling of hope ran through Peter's body. If anyone else had told him that the dragon world would be ready to take on Manson and his associates, Peter would probably have laughed in their face. But there was something about this guy, something about the way he talked, carried himself, spoke, the way he looked into your eyes. Peter had no doubt at all that if the old man told him to come up stairs to the top of the hospital and fight Manson all over again, he would, here and now. He wouldn't want to of course, but this old man, he seemed so ordinary and yet, Peter decided, he would follow him into battle at a moment's notice.

"And that, my young friend, is all I have to tell you. Do you have any questions at all?"

"One thing that really bothers me," croaked Peter, taking a small sip of his drink, "is the matter of how Manson knew I was going to cure Garrett on that particular Friday. I'd worked so hard and planned it all out to the very last detail. I even watched as his car left the facility to go to the awards ceremony."

"And you're sure you didn't tell anyone?" said the old man, stony faced.

Peter concentrated, thinking hard about the events leading up to all of that. "I'm sure I didn't tell anyone of my intentions. Tank delivered the cure to me, but had no idea what I was planning to do or when." Suddenly something crossed Peter's mind.

"I do seem to remember sending a brief message to Councillor Rosebloom though. He sent me a message asking for an update on my progress, as I hadn't been keeping him informed on what was going on," said Peter, more than a little guiltily.

"Did you tell him about your plan?" said the old man seriously.

Peter thought for a moment.

"No, no I didn't. I sent him a quick message telling him when the whole thing would be resolved by, but I didn't give him any details."

The old man twiddled the ends of his unkempt hair in thought.

"What I tell you next must be kept in absolute secrecy, between you and me. Do you understand?"

"Of course."

"I and some of the other members of the council have had doubts about Rosebloom for some time. Some of his actions in the past have proved dubious to say the least, but nothing has ever been proven against him." The old man looked deeply troubled as he was telling Peter all of this. "He's also related to a rather treacherous fellow from very far back in the past. A person called Osvaldo."

Peter thought he recognised the name, but maybe whether due to the drugs, or just the fact that his body was still recovering from the beating it had taken, he couldn't quite put his finger on it. The old man continued.

"Osvaldo cost the lives of many good dragons, a long time ago. It's been generally believed that he's been dead for a very long time indeed, but every now and then something comes up that has all the hallmarks of Osvaldo. I don't believe for one second that he's dead. What I do believe is that he is in some way connected to Councillor Rosebloom. I don't know how, and more importantly, I can't prove anything, but I would in fact stake my life on it. While you've done the right thing Peter, I think it's best and also safest for you if you give Councillor Rosebloom a wide berth. If he or anyone else asks, you're to say that I've asked you to report directly to me. Is that okay?"

Peter stared wide eyed at the old man, hardly able to believe everything he'd heard.

"Of course, of course," he croaked in reply.

Peter mulled everything over in his mind. He felt tired, drugged, bruised, battered and overwhelmed. He couldn't think of anything else immediately that he wanted to say, but before he got the chance to say anything, the old man spoke up once more.

"Oh the one thing I didn't tell you, but you've probably figured out by now, is that you are being guarded by a whole host of police down here in the basement. All of them are dragons of course, along with any medical staff that may come your way. You haven't been allowed any visitors I'm afraid, due to the seriousness of the situation, but I've a funny feeling there might just be some visitors waiting to see you now."

Peter felt tired and thought to himself that he really couldn't face any visitors at this present moment, but before he'd had a chance to say anything, the old man had closed his eyes and whispered,

"Send them in."

Peter stretched out with his dragon senses, which were limited at the moment due to the severity of his injuries. He could just about sense some of the guards who manned the corridor and two of whom he felt hiding in the recesses of the ceiling. Just as he felt his strength waning, right at the limit of his sensing ability, he felt a familiar presence, no make that two familiar presences. HIS FRIENDS!!!!!!!!!

Seconds later, Richie and Tank burst through the door like a raging river,

357

smiling for all they were worth. They both ran straight to Peter's bed and crowded in beside him.

"You had us so worried," Richie said, as she bent forward and kissed him on the forehead.

Peter smiled a dreamy smile and squeezed Richie's hand tightly.

Tank leant in close and said,

"Yes so worried," and puckered up, ready to kiss Peter too.

Peter burst into laughter, something it seemed to him he hadn't done in an absolute age. Both his friends followed suit. As the laughing came to a gradual halt, the friends noticed they were not alone in the room. Silence overtook what should have been a joyous reunion. Tank and Richie stared at the old man. Peter couldn't comprehend exactly what was going on, and joined his two friends. He wanted to tell them that they had nothing to worry about as this was one of the council members. As Peter joined his friends looking over at the old man, he noticed for the first time the very special cane that he knew the old man always kept with him. Something about the cane nagged at the back of his mind, but for the life of him, he couldn't work out what it was.

It was Tank who reacted first. He shot down to one knee faster than a bullet from a gun. Unusual for Richie not to be first on the uptake, but she too dropped to one knee, as quick as a flash, right behind Tank. Peter sat up as far as he was able to, without passing out. He leaned over the side of his bed, watching his friends, both on one knee, with their heads bowed in the direction of the old man.

"What's going on?" he whispered towards Tank.

Tank brought his head round slightly so that he could see Peter and rolled his eyes slightly in the direction of the old man. Peter had absolutely no idea what was going on.

"Enough," said the old man sternly. "You may get up, both of you."

Peter was stunned as both Tank and Richie did what he said straight away.

The two friends looked towards Peter, who it had to be said, had the most confused expression since a certain weatherman went into work one morning in the late 1980's and said, "There was a storm, what kind of storm?"

Eventually, Peter had no choice but to ask,

"What the hell is going on?"

Tank turned to face Peter and nodded his head indicating the old man, while at the same time mouthing the word "King". Peter couldn't believe what he was seeing and gave Tank a confused look in return while enquiring silently, "King?"

Tank shook his head in disbelief.

"What he's trying to tell you," said the old man grinning, from ear to ear, "is that I'm the King."

Peter gulped as his stomach proceeded to do a somersault.

"The King?" he said sceptically.

"That's right," said the old man, still smiling.

"But you said you were from the council?" said Peter.

"Well technically, I am," replied the old man, standing up. As he did so, he pulled his cane from behind the chair and moved closer to the bed, beside Tank and Richie.

The cane, Peter saw now, looked magnificent. It reflected the light in a kind of purple hue. It looked flexible and strong, both at the same time. About two thirds of the way up its hilt, Peter noticed for the first time, a sparkling purple trident carved into it. The trident glowed as it continually pulsed on and off. Peter raised his head, looking along the entire length of the cane, stopping only when he reached the top, and the old man's hand. "Oh I can't believe it," he thought to himself. "It's just so obvious now." The old man's hand rested on the cane, covering the top of it. However, it wasn't the top of the cane that had caught Peter's attention. There was a ring on the middle finger of the old man's right hand. Not just any ring. This ring might as well have had big forty foot neon signs surrounding it, with huge fluorescent arrows pointing towards it. It was the most amazing, most fabulous looking and above all, most famous ring in the world. How on earth had he not spotted it before? Peter berated himself silently.

The old man, no, the king, spotted Peter gazing intently at the ring.

"Mesmerising, isn't it?"

"It certainly is," replied Peter, not taking his eyes from it for a moment.

"When I first joined the council, many hundreds of years ago, I was but a lowly knight. I was easily the youngest dragon there, by at least a hundred years, if not more," the king continued starry eyed. I attended council meetings, whenever my knight's duties allowed me to, and also had private audiences with the then king on numerous occasions. This went on for years.

During all of that time, I never once noticed this," he said holding up his hand, indicating the gobsmacking ring.

Peter drew breath, along with Tank and Richie.

The King held up his hand to stop the inevitable question being asked.

"You see, the ring itself, as well as containing an almost limitless supply of .... how would you put it................. mana, magic, mantra enhancing energy, has a sentience of its own, a mind, if you like. It can sense those all about it, good, bad, indifferent. And for some peculiar reason, which still isn't even known to me to this day, it chooses not to show itself to certain individuals. Ever since we first met, Peter, you've never been able to see the ring, not before just now, before your friends pointed out to you who I am, even when others all around you can.

"Why has it always concealed itself from me, up until now I mean?"

"That's what I've been trying to tell you, I have absolutely no idea. The crazy ring has a mind of its own. I can use it to power and enhance spells whenever I choose, although I wouldn't be surprised to find even then that it's in fact humouring me in some way shape or form, but I have absolutely no control as to who it shows itself to."

Off to the side, Tank began to open his mouth to ask a question. Before he could do so, he was stopped once again by the King.

"And before you all ask, hardly anyone knows what I've just told you, so I would suggest it remains our little secret."

The three friends nodded eagerly in unison. Well you would, wouldn't you.............for the King.

"Good, I know I can trust each and every one of you," said the King, stepping back a little from Peter's bed and taking in Tank and Richie.

Richie bowed her head as the King stared straight at her. She didn't want to appear rude and stare at him. In truth, she didn't quite know what to do.

The King took a couple of paces forward, and then reached out and gently tilted Richie's head at the chin, so that they could look into each other's eyes.

"No need to be shy, child," he said softly, all the time taking her in. It wasn't often Richie was lost for words, but this was definitely one of those times. Peter and Tank exchanged a little glance, knowing that in any other situation, they'd probably be laughing their socks off at their friend's dilemma.

"You would be Richie Rump, am I correct?" said the King softly.

Richie nodded in response and started to blush just a little.

"Hmmm," muttered the King, while studying Richie carefully. "So much paperwork comes my way that it's very often hard to pick out the trees from the wood. The names of individuals in all of that paperwork are so hard to remember, even with my near perfect dragon memory, but you.... hmmm............. I seem to recall being told all about you."

Tank and Peter both developed worried expressions at exactly the same time, knowing that all of Richie's antics, standing up for everyone all the time, showing off, arm wrestling rugby players, that sort of thing, was just about to bite her in the ass in the biggest possible way.

Richie's blushing had faded, to be replaced by a more defiant expression of sorts.

"Yes, that's right," said the King, suddenly seeming to recall something. "The last report with your name on it quite recently mentioned something about...... what was it again........ arm wrestling big strong sportsmen of some sort, I think. Would that be correct?" he asked Richie.

Richie jutted out her chin, keeping her defiant expression and looked the King firmly in the eyes.

"Yes," she said nervously.

This was it, thought Peter. Richie was going to get carted off and be forced to stay in the dragon domain, with little or no chance of ever getting to see the humans and enjoy all of their activities ever again. "Perhaps," he thought, "if I could just beg forgiveness on her behalf, then just maybe she'll be allowed to stay."

Before he had a chance to act, the King burst into the biggest belly laugh Peter had ever heard in his entire life. The three friends stood bewildered while the King finished laughing. After half a minute or so, the King managed to regain his composure.

Peter wasn't sure what was going to happen next.

The King unexpectedly put his arm around Richie's shoulders in a fatherly sort of way.

"There's no need to keep up the expression of defiance," he said, still plainly amused. "I know all about most of things you get up to. Ever since you left the nursery ring, I've been getting reports with your name crossing my desk. Ohh, some of my advisors frown upon most of your actions, but then most of them are pushing four hundred years old and still think the streets up here are full of horses and carts. Much the same with some of the other dragons that live in Salisbridge, I'm afraid, which is probably why I see so many reports. They'd like to see me give you some sort of warning or dressing down I'm sure. But to be honest, you remind me of......." A thoughtful expression crossed the King's face. "Let's just say another dragon I once knew. He acted in much the same way and although many frowned on his actions, he only acted that way because he had the best interests of the humans at heart."

A little smile broke the steely facade of Richie's face momentarily.

"That's not to say that I'm giving you some sort of permission to embarrass and ridicule human kind on a regular basis, you understand," he said sternly.

Richie's smile disappeared faster than a rat out of an aqueduct.

"But, and if you tell anyone outside this room that I said this, ooooww they'll be trouble," said the King, now smiling, "I trust you to keep the humans on their feet, and bring the ones that get too big for their boots, down to earth once in a while." The King held out his hand for Richie to shake, and said "Deal."

Richie took the outstretched hand, her confidence having fully returned. Instead of shaking the King's hand, she walked right up to him and planted a soft kiss on his weathered right cheek.

Peter and Tank both winced as she did so. They were both pretty sure that kissing the King without permission wasn't royal protocol. However, the King just gave another of his giant belly laughs. The two friends breathed a sigh of relief, hardly believing anything they'd seen in the last few minutes.

When the King had finished laughing again, he turned his attention to Tank. Unlike Richie, Tank carried himself as always, with a cheerful expression and a larger degree of modesty. He stood happily as the King approached him and gazed up at his large smiling face.

"And you would be........ Tank?" said the King.

"That's right," said Tank, offering out his hand for the King to shake. "Pleased to meet you, Your Majesty."

A frown came over the Kings face.

"What ...... no kiss?"

For a split second Tank's face was an absolute picture. Richie burst into laughter first, quickly followed by the King and then Peter. Tank soon saw the funny side and joined in, always happy to appreciate a joke, even at his own expense.

"Sorry son," said the King, when they'd all stopped laughing. "Couldn't resist I'm afraid."

"That's okay," replied Tank in his normal friendly voice.

"You're the one that nearly made a laminium ball player, is that right?"

"Yes Your Majesty."

Peter and Richie shared a glance that said, "That's news to us."

"And now you work for Gee Tee?"

"Yes Your Majesty."

"Less of the majesty," said the King, softly. "We're all friends here."

Tank nodded his big head in agreement.

"How do you like working for Gee Tee, son?"

"It's fascinating," Tank said thoughtfully. "I never knew that so many different types of mantras and magical artefacts existed. I've only seen a fraction of the things in the shop, but they would make most dragons' eyes pop out."

This time it was the King's turn to nod in agreement.

"Not to mention the things Gee Tee himself knows. Some of it's mind boggling, it really is, but mostly it's just absolutely brilliant. I'm sure with more time and research, the mantras combined with Gee Tee's amazing knowledge could have astounding beneficial effects on the human civilisation."

The King held up his hand to stop Tank from going any further. Although never having met him, he got the distinct impression that Tank would be able to talk for a whole day and beyond about his work.

Peter smiled, noting how quick on the uptake the King was. Clearly one of the qualifications of being King was to be able to distinguish somebody that could talk for England, and to know just when and how to stop them.

"I hope before you use any of your newfound knowledge topside that you'll run it by the planetary development department at the council."

"Of course Your Majesty," replied Tank instantly, as the King smiled.

"You could also perform a small act for me," said the King, "and don't worry, there's no kissing involved."

The three friends smiled at the King's joke as Tank replied,

"Anything, Your Majesty."

"You could thank Gee Tee for helping out in this instance, from me personally. Also, perhaps you'd be good enough to tell him that I'm sorry it's been so long, but I will pop in just as soon as I get the chance. I look forward to examining some of his.... mantra ink again."

Peter had just been taking a sip of water from the plastic glass as the King said these last few words. On hearing "mantra ink", he sprayed the water down the length of the bed and proceeded to have a small coughing fit. Richie came over and patted him hard on the back, which didn't stop the coughing, but was hard enough to take his mind off it. The King meanwhile gave him a knowing look.

"You do know, Peter, that certain mantra ink has an age limit before you can use it?" said the King, in a tone that Peter wasn't quite sure was serious or in jest. Peter just finished coughing, pretending not to know what the King was talking about, while it was abundantly clear that neither Tank or Richie needed to pretend. The King turned his attention back to Tank.

"I'll certainly pass the message on, Your Majesty," said Tank, letting all the stuff about 'mantra ink' go over his head.

"Good dragon," said the King slapping Tank on the shoulder.

Tank smiled in return, but thought to himself, "Great strength for such a small man."

"You know Gee Tee?" Peter enquired.

"Who doesn't?" said the King quickly.

Peter eyed him suspiciously, suspecting that there was more to it than that.

"Truth be told," said the King, looking around cautiously, "the old shopkeeper has helped me in much the same way as he's helped you, on more than one occasion. In fact, I'm pretty sure that I wouldn't be standing here if it wasn't for his help. I owe him my life many times over, as I'm sure many other adventuring dragons down the ages do. Once again, I feel I'm trusting the three of you with one of my innermost secrets."

"Don't worry, Your Majesty," the three of them replied in unison.

The King nodded his head, acknowledging that he could trust them, and then stepped back so that he could address all three friends at once.

"I think now might be a good time to take my leave and let the three of you catch up."

Richie and Tank felt quite relieved at this announcement. Although they were honoured and quite gobsmacked to meet the King in person, something that very few dragons ever got to do, they were also more than a little unsure of how to act and behave. Peter, on the other hand, felt panic sweep across him. At first he wasn't quite sure why, but after a split second he knew. He wanted answers, answers that perhaps he would never have the chance to get again. He quickly swung his legs down to the floor from the bed, ignoring the searing pain. Standing up, his head spun but despite this he still managed to wobble over towards the King. Tank and Richie rushed to his aid, but he waved both of them away and stood firmly in front of the King on his own two feet. The King looked at him bemused.

"Please don't go just yet," pleaded Peter.

"I'm afraid I have some serious unfinished business to attend to," replied the King.

"I............I....I have some questions to ask you," said Peter, looking down at the floor.

The King reached into the inside pocket of the brightly coloured jacket he was wearing. He pulled out a rainbow coloured pocket watch and studied it intently. After a few seconds, he nodded to himself and put the watch away.

"Sure," said the King. "What's on your mind, son?"

With the undivided attention of the dragon King, in this small hospital room, Peter suddenly seemed to feel under quite a lot of pressure and wished he'd kept his mouth shut.

"Don't be shy son. You can ask me anything you like."

Peter could feel the steam rising off him like it would off his favourite steam train at Swanage. He felt so nervous he thought he might pass out. The King grabbed his arm and led him back to the bed. Peter gratefully sat down on the edge of it.

"Is it something you'd rather not have your friends hear?" the King said glancing round at Tank and Richie.

"No, no, no, not at all," mumbled Peter.

"Then ask," said the King. "I don't bite, well......... not in this form anyway."

Peter managed a smile, put at ease by the King's attempt at humour.

"It's just that, it's just that............. why me?"

The King looked questioningly back at him. Peter knew he hadn't made himself clear.

"I understand the whole Cropptech, Manson thing. He was after the laminium and I was just in the wrong place at the wrong time. It's just, well I was wondering why you've sought me out all of those times in the past. Do you do that for everybody or is there some sort of reason?" said Peter, not being able to look at the King directly.

"Aahhhhh," sighed the King. "I did wonder if you would ask."

Peter lifted his head expectantly.

"Perhaps the three of you should sit," said the King, indicating the bed with his right hand.

Tank and Richie moved over to the bed and perched down on the edge, one either side of Peter. The King, in the meantime, looked as though he was doing some serious thinking, deciding no doubt how much he could tell the three young friends.

After pacing the length of the room twice, the King stood in front of the trio, and began.

"I haven't always been King, as I'm sure you are all aware. I've already mentioned that at the start of my career on the council I was also a knight. What you probably don't know, and only a few do, is that I wasn't just any knight. In fact, I'm guessing with a little help maybe Peter can tell the two of you exactly who I once was, before I became King."

Tank and Richie both turned their heads towards Peter, waiting for him to work it out.

Peter felt the pressure of expectation mount. He wasn't quite sure how he was supposed to figure it out. He'd never met a genuine knight, only heard the stories that so many dragonlings hear in the nursery ring. He sent a puzzled look in the direction of the king, hoping for the tiny bit of help the King had alluded to.

The King took pity on Peter straight away, giving him the clue that he so hoped for.

"What would be the most ironic thing, bearing in mind your favourite tale from the nursery ring?"

Peter racked his brains, trying desperately hard to think what the King meant. He hated quizzes at the best of times, and this most certainly wasn't the best of times. He could feel the breath of his two friends, caressing either cheek, waiting expectantly for him to make the breakthrough and put the missing pieces together. Steam poured off him as he sought the answer. He gazed up into the King's worn but kindly face. It looked as if it had seen terrible tragedies and remarkable sorrow. "What would be ironic?" he thought over and over to himself. His favourite tale, with or without a knight, was easy. George and the Dragon. He heard it so many times that he knew it off by heart, but ironic?

From out of nowhere it hit him like speeding bullet. "You've got to be kidding me," he thought. He smiled at the King, trying to gauge if it could be true. The old man had a perfect poker face and gave absolutely nothing away.

"Are you really him?" Peter asked quietly.

The King gave a gentle nod in return.

"I've always thought it ironic that your favourite tale was that particular one."

Richie and Tank were almost bursting with anticipation.

"Is anyone going to put us out of our misery?" said Tank, feigning annoyance.

The King smiled at them all.

"As a knight, I believe you would have known me as George. You might even remember a little encounter I had with a....... dragon."

It took a couple of seconds, but for anyone who was watching, the wait would have been thoroughly worth it. Richie's eyes nearly popped out, while at the same time Tank's jaw nearly hit the floor.

"*The* George, from George and the Dragon," the two friends said at once.

Once again the King nodded and smiled, remembering fondly his days as the knight George. "So long ago," he thought, "but simpler times."

"All my secrets seem to be coming out today, it would seem. You may all address me as George, in private. Otherwise you'll have to stick to 'Your Majesty', understood?"

The three all nodded at once.

The reason that I've followed you with interest, Peter, is that your grandfather, your father's father, was one of my most trusted comrades. We fought side by side for decades and developed something of a friendship, you might say.

Peter looked shell shocked. He'd never met his grandfather. He'd inherited the house and all its contents from him, but never knew what became of him, or anything else about him.

The King, seeing the look on Peter's face, decided to carry on.

367

"I first met your grandfather the day after I fought Troydenn. He was one of the first to arrive in the City. He was a seasoned warrior, but what impressed me most about him was his ability to recognise what needed to be done, and just get on and do it. He helped set up the first of the emergency hospitals, and had no trouble mucking in helping the patients. In the darkness of night, when all others had given up and gone to bed, he wandered the huge areas of rubble, moving large chunks of it searching for survivors that may still have been trapped. Most thought him mad, including myself at the time. However we were all proved wrong when, in the middle of the night, he started shouting out for help. The knights and the townsfolk all raced to the scene, myself included. What we found shamed me for even thinking he might be mad. Your grandfather had moved a huge amount of rubble and found a pregnant woman trapped underneath, still alive. The woman, it seemed, was about to give birth, and was trapped in a hole about fifteen feet deep. It didn't seem like much, but the whole structure was unstable and could have collapsed at any moment. The city folk were wary of getting too close in the dark because of the risk of collapse. The woman was screaming in pain, her child ready to spring into the world. Without thought for his own safety, your grandfather tossed me the end of a rope and threw it into the hole. With me holding onto one end, he clambered down into the hole, one handed, carrying a lamp in the other hand. The lamp, miraculously, stayed alight all the way down. While I and a few others watched from atop the rubble, your grandfather delivered the baby, a girl in fact, if my memory serves me. He then, calmly as you like, tied the baby to the rope, wrapped in his own clothing and let us bring her out. He did the same with the mother shortly after, and only after they were safe did he come out himself. To this day, I can honestly say I've never seen bravery quite like it."

Peter had a tear in his eye, and was trying to hide it from his two friends who were listening intently.

"After that night, I made a point of finding out about your grandfather. He was the kind of dragon that I wanted by my side. Brave, fearless, inventive, all of these qualities and more he possessed. He helped transport Troydenn back underground, and but for a quirk of fate would have been one of the guards that accompanied the conspirators on that fateful journey to the South Pole. The King of the time had heard about his heroics in the city, mainly from me, but others as well, and rather than let him go with the others to the South Pole, the King wanted him to stay and be promoted. Well, the rest is history, as you say. He stayed, avoided death at the Pole, got promoted and we became the best of friends."

The King stopped all of a sudden, rubbing his forehead, looking as sombre as any of the three friends had seen him that afternoon. By now tears were streaming down Peter's face, thinking of his grandfather performing such valiant deeds alongside George, all those years ago.

The King started pacing again, continuing where he left off.

"As the years went by, I became enthralled by the politics of the dragon kingdom, looking to make an impact and shape the world in that particular forum. Your grandfather had little time for politics and especially politicians. He thought them time wasters and frauds. Many a night we would share some ale, nibble on some charcoal and fight like cat and dog about how best to serve the dragon world. God, I miss those nights so much," sighed the King. "Although our careers kept us apart for long periods of time, we always reunited whenever possible. The bond between us remained strong even though we went for long periods of time without seeing each other. Eventually I was crowned King, not in the most pleasant of circumstances it must be said. Even so, one of the first things that I did was to recall your grandfather from the mission he was on. When he arrived in my chambers, he was livid," said the King, smiling. "He raged about how important the mission had been and how it had been wrecked by me calling him back here at a moment's notice. It took some time for him to calm down, and many broken relics it must be said. But eventually he listened to what I had to say. Most rulers have their own emissaries, right hand dragons, call them what you will. I explained to your grandfather that I wanted him to be mine. He scoffed and laughed at me for what seemed like forever. Finally however, after I explained to him that he was the only dragon in the whole of the world that I trusted completely and utterly, he started to listen. I explained that not only would it be diplomatic matters that he would deal with, but also delicate matters that might require a more...... covert approach, shall we say. This got his attention, and somewhat reluctantly he agreed to take the position I had offered him.

From my point of view, I never looked back. Despite his reservations, he was a wonderful diplomat: courteous, understanding, intelligent and tough as nails when he had to be. He carried out the covert operations with such cunning and skill that nobody ever suspected he'd even been there. In the process he saved tens of thousands of human lives, making the world a better and much more civilised place.

The King was pacing across the hospital room quickly now. As he recounted events, his bottom lip began to wobble just a little. Peter wiped away the tears, determined to hear the rest of the tale. He'd always felt a connection with his grandfather, even though he never knew him, and all the things the King had said about him made Peter so proud.

"About forty or so years ago," the King said, clearly starting to become overwhelmed by the situation, "I sent your grandfather on one of these covert missions. At the time it didn't seem anything too special; neither of us had any major concerns about the outcome or how it would be carried out. Anyhow, the mission went wrong. To this day, I'm not quite sure how, but it did. Neither your grandfather or any of the dragons with him returned. I sent other teams out to find them and bring them back, but all to no avail."

The King had wandered round the other side of Peter's bed and had slumped in his chair, eyes closed, running his hands through his long grey hair.

"I wish to God I'd never sent him on that blasted mission," said the King angrily. "There were others that could have gone in his place, but none were as efficient or effective as he was. He always got the job done, no matter what. I still have no idea to this day what happened to him. I've done everything I can to find out. I'd give everything I have just to know," said the King, looking straight at Peter.

Richie and Tank sat rigid on the bed; the only sound they could hear were the sobbing noises emanating from Peter and the King.

Time went by and the two dragons eventually stopped crying. The King, to his credit, although upset, was determined to carry on and tell Peter the rest of the tale.

"Some time before all of that, a few years in fact, your grandfather had taken me to the nursery ring at Purbeck Peninsula to see you. It was difficult not to recognise you by that bent whistle marking, that even as a young dragon, stood out very clearly. While we were there, perched on the wall by the side of the walkway, listening to you have your lessons, he asked a great favour of me. He asked that I should look out for you, should anything happen to him.

He was very serious about it. He told me how he had left his house and all the belongings inside it to you. He was passionate about making sure you were looked after. How could I possibly refuse?

The other thing he went on to mention was the fact that he'd fallen out with your parents. He didn't go into any specific detail as to why, but something very bad had happened between them. So much so, that when they left your egg at the nursery ring, before disappearing, they left instructions that specifically said they didn't want your grandfather to have anything to do with you as long as you were at the nursery ring. Then they upped and left as so many parents do."

Peter put his hand over his eyes because he thought he might cry again. It was all so much to take in. He felt sad that his parents had left him. Why couldn't he have grown up in their company? Where had they gone? He'd known their names when he left the nursery ring, and had looked them up on the dragon register. But there was no sign of them anywhere. They seemed to have abandoned him and then just disappeared into thin air.

He felt love and pride for his grandfather, mixed in with the sadness. His grandfather seemed such a decent dragon, making sure the house and its contents were left to Peter and that his best friend would look out for him. It made Peter wish desperately that he could have met him, just once, just to see what sort of a dragon he really was. As Peter delved deeper into his thoughts, anger leapt up inside him and threatened to overwhelm the other emotions. "Why would they not want my grandfather to come near me? What did they fall out over? It must have been something really bad to have caused all of that. Did it have something to do with them leaving and disappearing?"

The sound of the King clearing his throat startled Peter back to the present.

"Despite the instructions that he wasn't allowed to have anything to do with you, I know for a fact that your grandfather would spend most of his time when he wasn't working for me, sitting alone on that wall next to the nursery ring, watching your development, and looking over you in his own special way."

Peter's head was in his hands, the tears flowing readily down his cheeks, dripping onto the polished, clean, white floor.

"Only a month or so after he took me to see you at the nursery ring, your grandfather left a large trunk with me, to be given to you when I thought you were ready for it. To this day, it remains untouched in my home, waiting for you..... young Peter. Perhaps when you've fully recovered you can come and claim it; you and your friends would be more than welcome any time."

Peter continued crying, giving a large "sniff" as he nodded his head in reply.

The King's mood lightened a little; a weight seemed to have been lifted from his shoulders.

"Have you ever wondered why your grandfather's house is in Salisbridge, son?" he asked cheerily.

Peter shook his head, as both Richie and Tank looked on.

"It seems he fell in love with the place while working there. I bet you can't guess when that was?" he said to all three of them.

Peter was still clearly distraught, but had at least stopped crying. Tank thought he'd try and break the silence, so he said,

"During the George and the Dragon incident?" trying to lighten the mood.

"Exactly!" roared the King, much to Tank's utter astonishment. All three friends looked up at this announcement, thinking the King was building up to another of his so called jokes.

"It's true," said the King. The history books only ever mention that I battled Troydenn in some rural part of England. They never actually say where, but it was in fact Salisbridge. Your grandfather once told me that from the moment he arrived there to help with that unfortunate event, he felt a connection of some sort, not just to the people, but to the city itself. Throughout the years, whenever he was off duty or recovering from some injury or other, he would always be found in Salisbridge. Eventually he bought his own human house, around the turn of the century I believe," said the King, wistfully. "And he remained in love with the place right up until the day he........ until the day he undertook that fateful mission."

Peter's head sprang up and he looked the King right in the eyes.

"Can I ask what the mission he set out to do was.......... please?"

This had clearly caught the King off guard. He hadn't for the life of him been expecting this particular question, but perhaps he should have been, he thought. He wandered over to Peter slowly and crouched in front of him.

"I'm afraid it's not quite that simple, my young friend. You see, the mission and all information pertaining to it is 'top secret'. And while I would be quite happy to tell you and trust you with that information, if it ever got out that I told you without permission from the council itself, my political enemies would use it against me. I can, however, put a request to the council on your behalf, asking if you could be told, so that you may put to rest the memory of your grandfather. Would you like me to do that?"

Peter nodded vigorously and said,

"Yes please."

"Okay son, I'll do that for you. Hopefully by the time you come and visit me to pick up your grandfather's belongings, I'll have had some sort of decision as to whether you can be told about the mission he was on."

The King looked as though he was just about to make his excuses and leave, but before he could, Tank raised his hand politely to ask a question that had been bugging him for a little while now.

The King smiled at Tank's manners and said,

"What is it son?"

Moving his head to one side and giving the King a lopsided grin, Tank asked,

"We were always taught in the nursery ring that the dragon King wasn't allowed on the surface..... ever. If that's so, how is it that you're here?"

"And I thought it was this young lady here, that was the smarty pants of the group," said the King laughing and gazing at Richie.

Richie just blushed, lost for words once again.

"It would seem that I've been busted," said the King, opening his arms wide. "Guards, guards, come and arrest me,"

Tank sat on the hospital bed wishing he'd never asked.

"Let me tell the three of you something," the King whispered. "I'm not supposed to be on the surface," he said tapping his nose. "But I figure since I'm the King, I'll do as I damn well please."

The three friends laughed together at the attitude of their ruler.

"And let me tell you another thing, I haven't been above ground for nearly a hundred and fifty years, and I'm not sure I care for it too much. It's all so..... fast. Everyone's in a hurry. The cars, the people walking, even the hospital porters, dragging patients at top speed everywhere and driving those little electric trucks throughout the hospital. Five times I've nearly been run over by them since I've been here. Five times!"

The three friends were beside themselves with laughter now, tears for very different reasons rolling down their cheeks.

"It's all true," said the king indignantly. "Seriously though, Tank, you're right, I'm not supposed to be here. However, at this present moment, as well as the seventy or so dragons that are here, guarding the hospital, I would also guess that in a five mile radius of where I stand, there are another five hundred or so ready to come to my aid at a moment's notice, if required."

Tank whistled to himself. That, he thought, was quite an impressive number.

"So you see, my young friends, I always think of myself as the knight I once was. And while, at this present time, we as a community face a very real threat, part of which you all thwarted, I will never be afraid to go anywhere or do anything that I have to ask of another dragon.

Anyhow, I have to depart now. There are some rather pressing issues that have developed in the South Pole that I have to go and deal with. No doubt you will learn soon enough, through the media. Another of our expeditions has gone missing, the second in a row. The first was very low key that nobody really knew about. This time however it's much more serious. I bid you all farewell and look forward to meeting you all again. Your friends are welcome to accompany you when you come and pick up your grandfather's belongings, Peter. The whole community owes you a debt of gratitude for what you've done in stopping the dragon Manson. On their behalf I thank all three of you." The King bowed and as he turned to leave said,

"Farewell."

The scuffed wooden door closed silently as the King left. The three friends sat in silence next to each other on the hospital bed, barely able to believe what had gone on. To have caught a fleeting glimpse of the King through a crowd was one thing; this was something else altogether.

Tank spoke first.

"Your grandfather sounds like one hell of a guy."

"He sure does," replied Peter, with just a hint of sadness in his voice.

"Fancy having the King looking out for you," said Richie playfully. "What's that all about?"

Tank smacked his friend playfully in the arm.

"Do we have to bow now? I'm not quite sure what the protocol is," he said towards the other two.

Peter shook his head, smiling as he did so.

"There's going to be no end to this is there?"

"Whatever do you mean, majesty?" said Richie.

"Sire?" said Tank, grinning.

"Bugger!" said Peter, loudly.

Richie and Tank burst out laughing at exactly the same time.

As Peter sat on the bed, looking forward to weeks, if not months of abuse, a sudden look of realisation crossed Peter's amused face.

"Hang on a minute," he said. "What happened in the final?" he asked excitedly. "Did they win, ohh............tell me they won, pleeeeasssssseee tell me they won."

Richie and Tank looked at each other. Their smiles slowly disappeared. In unison they shook their heads at Peter's question.

"They lost!" Peter exclaimed, heartbroken.

"Afraid so," said Tank.

"Did you...... did you...... go to the match?"

Richie stifled a laugh.

"What do you think?"

"We've been here all the time," said Tank. "All the time."

Peter hung his head in shame.

"Sorry, I should have known. That's what I would have done for either of you."

"You know I do believe his majesty would have attended the match," said Richie in a pretend posh voice.

"I'm pretty sure you're right, sire would have gone to the final of the Global Cup."

"Oh right, very funny," said Peter.

"We did at least get to hear a live running commentary though," sighed Tank.

"No way."

Tank and Richie both nodded.

"The brother of one of your guards was at the match. His brother phoned him and we all got to listen to it live. Don't worry, from the sounds of it we didn't miss much as Indigo Warriors fans. They got their asses kicked."

"Oh well, there's always next year," said Peter hopefully.

"Yeah right," said Tank. "Do you have any idea what the likelihood is of the Warriors getting to the final two years in a row?"

"Yeah," said Richie. "You've got a better chance of sprouting wings and flying out of here."

The three friends laughed their socks off.

Thank you for reading

We invite you to share your thoughts and reactions

Bentwhistle the Dragon will return in

'A Chilling Revelation'

1135

Lightning Source UK Ltd.
Milton Keynes UK
UKOW04f0856011014

239411UK00005B/137/P